Pr...
*Ellie P...*

'**Hilarious and heart-warming.**'
Aisha Bushby, author of *A Pocketful of Stars*

'**Frank, funny, warm-hearted and wise.**'
Simon James Green, author of *Gay Club!*

'**Warm, funny and hopeful!**'
A. M. Dassu, author of *Boy, Everywhere*

'**A fresh, funny, feel-good story.**'
Rashmi Sirdeshpande

'**Heart-breaking and hilarious.**'
*Brown Girl Magazine*

'**I loved the fresh and original voice.**'
*Bookseller*, Highlights of the Season

'**Hugely enjoyable.**'
*The Scotsman*

'**Funny, heartfelt, true-to-life,
coming-of-age page-turner.**'
*LoveReading*

# ABOUT THE AUTHOR

Christine Pillainayagam is a writer and retail strategist, who lives in Kent with her young family and a collection of records, CDs and minidiscs. A mild obsession with the Beatles and the desire to write a story that reflected her own experiences growing up as a first-generation immigrant led her to put that love of music and words into a book. *Ellie Pillai is Not Done Yet* is her third novel.

A singer-songwriter, Christine also writes a blog: thelittlebrownbook.co.uk

# ELLIE PILLAI
## IS NOT DONE YET

# CHRISTINE
## PILLAINAYAGAM

Illustrated by Trisha Srivastava

**faber**

First published in the UK in 2024
by Faber & Faber Limited,
The Bindery, 51 Hatton Garden
London, EC1N 8HN
faber.co.uk

Typeset in Mr Eaves by MRules
Printed by CPI Group (UK) Ltd, Croydon CR0 4YY

A CIP record for this book is available from the British Library

ISBN 978-0-571-38725-0

**MIX**
Paper | Supporting
responsible forestry
FSC® C171272

Printed and bound in the UK on FSC® certified paper in line with our continuing
commitment to ethical business practices, sustainability and the environment.
**For further information see faber.co.uk/environmental-policy**

2 4 6 8 10 9 7 5 3 1

You can listen to the *Ellie Pillai Is Not Done Yet* album by scanning in the link below – hear Ellie's songs come to life!

There are song chapters throughout the story that reference specific songs on the album.

For Mum, Dad, Michele and Terence – the family that made me. For Ian, Theo and Miles – who made me a family.

# 1

# A Girl Called Ellie

My name is Ellie. Ellie Pillai.

And I choose me.

Which, I appreciate, doesn't make sense to a lot of people.

It's just, I sort of fell in love, and then I fell out of it, and I feel like falling, when you're not sure where you're going to land, is how you end up with the words SPLAT and WAH WAH WAH above your head in a speech bubble, like you're a cartoon character instead of a real human girl.

So, when it's a choice between your ex-boyfriend, your current bandmate, or yourself – you choose you. Because real human girls don't bounce as well as cartoon ones. They tend to crumple. Or split into pieces. And I've found pieces don't really suit me. Like the one-shoulder top my cousin made me buy, which makes me look like an octopus that's missing a tentacle.

My name is Ellie. Ellie Pillai.

And I choose me.

Which means no falling, no crying, no kissing and definitely – no drama.

Or at least, that's the plan.

Although.

I've never been that good at sticking to plans.

# 2

# Pride & Prejudice or Prejudice & Pride

**London Cousin – Not Annoying:**
WHAT IS HAPPENING??

**Ellie:**
nothing

**London Cousin – Not Annoying:**
who do u love??

**Ellie:**
no 1

**London Cousin – Not Annoying:**
ELEANOR. Y R U TORTURING ME?

I can only guess my cousin's reference to torture is the quasi-love-triangle I appear to have found myself in with my ex-boyfriend Ash – aka the boy in the yellow rain mac – and my bandmate Shawn – aka Dirty Blond – and the fact they've both asked me out, but I refuse to go out with either. And before you ask: I have no idea what a quasi-triangle looks like. I can only assume, a smaller triangle.

**Ellie:**
i choose me ❤

Which, I'm not going to lie, isn't exactly easy when you like both of them, but you're not entirely sure how much you like yourself.

But here's the thing about falling out of love/getting your heart broken: at some point, you have to get unbroken. You have to get back up and think about yourself. Work out who you are on your own. What you want on your own. You have to learn to like you. Love you.

**London Cousin – Not Annoying:**
what does that mean??

And what that means is . . .

**Ellie:**
☠ no romance ☠

So, I am now officially entering my No-Romance Era, a strictly Self-Improvement Zone. Because therein lies my problem. Romance. Distracting myself with yellow rain macs and dirty blonds and missing the bigger picture. The future. Real stuff.

**Ellie:**
i need to focus on me

I check my reflection in the mirror and imagine myself metamorphosising into a mature, better version of me. A butterfly Ellie. An Ellie 2.0 who focuses on exams and family and friends. An Ellie who doesn't have chin hair like her thousand-year-old granny.

Note to self: find tweezers. Also, find out how hairy caterpillars are when they become butterflies.

**London Cousin – Not Annoying:**
👍 it's not a *terrible* idea 🙅

**London Cousin – Not Annoying:**
I give it 2 weeks

**London Cousin – Not Annoying:**
3 tops 🍟

I ignore her tone in the manner of a mature, better version of oneself, and throw my phone down on the bed, jumping spreadeagled behind it. Then I smash my head against the headboard – because unfortunately, butterfly Ellie does not have new and improved spatial awareness.

I rub my head for a minute then I turn over on my back and press play on my new favourite podcast, my pyjama-clad legs and white socks neatly crossed beneath me.

I will no longer be drawn into pointless childish romantic entanglements. I am Ellie 2.0. Fearless, formidable warrior of a new world.

Ooh, that sounds good. Must write it down.

I type the words into my Journal app and listen as the sound of Dr Jada's American accent fills my room. It may be the twelfth time I've listened to this particular episode but it's the sound of the words being said, sort of staccato and firm and unapologetic. *Heartbreak is a pointless exercise.* Just like that. Heartbreak. Is. A. Pointless. Exercise. It's sort of rhythmic. And soothing. I listen to it like it's a song. As though it's lyrics I can memorise. Wisdom I can absorb.

Heartbreak.

Is.

A.

Pointless.

Exercise.

**London Cousin – Not Annoying:**
ru listening 2 that Jada person again??

How does she know? I sit up and eye the corner of my wardrobe suspiciously. Maybe there's a hidden camera in there. I wouldn't put it past my parents; a hangover from their Ellie Is In Need of Watching at All Times phase – or maybe Ellie's Actual Hangover phase, which, I will admit, was not my finest hour. But all I can see in the vicinity of my wardrobe is clothes. And records. And books. And a bowl with some leftover ramen noodles from when Mum 'cooked' last night. Which makes it sightly tricky to spot a camera, or in fact anything I need, at any time I might actually need it.

**London Cousin – Not Annoying:**

u need 2 clean ur room

I slide my eyes from side to side.

**Ellie:**

where ru??? 👀

**London Cousin – Not Annoying:**

i. am. everywhere . . . 👀

**Ellie:**

this feels like the start of a horror movie

**Ellie:**

where the brown girl dies 1st

Soon, a masked clown will come and kill me.

**London Cousin – Not Annoying:**

ur mum may kill u if u don't clean ur room

Mum, dressed as a masked clown may kill me.

**Ellie:**

. . .

**London Cousin – Not Annoying:**

hrd her telling my mum u haven't left ur room in a week . . .

**London Cousin – Not Annoying:**

it's not the quasi-love-triangle is it?? ⚠

But if she means the fact I was once in love with Ash Anderson, and now I am not in love with Ash Anderson, because he broke up with me on my birthday and had a weird inappropriate relationship with his best friend that he also used to date (ugh, Rebecca) then didn't bother to visit me in the hospital when I almost died – then the answer is no. Or if she means the fact that after Ash and I broke up I kissed Shawn, and it may have felt like one of those fairy-tale kisses where space and time cease to exist and you are the only two people alive in the universe – then also, no.

These are just Things I Can't Think About Right Now, because I'm focusing on becoming Ellie 2.0. Someone who thinks about things other than kissing, and what songs are playing in your head when you're kissing, and has a firm grip of quadratic equations and the French perfect and pluperfect tense.

**Ellie:**

hav been revising!

Which Mum knows, because I've told her this, like, multiple, multiple times. It's not my fault that every time I use the word 'algebra' she just switches off and goes on about how I need to have a shower and leave my room.

**London Cousin – Not Annoying:**

ru sure? because that kiss w dirty blond ... 😨

8

Exactly. Head-blown emoji. This is why my love life carries a triangular hazard warning sign.

Note to self: heartbreak is a pointless exercise. Heartbreak is like doing circuits around a running track, just, you know, *because*. So, it's weird. In a bad way.

So, even if Ash did secretly drive my mum and granny back and forth to the hospital when my dad had a heart attack and he says he's sorry, and he still loves me, and he'll wait for me, It Doesn't Matter. And even if Shawn says he likes me, and he'll wait for me too, That Doesn't Matter Either. Because as Dr Jada, Spotify's number-one emotional well-being podcaster keeps reminding me, I need to focus on Me.

**Ellie:**

as previously discussed. i choose me.

**London Cousin – Not Annoying:**

i'd choose u 2 ♥

**London Cousin – Not Annoying:**

altho dirty blond would come a close 2nd

So, I've been trying to focus on finding my own path. Which in my case is paved with algebra and trying to understand whether Elizabeth had the pride and Mr Darcy had the prejudice, or Elizabeth had the prejudice and Mr Darcy had the pride – one of life's most important and eternal questions.

**London Cousin – Not Annoying:**
time 2 think abt U snack 🐵

**London Cousin – Not Annoying:**
also me . . . can i borrow ur yellow top??

Stuff is happening in the world. Real stuff. Important stuff. Things that need my attention. Like my GCSEs and my dad recovering from heart surgery, my mum having a baby and my lovely but brutal granny (aka a brown, old-woman version of Jon Snow, *Game of Thrones*) currently living with us and obsessing over what we should all wear on Saturday to meet my aunt's soon-to-be husband's parents, at possibly the world's most awkward lunch. My fear is she's erring towards sari, which I never feel like myself in. I have a tendency to fall over in them, and if I'm going to fall over, I'd at least like to look like myself when I'm doing it. Or maybe I wouldn't. Maybe I can pair my sari with sunglasses and a fake beard.

**Ellie:**
👍

**London Cousin – Not Annoying:**
c u on sat 📹

**Ellie:**
stop being creepy

**London Cousin – Not Annoying:**
👀

I stroke the hair on my chin, the feeling annoyingly soothing. At this rate, I won't be needing the fake beard.

# 3

# Ellie 2.0

My brain is now thinking in French.

*J'ai le menton d'une femme cinq fois mon âge.*

Which I'm taking as both a win, and urgent reminder to find my tweezers.

I take a break from revision and decide to alphabetise my records while Dr Jada plays in the background, telling me to release the need to criticise myself.

'Ellie?' Mum says, poking her head through the doorway.

'Uh-huh?' I reply, sat on the floor trying to work around the mountain of washed clothes in need of a home.

I mean, *I* release the need to criticise myself, now Mum's here, that's an entirely different story.

'Are you listening to that woman again?' she asks, side-eyeing the pile of clothes I was planning to put away as soon as I worked out whether to organise my records by band, album, genre, era or experience. It's a lot. I'm having a lot of thoughts about it.

'It might be easier to do that first,' she says, pointing at the clothes.

12

'Her name's *Dr* Jada, Mum.' I roll my eyes as I press pause on my phone, which takes several minutes due to having to find it beneath the aforementioned washing.

'She's not a *real* doctor, Ellie.'

Mum. Six months pregnant. Wants me to leave my room. Doesn't rate Dr Jada and more often than not, me either.

'She is,' I insist in a high-pitched voice. 'She has a PhD in Resilience.'

'Resilience?' Mum scoffs, and I know, as soon as she's alone, she will immediately google whether or not that's a real qualification.

'Do you need something?'

She's stood at the door looking gloriously, beautifully round, in a long denim skirt and black vest top. Because only my mother could look this beautiful whilst appearing to smuggle a beach ball.

'I was going to ask you the same thing.' She rubs her stomach in smooth circular motions. 'When was the last time you changed your clothes, *en anbe*,' she asks, trying not to look like she's been keeping track of my daily outfit choices in a diary entitled WHAT ELLIE IS NOT DOING WELL.

I sit up and brush the crumbs of toast Granny brought up for me off my favourite Strokes T-shirt.

'I've changed my underwear,' I mumble, 'and this is a new T-shirt.'

Yesterday I was wearing a Queens of the Stone Age T-shirt. I remember because I kept hearing 'Fortress' and wondering what wilderness behind your eyes looks like and if I had it when trying to understand quadratic equations.

'Granny says I need to revise,' I state. 'In fact, I was just trying to work out . . .' I pick up a mock paper I've stuffed into a shoe and start reading out an algebra problem that involves x's and y's and whole numbers, and watch her eyes lose focus. Mum is annoyingly good at everything, but even she can barely feign interest in the completely irrelevant, unrelatable, useless questions of a GCSE maths paper (her words, not mine). I hope the problem will be enough to dissuade her from further conversation re the state of my room/life in general, but she clearly has an axe to grind.

'It's thirteen,' she says, staring at me.

'What?'

'The answer. X is three and y is four.'

'How did you do that?'

'Do you really need me to tell you?' she asks suspiciously. 'Because you're pretty good at maths, Ellie – and that wasn't a hard question. Or are you just hoping my dislike of algebra will make me go away so you can carry on doing whatever it is you're doing in here?'

Mind reader. Witch!

She watches me carefully, her face contorted with a mix of wariness and concern.

'And since when did you listen to your grandmother?' she continues. 'Or anyone, for that matter? You need to take a break, *en anbe*. See some friends.'

She looks exhausted. She looks like she's got enough on her plate with the pregnancy and working and looking after Dad and Granny. Because Granny alone would be enough to make anyone's plate feel more than full. I feel suddenly guilty for making her worry. For making her think there's something wrong with me. That she needs to watch me, the way she used to watch me.

'I'm fine, Mum,' I reply, trying to look Alive and Vital and Powerful, as Dr Jada tells me I am daily, so it must be true. 'But I was going to

14

invite Jess and Hayley over later, so you can stop worrying that I'm some kind of crab hermit.'

Note to self: invite Jess and Hayley over later.

'A what?' she smiles.

'A crab hermit,' I offer imperiously, not enjoying the look she's giving me.

'I think you mean a hermit crab,' she says, trying to hold back a laugh, which seems to me to be the exact same thing.

'That's what I said.'

'OK,' she says, trying to keep a straight face.

'Look. Can I help you with anything, Mum?' I ask, sitting up on my knees.

She shakes her head.

'I came in here to help *you*,' she says, rubbing her belly for the hundredth time. I'm starting to think there's a genie in there.

'Is everything OK?' I ask, nodding towards her stomach.

'Fine,' she says. 'Just itchy.'

Gross. Remind me never to get pregnant.

'Seriously,' I say, looking at her. 'Can I do anything to help, Mum? You look tired.'

'I'm fine,' she repeats, sounding like me. 'I don't need anything. I just wanted to make sure you know I'm here. If you need me.'

'I don't need you.'

'Oh,' she says, sounding hurt.

Ugh, well done, Ellie.

'I mean, *I* should be helping *you*. Let me take something off your hands. Something you don't have time for,' I insist. Because this is how you become a better person. An Ellie 2.0.

15

She walks in, arching her back slightly as she lowers herself down on to the bed.

'Well,' she breathes, 'you *could* help your grandmother organise her table setting. For the lunch.' The lunch being the meeting on Saturday between the Sòng family and the Pillai family before my aunty Kitty and her fiancé, Charles, get married next month. The reason I'll see Hope this weekend – and probably never see my yellow top again. A marriage Granny took her time coming round to, because Charles is British Chinese and not Sri Lankan Anything. Mum rolls her eyes, clearly exhausted by the idea of the lunch, let alone the lunch itself.

'Like helping her buy stuff and organise, that kind of thing?' I ask.

'Yes,' she says, fixing me with a piercing look. 'That would be great.'

'Anything else?'

'You could get Dad's records out of the cupboard? He wants them in the lounge so he can listen to them while he works.' Since Dad's heart surgery he's been listening to a lot of Tim Buckley. Which says a lot about how he's feeling. He's usually more of an AC/DC man.

'No problem,' I respond cooperatively. I love Tim Buckley.

'So, how are you getting on with all this?' she asks, gesturing to the chaos around me.

'Fine. Yeah. Good.'

'Great,' she says slowly.

'Then why are you looking at me like that?' I demand.

'I'm worried about you, *en anbe*.'

'You should worry about you, not me,' I say calmly.

'Me?' she asks, surprised.

'You've got work and the baby, and Dad, and Granny. You've got a lot going on. You don't have to worry about me too, Mum.'

Ellie 2.0 notices when her mum looks worn out. Ellie 2.0 is helpful and mature, with a soon to be excellently organised record collection.

'Yes, but you're going through all that with me,' she says gently. 'Don't think I don't know that.'

But I'm not going through anything other than a hairy caterpillar (must find tweezers) to powerful butterfly glow up.

She stands up and leans down to kiss me on the forehead.

'I'll talk to Granny about the table stuff,' I reply officiously. 'Get it all sorted.'

'OK,' she says heavily.

As she leaves, I close my eyes and un-pause Dr Jada.

*You are Alive and Vital and Powerful*, Dr Jada intones.

*You are a Woman, tapping into your Power*, she continues.

Yes. Yes, I am.

I just need to work out what my Power is, and where I can find it.

I am Ellie 2.0.

Watch out, world. I'm coming.

# 4

# Convince Mum Am Normal

**Ellie:**

need u 2 come over & convince mum am normal

**Hayley:**

not. possible.

Hayley. Best friend, pessimist, dealer of excellent levels of sarcasm, apart from when they are aimed at you. Amazing actress, person of whom I am genuinely afraid.

**Jess:**

what hav u done now?

Jessica. Best friend, optimist, sunshine in human form. Clever, beautiful, popular and, for some reason, friends with me. And Hayley.

**Ellie:**

nothing!!

**Hayley:**

literally . . .

**Hayley:**

when was the last time u left ur house??

**Ellie:**

. . .

**Jessica:**

@HayleyAttacksFilms when was the last time u saw ur lovers??! ☺

**Hayley:**

. . .

In the silence that follows Jess's message, I sense Hayley's thorny irritation. As if even her ellipsis is gifted with dramatic flair. Which makes sense because Hayley Atwell is a drama queen. As in, a Queen of Drama in both the literal (on course for a 9 in her drama GCSE) and metaphorical (extremely dramatic in everyday-life situations) sense.

At the end of last term Hay got caught up in quasi-love-triangle too – with her ex-boyfriend James and my bandmate Benji. It's just her sphinx-like inscrutability when it comes to feelings of all kinds has made it impossible for Jess and me to work out which one she likes back.

**Hayley:**

ignoring u

**Jessica:**

jk

**Jessica:**

but how r ur lovers??

Jess and Hayley haven't always been friends. Mainly because Hayley assumed Jess was the reason I wasn't living my best life, when the truth is, *I'm* the reason I wasn't living my best life. I was trying to be invisible, afraid of being noticed for all the wrong reasons, because I'm brown and 99.9 per cent of my school are the opposite of any colour whatsoever. But I've put *that* Ellie, the one who was afraid to be seen, away. It's the reason I joined Shawn's band last term. That, and the teeny-tiny crush I had on him.

Note to self: stop having teeny-tiny crushes. Mature, better versions of oneself do not have crushes.

There's been a lot of quasi-love-triangles/teeny-tiny crushes going on this year.

Me, Ash and Shawn.

Hayley, James and Benji.

Ash, Rebecca and me.

Jess, me and Ash.

And yes, I'm aware Ash and I are in, like, three of these.

But technically, Jess did go out with Ash before I did. He was her fake boyfriend while she and Elina, his sister (her now girlfriend), were first getting to know each other. No one knew it was a fake relationship at the time though, which made things somewhat *complicated* when Ash and I caught feelings for each other. Which is why when Jess came out, and Ash and I got together, I thought That Was It. Happy ending. Cue theme music – and there was theme music – but it was Roy Orbison, 'Crying'.

**Hayley:**
i don't hav any lovers taylor swift

**Jessica:**
i ♥ taylor swift

**Ellie:**
me 2 ♥

**Ellie:**
you're my, my, my . . .

**Jessica:**
*Lover*

**Ellie:**
*Lover*

**Hayley:**
u r both hilarious

**Hayley:**
hav died from laughing. u will find me in hell

**Ellie:**
k drama queen 😈

And now Taylor Swift, 'Lover', is playing on repeat in my head, as

Taylor serenades me from the end of my bed. Because my life is one long soundtrack no one else can hear.

Note to self: hallucinating Taylor Swift in my bedroom is something a mature, better version of me would still do.

**Ellie:**
I NEED 2 LOOK NORMAL

**Hayley:**
caps not helping u

**Jessica:**
be there in an hour lover

**Ellie:**
you're my, my, my

**Hayley:**
r u done yet?

**Ellie:**
*Lover*

**Jessica:**
*Lover*

**Hayley:**
GUESS NOT THEN

**Ellie:**
CAPS. HA.

**Hayley:**

normal ppl r boring.

**Ellie:**

tru. but come anyway.

**Hayley:**

FINE LOVER

**Ellie:**

🏇🏇🏇

**Ellie:**

c u soon ♥

This past year, I haven't really been there for Jess and Hayley as much as I should have. I've been too fixated on quasi-love-triangles and teeny-tiny crushes. Throwing my heart against a wall until it turned into one of those bloody steaks my dad is obsessed by, now he's no longer allowed to eat them. But now I'm a better Ellie. An Ellie 2.0. And Ellie 2.0 would notice when one of her friends stopped eating like Hayley did last term. Or when they're a carer for one of their parents, the way Jess was with her mum's bipolar disorder.

Ellie 2.0 knows that since Hayley was diagnosed with anorexia and Jess's mum walked out on her, she has to be a Better Friend. She has to start noticing stuff. The important stuff. The real stuff.

She also has to:

- Revise.
- Organise a table setting for Granny.

- Stop using caps.
- And most importantly – convince Mum she's normal.

# 5

# I Blame the Crystals

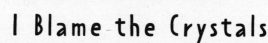

'Ellie, you're giving me a weird vibe,' Jess says, staring around my bedroom.

'You're giving me serial killer energy,' Hayley adds, poking the crystals I've placed at intermittent points throughout the room. 'Where did you get these?'

'Oh, I had a bunch of them from when I was going through my crystal healing phase,' I remark casually.

'Crystal healing phase?' Jess responds, throwing Hayley a look.

'It was ages ago. I was, like, eight or something,' I say, looking away.

'Oh,' she says suddenly.

'What?' Hayley asks incredulously. 'Why were you into crystal healing at *eight*?'

'I heard it could make people better, you know, when they were sick.'

'Right,' she continues, rolling her hands. 'I'm still not . . .'

'My brother.' I swallow. It never gets easier talking about him, however much I think it will. 'I thought it would help.'

I was seven when my brother was diagnosed with leukaemia. Two years later, he died. In that time, even Mum got into crystal healing. I'd bought them from a lady at a local market who sold incense sticks and clothes with tiny mirrors stitched into them. She told me crystals had powers. That they could change the energy around us. So, I saved my pocket money. Hid them in Amis's bedroom. Mum was angry when she found them, but then she got desperate. We'd tried praying, tried oils and therapies and holy water. We'd tried everything – so why not crystals too? And even though in the end the crystals didn't help either, they made it feel possible to have some kind of control. Even though I couldn't. None of us could.

'Oh,' Hayley says quietly.

Jess swallows messily, the lump in her throat evident.

She's been more emotional since things came out about her mum. Like she's finally let go of trying to hold everything in. She's staying with her dad now, but I know it hasn't been easy. Trying to re-establish a relationship with her mum, trying to learn to trust people again.

I reach out and stroke her arm.

'Anyway,' I continue, 'Dr Jada was talking about crystals in her last podcast. These ones are supposed to be for positive changes.'

'Cool,' Hayley says, avoiding eye contact.

'Oh, so now they don't have serial killer vibes?'

'To be fair, I meant you, not the crystals,' she says, eyeing my stained Strokes T-shirt. At least I've changed out of my pyjama bottoms into a pair of flared black leggings.

'I feel weird about leaving Dad, and I've had loads of revision and stuff, and Granny's been, like, Granny.'

26

And what I don't say is: *I chose me*, which I thought would lead to something more powerful than lying around in my pyjamas listening to Fleetwood Mac, *Rumours* on repeat. But it didn't. So, I've sat around in my pyjamas listening to Fleetwood Mac *Rumours* on repeat.

'Benji said you've missed the last couple of band rehearsals,' she continues carefully.

'Benji *your lover*,' I joke.

'He's not my lover,' she sighs.

'Who *is* your lover?' Jess asks, giving her a sideways glance. 'Because I saw James on the way here. With Sadie. From Year 12. She's on the girls' football team.'

'The redhead?' I ask reverentially. 'I love red hair.'

Jess gives me a look. As if to say, now is not the time to show your appreciation for red hair. I look at Hayley's face and silently concur. Ellie 2.0 may be an improvement on the original Ellie, but she still has her foot in her mouth.

'What do you mean *with* her?' Hayley asks, collapsing on to the bed dramatically.

'They seemed . . . friendly.'

'They probably just know each other from football,' I say, trying to placate Hayley, who looks like she might be on the verge of tears.

'They were kissing,' Jess says, looking away. 'I'm sorry, Hay. I thought you should know. I feel awful after that whole lover thing we were doing earlier.'

'It's fine,' Hayley says, tossing her dark hair back. It's getting longer. Not a chin-length bob, but at her shoulders now, her fringe almost grown out. 'He's not my boyfriend. He can kiss whoever he wants.'

'Are you sure about that?' I probe.

'Yes,' she snaps. She's playing with the buttons on her black denim minidress, her fingers tracing the edges of the silver rivets, over and over, like she's trying to distract her mind with her fingers.

'Because I don't want this to affect you,' I add euphemistically. Because it's hard when you're going through what Hayley's going through. Food is control and emotion, a way of loving or hating yourself, and I need to know if she can cope with this.

She looks uncomfortable for a moment. The way she always does when anything personal comes up.

'I'm OK,' she responds quietly.

I sit down next to her, pulling her hand away from the rivets before squeezing it.

'Sorry about the lover thing,' I say, putting my head on her shoulder.

I'll just keep an eye on her. A really close eye on both of them.

Jess sits down and puts her head on Hayley's other shoulder.

'I think I have to break up with Elina,' she says out of nowhere.

'What are you talking about?' I ask, sitting forward and turning to look at her across Hayley. Her long blonde hair is loose around her shoulders. The black, sleeveless T-shirt she's wearing tucked into straight-leg grey jeans. 'What happened?'

'Nothing,' she says, turning away. 'But she's going back to London soon, and I'll be . . . here. I don't want to hold her back. I don't want us to hold each other back.'

'Jess, no,' I say, reaching over to grab her hand. 'You've got months together yet. The whole summer. You love her. You can make it work, I know you can. Have you talked to her about it? What did she say?'

'It'll just make everything harder,' she says slowly. 'The longer we're together. She'll go. Things will change.'

'You sound like me,' I say glumly. 'When I first got together with Ash. Everything ends, blah, blah, blah.'

'But you were right,' she says calmly. 'I'm not being dramatic. We've both got things we need to focus on. I love her. I *really* love her. But we're sixteen. I want her to have the best time at uni. I don't want her to worry about me, or us . . .' She trails away.

'This is not the change of energy I was hoping for,' I say, lying back on the bed. But I don't try and talk her out of it. Because I've learned my lesson. That people need to come to decisions on their own. When they're ready. Not when I think they should be ready.

'Why does everything feel like such a mess?' Jess says, lying down too.

'It does, doesn't it?' Hayley says, dropping down between us.

We stare at the ceiling.

'I blame the crystals,' Hayley says, deadpan.

'Definite serial killer energy,' Jess ripostes.

'Shut up. You're both annoying.'

Hayley sniggers.

'Should I put an episode of Dr Jada on?' I ask. 'I feel like the one on emotional intelligence could be just what we need right now.'

'NO,' they both shout simultaneously, before descending into fits of giggles.

What is everyone's problem with Dr Jada?

'Ellie?' Granny's knocking on the door, keen to see if we're doing any actual studying. 'What is going on in there? Is herd of elephants arrived?'

'Sorry, Granny,' we all chorus.

'Chkkk,' I hear her tut from behind the door.

We giggle again, before I notice we're all holding hands.

Whatever happens, crystals or otherwise, my heart will never be broken, not while I have these two.

'You're my, my, my,' Jess sings.

'Loverrrrrr,' I finish.

'I hate you two,' Hayley responds. 'You've ruined that song for me.'

'I love you too,' I reply, squeezing her hand. Because that was Hayley's version of = that song will always remind me of you clowns.

'We should probably do some revision,' Jess says from beside us.

Hayley makes a noise that suggests she disagrees.

Some things never change.

For some reason, I find the thought soothing.

# 6

# The Moment

When you write a song, sometimes you don't even write it. Not really. There's nothing conscious about it, nothing intentional.

It just happens.

Appears suddenly, as if it always existed.

Digging some weird passage through your brain and out through your fingertips. Making sense of things you had no idea made no sense to begin with.

When Ash and I broke up. When Shawn and I kissed. When Dad had a heart attack and the world felt like it was ending.

Suddenly, all those feelings you couldn't quite articulate seem small and manageable and simple. The answer to a question, a chorus or a middle eight.

And that's what writing a song is about. That moment. *The* moment.

Because sometimes, the song knows before you do.

# 7

# A Cake Made of Cheese

Granny has lost the plot. Like, seriously. And not in a cute, adorable, she can't remember which day of the week it is or where she put her phone way. In a stress-eating Bombay mix while screaming in Tamil at someone about the food she's ordered for the lunch with Aunty Kitty's soon-to-be in-laws way.

She's decided to go for a Sri Lankan/Chinese buffet, which consists of too many egg rolls, some suspect-looking spare ribs, fried rice, kung pao chicken, chow mein, mutton kottu roti, dahl, aubergine curry, string hoppers, kiri hodi and for some reason – Bombay mix. It's a weird combination of foods, but it's also Granny's attempt at being welcoming. Hospitable. As if Chinese people can only eat Chinese food. I try to point out to her that this is our chance to introduce them to Sri Lankan cooking, not that any of this is home-made, because my parents are useless at cooking and she's too nervous to wait for the London family to arrive with food in case the Sòngs should enter to an empty table and judge us unworthy of their son, as she would if the situation were reversed.

The Sri Lankan food, ordered from a newly set up catering company, is missing the wattalapum and milk toffee Granny ordered for dessert, and she's screaming at the poor man who's saying it will take at least a couple of hours for them to get it here. A couple of hours, in Granny's world, is the end of time. Her daughter will be rejected and die old and alone, due to the lack of a creamy tropical custard and cardamon-and-rose-based toffee.

At least the table, which I've helped her shop for and style, looks good. We've gone for cream linen with a delicate green-and-gold table runner and a set of copper karahi dishes that make the whole thing look a bit like a picture on Pinterest.

'*Amma*, it's fine,' Dad says, trying to coax her away from the phone. 'I can pick up a cheesecake or some brownies.'

'Cheesecake,' she shrieks. 'What is this cheese *cake*?' And you'd think after living in the home of cheesecake (New York, New York) for several years, she might have picked up that it isn't a cake made of cheese. Although I suppose it is.

Dad stands up to collect his car keys.

'Noel, you know you can't drive yet,' Mum says, pushing him back down on to the sofa. 'I'll go.'

'You cannot go,' Granny says hysterically. 'You are tired. They will not want cake cheese. We must make the wattalapum.'

Mum looks panicked. '*Amma*, we don't have the ingredients or the time. They'll be here in a few hours.'

Granny stamps her tiny foot angrily.

'I'll go,' I offer. 'I can get the bus and be home before they get here.'

Mum stares at me, impressed and possibly disturbed by my sudden helpfulness.

The doorbell rings, and I think Granny might be about to have a coronary.

33

'They are here. They are HERE! We are not dressed. Nimi! NIMI!' she shouts in terror.

'I'll get it.' I stand up, smoothing the legs of my black-and-blue two-tone jeans down, thankful to leave the hysteria behind momentarily. It's starting to make me feel slightly sick. That or the combination of spare ribs and Bombay mix.

I open the door and it's him.

Him.

And all I want to do is wrap my arms around his waist and put my head beneath his chin and ask him how he organises his records – but then also punch him. Because he's him, and I'm me, and even though I loved him, he didn't trust me enough to be honest.

Note to self: violence is never the answer.

'Hi,' he says, looking almost as uncomfortable as I feel. 'Your granny called me.'

'Oh,' I say stupidly, pulling at my black crop top, which I fear may be showing off more stomach than I intended. 'Come in.'

My ex-boyfriend. He of the green eyes and long lashes, and dark blue jeans and knitted yellow polo shirt and Converse high-tops, who told me he was going to wait for me the last time we spoke. Wait for me. Meaning, I don't know. Waiting for me. To do something. I don't know what.

As he moves to step past me, we turn towards each other, suddenly uncomfortably close.

'Er, sorry,' I say, slipping past him as my heart skips a beat. Why does he make my heart skip a beat?

'It's OK,' he stutters.

'Ashar,' Granny calls. 'Is that my Ashar?'

He blushes.

'Oh. So, you're *her* Ashar now, are you?' I joke.

'Jealous?' he smiles.

And I want to say, yes. Yes, I am. But I just blush instead.

'I meant because she's your granny, not because I'm yours, or you want me to be yours.' He cringes.

I wave him ahead of me, ignoring the sentiment. Remembering I'm Ellie 2.0 and I choose me, but looking at him, it's hard to remember why. Because I want to kiss him. I want to put my hands in the back of his hair and feel his arms tightening around me. I want him to smile at me, the way he used to smile at me. Like we're sharing a joke only the two of us understand.

But also, I don't.

Because I want to punch him.

'Hi,' Ash says, poking his head into the kitchen and sounding relieved to no longer be talking to me as I stand in the doorway behind him.

'My Ashar,' Granny says warmly. 'You will take Ellie to shop, please? Must buy sweets for lunch. Is bad luck to have no desserts.' And I'm pretty sure she's making this up.

'Um, yeah. Sure,' he says, turning around to look at me.

'I'm not sure that's such a good idea,' Dad says uncertainly. And I can tell by looking at him that he's remembering the last time Ash and I were in a car together. When we got in an accident that resulted in my heart ceasing to beat for thirty seconds.

'Noel,' Mum says forcefully.

Ash looks at his feet, and I'm pretty sure Dad's now also remembering that even though the accident wasn't Ash's fault, he accused him of trying to kill me, and told him his dad, who passed away a couple of years ago, would be ashamed of him.

Without meaning to, I step behind Ash, using my finger to draw a circle on the palm of his hand. My code for: it wasn't your fault – you know that, don't you?

Granny glares at Dad until he shakes his head suddenly, clearing his throat.

'I'm not sure why *Amma* bothered you, but it was good of you to come, Ash.'

Mum smiles at Dad and walks over to sit next to him.

'And, thank you,' Dad continues, clearing his throat again. 'For everything you did for my family while I was in the hospital. Your father would have been very proud of you. *I'm* very proud of you,' he says, meeting Ash's eyes.

I can feel the lump in Ash's throat as if it was in mine. As if I'm feeling what he's feeling.

'It was nothing,' he says in a small voice.

'It was everything,' Dad says, sounding slightly wobbly.

They look at each other. The way people do sometimes. Like there's something to say that can't be said with words.

They nod at each other as I pull Ash backwards into the hall, my hand suddenly around his.

'I just need to grab my bag.' I let go of him, painfully aware of him watching me. Remembering the feel of his palm next to mine, like an electric pulse passed between us.

I remind myself of the way it felt on my birthday. When I found out he'd been seeing Hannah. The way he ghosted her when we started going out. I remember his best friend, Rebecca, and their

36

whole weird relationship and how insecure it made me feel. Maybe he makes my heart skip a beat, but it doesn't mean we belong together.

I take a deep breath when I get to my bedroom and jump up and down on the spot. Dr Jada says the best way to get out of your head is to get out of it. Literally. Shake it out. Like Florence and the Machine. Which is when I start hearing Florence and the Machine, 'Shake It Out', in my head, as I grab my bag and head down the stairs to where Ash is stood by the front door, Granny issuing instructions at him.

*Shake it out, Ellie,* Florence croons. *Regrets do not need to collect like old friends.*

'Here's some money,' Mum says, handing me a couple of notes.

Ash opens the door for me, and we step outside on to the street.

'So, how are you?' he asks, looking over at me. 'How's revision and stuff going?'

'Yeah. Fine. Good.'

'How's your dad doing?' he asks, as he opens the car door and I slide inside.

'Yeah. Fine. Good.'

And I'm now concerned I may only have three words to say to him for the rest of my life. How many minutes until we get there? How many times is too many times to say: Yeah. Fine. Good.

'Ellie,' he says, turning to me when he's sat in the driver's side. 'I meant what I said to you a few weeks ago. I messed everything up. But I care about you, and I want you to be happy, and if I'm ever doing anything to make you *not* happy, then I want you to tell me.'

'OK,' I reply, and I've made it to four words now, which seems like progress.

'I mean, me being around. Waiting for you. I don't want you to feel pressured. I don't want this to be awkward for you if you don't want me to wait.'

'I–it's not,' I stammer.

But clearly, it is.

'Shawn said you didn't make it to the last band rehearsal.'

'Shawn?' I ask awkwardly.

'He's worried about you. I'm worried about you.'

Why is everyone worried about me? I've been revising. I'm fine. I'm Alive and Vital and Powerful. I'm choosing me. I'm focusing on exams and family and not the fact that being this near to him is making me want to hyperventilate. Not the fact that everything is changing.

'You don't need to be worried about me. I'm fine.'

'OK,' he says, turning towards the road. 'But if you ever need to talk . . . Unless I'm the thing you want to talk about, because I'm making you unhappy and you want me to go away,' he says worriedly.

'I don't want you to go away. I want you to drive to wherever Granny told you to, so she doesn't kill me. Or you. Or us.'

He smiles.

'And – I want to be friends again,' I say, looking at him. 'Because I miss being friends with you.'

'I miss it too,' he says softly.

'Good,' I smile. 'Now drive. Before Granny explodes.'

'You paint quite the picture,' he grins.

He drives. We buy a cake made of cheese, some profiteroles and a strawberry milkshake, mostly because Ash keeps singing Kelis, 'Milkshake' at me and making me laugh.

When we arrive back at the house, an air of calm appears to have descended as Granny and Mum get dressed for our guests.

'Thanks,' I say shyly, as Ash walks me to the door.

'No problem,' he says, inspecting his shoes. 'Enjoy your lunch thing.'

'I think we both know that isn't going to happen.'

He grins again.

I open the door and step inside the house.

For a second, and no longer, we both just stand there hovering, our fingers inches apart.

'ELLLLLLLLIIIIIEEEE,' Granny shrieks from upstairs.

I am Alive and Vital and Powerful. I am Ellie 2.0 and I choose me.

'I'd better go.'

He nods.

'Bye.'

'Bye,' he returns.

I close the front door and walk into the kitchen, putting the newly bought desserts down on the table.

'We got a cheesecake and some profiteroles,' I offer, as Granny walks in.

'Ah, ah. Good,' she says, giving me her Sri Lankan head shake and taking the wattalapum out of the fridge.

'Um, is that wattalapum?' I ask, staring at it.

'Arrive just after you and Ashar leave,' she says, not looking at me.

'Why didn't you call me?' I ask, clutching my half-drunk milkshake.

'You have fun?' she asks slyly.

And I think I've just been set up by my grandmother. Which is sort of badass, and sort of *not*.

'Now go put on sari,' she says sternly.

And for a minute, I just wish I could put on something that feels like me. The real me.

If I knew who the real me is.

**8**

# I Hate That I Have to Wear This

**Ellie:**
i look 😫

**London Cousin – Not Annoying:**

**London Cousin – Not Annoying:**

**London Cousin – Not Annoying:**

**Ellie:**
stop calling me a snack. am not a snack.

**London Cousin – Not Annoying:**
u r

When I trip over my sari on the way down the stairs, Mum rolls her eyes.

'You did that on purpose, Eleanor,' she says, raising her eyebrows.

'I didn't,' I hiss.

But I did.

I hate that I have to wear this. That I have to pretend to be something I'm not. Some Proper Sri Lankan Tamil Catholic Girl. Which I am, just my version, not some version Granny approves of. I even had to put a gold cross on my necklace instead of the E charm I got for my birthday.

Granny's fussing around the table, setting and resetting the dishes. She looks at me.

'Turn,' she says, indicating I should do a twirl like the world's most awkward ballerina. I turn. Like the world's most awkward ballerina.

'Look nice,' she says approvingly.

Note to self: you are Ellie 2.0. You are a helpful, mature Better Person who doesn't make an issue of having to wear something that makes you feel like a deepfake version of yourself.

I spy myself in the glass of the hallway mirror, something I usually try to avoid unless I'm looking for chin hair. I'm wearing a light pink sari with an embroidered bronze crop top. The outfit itself is beautiful, if a little much for lunch in my own house – but something about wearing it makes me feel uncomfortable. Like my parents are trying to hide who I really am. That I'm not like the rest of my family. That I'm not a real Tamil.

'You look beautiful, *en anbe*,' Dad says, putting his arm around me. Which is nice but also: why? Why do I look beautiful when I'm pretending to be a version of myself that I'm not?

But Mum's the one I can't take my eyes off. Her skin and hair are glowing, her sari, a pale peach with silver thread, draped flatteringly over her elegant frame. Next to her, I feel like a child playing dressing up.

'Nimi look very nice too,' Granny says, looking her up and down. 'Noel, you need tie.'

'I can't breathe if it's buttoned that high,' he says, playing with his collar. Mum and Granny look distraught, while I eye Dad suspiciously. He's playing his recent heart attack for everything it's worth.

'You OK?' Granny asks worriedly.

'Fine, *Amma*. Just need to be able to breathe.'

I'd also like to be able to breathe. Which feels difficult right now, and I don't know why.

The rest of the family are due to arrive later this afternoon, but lunch is a smaller affair. Just us and Charles's parents and sister.

When the doorbell rings, we all jump, apart from Granny, who suddenly appears to have found her zen. She opens the door and greets Charles first.

'*Amma*,' he says, leaning down to hug her. She pinches his cheek.

'*Amma*,' Kitty says, looking lovely in a striking red sari. It's as if my aunt – who for as long as I've known her has played a side part, an accessory to Granny's main character energy – is suddenly the hero of her own story. She looks confident and happy and completely herself, in a way I can't ever imagine feeling.

'This is my mother, Mei; my father, Bo; my sister, Diana, and her children, Ethan and Lina,' Charles says. One by one they all embrace Granny and then us, like some kind of weird royal line-up.

43

'Hey,' I say, as I reach Charles's nephew, Ethan, who refuses to touch me.

'Hey,' he says, looking bored.

'Hi,' I say to Lina, his sister, who's eight and incredibly cute, with long dark hair in two neat plaits.

She grabs me around the waist. 'I like your dress thing.'

'Thanks,' I say, patting her on the head.

'What's up with your brother?' I whisper, as I watch Ethan skulk to the corner of the living room while the two families speak over each other in loud, bright accents.

'Nothing,' she says sunnily. 'He's always like this.'

'Great,' I remark, trying not to roll my eyes. I wish Hope was here. Hope, my cousin from London, makes everything better. At least she's arriving later.

Charles's family are all tall like him, apart from his mum, who's petite and pretty, wearing white jeans and an expensive-looking blazer with gold buttons. She's probably not much younger than Granny, but she looks it. Cool and modern with her hair cut to her shoulders, perfectly straight and parted down the middle. His dad is tall and stocky, dark eyes and dark straight hair, smartly cut in almost exactly the same way as Charles's in navy trousers and a light blue shirt. They look preppy. Like the kind of people who eat in nice restaurants and take taxis when it rains.

His sister seems smaller than the rest of them, even though in reality she's tall too. She seems sad. Like she's reducing herself through sheer force of will.

'Ellie,' Dad says, turning to me. 'Can you take care of Ethan and Lina? Get our guests some drinks?'

44

'Sure.' I nod. 'Come on,' I say, taking Lina's hand and leading her towards the kitchen. Ethan trails behind us, his hands deep in his pockets.

'What would you like?' I ask, opening the fridge.

'Do you have any apple juice?' Lina asks, peering inside.

I nod, taking the carton off the shelf and finding a glass to pour it into.

'Got anything stronger?' Ethan asks, looking over his shoulder.

'Sorry?'

'Where do your parents keep the alcohol?' He asks slowly, as if I'm speaking a different language.

'How old are you?' I ask, passing Lina the glass.

'He's sixteen. He'll be seventeen in six weeks,' she responds for him.

'Li, what have I said about answering for me?' he huffs.

'I guess you'll be having juice too, then,' I say, pouring him a cup.

'I knew you were a square as soon as I saw you,' he replies, rolling his eyes.

'Whatever.'

Like his grandad, Ethan is tall and stocky, where Charles is leaner. His dark hair is long, and he has what seem like grey eyes, although with the amount he keeps rolling them, it's hard to get a decent look. He's nice-looking. Cute in a sort of angry way. He's wearing a lot of black. Straight black jeans, black boots, plain black T-shirt. I wonder why he gets to wear jeans and a T-shirt while I have to dress like Cinderella on her way to a ball she isn't even interested in attending.

He stalks off as Lina looks up at me.

'Can we go to your room?' she asks, taking my hand. I've never been good at saying no to cute kids. It's why Jess's little brother Alfie

45

basically sits on me whenever we're watching a movie, his curly little head directly in front of mine until I can't see anything. But all he has to do is say *plllleeeeeasssssee, Ellllliiiiiie* and I'm basically a living chair.

'Come on. Mum,' I say, as we walk past. 'I'm taking Lina up to my room.' She nods gratefully.

Upstairs, Lina wants to play all my records, look at every single book I own and try on every item in my wardrobe. I let her. Because I've found the easiest way to deal with her is to say yes; because it appears to be the only word she responds to. I stand by the window, looking out on to the street while she tries on my aunty Kitty coat. The one that makes me feel like Ali McGraw in *Love Story*, trying desperately not to sound like Mum when I keep begging her to be careful, because it stains easily.

Just as I'm looking outside, I notice the shadow of a black coat against the grass by the garage. I crane my head to get a better look and see Ethan pouring some of the vodka my dad's lab partner brought back from her trip to Minsk into a plastic water bottle. He puts the bottle down and screws the lid back on, placing it under his jacket. The idiot has no idea that Mavis from next door can see him, and if she catches him, the first thing she'll do is march over to our house to complain about the Irresponsible Youth of Today (which, in fairness, he deserves) and ruin the lunch Granny's spent weeks obsessing over and which apparently, according to her, could make or break Kitty and Charles's marriage.

'Er, hang on a sec. I'll be back,' I say, turning to Lina. She says nothing. Already nose deep in a box of my *Beatles Book* magazines.

I walk quickly down the stairs, out the front door and down the side of the house.

'Er, hey,' Ethan says, looking up guiltily.

I grab him by his arm, pulling him into the garage by the side door.

'What are you doing?' I demand.

'Nothing.' He shrugs nonchalantly. 'Chill. You're like an uptight stick of cotton candy,' he says, motioning at my sari.

'What?' I demand. 'I. Am. Not.' Except now I feel like I am. Sickly coloured and puffy.

'I know what you're doing,' I conclude. 'I saw you from my window, and so did half our neighbours probably.'

'You people are so backward,' he huffs.

'You people?' I scream. 'What do you mean by *you people?*'

He blushes. 'I didn't mean it like that. I meant, like, people, as in *your* kind of people.'

'*My* kind of people,' I demand. 'And what's that? What is *my kind* of people, Ethan. Brown people, I assume? We're backward, are we? Not good enough for your family, are we?'

He looks slightly terrified.

'You know, I am so *bored* of people making assumptions about what *kind* of people my family are. I don't make them about you. Why do you make them about me?'

'I didn't mean that,' he says, looking embarrassed. 'I meant this place, this weird little village where everyone's watching you. Or should I say watching *us* because we don't look like them.'

'Oh,' I say, suddenly realising what he meant. 'But still. I saw you put vodka in that water bottle and if anyone finds out, it's going to ruin today.'

And I am not doing it all again on a different day, in a different sari.

'Just don't say anything,' he says, looking up at me from where he's been inspecting his shoes.

47

'Hand it over.'

He passes me the plastic bottle.

'And the other one,' I say, my other arm out.

'Come on, don't be such a—'

'Square? Rectangle? Person who doesn't drink at lunchtime while their elderly grandparents are next door?'

He grins.

'Fiiiine,' he says, handing it over.

'What's this whole Marlon Brando thing you've got going on anyway?' I ask, as I take the bottles away from him and hide them in the back of the garage.

'Who's Marlon Brando?' he asks, screwing his face up.

'1950s Hollywood. Angry, brooding type. Difficult. Wore a lot of black.'

'I'm not angry,' he says defensively.

'No, no. You sound very happy,' I reply sarcastically.

'Well, maybe if your dad said he was taking you away for the weekend, then didn't bother to show up, you'd be angry too.'

'I'm sorry,' I say, embarrassed by the tears I suddenly see in his eyes as he looks away quickly. 'I didn't mean to . . . I shouldn't have . . . It's none of my business . . .'

'It's fine,' he says, turning back to me. 'He's a loser.'

'Yeah. He is,' I offer half-heartedly.

'I mean, it's all my mum anyway, you know.' He shrugs. 'It's not like I should expect him to start caring now he's gone. He didn't care when he was around.'

'Ethan, I—' I begin.

'It's OK,' he says, giving me a look. 'You don't have to feel sorry for

48

me. I look good in black.'

'What?' I ask, wondering if I've misheard him.

'It works for me,' he says dismissively. 'This whole Marlon Brando thing.'

'What?' I ask incredulously, my mouth now so wide open I could catch flies. 'I thought you didn't know who Marlon Brando was?'

'I don't. But I assume he was good-looking and charming.'

'What?'

'What?' he says, mocking me.

'You are *not* charming.'

'But I am good-looking?' he teases.

'Er, er, er,' I splutter.

'I'm sure Marlon was a very popular man,' he says smugly.

'He was,' I say curtly, 'but I don't think he was ever happy.'

He looks sick. The glint in his eye suddenly black.

'I don't mean you'll never be happy,' I offer quickly. 'Sorry, I was just saying Brando was complicated. Not that you actually care about Brando.'

'Who said I didn't care?'

I raise an eyebrow at him.

'You're just comparing yourself to him because it makes you feel superior. And OK, yes, he was undeniably one of the greatest actors of the twentieth century, and a very comely man.'

'Comely?' he asks.

'Yes, you know, attractive to look at. Agreeable-looking.'

'Agreeable-looking?' he laughs. 'Are you from the 1950s as well?'

'Anyway,' and I can't remember where I was going with this, other than listing all of Brando's greatest points, which I do not believe Ethan shares because he is definitely not agreeable. 'You can feel as superior as you like, but—'

'Trust me,' he cuts in darkly. 'I don't feel superior.'

'Oh,' I say, not knowing how to respond. 'Well, you're not *that* bad.'

'Listen, Freud,' he says, staring at me. 'I just like black, all right. And I wanted a drink. Why'd you have to come outside anyway?'

'I'm guessing your mum's pretty stressed about your dad not showing up. Maybe it'd be better if she didn't have to deal with you as well.'

'Whatever,' he mutters, but he's staring at his feet, looking slightly mollified.

'Come on, let's go find Lina,' I say, pulling him out of the garage and on to the driveway.

He grins suddenly. 'You should check your drawers. She likes to steal things.'

'What?'

'What?' he responds, imitating me again. 'Are we not perfect enough for your perfect little family? I know what happened with your grandmother. I know she didn't think they should get married.'

'People make mistakes,' I say, turning to face him.

'Hey, Ellie.'

I look over my shoulder at the sound of my name. The human cotton candy who is about to join forces with Marlon Brando's family, for better or worse.

'Wow. You look . . .' he says, waving his arms around as I move towards him.

'Like an uptight stick of cotton candy,' I say, glancing at Ethan.

'I was going to say really pretty.' He blushes.

God, he's hot.

Shawn. My Shawn. Or *not* my Shawn. That's the point.

'What are you doing here?' I ask, staring at him.

Stop staring at him.

'I was just in the area, and I thought I'd say hello. Who's this?' he asks, looking at Ethan.

'Marlon Brando,' he says disparagingly.

Shawn glances at me as I roll my eyes.

'It's a long story. I'll tell you another time. But I can't talk right now. We have a family thing.'

'OK,' he says simply. 'Are you coming to rehearsal tomorrow?'

'I don't know,' I say, looking over my shoulder at the house. 'Like I said, family stuff.'

'Come on, Ellie,' he says, his blue eyes watching me. 'We miss you.'

Why do I like his blue eyes watching me?

'I'll let you know,' I capitulate.

'Cool,' he says.

'Cool,' I reply, blushing. Thinking about the last time we sang at a gig together. About how that felt.

'*Cool,*' says Marlon Brando in an irritating voice.

For a second, Shawn leans down to hug me and I lean up into him. It feels warm and soothing, like a cup of tea on a cold day. Like just the thing you need at just the time you need it. But he does something weird when he lets go, or he gets caught on me, or pulls at my shoulder. The part that adjusts the top half of my sari from where it's tucked in and pulled together. And it starts to fall apart. A lot.

'Oh God,' I say, as he tries to let go of me. 'Don't let go just yet.'

He pulls me back into him. Like I'm being coy. Like he thinks I want another hug.

'I think you've undone my sari. I haven't put it on properly. I'm not very good at it.'

'Oh,' he says loudly.

'Just don't let go for a minute.' I reach around myself, trying to gather the fabric at the back.

'Ellie?' Dad says, poking his head out the front door and eyeing Shawn and me embracing on the driveway. 'What's going on out here?'

'Nothing,' I say, letting go of Shawn and turning towards him while he desperately tries to hold the cloth together behind me.

'OK. Well, come in. We're about to eat,' Dad says suspiciously, before going back inside.

'I'll take it from here,' Marlon Brando says, taking the sari out of Shawn's hand. 'Shuffle forward in front of me.'

Shawn lets go, staring at Ethan as he holds the shimmering cloth tight behind me.

'Boyfriend or ex-boyfriend?' Ethan asks, as Shawn leaves and I wave goodbye.

'Neither,' I reply. 'Anyway, why are you helping me?' I ask, as we reach the front door.

'Don't mention the vodka and we'll call it even,' he smirks.

God. This guy is the worst.

# 9

# I Got You, Snack

'Hope!' I hiss, as soon as she walks through the front door.

'E!' she says, hugging me. 'What's going on?'

'My sari,' I say, motioning towards it. 'I messed it up. It keeps coming undone.'

'What?' she says, looking confused.

'My sari,' I repeat. 'It's gone weird.'

'Come on,' she says, dragging me up the stairs. 'Let's have a look.'

'You really weren't joking,' she says, walking behind me, trying to hold it together. 'Did you use a safety pin?'

'Of course I did,' I say, exasperated. 'Mum usually helps me, but Ash and I got back late, so she didn't have time.'

'Ash?' she asks, widening her eyes. 'I thought you two broke up?'

'We did. He just gave me a lift to the shop. It was for Granny.'

'For Granny?' she says under her breath, raising a perfectly plucked eyebrow as we enter the bathroom.

'Don't look at me like that.'

'Like what?' she responds innocently.

She looks beautiful. Her lime-green sari perfectly tied, accentuating her tall, slim frame and annoyingly chiselled face. She looks like she's made out of marble. Like she belongs on the steps of a temple.

'You look nice,' I say glumly.

'So do you,' she says, unwinding the cloth and starting to right the mess I made putting it on in the first place. 'I think we need to start again,' she says, trying to keep the amusement out of her voice.

'I look horrible, Hope. I *feel* horrible.'

'Don't say that,' she says, looking up at me from where she's now perched on her knees, trying to fix me. 'Why do you feel horrible?'

'I feel like a fraud,' I say, my eyes filling with tears. 'I feel like everyone wants me to be someone else. Someone I'm not. Because I'm not good enough as I am. Because I don't fit in.'

'Whoa, whoa, whoa,' she says, reaching up to grab my hands. 'Where did this come from? What happened to the Boss Ellie I saw at Christmas?'

'I don't know,' I say, suddenly snivelling. 'I think it's just exams and stuff. I feel really stressed.'

She stands up and gives me a hug. And it dislodges the knot in my chest. Just for a minute.

It feels like one of the hugs I used to get from Hayley. Our tall girl, small girl embrace. It's just Hayley got so thin it stopped feeling the same. Hayley, who I should have noticed was struggling.

'Ellie, you've been through a lot this year.'

'Why does everyone keep saying that?' I ask, exasperated.

'Because it's true,' she says slowly. 'Your accident, your dad's heart attack, the stuff with Ash, and now the exams and the new baby. It's a lot. You must be feeling stuff.'

No.

No.

No.

I am Ellie 2.0.

She strokes my hair as I lean into her.

'It's all right, my little snack. You're beautiful and special and funny and brilliant and everything's going to be OK when I get this sari done up properly.'

'OK,' I monotone.

'Next time, just tell Granny you're not wearing it.'

'Have you *ever* tried telling Granny *anything*?'

She grins. 'True. Just turn up not wearing it.'

'I wish I was that brave.'

'Come on,' she cajoles. 'Fill me in on the goss. I need details about these people. The boy's cute. Bit emo for my taste, but cute. The granny's très chic. Makes our granny look . . . less chic.'

'Don't be mean, Hope.'

'Listen, I'd take our granny over très chic granny any day of the week. I'm just saying the woman knows how to dress.'

'I've missed you,' I grin.

'I know, snack. But I got you. I'm here.'

She takes my hand. 'Now let's go eat some of those leftover spare ribs and Bombay mix. Looks special.'

I messaged her a picture of Granny's banquet earlier.

I start laughing just as she does, so grateful to have her here.

'I've got band practice tomorrow if you want to come?' I say, as we head down the stairs, my sari now perfectly tied.

'With Dirty Blond?' she asks, winking. 'Why not.'

# 10

# A Disturbing Turn of Events

In a disturbing turn of events, Hope appears to be flirting with Ethan. While this is a welcome change of routine from her usually inappropriate crushes on people I consider far too old for her, other than being the right age, Ethan hasn't exactly proven himself to be a catch thus far.

'Hope!' I hiss at her for the millionth time. She looks over her shoulder at me, deliberately ignoring my tone.

'What?' she hisses after I finally separate her from her new inappropriate crush.

'What are you doing? I thought you were seeing someone?'

She shakes her head.

'He's being . . .' she says, trying to find the right word. 'Annoying,' she finishes.

'That's not a reason to lead Ethan on.'

'Lead him on?' she laughs. 'We're talking about the latest series of *Euphoria*. Chill.'

'I will not *chill*,' I hiss back. Why does everyone keep telling me to chill? I am a perfectly even temperature.

'Clearly,' she grins. 'E,' she says slightly more seriously. 'I haven't seen you this uptight in a while. I'm worried about you.'

'Are you telling me,' I respond slowly, ignoring her comment, 'that you're not doing *anything* to make that boy think you like him?'

'I didn't say that,' she smiles, like a wolf with a baby rabbit caught in its jaws. 'He's cute. I'm single. We're both going to the wedding. It might be fun.'

'*Fun?*' I screech.

'Ellie, you sound like your dad . . .'

I try to change the tone in my voice to one that suggests I am not a middle-aged, well-meaning but grumpy Sri Lankan man who thinks fun should be licensed, so you can justify and regulate what fun looks like and who should be allowed to have it.

'I found him outside with a bottle of vodka earlier. I had to hide it in the garage.'

'Ooooh, vodka,' she says, sounding interested.

'Hope! He's not going to be a good influence on you!'

'All right, Captain Fun. Let's get back to the party. And when I say party, I use that word in the loosest possible sense. Because it's not that fun, is it? Although you and Ethan and I *could* be having some fun – so, why don't we?'

'Bleurgh,' I reply.

'That's not a word.'

'It is now.'

'OK,' she says, taking my arm. 'Let's go. I'm staging an intervention. You need to calm down.'

'I am calm!' I say in a Mary Poppins-esque tone. I love Mary Poppins. She's practically perfect in every way.

We walk back into the living room, where the grown-ups are drinking wine, including Dad, who's claiming red wine is good for his heart. Mum looks irritated with him, and like not being allowed to drink wine is making her even more irritated. Granny is talking to très chic granny, looking slightly pink in the face, which is sweet but also terrifying – because what is Granny like with a hangover?

Shudder.

Kitty and Charles and Diana (OMG, Charles and Diana . . . did the Sòngs do that on purpose?) are talking to Mum and Dad, while Lina sits on the floor playing with her mum's phone. Ethan seems to be looking for someone who I can only assume is the marble beauty to my right.

'Hey,' Hope says, sidling up to Ethan. 'Should we go up to Ellie's room?'

He nods, ignoring me.

'I will be joining you,' I add, like a chaperone in one of those period films Mum's obsessed by. The ones that never seem to have anyone that looks like us in them.

'I figured,' he says, not smiling.

At the top of the stairs, as we turn into my bedroom, he looks at the peeling Blur poster on my wall.

'Blur?' he queries.

'Yes. And?' I ask primly.

'I love Blur,' he says, shaking his head.

'I thought you'd be more into, like, something more . . . I don't know . . .' Hope says, being entirely unsubtle.

'Dark?' he grins. 'Angry?'

She smiles back. 'Yeah, kind of.'

58

'Can I have a look at your records?' he asks, pointing towards my bookshelf, piled high with albums.

I nod.

He pulls a few out and I have to admit his taste isn't awful. And maybe he isn't awful. Then he pulls out the vodka he clearly went back and took from the garage, and I revise my opinion. He is awful.

'What are you doing?' I hiss. I have become a hisser. He's made me into one of those people who spit words instead of saying them.

'Relax,' he says, as Hope looks uncomfortable.

'Ethan, our parents are going to lose their minds.'

He laughs. 'My dad *literally* doesn't care,' he says, taking a swig from the bottle.

Hope and I shake our heads when he offers it to us.

'What do you mean?' Hope asks sympathetically.

'Ever since my parents separated, he's just, like, disappeared,' he says, staring into space.

Hope and I share a look.

'So, what happened this weekend?'

'Lina and I weren't even supposed to come to this,' he says, gesturing at the room. 'We should have been with my dad, but he never showed up to get us.'

'I'm sorry,' I say quietly. 'That's horrible. Have you heard from him?'

He shrugs, which we take to mean no, and takes another swig from the bottle.

'I don't think that's going to help,' Hope says, sounding wise.

'Probably not,' he laughs, and takes another gulp.

I walk over to my bookshelf and pull out one of my favourite new albums. A band Shawn introduced me to. I take my copy of *1* by the

59

Beatles off the record player and replace it with the new vinyl, sliding it carefully from the sleeve and placing it gently on to the turntable.

I put the needle on the final song, letting the music swell inside the room. It's classic indie rock. Beautiful and fragile. Angry and hopeful. Like the sound of guitars and drums and vocals might shatter, as if it were a thing you could pick up and drop that would break into a thousand pieces. Inhaler, 'If You're Gonna Break My Heart', from an album called *Cuts & Bruises*.

To me, this is the sound of a heart in pieces. A heart trying to find its light.

Ethan just sits there listening to it, swigging at his vodka, his eyes momentarily as black as his T-shirt. When it ends he puts the bottle down, so I collect it and hide it behind my bed.

Hope puts her arm around him.

'Time for something a bit more upbeat,' she smiles. He turns towards her and half smiles back.

I put Billie Eilish, 'Bad Guy', on, and Hope jumps up and starts bopping around in her sari. Ethan and I try to ignore her. Resolutely staring at the floor, like the two clearly awkward people we are.

But it's impossible. Because Hope won't allow it.

'Come on,' she says, pulling us both up breathlessly.

And so, we do.

Because resistance, much like heartbreak, is futile.

# 11

# REVISE! First Exam in 4 Weeks!

I'm in the main hall at school, during what should be the Easter holidays, wearing a dress Hope made out of an apron. It's white-and-yellow striped with a big, wide skirt, like I should be twirling in a field somewhere, singing to no one about the hills being alive. My ankle-length white socks are embroidered with tiny daisies, and I'm wearing my new Converse high-tops. Butter yellow with white laces.

The last time I was here, I was singing onstage with the band. Shawn and Benji and Elliott and Lucas. The coolest people you've ever seen close up. And I was one of them. Part of the band. Me, Ellie Pillai, welcomed to the inner circle. It felt amazing. It felt like I was declaring to the world that I'd arrived. That I was finally where I was supposed to be. In the hallway outside, just by the girls' changing rooms, Ash told me he'd wait for me. That he was still in love with me. Then Shawn and I stood onstage singing to each other, as if we were the only people that existed. I felt in control. I felt like I had choices that were mine to make.

I remember the night vividly. The feel of Jess and Hayley as I danced next to them when Elina started DJ'ing the band came offstage. The feeling that everything was just beginning. That it was all going to be OK.

And then I went home, and the euphoria of it all just seemed to disappear. Dad was building a cot when I got in. In Amis's room. Granny carefully unpacking some of his baby things to put away in the new baby's drawers, as if Amis was being replaced.

I watched Dad as he made the cot. Huffing and panting, a sheen of sweat on his forehead like he was doing too much. Getting tired. Like he was going to have another Thing I Can't Bring Myself to Think About. I felt scared. I felt like everything I'd ever known was suddenly changing, and then I woke up the next day to my phone alarm announcing *REVISE! First exam in 4 weeks!* – and the breath in my chest started to constrict. My lungs started to collapse.

I wanted to call Ash. Or Jess or Hayley or Shawn. Hope. I wanted to say: *I don't like this. I don't like the way I feel today.*

But I didn't.

I found a podcast to help quieten my mind, because I didn't want to worry Mum or Dad or Granny. Because they're worried about the baby. Because I know they're not replacing Amis, I know he'll always be our family, I just also know we have bad luck sometimes. Really bad luck. And my new brother, this new baby, he has to be OK. Which means I need to not stress anyone out. Especially Mum or Dad or Granny.

Thank God for Dr Jada.

Suddenly, standing here in this hall, the last few weeks feel like a weight. Like I'm carrying an enormous invisible backpack.

I look around at Elliott and Lucas unpacking their guitars, and feel an intense sense of belonging, coupled with a desire to run away. To make everything disappear by moving as far away from it as possible.

'Hey, Ellie,' Lucas says, pulling me into a hug. 'It's good to see you.'

I blush. He's wearing a light purple sweatshirt and loose ankle-length jeans. Looking like he always looks. Too cool to be talking to me.

'Who's this?' he asks, looking at Hope.

'Hope!' Shawn says, picking her up. 'I didn't know you were going to be here.'

'Well. I am,' she announces imperiously.

Shawn and I grin at each other.

'Hey,' he says, leaning down to hug me.

'Hey,' I reply. 'Listen, I, er,' I try to say.

'You, er,' he mimics, smiling.

'ELLIE,' Benji screams, as he enters the room.

Benji. Shawn's best friend. Frenetic drummer. Expert in sarcasm. Enjoys mocking me far too much.

'You are looking . . . much the same as always.'

'Thanks,' I remark, rolling my eyes.

'Who's the groupie? She can stay,' he says, opening the doors to the cupboards and pulling out an assortment of musical instruments.

'Are you sure Hayley won't mind?' I tease. Even from behind, I can see his ears turning pink. Benji blushing seems almost sweet. He mutters something inaudible into the cupboard, and I decide not to do that again. He doesn't need reminding that he likes Hayley and has no idea how she feels about him. Been there. Done that.

'Hey, Ellie,' Elliott says, all flame-red hair and intense blue eyes, as he walks in and goes straight to help Benji pull the rest of his drum kit out. 'We missed you. Have you been away or something?'

'Er, no,' I mutter, as Hope gives me a look. 'Just revising. Couldn't get away from the old books,' I say, affecting a jolly-old-man tone.

Really, Ellie? REALLY?

'We've got a gig at Blues Factory in a couple of weeks. Can you make it?' he asks, popping his head back out of the cupboard.

'I mean, yeah. Sure.'

I wish Shawn would give me another hug.

'So, um,' I say, reaching down to my bag and pulling out a piece of paper. 'I wrote a new song. I thought maybe we could give it a try.'

'Cool,' Lucas enthuses.

'Do you mind if I play it to you on the piano, instead of using the keyboard? I know we won't have one for gigs, I just want you to get a better sense of it.'

They all nod, their instruments now set up, watching me as I walk towards the piano by the side of the stage.

A few months ago, the thought of this would have terrified me. The idea that anyone was watching me. That anyone was listening to me. But all that's changed now, and I'm so proud of myself for being here. For being Ellie 2.0. The Ellie that can handle anything.

I can handle anything, I remind myself. Anything. Maybe.

I ignore the feeling edging at my consciousness and put my fingers on the keys. It feels soothing and peaceful, like my worries disappear beneath the weight of the notes. I sing like I'm trying to tell them something. Like sharing my words can fix me. Explain it all. And when I finish, they ask me what key it's in and we start playing it together. Trying out different rhythms and sounds until it starts to feel like something more than it is. Something special.

When rehearsal is over, Hope tells me she filmed the final take. We watch it back as a group, and I wonder how I can look so confident, so at ease. How I can look as though nothing could hurt me, when for some reason, right now, it feels like anything can.

Like everything can.

# 12

# A Girl Called Ellie

My name is Ellie. Ellie Pillai.

And I hurt, but I don't know why.

Or maybe I do, I just don't want to say it. Because saying the words out loud makes them real. Saying the words out loud makes them impossible to ignore.

I want to be better. I want to try harder. I want to be the version of myself I told myself I am.

My name is Ellie. Ellie Pillai.

When does this feeling stop?

When do I begin?

# ♡ Song 1 ♡

## As It Seems – Intro, Verse, Chorus, Middle Eight

It means everything because it is everything. The way I feel now. The way I've always felt, even if I couldn't say it.

> *All is not as it seems.*
> *I have to find my way back to me.*

It's all piano. All ballad and heartbreak. It's all me – even if I don't want to be all ballad and heartbreak.

It's the sound of moving on, but not moving on. Of wanting to stop thinking about things when you just can't.

It's confusion, and love, and light, and all points in between.

It's the space between words.

The silence between notes.

It's me.

Just me.

*All is not as it seems.*

# 13

# The Beginning, All Over Again

When the Easter holidays are over and it's time to go back to school, I'd like to say I'm happy about it. But exams are starting to feel real. Like, really, really real; and as exams get closer, so does the end of the year. The end of GCSEs and everything we've worked for over the last three years. Then comes the start of something new. The beginning, all over again.

I've never been good with beginnings.

To make matters worse, Hayley delivers the following news.

'I'm applying for a place at BackStage. In London. Mrs Aachara said a couple of spots have opened up, and she thinks James and I should try out.'

Dear gods. NO.

'What does that mean? Are you moving? When? Why? Are you sure you're ready? Because it's a lot, Hay. It's a lot.'

And more to the point, *I'm* not ready for her to go.

'I'm just auditioning, E. I probably won't come close to getting in. I just can't believe she thinks I'm good enough,' she beams, and Hayley never beams.

'That's amazing,' I say, trying to breathe – and there I go again. Trying to do something that should come naturally to an ordinary human body.

'So, you *and* James?'

'Yeah,' she says awkwardly. 'I know.'

'What are you going to do?'

'I'm going to come up with an audition piece.'

'Great,' I smile, despite my reservations. Because my mission this term is to be the friend I wasn't last term. Which should be easy, because I was a terrible friend last term.

'If they don't give you a place, they're idiots,' I say loyally, even though the idea of her leaving is making me want to put my head between my knees and breathe into a brown paper bag.

'Speaking of James . . .' I say, watching him approach.

We're stood in the corner of the corridor, not far from the Cool Girls' Wall, where Jess is talking to Billie and Addy McQueen. When Jess came out a few months ago, the McQueens didn't bother talking to her until they knew it was OK with everybody else, as if they needed permission to be her friend – so Jess stopped being friends with them, and I was happy with that. That she'd seen they don't treat everyone the way they treat people like her. But she broke up with Elina last week, and in typical understated, undramatic Jess style, only mentioned it to Hay and me yesterday, when it happened days before. But I know Jess. I know her heart's broken; I know she's vulnerable. I just really hope she can still see the McQueens for what they really are.

'Hi, James,' Billie and Addy chorus, as he walks past them. 'Hi, Sadie. Love your bag!'

James and what appears to be his new girlfriend, Sadie, walk towards us holding hands. I glance over at Hayley, just as Jess does. Our eyes meeting in the middle.

'Hey,' James says, looking at the floor. 'How was your Easter?'

'Fine,' Hayley says, also looking at the floor.

'Cool.'

You could cut the tension with a knife. As in, the air around them feels thick with feelings, and I don't know what the feelings are, but they are *awkward*.

'I'm Ellie,' I say, looking at Sadie. She's average height and build with long red hair, freckles dotted prettily across her nose, like one of those Strawberry Shortcake dolls I wanted when I was little.

'Hi,' she says sweetly. 'You're Ash Anderson's girlfriend, right?'

'No,' I reply quickly.

She blushes. 'Sorry. You're with Shawn Kowalski now, aren't you?'

Really, gods, REALLY?

'No,' I respond again. 'Shawn and I are just in a band together.'

'I love you guys,' she says kindly. 'I love that song you do together.'

'Cooooool,' I respond, noticing Hayley's stone-like face. 'It's really nice to meet you, but we have to, um, go to, um . . .'

*Where?* Where do we need to go to? Somewhere. Anywhere but here.

'To the library,' Jess says, appearing next to us and grabbing Hayley's arm. 'To return some books,' she adds unnecessarily.

'Byeeeee,' I shout, as we drag her away.

Out of the corner of my eye, I watch Sadie squeezing James's arm as she kisses him on the cheek.

'You OK?' I ask Hayley cheerily.

70

She says nothing.

Jess and I look at each other.

'Hay?' Jess says. 'You still with us?'

'Hmmmmn,' Hayley says, looking up at her.

'Are. You. OK?' I repeat.

'Yeah, yeah. I'm fine,' she says, shaking her head. 'I really think I'm *fine*,' she smiles. It looks genuine. Really, truly genuine.

'Good,' I say, surprised. 'That's good.'

Then I see the colour drain from Jess's face as Elina and Ash round the corner; and I haven't seen Jess's face do this since she and Elina broke up the first time round. Before she came out. Before she swore she wasn't going to run away from things any more. And it feels like that's what this is. Running away from things.

But I remind myself that this is none of my business.

None of My Business.

And Do Not Get Involved.

Just Be a Good Friend and Listen to What She Wants and Feels, and everything will be OK.

'Hi,' Jess says, strangled. Elina gives her a look. One that seems to say: Don't Talk to Me. Ever.

'Um,' I say awkwardly.

'We have to go,' Hayley says, pulling Jess away. 'Library,' she continues, shouting over her shoulder.

Elina turns to hug Ash goodbye. 'See you later,' she says to him.

'Bye, Ellie,' she says, looking down at me.

'I'm sorry about you and Jess,' I say stupidly.

'Me too,' she says, her eyes filling with tears.

She leans down into me, and I hold her close, her hair tickling my

71

ear. It's slightly longer now, a messy ear-length bob, her dark roots showing through her blonde dye job. As always, she looks effortlessly chic in a canary-yellow silk slip skirt and red vest top with matching lipstick, her feet in pink satin ballet slippers. Not for the first time, I'm glad that when I wear non-uniform next year, she won't be here to witness my attempts at fashion.

'It's OK,' I murmur. 'It's going to be OK.'

'Why is she doing this?' she asks, pushing herself away from me.

'Because she loves you,' I say stiltedly – and admittedly, it does sound weird when you say it out loud. That she's hurting someone because she loves them. 'She doesn't want to hold you back.'

'Don't I get a say in any of it?' Elina asks angrily. 'She wouldn't even listen to me. She won't even talk about it.'

'Sounds like Jess . . .' I trail away.

Note to self: None of My Business. Do Not Get Involved.

'I have to go,' she says flatly.

As she walks away, I look at Ash.

'Who would have thought we'd be the only ones who could talk to each other without any drama,' I say jokingly.

He grins, his hands in the pocket of his ankle-length dark grey trousers. He's wearing a short-sleeved black shirt covered in tiny white smiley faces over the top of a white T-shirt tucked in at the waist. No sign of paint anywhere on his clothes.

'How was Granny's lunch?'

'*My* granny's lunch?' I joke.

He touches my arm lightly. 'Yes. Your granny.'

'It's OK,' I laugh. 'I don't mind sharing. It was good. I mean, my cousin came for the weekend, and it was, you know, not terrible.'

'Sounds like a good time,' he teases.

'I really want you to meet her,' I say without thinking. 'I think you'd like her.' And then I think: Hope. Beautiful, perfect, marble-faced Hope. Maybe not. Maybe he'd like her too much.

'I'd like that.'

'I'd better go too,' I say, throwing my thumb up behind me. 'Or I'll be late for registration.'

He nods.

'Ellie,' he says, grabbing my arm as I try to walk past him. 'There's this exhibition on at the Shelley. Beatles paparazzi pictures,' he explains quickly. 'But of the fans, not the band.' I widen my eyes interestedly. 'I wondered if you wanted to see it?'

'With you?' I ask stupidly. 'Like, a date?'

'No,' he says hastily, and it feels a bit too hastily. Like I wanted him to say yes, even though I didn't. 'Just friends. No pressure. I couldn't think of anyone else I'd like to see it with more than you.'

'Oh,' I respond.

Try another word, Ellie. Like yes. Or no.

'Um.'

Not that one.

'Er . . .'

Or that one.

Come on, brain!

You're revising.

You can't.

You're having a miniature meltdown about how much everything is changing. There's a new baby coming, and Hayley might be leaving, and Jess is sad, and there is Too Much Change.

73

The word you're looking for is no. You'd love to. But you can't.

'OK.'

*What?*

You are a traitor, brain!

'Great,' he says warmly; and it feels like his face is lighting up against his will. Like my face may be doing the exact same thing. 'I'll message you,' he says, saluting me.

What. Just. Happened? This is not focusing on me. This is not being Alive and Vital and Powerful. It's just, I'm not sure I really want to focus on me. If I really want to think about things at all.

I walk down the corridor on my way to form room and do what I always do in situations like this.

**Ellie:**
jus agreed 2 to go 2 shelley w ash . . .

**Ellie:**
is this a *terrible* idea???

**Jess:**
why wld it b?

**Ellie:**
dr jada says clear boundaries r important

**Hayley:**
do u want to c whatever it is?

**Ellie:**
. . .

**Jess:**
jus b clear is as friends

**Ellie:**
he already said that

**Hayley:**
i'm 4 anything that gets u 2 leave ur house

**Ellie:**
feels weird

**Hayley:**
then don't go

**Ellie:**
but nice. i miss him.

**Hayley:**
then go

**Ellie:**
is it bad that it feels nice??

**Hayley:**
r u coming 2 registration?? ur late

**Ellie:**
omw

**Ellie:**
ru ok @JessKing?

**Jess:**
👍

But something about Jess's thumbs-up emoji makes me feel like she's the exact opposite of the feeling she's trying to convey. Something I understand more than I want to admit.

Be a better person, Ellie. Stop thinking about Ash, Ellie. Stop getting distracted, Ellie. Or at least get distracted by the right things.

Your best friend needs you.

Even if she doesn't want to admit it.

# 14

# Scary-Looking Aunties

When I get home from school, there's a scary-looking aunty in the living room.

'Ellie, this is Aunty Agnes,' Mum says, giving me a look that seems alarmingly warning-like. Alarming. Warning-like. These are not good feelings to associate with a Scary-Looking Aunty.

'She's a friend of your grandmother's. She's here for a holiday but she's back in London next week. We thought she might be able to help find you a sari.'

Aunty Kitty, who hadn't planned to wear a sari at her wedding, has finally given in to Granny's demands and said she'll wear a sari and a wedding dress for the Catholic ceremony, because apparently, she has to wear a qipao for the Chinese wedding, and Granny doesn't see why the Catholic wedding shouldn't include Tamil traditions too.

On the one hand, I don't see why Kitty and Charles can't just have the wedding they want to have, wearing whatever it is that they want to wear. On the other, I know it's more complex than that. That the reality of merging two cultures in a way that feels respectful to both families, to each heritage and its history, is about compromise. Creating new traditions, new cultures.

Which means: Hope and I have to compromise too. Which means: saris because Granny says so. Ugh.

'Come, come,' Aunty Agnes says, giving me her Sri Lankan head shake.

I move towards her slowly. Carefully. Like she's a horse that might spook and kick me in the face.

'Hmmmm,' she says, as I approach. 'Turn, turn.'

I turn.

'She is dark,' she says, looking over at Granny. Granny nods disloyally, while I burn with rage.

'I like my skin,' I say through gritted teeth. 'I think it's a very nice colour.'

'It's beautiful,' Mum says, putting her arm around me.

'Chkkkk,' Aunty Agnes responds. 'Why this generation soooo sensitive? You are very pretty. A little dark, but Tamil, no? All dark!' she says, suddenly giggling.

'Like night!' says Granny, suddenly guffawing.

'Tamil nights!' Aunty Agnes says, fountains of saliva spraying from her mouth.

'Hahahahahahaha,' Granny continues – and I think Aunty Agnes might be to Granny what Hope is to me.

'Anyway,' Aunty Agnes says, wiping her eyes. 'Come, come,' she says, pulling me towards her. 'I do not mean upset you, Ellie. We all Tamil. We all being told we too dark by our aunties,' she says, winking. 'You know, your grandmother very proud of you. She tell me very often about you.'

Granny? Proud? Of *me*?

'Some colours are better than other, though. For your skin,' she says with a flourish. 'Gold and turquoise,' she says to Granny, 'will suit both their complexions.' She looks to Mum for affirmation.

'Sounds fine to me,' Mum says, stroking her ever-expanding belly. 'If that's OK with Ellie and Hope – and Kitty, of course.'

Granny chkkkkks, as if the opinions of these people (the ones wearing it, and the one whose wedding it is) mean nothing in comparison to hers.

I shrug. 'I mean, I'd rather not wear a sari at all, but . . .'

They all ignore me.

'You will be my eyes, Agnes. Go with Kitty and Christine this weekend?' Granny asks her.

'Why you not come with us?' Agnes says, looking over the teacup she's sipping from.

'Cannot leave Nimi,' Granny says, scandalised. 'She is pregnant! At her age! Also, Ellie has important exams. I cannot go until wedding, when all go together,' she says firmly.

'No, *Amma*,' Mum says, shaking her head. 'Kitty's your only daughter, you have to be there. You'll regret it if you don't go.'

'Mmmmm, mmmmm,' Agnes murmurs in agreement.

'Is not *only* daughter,' Granny says, eyeing Mum, who puts her hand out and places it on Granny's momentarily.

'Ellie can go with you,' Mum says, her eyes widening as if she's had a brilliant idea. 'For the weekend.' She turns to look at me. 'That way you can choose the sari yourself.'

'What about you?' I ask.

'I need to look after Dad. Plus, I've got some things to do in the baby's room.'

The baby's room.

The baby.

I make a face involuntarily, Mum pretending not to have seen me.

'What about revision?' I ask her.

She waves me away. 'I've never seen you study as hard as you have been this year, Ellie. You can always revise on the train there and back.'

'It *would* be nice to see Hope,' I say, thinking it over.

'See?' Mum says excitedly.

'Cannot leave Noel,' Granny says stubbornly. And I hadn't thought about that either. About leaving Dad when we almost lost him.

'I'll be fine,' I hear Dad shout from the room next door. Clearly, nothing wrong with his hearing.

'He'll be fine,' Mum confirms, soothing us both.

'I mean,' I say, looking at Granny, 'I will if you will?'

'Would be nice to see Kitty,' she admits. 'She is only in London for one night.'

'Go,' Mum says cheerily. Too cheerily. Like she wants to get rid of us.

'We will book first class!' says Aunty Agnes. 'Anton will get us discount.'

'Ooooooh,' Granny says, matching her Sri Lankan head shake with her friend's.

And it's decided.

We'll travel Saturday morning. Me, Aunty Agnes and Granny. A winning combination, or a living nightmare.

The world will soon find out.

# 15

# The Best at Impressions

At the end of Tuesday, I hang around the playground, waiting for Jess to emerge. I tried to catch her after school yesterday, but she ran off to get a lift home.

'Hey,' I shout when I see her.

'Hey,' she says, smiling.

'How's it going?' I ask.

'Fine . . . since the last time you asked me.' She smiles warily. 'You don't need to keep asking, E.'

'Yes, but I mean in person. You know, in real life, how are you?'

'Still fine.'

I try a different tack.

'Could you help me with French?' I plead. 'Madame Keener was screaming at me about something, and I can't work out what it is.'

She makes a face. Jess has a never-ending capacity for helpfulness. Although truthfully, I know why Madame Keener was screaming at me. It's because she asked me to spell my name out loud in French, and I kept missing out the 'i' in the middle, and she kept saying that was a better name, but not actually *my* name, and that this was Year 7–level

French and I'm supposed to be Year 11–level French – and I'm probably going to fail French.

'She can be such a bully,' she sighs. 'Try not to worry. I'm sure you're better than you think you are.'

'I'm not,' I insist. 'You never get anything wrong. Why can't I be more like you?'

She exhales again. This time more audibly.

'Maybe I do,' she says irritably. 'I'm not perfect, Ellie. I get stuff wrong all the time . . .' She stops mid-sentence as Elina wanders past with Jane Fuller, one of the Year 12 student librarians.

I watch her visibly wither, her face crumpling like the piece of paper I wrote my French homework on, which inevitably ended up in Madame Keener's bin.

'Jess,' I ask carefully. 'Are you *sure* you're OK?'

This time, she doesn't fight it.

'No,' she says dejectedly. 'I don't think I am, actually.'

I take hold of her arm and squeeze it.

'You don't have to pretend with me,' I say, pulling her towards me. 'Just talk to me. You'll feel better. Is it school or home or Elina?' I offer.

'All three,' she whispers.

'OK.' I nod encouragingly.

'I've just got so much to prove, E,' she says, staring ahead of her. 'All the teachers have such high hopes for me – and so do my dad and Barb. And Mum. It's . . . a lot, you know. A lot of people's happiness, resting on me,' she says, watching Elina's retreating back.

'All you can do is your best, Jess – and I promise you, that's enough. I know that's enough. You just need to know it too.'

She turns and hugs me. 'Thanks,' she says tearfully.

'So, what's going on with your mum?' I probe.

'I'm seeing her next week.'

'Wow.'

'I know,' she says, looking happy. Or *is* it happy? Maybe it's more worried. Unsure.

'So, how's she been?'

'I don't know,' she says, embarrassed. 'She didn't turn up the last time we were supposed to meet.'

'Oh, Jess,' I breathe. 'Why didn't you say anything?'

'It's OK,' she says, her eyes shining. 'She definitely will this time, she just had some . . . some stuff going on. With her boyfriend.'

I stroke her arm sympathetically.

'You're allowed to be angry, Jessica. You're allowed to say you're disappointed.'

'I'm not disappointed,' she says quickly. 'How can you be disappointed when you're expecting something?'

I don't respond, unsure of what to say. She loves her mum, and I know her mum loves her. It's just, families are complicated. People are complicated. Mental health is complicated.

'It's just, I know we're broken up now,' she says quietly, 'but the one person I really want to talk to about all this is Elina.'

'I won't take that personally,' I joke softly.

'You know what I mean,' she says, staring at the floor. 'She's my best friend too. Or at least, she was.'

We walk out of the playground and towards our favourite coffee shop. Or Jess's favourite coffee shop, and for me, a place I drink tea.

**Ellie:**

going to the spoke w Jess. u around?

**Hayley:**

working on audition pieces. srry. ☹

**Ellie:**

👍 spk ltr.

'*You* broke up with *her*,' I remind Jess gently. 'You can't expect her not to be upset.'

'I don't. I just miss her,' she says glumly. 'You know what it's like.'

But I don't. Or I tell myself I don't.

'I'm sure she misses you too.'

'It didn't look like that earlier.'

'I'm sure they're just friends.'

But I don't know if that's true.

'If you miss her this much, then maybe you shouldn't have broken up with her,' I suggest softly.

'I told you,' she says angrily, as we get to the Spoke and join the queue that's formed outside. 'It was the right thing to do. For both of us. It might hurt now, but it would be so much worse in September, or at Christmas, or next summer.'

'You don't know that. You don't know that you'd break up.'

'I do, Ellie. You're not naive. You must feel the same way about Ash. Or Shawn,' she says suddenly, as if unsure of which person I'm truly attached to. Ditto.

I notice her blush slightly as she nudges me, then look up to see Shawn stood a few places in front of us.

84

'Do you think he heard me?' she whispers. I blush myself, hoping against hope that he didn't. That he doesn't think I feel anything about anything. But there's only way to find out.

'Hey,' I say, leaning forward and tapping him on the shoulder. He turns around.

'Hi,' he says stiffly.

Oh God. He heard us. He must have heard us.

'You guys know each other, right?' I say, pointing between him and Jess. They smile at each other, Shawn's eyes lingering on Jess the way people's do without even meaning to.

Then.

'Hey, Ellie,' comes the voice.

'Oh,' I say, shocked, looking from her to him, then back again.

Clearly he was too busy to hear anything about anything.

'Hi, Hannah,' I reply. I take in her low-slung loose white jeans, black tube top and light pink bomber jacket. I want to hate her, but she looks so herself, so effortlessly who she is without question.

Jess looks between all of us and clears her throat uncomfortably.

'Hi, Jess,' Hannah says, because everyone knows who Jessica Leigh King is.

'Hi.' She nods back. 'Anyway, E,' she says, drawing me back into our conversation. I widen my eyes at her gratefully, Hannah holding on to Shawn's arm.

'Are you OK?' she mouths silently.

I nod vigorously. Like my head might fall off. I hope my head falls off.

When we get inside, we get a table on the other side of the room from Shawn and Hannah.

85

'And as *you* said to *me*,' Jess says quietly, 'you're the one who said no when he asked you out.'

'I know,' I whisper, 'and it's for the best. He's clearly not over her, and I need to be on my own. But,' I say, turning back to her, 'this is about you, not me. I want to be there for you, Jess. I don't want to keep missing things.'

She rolls her eyes. 'I'm fine, Ellie. At least, I'm trying to be. But focusing on other people isn't going to make things any clearer for *you*,' she lectures. 'It isn't going to help you work out what you want. Like choosing your A levels,' she says pointedly, sipping her coffee.

'I've got ages, Jess.'

'No. You don't. It's the end of next week, E.'

I inhale messily. How did it come round so quickly? I got an extension at the end of last term because of everything that happened with Dad, but now I need to decide. I need to talk to my parents about what I decide. I need to know what my future is, when I can barely decide what to wear this weekend.

'Oh God,' I intone.

'It's OK,' she says, reaching across the table.

'I'm supposed to be looking after *you*,' I grumble.

'How about we look after each other?'

Out of the corner of my eye I catch Hannah's hand across the table, strategically placed over Shawn's. He's wearing that T-shirt I like. The one with *Talking Heads* written in garish black and white and red. My heart aches suddenly. Talking Heads, 'This Must Be the Place,' playing on repeat in my head. That line about feeling numb and burning hearts and having fun, pulling at my brain.

I nod my head at Jess's suggestion, trying to concentrate.

'We need to focus on us,' she says lightly. 'Not Elina or Shawn . . . or Ash,' she adds hurriedly. 'And not on each other. On our own stuff.'

'I know.'

'So, French,' she says, waving her hand in front of my face. We spend the next hour revising, by which time I understand my name is not Elle but appreciate maybe it would be better if it was. Then I do my best impression of someone who doesn't notice Shawn and Hannah leave together, and Jess does her best impression of someone who hasn't seen an Instagram post of Elina and Jane revising in the park.

We are both excellent at impressions.

We are both probably not OK.

But at least, I think, as we order a piece of cake, we're not OK together.

# ♡ Song 2 ♡

## Intro, Verse, Chorus, Middle Eight

It's fighting me, and it never fights me.

I've never found it hard to put the words down. To get the words out. Not here, with the notes in black and white in front of me. Maybe other places. Real life. Faced with real things and real consequences. Those are the places words fail me. But not here.

I wait for a line to emerge, the way it usually does. The song writing itself, channelling through me without intention.

*I'm not ready to let go*

A single line without warning. Nothing more. The tune simple and sweet and beseeching.

*I'm not ready to let go*

Of what?

I try to push through it. But the words aren't writing themselves. The song isn't singing itself.

The words are gone.

I just wish I knew where.

# 16

# The How Can I Help You Robot

In drama, Hayley is doing an excellent impression of not caring that James has a new girlfriend, and James is doing a not-very-excellent impression of not caring that Hayley doesn't care that he has a new girlfriend.

Turns out some of us are good at impressions, and some of us are not.

'Sadie seems nice,' I venture, in an effort to see whether Hayley's as OK with everything as she claims to be.

'I don't know her,' she replies dismissively. 'But I'm sure she's fine.'

'Cool, cool,' I say to no one.

'So, I'm thinking about writing my own audition piece,' she continues.

'Cool, cool,' I repeat. In my head I'm Danny Zuko from *Grease*. Wearing a biker jacket, slicking my hair back with a folding comb. My hair does feel particularly greasy today.

'Ellie, are you listening?'

'Yes. Totally. Listening. Cool,' I say, staring at her.

Note to self: stop having *Grease* fantasies.

'Stop staring at me like that,' she says, appalled.

'I'm just trying to convey with my face how much I'm listening to you, and how much I want to help.'

Because I do want to help her. Except I don't. Because I don't want her to leave. Even though I want her to succeed. Which are very confusing, conflicting thoughts.

'OK . . .' she says, looking disturbed.

'So, what are you thinking about? Writing wise?' I ask, focusing.

'Something personal,' she says, looking at her feet. 'Contemporary.'

'Sounds like you,' I smile. 'Can I do anything?'

'I'm not sure,' she says, looking away. 'Maybe I'll show it to you when I've written it.'

'Whatever you need.' I smile again. 'I'm here for you.'

'That smile's creepy, E.'

'Oh. Thanks,' I reply sarcastically.

'Seriously,' she says unkindly. 'You're turning into a How Can I Help You Robot. What's going on?'

'Nothing. I'm just trying to help. People. Like you. And others,' I offer.

'Try helping yourself,' she says annoyingly astutely, 'by picking your A level options. Which would help me. Because I'm worried about you.'

'I'm the one that's worried. About *you*,' I exclaim.

She gives me a look.

'Do you want to take drama?' she demands. 'Are you worried about telling your parents?'

'I don't know,' I admit. 'I mean, I love it, but I don't know if it's what I want to *do*.'

How is *anyone* supposed to know what they want to do yet?

'Ellie,' she says, putting her arm around me. 'You're supposed to be focusing on you. On figuring out who you are and what you want. That's what you keep telling me your friend Dr Jada says. But all I keep hearing from you is how is *everybody else*,' she says, again too close for comfort.

'I'm figuring it out,' I say through gritted teeth.

'Jess and I were thinking we could get together on Friday. Maybe talk through your options. Get something on paper.'

Ugh. The only problem with Jess and Hayley being friends now is that they know too much. I have nowhere to hide.

'I've got band rehearsal on Friday.'

'We'll do it after. You can come to mine.'

Great. Hayley's scary mum/our deputy head will be there. Probably to terrify me into making decisions about the rest of my life.

'I can't,' I reply quickly. 'I'm going to London this weekend. Mum and Dad will want me straight home after rehearsal to pack.'

'Hmmn,' she says sharply.

'I promise I'll think about it over the weekend.'

She gives me a look that says: *I will not forget this, however much you may want me to.*

'Hey, Ellie,' James says, appearing next to me. 'Is it OK if I bring Sadie to your rehearsal on Friday?'

Hayley glares at him.

'It's just a band rehearsal, James, not a gig. No one's coming to watch,' I say dismissively.

'Shawn invited me,' he says, surprised.

Probably so he can invite Hannah and hope there'll be too many people there for me to notice.

GREAT.

Whatever.

I don't care.

Clearly his whole 'I'll wait for you' thing was just that. A Thing he is now over, and he is no longer waiting.

'Whatever,' I say to James, mimicking my brain.

James nods as if I've given him permission to bring both himself and Sadie.

The only good thing about any of it is that Hayley's impression of Not Caring slips for just a second. She stares at James, looking slightly sick as he stares back, also looking sick.

At least I won't be the only one there doing a bad impression of Not Caring about someone.

# 17

# In with Love, Out with Anger

The first week back at school hasn't been too bad. In fact, it's been fine. In some ways, I wish exams would never end, because at least I know where I am with exams. Because exams are The Now. It's what they lead to. What's supposed to come next. The future. Change. Whatever it is they tell us we should be looking forward to. I'm not a looking-forward type of person. More of a looking-back-with-many-many-regrets type of person.

'E, are you just going to stand there?' Hayley asks, as she helps Benji lug his drum kit out of the cupboard and into the main hall for band rehearsal.

'That's what I usually do, yes,' I respond, watching them. She looks thin. So thin it still scares me to think I didn't see it before.

'Although, you know . . . do you need help? I'm not sure she should be doing that, Benji.'

'Why's that?' Hayley says, stopping to stare at me.

'Um . . .' I try to find the words. *Because you look too thin. You look weak. I'm worried I haven't seen you eat all day.*

'She's fine,' Benji says, pulling out the snare drum. 'She's got that angry look again. She only gets that when she's fine,' he says dismissively.

I think I might love Benji. Although not like that. Because apparently, I love too many people like that. Or don't love them, but might love them, or feel things for them that I shouldn't feel.

And at the exact moment I'm having these thoughts, Shawn walks in.

In with love, out with anger. In with love, out with anger. Dr Jada says it's important to acknowledge our anger, so we can let it go. Although I have nothing to be angry *about* because Shawn is entitled to do whatever he wants, with whoever he wants. Would I prefer if he wasn't back together with someone who clearly hates me and used to go out with my ex-boyfriend? Yes. Probably.

'Hey,' he says, walking over to me. 'I've been trying to get hold of you all week.'

Which is true. He's been messaging me ever since we bumped into each other at the Spoke. But I've been focusing on exams. On Jess and Hayley. On not getting distracted from the task at hand. Although I haven't exactly been embracing the task at hand either. Like thinking about my A level options, or me, or why I feel the way I feel.

'Sorry. I've been busy. Revising and stuff.'

'About Tuesday,' he begins.

'Tuesday?' I say quizzically, pretending I don't know what he's talking about; and this is why I'm not the one doing an audition for BackStage – I enjoy acting, I'm just not that good at it.

'When I saw you at the Spoke,' he says quietly. 'With Hannah.'

'Oh, Hannah,' I say indifferently. 'Sure, yeah, OK.'

94

I look around for any excuse to leave the conversation.

'Hayley,' I say loudly, waving at her. 'I'm coming!'

She stares at me, perplexed. But I'm not looking where I'm going, and there are cables everywhere, and bits of kit like amps and mics lying on the floor from where unhelpful people like me don't know what to do with them.

I imagine I'm walking away to Janelle Monáe, 'Make Me Feel'. Cool and in control. Powerful and a little bit tender.

But I'm not Janelle Monáe. I'm Ellie Pillai.

I fall forwards, spreadeagled, my foot stuck under a cable as the rest of me crashes down, my chin landing at James Godfrey's foot.

'OW,' I exclaim.

'Are you OK?' James asks, leaning down to pull me up, the hint of a smile playing at the corner of his mouth.

'Shut up, James,' I manage, as I look at his face.

'I didn't say anything,' he laughs.

'Your *face* says it all,' I hiss.

'You're bleeding,' Hayley says, rushing over.

'You're bleeding,' Shawn says, as he arrives next to her.

'You're bleeding,' Ash says out of nowhere.

Ash. With Hannah. For the love of God. Can she just make up her mind?

'I'll take you to the nurse,' they all say at once.

'No, no. I'm fine,' I say, putting my hands up in front of me. 'I can take myself,' I say, dabbing at my nose with my shirtsleeve.

I look around me, at all the people who've assembled like it's a gig rather than a rehearsal.

'What are all these people doing here?' I ask Shawn.

'I just figured it's our last term. We might as well make it an event. Hang out with our friends.'

'Cool, cool.'

I am Danny Zuko.

I am all the T-Birds combined.

I am coolness personified, not someone stood here bleeding in front of both my closest friends and the closest thing I have to an enemy.

'I'll just, er, go to the nurse now.'

I walk towards the door. My face burning. Our last term. That's what he said. Last. Term. As in, the end. He's going. It's all changing. Ending. And I don't like it. I don't want to think about it.

I push the door open and walk quickly, my heart rate accelerating.

'Ellie!'

I stop at the sound of my name and turn as she runs to catch up with me in the corridor.

'Hey, Hannah,' I manage. I'm starting to think she's stalking me. Or I'm stalking her. Because we're running into each other way more than feels necessary.

'Hey,' she says when she reaches me. She shifts uneasily from side to side. 'I just wanted to say – I'm sorry. About what happened on your birthday. What I said about you.'

'You didn't say anything about me,' I say through gritted teeth. I have to grit them. My mouth is literally bleeding.

'Not to your face,' she mumbles. 'Look. I know it was you who told him to talk to me.'

'What?' I ask, confused.

'Ash,' she states. 'He apologised. We went for coffee.' And she seems to be drinking a lot of coffee, with a lot of people, which is good if you like coffee. 'He said sorry for what happened between us. The way he ghosted me.'

'Oh,' I say, surprised. 'That's great. I'm so glad.'

'I didn't realise how much it was bothering me,' she says, raising her shoulders and looking away.

I nod, feeling slightly guilty for my internal monologue.

'Anyway,' she says, looking at me. 'I wish we'd never . . . you know . . . But we did, and at least he's sorry, and he knows what he did.'

I'm softening towards her, even though I really wish I wasn't.

'I know you talked to him, and I know it was you that made him see what he'd done, and that's really cool, Ellie. Especially after the way I've treated you.'

I shake my head. 'I'd love to take credit for that, but I didn't do anything. It was all him.'

'That's not what *he* said,' she replies, watching me.

I push my nose up my sleeve, partly to hide the purple I'm turning and partly to stem the blood that seems to be working its way down my chin like an unattractive line of red snot.

'Oh, God. Your nose,' she says, pointing at it, 'and your *mouth*.'

'I should go,' I say, throwing my thumb up behind me.

'Can I walk you to the nurse?' she offers – and I let her. And I think: *If you're back together with Shawn – or Ash – I'm not going to hate you.*

We talk about music. About the band she wants to start and how much we both love Miss Mason, and when my mouth has stopped bleeding and Nurse Dave has put half a tampon up my nose to soak up the remaining blood, we go back to rehearsals.

'Nice,' Benji sniggers, as I walk back in. Hannah shoots him a look which I feel annoyingly grateful for.

They play a couple of numbers without me, then I pull the tampon out to see what happens. It appears to have stopped bleeding, so I join in with the rest of the set.

At the very end of the session, before the caretaker throws us out, we try the song from last week. My song. There's no one there but the five of us by then, and it feels magical. Like we've finally found our sound. Just as the *we* in this scenario are about to be over.

'Ellie,' Shawn says, as we pack away the last of the equipment; I've decided to learn how to be helpful, if only so I know where the cables are to avoid them. 'Can I talk to you for a minute?'

Benji looks at him, while Lucas and Elliott pretend to be unnaturally interested in their guitars.

He takes my hand and pulls me out of the room and into the corridor. We've never really held hands before, not like this. Not so intentionally. It feels weird, but also not weird.

He leads me towards an empty classroom, and we step inside.

'About Tuesday,' he says firmly. 'When you saw me with Hannah.'

'Shawn, it's fine,' I say, letting go of his hand and taking a step backwards. 'Let's not make a big deal of it. It's fine if you're back together. She seems . . . not as awful as I thought she was.'

He smiles uncomfortably.

'I still care about her,' he says to no one.

'Like I said . . .'

'Can you stop talking?' he asks, the space between us closing.

'I mean, yes,' I mumble. 'I am *capable* of not talking. Or do you mean you want me to stop talking, like, right now?'

'Right now,' he says, moving towards me. 'Ellie, I like you. You know that. I don't want to push you or pressure you, and I know you want to

98

figure some stuff out by yourself, but I just want you to know I'm not with Hannah. We're not back together. We're never getting back together.'

'Oh,' I say, feeling slightly seasick.

'So, that's it really,' he says, looking down at me.

'Oh,' I repeat.

'Is that all you want to say?'

'What do you want me to say?' I ask weakly.

He's stood too close to me. I can feel his breath on the top of my hair. He's holding one of my hands again.

I look up at him, as he looks down at me, and before I know it, we're kissing. His hands searching the sides of my face, my fingers in the back of his hair.

Damn. It.

I want to stop. I want to push him away. But also, I don't. I don't want him to stop. Because while he's kissing me, I don't have to think about anything else. I don't have to think about me.

I hear the door open and shut again quickly as we pull away from each other. See his navy-blue bomber jacket as it disappears through the doorway. His dark curly hair under the dim school lights.

I want to run after him and explain. I want to run after myself and explain why I'm doing this. Why I can't stop for just one minute and really think about *me*, like I promised I would.

But I can't.

Because I have no explanation. I have no reason. Nothing other than this. Sabotage. Fear. Change. Everything, everything, nothing.

So, I allow myself to get distracted. I lean up and kiss Shawn again and again and again, until his arms are wrapped around me, and I can hear Benji making jokes in the corridor. And I know it's all a terrible idea, but that's me at the moment. Bad impressions, and terrible ideas.

# 18

# Kundi

The train into London with Granny and Aunty Agnes the next day is pretty much exactly as I expect it to be. They're deep in conversation, barely aware I'm there. Speaking loudly in Tamil and shooting dirty looks at anyone who dares to look at them.

I'm always aware of being looked at when I'm with my family, especially my grandmother. She never tries to fit in. She's just innately, herself. Her, but in a different country to the one in which she was born, whereas I feel like I'm two people, two versions of myself, in two different countries to which I only partly belong.

Across the aisle a man is reading that paper Dad hates. The one it feels like I see people reading all the time. On the cover is a picture of a boat. Kids with teddy bears and mothers with babies in arms. Small boats, they call them. As if they're vessels instead of people.

Dad says it's the language they use. The way they show immigrants as less than, when the world they're leaving is their home. When no one leaves their home unless they have to. Like Granny left her home. And Aunty Agnes and Dad and the uncles and Aunty Kitty had to. It's like that poem we read at school. No one leaves home unless home is the mouth of a shark.

Granny was living in the mouth of a shark – and she was scared. Scared of living in the teeth of something frightening and unpredictable. Scared for her family, and she just wanted better. The right to do better, to work harder, to feel safe. And I wonder why, when it's just luck really, where we're born and who we're born to, that people like Granny and the people on those boats don't deserve the right to those things. To be welcomed somewhere by someone who says: it's not your fault. You didn't deserve to be born in the mouth of a shark.

But I suppose I know, really. Why they're not welcomed. Why if I was on that boat, I wouldn't be welcome either. It's what we are. Me and Aunty Agnes and Granny. And there's a lump in my throat when I think about it. About how lucky I am not to have been born in the mouth of a shark, even if sometimes, jaws come in different shapes and sizes.

Because the man across the aisle reading his newspaper has sharp teeth too. We're in first class, and almost as soon as we sit down, he tells us so. That this is first class. Multiple times. As if it's clear we don't belong here. That we can't read. As if we're chancing it, our seats for somewhere else on the train.

But then there's Granny, and her curt yes, we know, thank you, and her sudden overuse of the word *kundi*, which is one of the few Tamil words I know because it's rude and means bum. Because she's seen real sharks, so his teeth don't scare her. Or when Aunty Agnes gets out the Tupperware with her home-made fish cutlets and the aisle man sniffs dramatically, puckering his face up as if he can't believe we have the audacity to not be eating white bread sandwiches devoid of any kind of flavour, but then she gives them out to the other passengers, who ooh and aah in delight until the conductor comes down and we think we're going to get told off, but he asks if he can have one too.

And these are the two sides of feeling othered. The side where you feel shamed for not conforming to standards you can't possibly meet, for letting someone else decide who you are and what you stand for; and the side where you feel the brilliance and beauty of rejecting the standards you don't want to meet. In being who you are, regardless of what the world tells you to be.

All through the journey I keep watching them. These two women who've been through so much to get here. Who have lived in the mouth of a shark. Who speak unashamedly in their own language. Who fit in, only as much as they feel comfortable and want to fit in. And all I can think is: I want to be them when I grow up. I want to be that strong and courageous and unafraid to be myself.

I just need to know who that is first.

When we get off the train, after barely speaking a word for the last two hours, I throw out a *poda madayan*. Granny and Aunty Agnes look over at me quickly, then grin. I may not know about much, but this much I do know. Aisle man is an idiot – and whether you say it in Tamil or English, a fool is a fool is a fool.

# 19

# The No-Romance Policy

I haven't been to Hope's house in over a year, and definitely not since we've become close again. Going into her room without wanting to strangle her feels like we're both still seven. Like there are secrets being kept, and games being played, in a world only we belong in.

'Oh my God,' she says, jumping on to her bed. 'You *kissed* him! I knew it. I knew you were going to end up together.'

'No. We're not,' I venture irritably.

'What happened to your whole No-Romance Finding Myself Thing?' she asks, rolling her eyes. 'I knew it wouldn't last.' And it annoys me she's right. That I've done the exact opposite of what I said I was going to do.

I sit down on the bed next to her. 'I'm confused, Hope.'

'That tends to happen when you kiss people you say you're not interested in,' she says, picking at her nail polish.

'*He* kissed *me*,' I insist.

She gives me a look.

'First,' I admit. 'He kissed me *first*. I may have kissed him a bit after that. I can't remember.'

She gives me another look.

'Fine. I kissed him. I am a terrible person, and I have no idea what I'm doing with my life.'

'Whoa there,' she says, sitting up, concerned. 'Stop being so hard on yourself.'

I can smell the sweet, delicious scent of milk hoppers. Something I never eat unless I'm at a restaurant, because my parents are not exactly the world's greatest chefs or in any way in the region of chefness at all.

'That smells amazing,' I say, ignoring her.

'I know,' she says, rolling her eyes. 'Mum only makes them when Granny comes to stay.'

Granny. The terror and fear and need to please this tiny Sri Lankan woman is both impressive and sad in equal measure.

'Poor Aunty Christine.'

'You know, I think Granny's chilled out a bit since she moved in with you. She seems more . . . relaxed.'

'Does she?' I ask, surprised.

'I mean, for starters, we're here. About to go to a wedding dress fitting, for a wedding she claimed she would never go to.'

'True,' I murmur. 'Speaking of which, how are you feeling about wearing a sari?' I'm hoping she'll feel the same as I do, i.e. wish she could wear something that feels more like *her* and doesn't show off her midriff, although her midriff is annoyingly taut.

'Fine,' she says, inspecting her nails. 'What do you think of this colour?'

'Fine,' I say, wishing she'd say more than fine.

'How are *you* feeling about it?' she asks, looking up. 'After last time? In fact, wasn't it Shawn who undid it in the first place?' she grins. 'It's a sign. You're meant to be.'

'The fact I don't know how to tie a sari properly is not a sign of anything other than my inability to tie a sari properly.'

'All right, be negative,' she huffs.

'Hope, can you *please* support my No-Romance Policy and stop trying to set me up with Shawn?'

'I want to,' she says, eyeing me, 'but you need to support your own No-Romance Policy by not kissing people.' She arches an eyebrow. 'Also, I'm worried this whole no-romance thing is actually because you still like Ash, and you're scared of getting hurt so you're just saying no to everybody.'

I feel suddenly winded. Like she's punched me in the gut. 'That's not true. I just want some time to work out what I want for myself.'

'What *do* you want?' she asks seriously. 'Don't you have to submit your A level options this week?'

'Heebeejeebee.'

'Oh. It's like that,' she says wisely. 'That's bad.'

'It's not bad, it's just . . . confusing.'

'Drama. History. Maths,' she says matter-of-factly.

'What?'

'That's what you should take. Those are the only subjects you talk about, or, like, enjoy.'

'I do not enjoy maths,' I lie. Because I kind of do. I kind of like the challenge. The way numbers can't lie. Apart from when Mr Potts is spitting on me when explaining how numbers don't lie.

'It's a good mix to have on your uni application. It shows a breadth of skill.'

What. Is. Happening.

'You sound really knowledgeable about all this. I thought you hated school?' I say, surprised.

'I don't hate school,' she says, rolling her eyes. 'I might not be the engineer or lawyer my mum wants me to be,' she says, making a face, 'but uni is a chance to work out what I am – and A levels are a stepping stone to getting there. I mean, I kind of think I want to go into fashion, but —'

I cut her off. 'You *need* to go into fashion,' I confirm. 'You are seriously gifted. I mean, that top–' I point at the shirt she's wearing. An oversized man's button-up she bought in a charity shop, over which she's stitched a fitted bodice, black and stern looking. It looks like something Madonna would have worn in the eighties, but she's embroidered tiny little cherries all over it, like something you'd find on a picnic tablecloth. It feels just the right side of fashion. Cool, but effortless.

She blushes. 'I mean, it's not the best stitching, but I like it,' she says, playing with the hem.

'Hope, you *designed* it. I think it's amazing,' I gush.

'So,' she continues, 'I'm thinking of taking art, English and maths, because that's what most design schools are looking for.'

'Wow,' I say, impressed. 'You've really done your homework.'

She nods her head, proud. 'Christmas just made me realise I could be so much more,' she says, her eyes sparkling. 'Like, I thought, I'm not good at school. I'm never going to make Mum and Dad happy, so I'll just marry an engineer instead of being one. Or I'll find a doctor . . .'

'Or a dentist,' I chime in, thinking of her awful ex-boyfriend Vikash.

'It's like I thought I couldn't *be* anything, unless it was by being attached to someone who was all the things I thought everyone else wanted me to be. I'm sixteen. When did I start thinking like a 1950s housewife?'

I nod wisely when I am anything but wise. She's got it all figured out. Why don't I have it all figured out?

'Ellie, I want to do stuff. I want to show my parents and Granny and everybody that success isn't just about getting a PhD. We can be whatever we want, even if that's . . .' she stops with a flourish and makes a little noise, as if to announce something spectacular, 'something in the arts.'

I hug her. She always seems to be one step ahead of me. I wish I could keep up.

'Don't forget me when you're Stella McCartney.'

'I'm going to be Masha Popova.'

But I don't know who that is.

'I'll dress you for your tour.' She winks at me.

I make a face.

'Why not?' she says, nudging me.

'I don't know what I want to do yet.'

'You do,' she says wisely.

But how does she know when I don't even know yet?

'Poor Aunty Kitty,' she says suddenly.

And we're both thinking the same thing as we hear Hope's front door open and a multitude of screams from both inside and outside the house. That Aunty Kitty and Charles are flying in just for the weekend, just for this dress fitting, and they're going to be exhausted, and dealing with Granny, Aunty Agnes and various members of Charles's family who are coming to Hope's for dinner this evening. Which sounds stressful, and not fun when you're jet-lagged and working a seventy-hour week.

'I know,' I concur. 'I don't know how she's going to survive this.'

'She's marrying a hot guy who also happens to be the love of her life. It could be worse,' Hope surmises.

'HOPPPPPPPEEEEE, ELLIIIIIEEEEEE,' we hear Granny scream. 'Come, cooooooommmmme!'

We turn to each other, giggling.

'I guess we should go downstairs,' Hope smiles.

I give her another hug. 'I'm really glad I don't hate you any more.'

'I'm really glad I don't hate *you* any more,' she says, hugging me back. 'And don't forget what I said. About your options. It doesn't have to be scary, Ellie. It's just one step on a really long journey.'

I nod, thinking a really long journey actually sounds terrifying. Too Long and Too Far and Too Much Change and thinking about it makes me feel like I've forgotten how to breathe.

'Come on,' she says. 'Into the tiger's den . . .'

'Isn't it the lion's den?

She shrugs.

Either way, someone's about to get mauled.

# 20

# Say Yes to the Sari

Aunty Kitty looks stunning. Breathtaking. Hope looks divine. Celestial. I look like one of those shiny blue chocolates from a box of Quality Street. The coconut one that nobody wants to eat.

Ugh.

'Look nice,' Granny says, while I try not to cry.

'*Amma*, can you have a look at the costume jewellery,' Aunty Kitty says, side-eyeing me. 'See if there's any pieces we can get for the girls?'

'Must wear Real Gold,' Granny mutters, but she dutifully follows Aunty Agnes as she goes to hunt down the unsuspecting shop owner.

'Are you OK?' Aunty Kitty says softly.

'I'm fine,' I say, trying to swallow down the lump in my throat.

'You don't sound it,' she says kindly.

Hope looks at me.

'You both look beautiful,' I say, turning to them.

'So do you,' Hope says, rubbing my arm.

And I know it's stupid. I know I'm not a shiny blue chocolate from a box of Quality Street; it just makes me feel so not myself.

I've worked so hard to be more confident. To be me. And I don't want to be a brat. I don't want to disrespect my culture, or choose not to honour my heritage, it's just this isn't the version of my heritage I feel I am. This person in the mirror is not who I am. Why do I have to wear this to prove I'm Sri Lankan enough? That I fit in.

'What's wrong? Tell me,' Aunty Kitty says, shining with happiness.

'It just doesn't . . .' I manage, 'feel like me.'

She looks at Hope worriedly.

'I just . . .' and now I'm starting to get that feeling behind my eyes, all hot and itchy, 'I don't feel good about myself.'

She grimaces. 'Well, I think you look beautiful,' she says thoughtfully, 'but I want you to *feel* beautiful. If it wasn't for you and Hope, I wouldn't even be here,' she says, untying my sari for me.

'That's not true,' I say.

'It is,' she says emphatically. 'You gave me the courage to tell *Amma*.'

She pulls Hope towards her and puts her arms around both of us.

'So, if you want to wear jeans and a T-shirt, I don't care. Wear what you want, OK? I'll deal with *Amma*.'

'Really?' I ask brightly.

'Really,' she confirms.

'How about you leave it to me,' Hope says suddenly. 'I'll make something. For both of us.'

'Have you got time?'

She waves me away. 'I want to. It'll be a stress reliever. Time away from my mum and her revision cards,' she says, making a face.

'I'll pay for the fabric and your time,' Kitty says, squeezing us both.

'OK,' I say happily.

'Now that's more like it,' she says, looking at my smile. 'Are either of you going to bring someone?' she asks.

'Can we?'

She nods.

'Kitty, jewellery here no good,' Granny says in a military voice.

Aunty Kitty smiles indulgently. 'Yes, *Amma*.'

'Ah, ah,' Granny says, looking pleased with herself. 'You are all . . .' but she can't quite finish the sentence, because Granny doesn't really do compliments. What she means is – she approves. That we all look acceptable under the Granny Clothing Treaty. Which makes me feel terrible in light of the conversation we've just had.

But not that terrible. Because I won't look like this.

'Should we go?' Kitty says to Granny. 'We need to go to the other bridal boutique.'

In the other shop, Kitty has a western wedding dress. A long white dress with a train, made of beautiful tulle roses, and even Granny has tears in her eyes when she looks at her, because she looks perfect. She looks perfect in everything because she's happy.

And I want to be her. I want to feel sure about something. I want to feel as if I'm not going backwards, crying in wedding shops and kissing boys with long hair and blue eyes who play guitars and tell you you're special, when really, you want to tell yourself you're special. You want to believe it when it comes from you.

'Are you going to invite Shawn to the wedding?' Hope whispers on the way home.

I shrug.

'You know Ash is coming, right?'

'No,' I say quickly, 'I didn't.' But of course, he would be. Of course

112

Granny would want her honorary grandson there. And Mrs Aachara, and probably Elina too.

Drama. History. Maths. Maybe it's that easy. Maybe I make things complicated when they shouldn't be.

Which sounds like me.

Just a version of me I really wish I wasn't.

# 21

# I Love That Green Cake

Ethan's here. At Hope's house. Annoying Ethan. Annoying Ethan who Hope is flirting with. Who seems to be reciprocating and enjoying the flirting, too much.

I want to come up with some credible reason for why this shouldn't be allowed. As though somehow they're going to be related through marriage. That it's incestuous and weird and wrong. But there's no viable reason for why they can't flirt, apart from the fact I'm not sure about him. That he keeps sneaking vodka into his Coke from a tiny bottle he's brought with him, and the more he drinks the more obnoxious he becomes. Interrupting us whenever we say anything, because what he has to say is obviously more important than what we have to say.

I want to say, I'm not done. I am not done talking. So, I do.

'I'm not done yet,' I say, as he interrupts me for the billionth time.

'Done with what?' he asks.

'Speaking. I was in the middle of a sentence.' He ignores me, covertly pouring another measure of vodka into his drink.

'So, what are you wearing to the wedding?' Hope asks, deliberately ignoring my tone.

'My uncle's got me in some kind of monkey suit,' he says, unimpressed.

'A monkey suit? What are you, seventy-five? A former member of the Rat Pack?' I ask moodily.

He gives me a look, and I feel satisfied I've made my point. Which is that he's annoying. And rude.

'Do you want some?' he asks Hope, proffering the vodka bottle. She shakes her head.

'Hope, Ellie,' Aunty Kitty says, walking over to us as Ethan hastily hides the bottle under his jacket. 'Chinatown for dinner?'

I nod. I've only been to Chinatown in London a couple of times before. I want to get one of those big green cakes.

'I love that green cake,' I say, turning to Ethan. 'What's it called?'

'Why are you asking me?' he says touchily.

I sputter.

'I'm Chinese so I should know the name of every item of Chinese food, right? Just like you know everything about Sri Lanka.'

I blush. Because he's right. Because I did assume. And I need educating sometimes just like anybody else.

'Sorry—' I say.

'It's called pandan cake,' he says, amused with himself for interrupting me again, but also having schooled me on my stupid assumptions.

Ugh.

'Are we ready to go?' Aunty Kitty says, waving from the other side of the room.

I stand up and grab my coat, just as Hope does the same.

She's wearing a sand-coloured trench coat and ankle boots that look like they're socks with a heel. They're cool. She's cool. Ethan's wearing a black leather jacket, black jeans, a black T-shirt. They look good together. Like one of those sexy young couples from a reality TV show. I try not to feel like an outsider in my black satin slip skirt and red stacked Vans, my oversized Stone Roses T-shirt hanging over my waist. I remind myself I am beautiful. That I'm the one who has to believe it. I play the Stone Roses, 'Waterfall,' to myself in my head, Ian Brown telling me I'll carry on through it all. And as always, the music lifts me up. Makes everything feel bright and purposeful and OK. Which is why I hate that I can't write at the moment. That I can't find the songs inside myself. The ones that usually come when I need them the most. You're standing on shifting sands, Ian says. The winds are going to lift you, Ian says. And I believe him. Even if Dad says he's a conspiracy theorist and should just stick to making music.

When we get to the tube station, Aunty Kitty tells us which restaurant we're going to in case we get split up on the train – which we inevitably do, because Ethan doesn't want to get caught drinking. When the rest of the family wedge themselves on to a carriage, he shouts through the doorway that we'll get the next one.

As soon as the train pulls out of the station, he gets his little bottle back out.

'Maybe you should slow down a bit,' Hope says gently.

'Maybe you should slow down a bit,' he mimics in a high-pitched voice.

Maybe I should push this kid under the train.

'Seriously,' I say, trying to take the bottle off him. 'Just stop. You're going to get us all in trouble.'

When the next train arrives, he refuses to get on, draining the last of his bottle.

116

'We're getting on the next one, whether you come with us or not.'

'Whatever,' he says catatonically.

FFS.

'Come on,' Hope says kindly. 'You need to eat something.'

He looks at her, as if inspecting every pore on her face.

'You're very pretty,' he says suddenly, as she blushes a deep shade of pink.

How does she do that? Look like a flower in bloom when she's embarrassed. I go purple. Like something having the life drained out of it, slowly and painfully.

'But you know that, don't you?'

'Hey,' I say, pushing him. 'Be careful what you say, pal.'

*Pal?*

He turns towards me.

'You,' he says viciously; and I'm waiting for the words that usually come in these kinds of situations. That I'm ugly, or fat, or that word that means you're from Pakistan, which isn't really an insult when you think about it, because there's nothing wrong with being from Pakistan, it's just the vileness with which it's said, with which it's intended, that makes it hurtful.

He steps backwards, raising his arm to make his point, but as he does, the train arrives in the platform and his foot's too far back, close to it, but not quite close enough. It disappears down the side, between the platform and the carriage, as he reels dangerously.

'Ethan,' I scream, grabbing hold of him and pulling him forwards.

'My foot,' he's shouting. 'My foot!'

And I don't know what to do. Because his foot's still there. Still stuck, and the train's about to move and the people inside the carriage are screaming.

'Move,' I shout. 'Move your foot!'

But it's like he can't hear me. Like the alcohol's dulled his brain to nothing but panic, and on the other side of him, Hope's gone white as a sheet, the seconds ticking by.

'Pull the alarm,' I scream at the woman inside the carriage. 'Stop the train! Now!'

She's just staring at me, her eyes glazed over in fear, and I can't rely on her to do it. I can't rely on anyone except me.

I fall to my knees and shove my hand down the side of the carriage.

'Ellie!' Hope screams. 'It's moving. It's moving!'

It feels like an age between the nothingness and the feel of his leather boot. I can feel a rush of wind beneath my hand, the thickness of the air around me, as though I could drink it like soup. I put my hand around his ankle and twist as hard as I can, until I feel his posture loosen, his foot moving as I pull it up and towards me. As I place it on the platform, panting, Hope grabs him, pulling him forwards. I hear the doors closing, the noise they make to warn you the train's about to depart. Hope's holding on to him, her arms around his waist, and he looks sick. His eyes black.

As the train disappears down the tunnel away from us, an older woman says heavily, 'I saw you drinking. You could have lost your foot, you idiot.' She narrows her eyes at him. 'You would have ruined both their lives as well as your own.'

He stares at her, his breathing ragged.

'I think the words you're looking for are *thank you*, young man,' she says brusquely.

Ethan gulps, then turns towards me, hugging me so hard I almost topple on to the track.

'Be careful!' the woman chastises him. 'That's the problem with alcohol,' she says wisely. 'It dulls everything you feel. The good and the bad.'

'I'm sorry,' he says to no one in particular.

When the next train arrives, we step into the carriage carefully, the three of us barely speaking. But the more time that goes by, the more what Ethan's drunk seems to affect him. As if, sitting down, the adrenaline and the vodka drain away, leaving his body hollow. We drag him out of his seat at Leicester Square, his chin on his chest, his eyes empty.

'I'm sorry,' he keeps saying. 'I'm sorry.'

'What are you sorry for?' I ask from where I'm stood under his arm, trying to move him alongside me.

'For what just happened. For being me. For disappointing everyone. Even people I've just met.'

Hope gives me a look.

'Don't be so hard on yourself,' I return, staggering under the weight of him.

'You hate me,' he slurs.

'I don't hate you.'

'You're very pretty too,' he says, staring at me. 'You don't think you are. But you are.'

I blush.

'Do you think coffee might help?' I ask Hope over his shoulder.

'It's worth a try,' she wheezes, pulling him along.

We drag him to a coffee shop just outside the station and order a double espresso and some water.

'I'm the reason my dad left,' he says suddenly. 'Because he couldn't handle me,' he slurs.

'That's not true. I don't know why your dad left, but I know it's not that,' I say surely.

'We're not the perfect Chinese kids he wants us to be,' he says flatly. 'He says my mum has no control over us. Over me.' And I think his dad sounds like an arse. As if his mum should be responsible for everything.

'Ethan, there's nothing wrong with you,' Hope says, holding the glass of water out to him.

'Although this whole drinking thing isn't The Best,' I say sternly.

'They want me to be something else. Something more than I am,' he says self-pityingly.

Now that, I understand.

I put my hand on the bottom of his glass and push it up towards his mouth gently, forcing him to drink it.

'You have to learn not to care. To be OK with what you are. Then it doesn't matter what anyone else thinks. Even your parents.'

'Basically,' says Hope, as he puts the glass down and stares at the table, 'you have to be kinder to yourself.'

'You sound like a self-help podcast –' and as he's being sarcastic and rude and not telling us how pretty we are any more, I'm assuming he must be sobering up.

'Drink this,' I say, picking the espresso up. 'Now, please. I've already had eight text messages from Aunty Kitty.'

He tips it into his mouth, swallowing it quickly, then hiccuping.

'Sorry,' he says again in a melancholy voice.

'You already said that,' I scold gently.

'That was really scary,' Hope says, looking at him. 'I thought you were going to die.'

'So did I,' he says, looking at the table again.

'You have to stop this, Ethan,' I say. 'It's not going to solve anything. My boyfriend used to drink like that, and it almost ruined his life.'

'Boyfriend?' he says, looking at me. 'I thought he wasn't your boyfriend?'

Hope raises an eyebrow as I blush that shade of purple I was talking about. The one that makes me look like I'm dying a slow, painful death, which I possibly am.

'That was Shawn,' I explain. 'He's just a friend.'

'That you kiss sometimes,' Hope finishes. 'Also, did you just call Ash your *boyfriend*? As in Ash, your *ex*-boyfriend that broke your heart?'

'I think we're getting our priorities out of order,' I say, motioning to Ethan, now falling asleep on his own chest.

'Ethan,' I shout, shaking his arm. 'We. Have. To. Go.'

He nods.

We stand him up, take him outside, and get him to jump and down on the spot until he starts to look slightly more alive.

'Ellie,' Hope says, turning to me quietly. 'Don't think I've forgotten what you just said.'

I try ignoring her.

'We'll talk about it later,' she says threateningly.

I try ignoring myself.

But I can't.

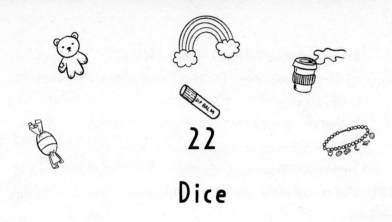

# 22

# Dice

I wake up in the middle of the night feeling strange. Like the actions of the last twenty-four hours have just caught up with me; the adrenaline kicking in.

I feel sick. The way you can only feel sick when something bad is about to happen. The way I felt in the months before Amis died, the way I felt when Dad had his heart attack, the way I feel all the time thinking about this new baby.

My breath is caught in my throat. Air trapped inside me I can't get out. I sit up, sweat pooling in my hairline, Hope looking angelic, fast asleep next to me. I don't want to wake her. I don't want to wake anyone.

I throw my legs over the side of her bed and pad softly to the bathroom. I sit on the lid of the toilet, my head between my legs, trying to remember what it feels like to breathe. To not feel afraid.

I can feel it getting worse. The feeling. The sense that everything's changing, and I can't stop it. That I have no control over anything.

I grip my phone in my hand. I count to a hundred, the way my therapist used to tell me to when this started happening after my brother died.

My brother. Who's still here somehow. In his room. In my life. On the edge of my consciousness, always.

But he's gone.

My brother is gone.

And now I'm having another brother. A different brother. What if I can't protect him? Protect any of us from the things we can't control? Like blood cancer or the moment your heart stops. Just like that. No warning.

No.

No.

No.

Breathe, Ellie.

Breathe.

I take my head from between my legs and sit up, pushing my shoulders back, gulping air in, sweat trickling down the back of my T-shirt.

I force myself to stand up, my legs shaking, and creep down the stairs to the kitchen, unlocking the back door.

I let myself outside and sit on the grass, feeling the dew wet against my legs. It feels soothingly cold, the air crisp.

My breathing slows down. Starts to regulate. The spaces between each one more and more consistent.

It's been a long time since I've had a panic attack, and I didn't think it was possible any more. I thought my panic was gone. All used up.

I feel a tear trickling down my cheek, and I'm surprised to feel it. Surprised because I've done so much not to be that person any more. To not feel like this.

I stare at my phone screen, scrolling through old messages. Trying to remember who I was before this happened. The person who wrote these messages, the person who received these messages. The person who hadn't had a panic attack in five years. Or at least was able to pretend she hadn't. Who hadn't gotten this bad.

There it is. In black and white. His name. The message I keep pretending he didn't send me. That I don't know how to answer. Because I want to, but I'm scared. Scared I'm not as strong as I thought I was. Scared I might be falling apart. Scared I'm broken and I'll never come back together again.

**Ash:**

www.theshelley/beatlesfans_unseen
fri?

Without meaning to, I press the phone symbol next to his name, listening to the dial tone as it rings out.

What am I doing?

*What am I doing?*

It's 3 a.m.

I'm about to hang up when I hear his voice half asleep on the other end of the line.

'Ellie?'

I say nothing.

'Ellie? Are you there?'

The tears are coming again. The tears I can't seem to swallow, even though I'm trying so hard.

'Ellie,' he whispers. 'What's going on? Are you OK?'

I hear him sit up in bed, his head moving against his wooden

124

headboard. The way it used to when we'd sit in his bedroom and he'd turn to look at me.

'Ellie,' he says again slowly. 'What are you doing? Where are you?'

'I'm on the grass,' I whisper; like it's our little secret, like he'll understand. 'It's cold.'

'Maybe you should go inside,' he says gently.

'I can't breathe inside.'

'OK,' he replies. No judgement. No questions.

'What are you thinking about?'

'Amis,' I whisper.

I hear him take a breath, sharp and immediate, his body adjusting as the bed creaks beneath him.

'There's a cot in his room,' I whisper.

'For the baby,' he states.

'For the baby,' I confirm.

'What colour is it?'

'It's white. Everything in his room is white now.'

'Did he like white?'

'I don't know,' I say, my voice cracking. 'I never asked him. There were so many things I didn't ask him, but I didn't know. I didn't know . . .' I trail away.

'Didn't know what?' he asks gently.

'That I'd never get to ask him. That there'd be so much I don't know. How am I going to tell the baby about him? How am I going to remember him?' I'm gulping again. The air thick with so many thoughts, so many feelings.

'It's OK,' he soothes. 'It's going to be OK, Ellie.'

But it's not. It feels like it won't be, ever again.

125

'I think I'm breaking,' I gasp. 'I think I'm broken.'

'Shhhh,' he soothes. 'Just breathe. Can you do that? Can you breathe for me?' And I wish his hands were stroking my hair. I wish his arms were around me, even though that wouldn't help, not really. 'You're allowed to break, Ellie. You're going through a lot. You don't have to be strong all the time. You don't have to figure it all out now.'

'I wish . . .' I sob, 'I wish you were here.'

'I wish I was too,' he says, sounding pained. 'But I'm glad you called me.'

'I'm sorry,' I say, calming down. 'It's three a.m. I shouldn't have . . . I didn't mean to . . .' Because I'm doing it again. Confusing things. Confusing myself. But I don't know how to make it stop. This merry-go-round inside my head.

'I'm always here for you, Ellie. If you ever feel like this, I want you to call me. I don't care what time it is, OK?'

'OK,' I say, quietened by his kindness. Breathing. Just like he told me I could.

'But you need to get some sleep. It's late. Or early,' he says, yawning. 'I'm not sure.'

I look down at my legs. Covered in goosebumps, the garden dark and eerie.

'I'm sorry for waking you.'

'Stop apologising. That's supposed to be my area of expertise.'

'Is it, though?' I tease him. 'I'm not sure.'

'And she's back,' he jokes.

'Roger that,' I smile.

'Did you just say *Roger that?*' and I can almost see him grinning on the other end of the phone.

'Roger,' I say officiously.

'I miss you,' he says suddenly.

'I miss you too. But I'm not . . . I can't . . .'

'As a friend,' he clarifies. 'I miss being your friend, Ellie. You were one of my best friends. I didn't know it until I didn't have you any more.'

'Me too,' I say quietly. 'You were one of mine.'

'Well, can we be friends again?' he asks hopefully.

'I thought we were.'

'You're right,' he says softly, and I can hear him smiling. 'We are.'

And part of me feels disappointed that he isn't confessing his undying love, telling me he'll wait as long as it takes for me to love him back. But a bigger part of me feels relieved that he can be part of my life, just like this. On the other end of the phone. Teaching me how to breathe.

'Do you think you can sleep now?' he yawns.

'I'll try,' I say guiltily. 'I'm sorry again for waking you.'

'Stop staying sorry.'

'Sorry, Roger.'

He laughs. 'Goodnight, Ellie.'

'Goodnight, Ash.'

I put the phone down and wrap my arms around myself, breathing in the fresh-as-it's-possible-to-get-in-London air. Seconds later a message arrives.

**Ash:**

'Dice', Finley Quaye, William Orbit

I creep back through the door, locking it behind me, and make my way up the stairs. Just before I climb into bed, I take my earphones out

127

of my jeans pocket and slip them into my ears. I lie down and press the link, listening to the song he sent me over and over and over. It's part beautiful ballad, part something more; something urgent and haunting and hopeful. And I fall asleep to Finley's low deep voice and Orbit's propulsive beat; as if they were always supposed to be here, to take me there. To a place I can finally breathe.

# 23

# A Girl Called Ellie

My name is Ellie. Ellie Pillai.

And sometimes I get this feeling. Like I can't breathe.

It happens when things feel heavy, or difficult. Sometimes even when they don't.

Sudden and unexpected fear. Overwhelming anxiety. Panic.

It used to happen a lot – and then it didn't. Things got better. The feelings disappeared. I hid them somewhere they found it hard to escape.

My name is Ellie. Ellie Pillai.

The feelings escaped.

# 24

# The Wise, Sage-Type Person

The next morning, I wake up feeling better. As though the night before were nothing but a bad dream, something at the edge of my consciousness that doesn't really exist. I wake up feeling happy. Sure it's going to be a good day.

'Morning,' I say to Hope cheerfully.

'Morning,' she groans.

Hope is not a morning person.

'Were you playing music last night?' she asks, rolling towards me. 'I feel like there's a song going round in my head.'

'No,' I lie. 'You must have dreamed it.'

'Hooooopppppppe, Ellllliiiiiie,' Aunty Christine calls. 'Breaaaaaakkkkkkfffassst–' and if it's milk hoppers, I might find another reason to be cheerful this morning.

**Ash:**

how r u feeling?

'Who's that?' she asks, peering at my phone suspiciously.

'Jess,' I say, trying to manoeuvre my screen out of her eyeline. And I don't know why I'm lying. Maybe because I don't want her to make this anything other than it is. Just two friends. There for each other.

'What time's your train?' she yawns.

'Eleven a.m.'

She checks the time on her watch. 'Do you remember what happened yesterday? With Ethan,' she says suddenly. 'I mean, he almost . . . you almost . . .' She stops, unable to go on.

'Yeah,' I say, feeling sick at the thought. 'It was scary.'

'Well, you saved his life. Or his leg. Or something.' She yawns again.

'Listen, about Ethan,' I say, trying to broach the subject of how she feels about him.

'What about him?' she says, eyeing me. 'No lectures, please. It's too early.'

'I just . . . I mean . . . do you like him? You know, like that.'

'Like what?' she asks facetiously.

I raise an eyebrow.

'I mean, he's not perfect, E, but he's not a bad person. He just thinks he's not good enough, and, like, don't we *all* get that?' she says pointedly.

'I know, but the drinking thing . . .'

'Yeah,' she agrees. 'We need to talk to him about that.'

'*We?*'

'We,' she confirms. 'You're the wise, sage-type person, Ellie. We all have our roles.'

I think about last night. About the dew against my legs. About not being able to breathe. I don't feel brave, or wise.

I push it to the back of my head. To the box where I put things I don't want to think about. Yesterday was yesterday. Today is today. Today is a good day, because I say so.

'Are you two coming?' Aunty Christine says, poking her head through the doorway. 'Granny wants to eat.'

'OK, OK,' Hope says, rolling her eyes.

'We're having milk hoppers,' she says, winking at me.

Today is going to be a good day.

# 25

# Love Is Love

When we get into the train station back home, I help Granny out of her seat. She's welded in, her tiny brown bottom stuck to the red fabric seats.

'Ah, ah,' she says, clutching her back dramatically. 'Am not sack of potato,' she says irritably. 'Must be careful with old people.' Which is funny, because Granny hates to be called old, or even to hear the word *old* used in any context about anything whatsoever.

'Sorry, Granny,' I say meekly.

She pretends to look dignified and ignores me.

When we get off the train and head to the car park, I look for Mum's car, but instead see Mrs Aachara standing by her little blue car, the one Ash borrows sometimes, waving at us.

'Hi,' I say, walking towards her. 'We're just waiting for Mum.'

'I said I'd give you a lift,' she smiles. 'Your mum had to take your dad to a hospital appointment.'

'On a Sunday?' I ask, panic-stricken. 'Is everything OK?'

'It's fine. Don't worry. The NHS never stops,' she says, taking my hand kindly.

133

I smile uneasily, the feeling worsening as Ash gets out of the passenger side and takes my and Granny's bags from me.

'Hey, Roger,' he says, smiling.

'Hey,' I say, surprised.

This is going to be a good day.

Today is today.

Yesterday was yesterday.

'You're here,' I say breathlessly.

'Hello, Ashar,' Granny says, grabbing his cheeks.

He leads her towards the front passenger seat, helping her inside, then slips our bags into the boot.

I get into the back of the car as he slides in next to me.

'I didn't expect to see you,' I whisper. 'I'm sorry about last night. I was being stupid,' I babble. 'I feel better now. So much better.'

He gives me a look.

'Anyway,' I continue, 'um, how are you? How's Elina?'

Why does this feel so awkward?

'Elina's . . . OK, and I'm not too bad, thanks for asking.'

'You're welcome,' I say formally.

'Why are you being weird?'

'Ashar, what is happening with your university application?' Granny cuts in from the front seat. 'When is interview?'

Interview?

'Next week,' he says, looking over at me tentatively.

'Next week?' I say, turning to look out of the window.

'Elina has hers the day after,' Mrs Aachara continues. 'I'm so excited for them.'

'That's great.' I feign enthusiasm. 'So, is Elina, um, is she seeing

134

anyone?' I ask unsubtly. Because I feel like I should find out. About the Jane situation, and the reason they seem to be in every Instagram post together.

'No,' he says emphatically. 'She's heartbroken. She doesn't understand why Jess broke up with her.'

'She does,' I say, suddenly annoyed. 'Jess is trying to do the right thing. Trying to give them both space. She doesn't want them to hold each other back.'

'I don't think being in love with someone holds you back,' he says obstinately. 'And I think that's a pretty immature way to think about it. Especially after everything Elina did for her.'

'Ash,' Mrs Aachara says warningly.

'Immature?' I say, outraged. 'You think Jess is immature after everything she's been through? She practically raised herself, not to mention looking after her mum — and coming out isn't some easy, breezy, everyone-finds-it-so-simple thing. Not everyone's family support them the way yours did. If you ask me, she did the right thing. Elina's leaving. It doesn't make sense for them to be together.'

He turns his head away.

'Clearly Jess didn't feel as strongly about Elina as she felt about her,' he says, shrugging, 'so maybe you're right.'

'What are you talking about?' I hiss. 'Jess loves Elina, and they *were* strong. But you can't fight hundreds of miles between you. It's immature to think you could,' I huff.

'If you really love someone . . .' he begins.

'Then you visit them in the hospital when they almost die,' I finish.

The car goes silent.

I can hear Granny and Mrs Aachara breathing in the front seat, Ash next to me, his eyes dark.

135

'And I guess,' he says quietly, 'you don't lie about the fact you have feelings for someone else, when it's obvious to everyone, including your boyfriend.'

I can feel my face turning purple, an oversized blueberry above my cropped denim jacket.

'True,' I say venomously. 'It wasn't love, then. But what Jess and Elina had. That was love.'

'Exactly,' he says angrily, 'and she threw it away.'

And I don't know how it got like this. How I got so angry. Maybe because being angry is easier than being sad. In having to admit I'll miss him.

'Maybe we should talk about something else,' Mrs Aachara says quietly.

But we don't talk. We don't say another word for the rest of the journey home. Or when I get out of the car and he carries our bags to the front door. Or even when they leave.

'Ellie,' Granny says, as we open the front door. 'You will never catch husband if talk like that.'

'I don't want to catch a husband, Granny.'

'Wife?' she asks, eyeing me.

'I don't want to catch a wife either,' I say, suddenly softening. Because this is Granny's way of saying it's OK to tell her. That she's OK with whoever I am, whatever I want. Presumably as long as I stay as light-skinned as possible and become a lawyer or, at the very least, an accountant.

'I just want to fall in love. With no complications or drama or hurt or anger or pain. Just love. Simple love.'

'But love is not simple,' she says kindly. 'Love is all you say. Love is

136

the good and love is the bad – but love is *love*,' she says wisely. 'Love is worth it.'

That night, as I'm falling asleep, a message appears on my phone.

**Ash:**
i'm srry

**Ellie:**
i'm srry 2

**Ash:**
friends?

**Ellie:**
always

**Ash:**
♥

**Ellie:**
♥

I remind myself to breathe.
And I do.

# 26

# Wow

I'm kissing Shawn in the computer room after school. I'm not sure how this happened. I think the fact my history teacher just told me I had a chance of getting an 8 may have done it. I think the whole I-may-not-be-terrible-at-school thing may have done it. He was just there, at the right time, asking what last Friday meant and did I want to go out sometime, and I kissed him. *I'm kissing him.*

His lips feel a bit like pillows. Which I'm sure is a comment he wouldn't appreciate. But they're sort of full and soft and comforting. Like something I could never not appreciate – because who wouldn't want pillows in their life? Everyone needs a pillow. Pillows make everything better. Even being murdered by a pillow has to be better than most other types of murder. Pillows are just innately Not a Bad Thing.

He's got his arms around my waist, my hands clasped at the back of his neck, up on my tiptoes. He lifts me up as though I weigh nothing and sits me on top of a desk, so suddenly I'm higher, taller, my face closer to his. He's standing between my legs as I pull him towards me, thinking: I probably shouldn't be doing this, however nice pillows are.

'Um, hey. Shawn,' I say, pushing him away. He tilts his head to one side and kisses me on the forehead.

'Ellie,' he says, watching me.

'I shouldn't be, I really *can't* . . .' I continue. 'I need to just . . .'

He stares at me.

'I'm sorry,' he says, putting his hands in his pockets. 'I said I'd give you time.'

'You don't have to be sorry. I kissed you. I'm the one that should be sorry. I'm not being very . . .'

But I don't get a chance to finish my sentence.

'Ellie,' Hayley screams, as she pushes the door open, Jess not far behind her. 'What are you doing in here?' she asks, looking around. 'I know you told your parents you were doing computer science, but this is taking it a bit far.' Jess elbows her, motioning unsubtly towards Shawn.

'Ohhhhhh,' Hayley says just as unsubtly.

'What do you want, Hay?' I ask through gritted teeth.

'Have you seen this?' she asks, brandishing her phone.

'Seen what?' I ask, turning into a blueberry again, Shawn playing with my hand.

'This thing your cousin posted. Hope, right?'

'Hope?' I say, jumping off the desk and walking towards her. 'Is she OK? What's going on?'

'She posted this video of you and the band doing a song,' Jess says. 'You were wearing something she made, so she put it up to show people.'

'But all anybody's talking about is the song,' Hayley says excitedly. 'It's been viewed, like, 500K times or something.'

'. . . and the comments.' Jess explains, 'they're just . . . well, here . . .' she says, handing me her phone, 'look for yourself.'

And right there, on her phone, is the video Hope made at the end of the Easter holidays. When she came to band practice. The first time we all played my new song. Underneath it are what seem like millions of comments asking who wrote it, and fire emojis, and various people saying how hot Shawn and Benji and Lucas and Elliott are. People saying I have a voice. People telling us their stories. About their heartbreak. About the first time they fell in love.

'Oh my God,' I whisper, as Shawn looks it up on his own phone behind me.

'You sound incredible,' he says, walking towards me. He puts his arms around me from behind and kisses the top of my hair.

Jess and Hayley are staring at us. Staring at his arms around me.

'Wow,' I say to no one.

'Wow,' they say, staring at us.

'I need to call Benji,' Shawn says, letting go of me. 'I'll call you later.' He kisses me on the cheek.

'Wow,' Hayley says again, watching him go. 'What happened to the No-Romance Policy?'

'Stop it, Hay. It doesn't mean anything,' I reply.

'Does he know that?' Jess asks gently.

And I want to say yes, he does.

But I can't. Because I know it's not true. Not for either of us.

# 27

# Friends That Sometimes Kiss

By the next morning, the video's been viewed two million times. By break time, that's doubled, and I'm being followed around by a group of Year 7s asking for my autograph. Which is deeply unpleasant but also quite flattering.

*We love you, Ellie,* they titter.

**Hope:**
i shld be ur agent

**Ellie:**
some of those people hate me

**Hope:**
only the jealous ones

'Hi,' Ash says, when he finds me hiding in the music room at lunchtime. 'I had a feeling I'd find you here.'

I smile thinly.

'You don't look too happy. For a celebrity,' he jokes.

'I feel sick,' I admit. 'People are staring at me.'

'People have always stared at you.'

'Thanks,' I say sarcastically.

'I meant because you're beautiful,' he states. 'People stare at beautiful people.'

'I think you might be the only person who thinks that.'

'I think Shawn might agree,' he says lightly.

Shawn, who I keep kissing.

Ugh.

'I . . .' But I can't finish the sentence.

'Why are you hiding?' he asks, coming to sit next to me on the piano bench.

I put my head on his shoulder. Which seems like it has a spot exactly the right shape and size for my weird blueberry head. Somewhere I feel safe – but is anything but safe. A place so heartbreaking I wrote a song about it that now has 4.3 million views.

'I don't know. It all feels a bit much.'

He puts his arm around me.

'Why does everything have to change?' I whisper.

'Change can be good, Ellie.'

'What, like Jess and Elina?'

'You know how I feel about that,' he says tightly.

I sigh. 'I know – and I don't want to fight about it, it's just, can't you see why she did what she did? Jess, I mean.'

'Would you have broken up with me,' he says quietly, 'if we'd still been together at the end of the year?'

I shrug my shoulders.

He sorts of gesticulates, as if talking to himself.

142

'So, how are things at home?' And really, he's asking me about the cot in Amis's room. How I feel about it.

'Fine,' I reply.

Because I've turned that switch off. That emotion. I have to, or I wouldn't have been able to get up this morning.

'You know Granny,' I gulp. 'Obsessing over this wedding.'

'You know we're coming, don't you? Elina and me and Mum.'

I nod, turning to look up at him from my spot on his shoulder, my chest tight.

'I'm glad you're going to be there.'

'Me too,' he says quietly.

'Ellie,' Benji barks, barging into the room as Ash and I spring apart. 'Some label guy just called me. He wants to meet with us.'

'What?' I ask, confused, as Shawn walks in behind him.

'Your hot cousin tagged us all in her post, and I'm the only one that checks my DMs and he asked for my number and he called me.'

'Whaaaat?' I repeat. 'Are you sure it's not just some dodgy rando making it up?' I'm having visions of some strange guy with a burner phone, surrounded by black tape and killing paraphernalia.

'We're not all going to be sold into white slavery, if that's what you mean. I've checked him out and he seems legit.'

'I'm not white, but OK,' I state.

He blushes, and I've never seen Benji blush.

'Um, I mean, you know, he's not going to coax us into a van with kittens and stuff,' he continues.

'Okaaaaayyy. What do you mean?' I ask again.

'He. Wants. To. Meet. Us.'

'What?'

'Ellie. I'm going to kill you if you ask me that again.' And in my head Benji's now the serial killer surrounded by black tape and killing paraphernalia. Which seems on point.

'I need to talk to my parents,' I begin. 'We need to double-check he isn't a serial killer. I need to think about it,' I babble. 'I need to, you know, think about *it*. Because it's a lot, Benji. This is, like, *a lot*. We've got exams and stuff, we've got things coming up, we can't just, you know, go meeting rando guys from record labels and hope we won't be murdered.'

Benji looks at Shawn. 'Can you talk to her, please? She seems to respond to you.'

He looks over at me, his blue eyes dark.

'I should go,' Ash says, standing.

Benji seems to notice him for the first time, throwing him a WTF look, closely followed by one in my direction.

'Yeah, me too,' he says, noting Shawn's expression.

When they're both gone, Shawn just stares at me.

'So, are you two . . . ?' he asks.

'No,' I say quickly. 'We're just friends.'

'Friends,' he says unsurely. 'Like us.'

I stare at his faded maroon T-shirt. It's a vintage Bowie print. I love vintage Bowie.

'Yes,' I say just as unsurely.

'But we're friends that keep kissing,' he states, his hands in his pockets.

'Well, we're not,' I say, alluding to Ash. 'We're friend friends.'

'What does it mean, Ellie, that we keep kissing?' he continues.

'I don't know,' I admit. 'Does it have to mean something?'

144

He looks hurt, so I try again.

'I just mean, right now, I'm not in the right place to start something. I've got exams and family stuff, and my friends.'

Also, sometimes I feel like I can't breathe. Which makes everything feel impossible.

'OK,' he says, looking at his feet. 'I don't want to pressure you.'

Pressure.

Pressure.

Pressure.

Even the word feels heavy.

'Do you want to come to a wedding with me? In London?' I ask suddenly.

'As friends that sometimes kiss?'

I smile and he smiles back.

'Sure,' I reply.

'I'd like that,' he says.

But I'm not so sure, not really, that I know remotely what it is I'm doing.

# ♡ Song 2 ♡

## Intro, Verse, Chorus, Middle Eight

I'm staring at the numbers, watching them tick upwards. Watching the comments veer from one extreme to another. Love. Hate. Love. Hate.

I put my fingers on the keys and sing the line. The only one that won't refuse to come to me.

*I'm not ready to let go*

I wait for something else to arrive. Another note, or word. A sentence. Something to make it make sense.

*I'm not ready to let go*

I put all the minor chords together and wait for the anger to turn into something else. Something meaningful to hold my hand.

But I'm stuck. Like a record on the same groove.

Stuck.

Like something that can't let go.

# 28

# Annoying and Unhelpful

'Ellie, I love you, but can you *please* stop following me around,' Hayley says, turning to me abruptly.

'What do you mean?'

'I mean, you're watching every single thing I do, and it's annoying.'

'Oh.'

'Like, really, really annoying,' she states.

'Hay, I'm just trying to help.'

'Please stop helping,' she begs.

'FINE.'

'What's going on, you two?' Jess says, as she approaches us after school on our way to the library.

'Apparently, I'm annoying and unhelpful,' I say irritably.

Jess shoots Hayley a look.

'Um, well, I mean,' she says, 'I think it's nice that you want to talk all the time, and check up on me and stuff, but you know, I'm OK, and Hay's doing OK, and maybe you should focus on yourself for a bit,' she says, linking arms with me.

'I chose my A level options,' I say sulkily. And frankly, that's as much thinking about me as I can cope with at the moment.

Thank all the gods for Hope and her drama, history, maths rant; because when Hayley's mum cornered me a week ago, I just repeated it, then wrote it down on a form and now I'm taking drama, history, maths and something called *general studies*, which seems vague and possibly not that useful.

Unbelievably, Mum and Dad didn't have anything to say when I told them what I'd chosen. Which partly felt amazing, but partly like they didn't care any more. Like they'd get another chance to get it right with the next kid, so what was the point in worrying about me.

Which isn't fair. I know it isn't fair. It's just everything feels so jumbled up and messy right now. This voice I can't separate from my own. That keeps telling me things are changing in all the wrong ways.

'So, I *have* focused on myself,' I lie. 'And Dr Jada says to celebrate each step, each accomplishment, so I've done something for me, and now I want to do something for you two.'

They exchange another look.

'What Jess means is you're being Too Much, E,' Hayley says unapologetically.

'You don't need to be so harsh,' Jess says, glaring at her.

'Really,' I ask, turning to Jess. 'Am I being too much?'

'No,' she says, shooting Hayley as much of a look as Jess is capable of giving, because she is fundamentally too nice to be shooting people looks even when they deserve it. 'But I don't want to talk about Elina any more. I don't need you to send me podcasts and articles and give me notebooks to write my feelings down in. I know you're trying to help. I know you're trying to be there for me, but it's just—'

148

'Too Much,' Hayley interrupts.

'That's not what I said,' Jess replies through gritted teeth. 'Anyway, how are things with Shawn?' she asks, changing the subject. 'What are you guys going to do about this record label thing?'

'I don't know.' I shrug.

'About which one?' Hayley replies.

'Either. I need to talk to my parents, but they've got all this baby stuff. I don't want to stress them out.'

'Why would finding out that their daughter is so talented she's written a song that almost six million people have listened to stress them out?' Hayley asks. 'You have to at least meet this person. See what they have to say.'

'Have you been talking to Benji?' I ask, thinking about how many times he's said practically the same thing to me in the last week.

It's been over a week since Benji told me about the label, and I've spent most of the time between then and now avoiding Ash and Shawn, revising, and apparently stalking my best friends in annoying and unhelpful ways.

'I don't like being viral,' I mutter ungratefully.

'You make it sound like a disease,' Hayley laughs.

We're stood outside the library, getting all our talking out before we have to go in and sit silently.

'I can't believe how quickly this year's gone by,' Jess says, looking at the doors.

Understatement. Huge.

In a couple of weeks' time, it's the first part of the wedding, and after that it's half-term, and study leave, and exams, and the second part of the wedding, and people leaving – and the baby is coming somewhere in the middle of all that. It's like everything's moving at twice the speed it should be, and I just want to get off this ride.

The library doors swing open, and Elina and Jane walk out, linking arms.

I can sense Jess's discomfort, the rays radiating off her like the sun. Elina, noticing Jess, lets go of Jane's arm and glares at her coldly. Jess looks away as Hayley stares at the ground awkwardly.

'Hey, Ellie,' Elina says warmly. It feels like we're in some kind of space/time vortex where everything's the opposite of the way it should be.

'Hey, Elina. Hey, Jane,' I say, as Jess and Hayley obstinately refuse to acknowledge them. 'Studying?' I ask pointlessly.

'We're trying to update the LGBTQIA+ section,' Jane says, looking at Elina.

'What do you mean?' I ask stupidly.

'I mean, books by queer authors about queer people. Books that might help people see themselves. We need more. I've been campaigning about it for ages, and now El and I are putting together a list of what we think we need.'

*El?* Since when did anyone call Elina *El?*

'Feel free to get involved,' she says, gesturing at Jess and Hayley. 'I mean, the more the merrier. The louder we can be, the better.'

'Sounds like you two have it all in hand,' Jess says, staring at the wall.

Elina looks away.

'You know, Ellie, maybe you could help me compile a list of authors of colour,' Jane says, looking over at me. 'We definitely need to update that section too.'

'I don't automatically know every author of colour because I'm brown,' I say out of nowhere.

'Oh, I, uh, I didn't mean it like that,' she splutters, while Jess and Hayley stare at me.

'Sorry.' I blush. 'I know you're the student librarian, and you're just trying to help, but I don't think it's my responsibility to educate people about this stuff. I mean, I want to help, I want to see more representation in the library, I just don't want to feel like it's *my* job to do that.'

'Of course, I'm so sorry. I should never have—' Jane says awkwardly.

I need to get better at saying things like this, even if it makes people feel uncomfortable. Because I've been uncomfortable for a really long time, and it's about time I stopped assuming that was my role. To make everyone else feel OK.

*Where are you from? No, where are you* really *from?* Unfortunately, I am *really* from the same place as you are.

*You don't sound Indian.* I'm not Indian, I'm Sri Lankan. But now we're on the subject, exactly *how* do the entire Indian diaspora sound?

*Do you know the guy that runs the corner shop?* Yes. I also know the woman that owns the greengrocer's and the man that makes gluten-free pastries for the café on the high street. I'm not sure what that says about me. That I like food, maybe.

'It's fine,' I say to Jane. 'I think it's great that you want to make the library better.'

I scan Jess's face for signs of disappointment at my disloyalty, but all I see is how pink her cheeks are. Like she's been for a run.

'Are you OK?' I ask, as Elina and Jane walk away together.

'Do you think they're going out?' she asks, staring after them.

'I mean, they seem quite close,' Hayley says unhelpfully. Which at least means I'm not the only unhelpful person in this triangle.

'Well, I've been kissing Shawn, and we're not together,' I insist.

'*Kissing?*' Jess says, stricken. 'You think they're kissing?'

Hayley gives me a look. Hayley is extremely capable of giving looks.

'I'm sure they're just friends,' she says more helpfully. At least she learns quickly.

'Exactly,' I reiterate.

'But to be fair,' Hayley says, 'you did break up with her . . .'

'I know,' Jess breathes. 'I just didn't want to wait until she left, and we had to break up over the phone, or I'd stop her from doing something she wanted to do because she'd made a commitment to me. I was trying to be mature,' she says desperately. 'I mean, it had to end, didn't it?' she asks us, wide-eyed.

And I want to say: you're right. That's exactly what I would have done. But I'm usually wrong about these things, so maybe you were too.

Because I sense this wouldn't be helpful, and I'm trying to learn quickly too.

'You did what you thought was right, Jess.'

'I have to go,' she says abruptly, 'I need to revise,' and she walks away, pushing the doors to the library open and disappearing inside.

'I'm telling you,' I say to Hayley, 'that notebook I gave her is going to save her life. Dr Jada says writing our feelings down helps us to detach from them.'

Hayley gives me a look. The one I will now coin Her Look. She's way too good at giving it. It says a thousand things without saying anything.

'She doesn't need to detach from her feelings. She needs to feel them and work out whether or not she made the right decision,' Hayley says matter-of-factly. 'Maybe you do too.'

But I don't have feelings. I've decided.

'How did you do it, Hay?' I ask her. 'You don't seem bothered by James and Sadie at all.'

'I'm happy for him. I love James.'

'That's my point. How do you do that? Jess can't let go of Elina; I can't let go of Shawn.'

'Or Ash,' she points out.

'That's not true,' I stutter. 'I've totally let go of Ash.'

She gives me Her Look.

'OK,' she acquiesces, not looking like she remotely acquiesces to my statement.

'I need to revise,' I say petulantly.

I push the library doors open, looking for Jessica, when I see the one thing I hadn't expected to see.

Ash sitting next to Hannah, leaning over her, explaining something about something in a way that feels too familiar. Too close.

I find Jess sat in a corner and pull a chair up next to her.

Note to self: detach.

# 29

# Not the Child Catcher from Chitty Chitty Bang Bang

Mum and Dad have cleared all Amis's things out of his room. They did a lot of it while Granny and I were in London a few weeks ago, and the rest of it's been coming out piece by piece, like they're hoping I won't notice.

It feels strange and painful, but they seem happy. As if this new baby is a chance to start again. And I want them to be happy. Even if I can't be.

'Ellie,' Granny says, coming into my room. 'Dinner is ready. I make kottu roti,' she says, giving me a kiss on the forehead. 'You like, yes?'

'I love. Thanks,' I say, putting my science book down and getting up.

'You are OK?' she asks, stroking my hair back from my face.

I nod.

'Hmmmn,' she replies, unconvinced.

'Are you looking forward to the wedding?' I ask her.

'Chkkkk,' she says dismissively. 'Wedding is good, but what comes after must be better. This is what you must understand. Marriage is not nice dress and nice dinner with friends.'

'I'm sure it's fun sometimes,' I insist.

I don't really know much about my grandfather, he died before I was born, but Dad says he liked to have fun. Too much fun. That he drank and smoked and gambled, and Granny loved him more than anything, but he didn't leave her in the best situation when he died.

'Hmmmn,' she responds glumly. 'Charles is good man. Will take care of Kitty. Not leave her in mess.'

'I'm pretty sure Aunty Kitty can look after herself,' I say, thinking of my formidable aunt.

'In my day, women are not supposed to look after themselves. Is not allowed. Is considered shameful, if they have to,' she says sadly. 'I am glad my daughter and granddaughters do not live like this,' she says thankfully. 'I am glad you are all strong.'

I shift uncomfortably. I don't feel strong. I feel the opposite of strong.

'How is revision?' she asks, as we walk down the stairs together. 'You are working hard. I am proud.' I'm not sure these words have ever crossed my grandmother's lips before. She seems uncertain. Like she might need to take them back.

Dad looks up as we step into the kitchen.

'Ellie always makes me proud.' I walk towards him and give him a hug, Granny trying desperately not to tell me off for touching him. She's been so nervous since he got out of hospital, almost as bad as I've been with Jess and Hayley. I suspect Dad thinks Granny is annoying and unhelpful too. Perhaps it's a family trait.

Dad kisses my head.

'I feel like I never see you any more,' he murmurs. 'I thought once you broke up with Ash, you'd be mine again,' he says, squeezing me.

'Ew, Dad. Stop. I'm not yours and I wasn't Ash's either.'

'Good girl,' Mum says, her belly entering the kitchen before she does. 'We don't belong to anyone but ourselves, am I right, *Amma*?' she says to Granny, who looks at her worriedly.

'Nimi, you must sit. Is not good to be running around when pregnant at your age.'

Mum sighs. 'I'm not that old.'

'Hmmmn,' Granny says unkindly.

'So, Ellie,' Mum says, sitting as requested. 'My colleague sent me this earlier today.' She takes her phone out and pulls up the video Hope took of me singing at the end of the Easter holidays.

'Oh, um . . .'

I wait for her to explode. To tell me I shouldn't be sharing myself online. That all sorts of perverts and murderers are looking for content just like this, of young girls like me, and I shouldn't be rushing to satisfy their needs.

'She wanted to know if it was my daughter, because the surname is quite unusual and she knew you were called Ellie.'

'Oh, um . . .'

'Seven million views and counting.'

'Seven million,' Dad shrieks. 'Let me see it,' he demands, as she hands over her phone.

He presses on the link, and I wait as the sound of the band fills the room. In the acoustics of the kitchen, my voice swells, filling every cupboard, every shelf, every cup and spoon and glass with sound.

I can see Dad starting to sway, his eyes bright with tears.

'Ellie,' he says, looking over at me. 'This is beautiful.'

'I know,' Mum says, looking at him. 'It is, isn't it?'

What. Is. Happening.

'Why didn't you tell us about this, *sina pillai*?' Dad asks.

'I didn't think it was important,' I respond.

'Of course it's important,' Mum says, bewildered. 'This is incredible. It's going to open up so many opportunities for you, Ellie.'

'Well,' I begin tentatively, 'it kind of has already. A record label wants to meet with us.'

'Really?' Dad says, concerned. 'Are you sure they're above board, *sina pillai*?'

'Not the Child Catcher from *Chitty Chitty Bang Bang*?' I joke.

Dad looks horrified. 'I mean, you haven't met with anyone, spoken to anyone yet?'

'No,' I reassure him. 'I'd never do that without talking to you first. I can give you their number. You can call and check yourself.'

And at least now Benji can stop harassing me to talk to my parents, as if he has any understanding of what talking to my parents looks like. Usually. I mean, they're being pretty cool. Or is it just that I don't matter as much any more, now there's a new baby coming?

'We'll have to think about it,' Dad says.

Or maybe not so cool.

'He means,' Mum says, watching my face, 'we'll call them tomorrow.'

'What is record label?' Granny interrupts.

'They're the people who look after musicians, *Amma*. Who help them make their music and get it out to people,' Dad explains.

'Ah, ah,' she says, as if this makes sense of everything. When nothing makes sense. How calm Mum and Dad are being, how calm I don't feel.

Over dinner, Mum and Dad are talking about the arrangements they've made for the birth. She's been offered a caesarean, but she wants to try something more natural. Granny and Dad are being understanding, but I can hear it in their voices. I can feel it in mine. That we shouldn't take any risks. That we should do whatever the doctors recommend as the safest option.

'But what if I have the baby here, at home?' Mum's saying. A water birth. A doula.

I'm thinking a) what's a doula, and b) I don't want to know what a water birth is because it sounds gross, and c) that doesn't sound safe, and I need her to be safe.

'I just want to do it on my own terms,' she's saying. 'I want to feel at one with the experience.'

'That sounds like something Dr Jada would say,' I say. Which I know she'll hate.

'Oh,' she says, deflated. 'Well, I haven't decided anything yet.'

Dad shoots me a grateful look as Granny takes a breath.

I sense the eggshells we're all walking on. I want to stamp on them. I want to scream: This isn't just about you. It's about all of us. What we all need.

'So, anyway, Ellie,' Dad says. 'I'll call these people tomorrow. See what they say.'

After dinner I head up to my room. Amis's door is open, displaying a new cot, bookshelf, drawers, artwork. A new room for a new baby.

I go into my room and sit on the end of my bed. There's only one person I want to call. But I don't call them.

I put my phone under my pillow and sit at my desk, pulling out the notes Jess made me for French.

I read them out loud.

Again.

And again.

And again.

Until the pulsing behind my eyes stops.

Breathe, Ellie. Just breathe.

# 30

# Jadie

Hayley and James are practising their audition pieces in front of the whole class today. Hayley seems unusually nervous for someone who isn't usually nervous at all. She keeps holding my hand and telling me how much she loves me and staring at James and being generally weird. I wonder whether she's going to confess her undying love, or do a withering takedown of Jadie, the James & Sadie moniker, which to be fair has so far only caught on with me and Jess.

'So, class, as many of you know, James and Hayley have been invited to audition for BackStage this year,' Mrs Aachara says from the front of the studio, 'and have both been busy preparing monologues. As their auditions are next week, I've suggested we use part of today's session to hear them and offer critical feedback. Now, remember,' she says, swinging round to Jeffrey Dean, 'critique and feedback are an imperative part of the creative process, but our job, always, is to be fair, open-minded and encouraging.'

James smiles as Hayley grimaces.

'James will be reading a monologue from *The Wolf of Wall Street*. James, are you happy to get us started?' she asks, looking over at him.

He nods.

As he takes to the middle of the room, I note how easily he seems to disappear into character between the moment he leaves his seat and the second he stands up to walk to the stage, like that scene at the end of *The Usual Suspects*. *James is Keyser Söze.* Except he isn't. He's Jordan Belfort, tapping into his testosterone and 1980s machismo to rally the room to do his bidding. He's sort of half shouting, half cajoling us. Telling us we can be just like him, that we too can drive a Porsche and have a big-breasted show wife.

And I'm not a fan of the character. I'm not a fan of the people who might genuinely consider this speech appealing, or rousing, something they aspire to – but I am a fan of James. Because this isn't him. It's someone else. Someone he is, for just the few minutes in which he inhabits him.

When he stops, I can see his shoulders loosening. The real James reappearing. The one who picked me up when I was a mess at the end of last term. Who sent me songs when I was heartbroken and sat with Hayley to make sure she was eating her lunch.

I clap until my hands hurt, and then I look over at Hayley. Hayley, who is now white with nerves because she has to follow this. This performance that even I have to admit is the best thing I've ever seen happen in this room.

'Well done, James,' Mrs Aachara beams. 'Any thoughts, guys?'

Jeffrey Dean proceeds to give James some advice on how to improve his posture, which has nothing whatsoever to do with the character, while the rest of us keep telling him how incredible he was.

'Let's chat later,' Mrs Aachara says to him. 'It's a good choice. Fresh. I think we can come up with a slightly different angle, though. Something closer to the book than the film.' He nods receptively.

'Hayley,' Mrs Aachara says, looking at her. 'Are you ready?'

She looks pale. I wonder if she's eaten today. I always wonder if she's eaten; but if I ask, she accuses me of being annoying and unhelpful.

'I haven't heard much about your piece,' Mrs Aachara says, 'so do you want to tell everyone what you've written, and why? Give us some context?' Mrs Aachara looks worried. And I wonder if this is too much for Hay. Too much pressure for someone dealing with what she's dealing with. Who's in recovery for anorexia, and barely any time's gone by since she was passing out at school.

'OK,' Hayley says quietly. 'The piece I've written is called "The Voice". I think you'll understand when you hear it.'

James smiles at her.

I smile at her.

She stands.

I'm not prepared for what happens next, but as always, I really, really, should have been.

# The Voice

## A monologue by Hayley Atwell

There's this girl I know. A girl called Hayley. She's that girl at school. The mouthy one. The one who has an opinion about everything. Who never seems to shut up.

I don't like her, even though I don't really know her.

But I can guess who she is by the way she dresses. I can guess who she is by the people she spends time with. These are the choices she makes. The things she deigns for you to see. She puts those choices out there for you to read her. Like a book, or a poem, or a song. One of those cheap greeting cards from your local corner shop. The ones you buy when you've run out of time to care.

Hayley is thin. Too thin, people tell her. But for the longest time, she thought she was fat. She is fat. Hayley is fat.

Hayley isn't that clever. Or special. Hayley is the youngest child of someone she worries doesn't like her. A father who ignores her. The sister to someone extraordinary when she, Hayley, isn't at all. Hayley was someone's girlfriend, but now she isn't. Is Hayley anyone at all?

Have I introduced myself yet?

I'm The Voice.

The one in your head.

That drives you to desperation. That makes you tear your hair out. Who tells you not to eat, because eating is the one thing you can control. Who tells you to binge, because you can get rid of it all, your fingers down your throat.

Put your finger down your throat.

I am The Voice.

Your voice.

Hayley's voice.

Hayley is the things we all are.

Hayley is a loser.

Hayley isn't the person you want her to be.

But she could be. If she would just try harder.

Why doesn't she try harder?

Hayley is tough. Like leather. Not the buttery soft kind of a rich girl's handbag, but scratchy and hard and difficult to love. Practical leather. Long-lasting leather. The kind of leather that protects you. That lets you feel nothing.

But Hayley is confused.

She keeps telling me to be quiet.

Fighting me when I've told her not to.

When I've explained that listening to me is easier.

Giving in to me is easier.

I am The Voice. The one who knows all, and sees all, and tells all, and is all. But Hayley can hear something else now. A smaller voice. Nagging and consistent. Brighter than it should be. The Truth, she calls it.

I've been trying to kill this truth. Smother it with pictures of good-looking actors, the kind I thought she liked, with long hair and jeans with holes in them. Tortured artists and wounded souls. Who star in films about important things. Things we need to talk about.

I thought that would be enough. But it isn't.

She doesn't want the actors I've shown her. She wants something different. Different actors. She likes the long hair and the jeans with holes in them. But she prefers them on girls. She prefers girls. She has always preferred girls. Loved girls, not boys. Not like that.

Hayley is a lesbian. Hayley is gay.

Hayley, whose boyfriend was the first person she came out to. Who told her not to be afraid, even though I told her he'd be angry. That he'd hate her. He didn't.

I've told her not to be the way she is.

I've explained this is wrong.

Unacceptable.

But she isn't listening to me.

Why isn't she listening to me?

I am The Voice.

Your voice.

Your voice.

Your voice.

Soothing and melodic and familiar.

I tell you the things you already know.

If you don't know who you are yet, then let me make it clear.

You're mine. What I tell you to be.

Don't listen to Hayley.

She doesn't know anything.

The truth won't set you free.

# 31

# I Love You Both?

I don't think it's possible for my hands to make any more noise. I'm clapping them together so hard it hurts. I clap and I clap and I clap; the whole class whooping and cheering and shouting.

Hayley's in tears. It started immediately after she came out of character. The character of The Voice. Silky smooth and undeniable. As though the words it's telling you are fact. As if it's the only voice. The only one that matters.

And it's not just the words she's spoken or the fact that she's just come out, or even the vulnerability it takes to write about yourself in the third person. It's the way she became someone else, The Voice. That she inhabited it, as though it were real – and I realise it is. I realise The Voice has been whispering to me a lot lately.

I want to grab hold of Hayley and hug her. I want to tell her that what she wrote spoke to me, in a way nothing ever has before. That I understand.

But I'll have to get in line, because James has his arms around her, and she's crying into his chest. And he knew. She told him first. Trusted him first. So, even though he still loves her, he accepts she can't love him back. Not the way he wants her to. Not ever.

So much makes sense to me, and so much doesn't.

'Well, Hayley,' Mrs Aachara says, wiping a tear from her eye. 'I have to admit I was worried. You hadn't shared anything with me before today, and I had no idea what to expect. But I can see,' she smiles, 'that I didn't need to worry at all. What an incredibly powerful piece that was. Well done.'

'Hay,' I say, trying to battle through her admirers. She turns to me from where she's hugging various members of the class.

'Hey,' she says shyly.

'I'm so proud of you,' I say, reaching up to her.

She leans down into me. Into our tall girl, small girl embrace. And I'm still worried about her, still worried if she's had any lunch and how she's coping, but I'm also not worried. Because she's fighting that voice, the one I need to fight too.

'OK, OK,' Mrs Aachara says, as the room continues to chatter. 'Any feedback?'

The class whoops again.

'I'll take that as a no,' she smiles. 'But we still have work to do, so can you get back into your groups and start working on your final piece.'

As Hayley and I aren't in a group together, we get separated before I can ask her anything else.

'James,' I hiss, because he is in my group. 'When did she tell you?'

'Last term. But I think maybe I always knew,' he says quietly. 'I just really liked her.'

'Liked?' I query. 'Past tense?'

'I've got a girlfriend, Ellie.'

I give him a look.

'Fine,' he admits. '*Like.* Present tense. But it's not going to happen, so I have to move on, you know?'

I wonder how Sadie would feel, knowing she's the one he's moved on with, when secretly he's in love with someone else. Not good, I imagine.

At the end of the lesson, Hayley and I walk out to the green together, the sun shining above us.

'I'm sorry I didn't tell you before,' she says, sitting on the grass. 'I was so confused. It's like as soon as Elina and Jess came out as a couple, I kept thinking, that's what it should look like, that's how I should look.'

'Why didn't you say anything?'

'I mean, James is amazing, and I thought if anyone could make me feel differently, it would be him. But it just didn't. I just couldn't. I broke up with him. I needed to deal with how I was feeling.'

'I should have seen it before.'

'Ellie, please don't make this about you.'

I stare at her. Shocked.

'I'm sorry,' she says, grabbing my arm. 'I didn't mean it like that. I just mean it's nothing to do with you being a good or bad friend – which, by the way,' she says, squeezing me, 'you're an amazing friend. I just had to be ready to come out in my own time. I had to know for sure. Which I did when I saw James and Sadie together.'

'Because it didn't bother you?'

'Oh, it bothered me,' she laughs. 'Because I missed him. He's my friend. One of my best friends. All of a sudden, I had to share him, and I didn't want to. I didn't want her to take my place.'

I put my arm around her, and she puts her head on my shoulder.

'It's going to be around the school in, like, the next five minutes,' I warn her.

She shrugs. 'When have I ever cared what people think of me?' she says – and I want to say always, because we always do, even when we say we don't.

'I met somebody at my group,' she says suddenly.

'What, like *somebody*,' I intimate, 'you *like*?'

'Yes, Ellie. I like *him*. As a friend. Rayden's gay, and he's so open about it. He's so free. I want to be that free.'

'Rayden, huh?'

'He's at Everly.' Everly is the sixth-form college on the other side of the city. The one for posh people.

'So, how did it go?' Jess says, throwing herself down next to us.

'Good,' Hayley smiles. 'I mean, I did it.'

'What? You knew?' I ask, my mouth open as my head jerks to look from one of them to the other.

'Ellie,' Hayley says warningly.

'I'm not making it about me. I'm just asking a question,' I insist.

'We've talked about it,' Jess admits.

Hayley gives me Her Look.

'OK, OK,' I acquiesce.

'I figured she'd get it,' Hayley says self-consciously.

'I'm sorry,' I say, leaning over to hug her. 'I just wish you'd felt like you could talk to me about it.'

'I did. I do,' she insists. 'If it wasn't for you, I wouldn't have got to know Jess. I wouldn't have seen her and Elina and known how it should feel to be in love.'

Jess's face falls.

'Oh God, Jess. I'm sorry,' Hayley says, looking torn. 'I didn't mean it like that. I totally understand why you broke up – I just mean, I've never had a queer friend before, and seeing how happy you guys were made it seem like it was possible for me to be happy too.'

And I think Jess is going to cry.

'Jess?' Hayley says, waving her hand up in down in front of her face. 'What I'm trying to say is – thank you. I couldn't have done this without you.'

Jess turns towards Hayley and smiles. One of those smiles only Jess can give. Like warm honey in a cup of milk.

'And E, you're always there when it matters. Always. I love you both.'

*I love you both?*

She *loves* us.

I look over at Jess worriedly.

'What's happened to you?' I ask Hayley. 'I mean, seriously. You're hugging people, and saying thank you, and I *love* you. It's weird. Unnerving.'

'Bone-chilling,' Jess adds theatrically.

'It won't last,' Hay replies caustically, 'but right now, I'm just really, really happy. I feel . . .'

'Like you can finally be yourself?' Jess finishes.

'Hay, I'm so proud of you,' I say, standing up, 'but I have to hand my history coursework in. I'll catch up with you after school. OK?'

I leave them sitting on the green, the rest of the school pretending not to be staring. But I don't hand in my history coursework because I did that this morning. Instead, I head to the girls' toilets and go into a stall. I sit on the seat lid, my breathing escalating.

170

I wait until the feeling passes and give myself a few minutes to collect myself.

Until I remember how to breathe again.

# 32

# Act Surprised

When I get home from the library after school, Mum's waiting for me by the door.

'You're home!' she says excitedly.

I jump, surprised to see her lurking in the hallway.

'Why are you lurking?' I ask, backing away from her.

'I'm not *lurking*,' she says, massaging her lower back. 'I'm just excited to see you.'

'Why?' I question. She has literally never been excited to see me before.

'Your father called the record label,' she says conspiratorially. 'They want to fly you out to New York! Granny's fretting, but I said you should go, Ellie. You've worked so hard for this opportunity. You have to see what they say.'

'Oh my God,' I say, falling back against the wall.

'He wants to tell you himself,' she whispers. 'So, act surprised.'

'What?'

'Ellie,' Dad says, appearing out of nowhere and shooting Mum a suspicious look. 'I need to talk to you. In the kitchen.'

I walk into the kitchen, trying to remember the breathing exercises from Dr Jada's podcast. The one I've been listening to all the way home.

I sit down as Mum bustles around, Granny cooking something on the stove.

Dad sits down opposite me.

'I called Sound Records,' he says formally. 'It's all above board.'

'OK . . .'

'They'd like you to play a showcase. Hear you in person.'

'Oh God . . .'

'In New York,' he finishes. 'Which is where they're based.'

I sit back in my chair, pretending to be shocked.

'She told you, didn't she?' Dad says, annoyed.

I look over at Mum, studiously pretending to help Granny cook, while Granny swats her away like a fly.

'Nimi, you are bad luck. You ruin my biriyani last week,' Granny says, glaring at her.

'I didn't do anything,' Mum protests.

'You'll stay with Kitty and Charles,' Dad says. 'Nimi's too late in her pregnancy to fly, and the doctor doesn't think it's wise for me at the moment.'

'So, I can go?' I say, my heart beating, because I know Mum said I could, but I think it's only just starting to sink in. That my dad's had a conversation with someone from a record label. Someone who wants to see what we can do. What I can do.

He nods reluctantly.

'This is your GCSE year, Ellie, so I'm not going to pretend to be happy about it, but Nimi was insistent,' he says, looking over at her, breathing heavily out of her mouth as she leans against the kitchen counter. 'And I can't fight your mother,' he grumps.

'Are you OK, Mum?' I ask, watching her.

'I feel like I'm carrying a beach ball inside my chest,' she complains. 'I can't wait for him to get here,' she says, rubbing her belly.

I nod. Pretending I can't wait for this event either.

The Event.

Dad crosses the room to kiss her on the forehead.

'So, when?' I ask, my breath catching in my throat. 'When do they want us to go?'

'Next week. I'll speak to the school. You're on study leave soon anyway, I don't think a couple of days will do any harm.'

'Next week?' I shriek.

Oh my God. I need outfits and I need to work out what to do with my hair, and we need to practise. So. Many. Things.

'Tuesday to Thursday. You'll be back in time for the wedding.'

The wedding, part one. So much to do. So. Many. Things.

I spring out of my chair and leap at him.

'Thanks, Dad,' I say, burying my head in his shoulder, then hug Mum, my arms around her neck, unable to meet around her middle any more. 'Thanks for understanding,' I say tearfully as she hugs me back, kissing my hair.

'We're so proud of you,' she says.

'Hmmn,' Granny says pointedly. 'Has enough pressure already. Is sixteen. Has time. Why must rush? Let child be child,' she harrumphs.

'I'm fine, Granny,' I insist.

'Hmmmn,' she says disbelievingly. Like she might know better.

But I'm too excited. Because I'm going to New York again. With

174

some of my favourite people. And I'm not going to let myself panic about how I'm going to sing in front of record label people, or spend that much time with Shawn without kissing him, or that exams are coming or that the baby could be here by the time I get home.

No. I'll just to listen to Dr Jada's breathing podcast again and remember I'm in control.

**Shawn:**

✈ tried 2 catch u at school but kept missing u

**Ellie:**

😱!!!

**Shawn:**

practice tomorrow?

**Ellie:**

YES

**Ellie:**

sit next 2 me ✈?

**Shawn:**

😎

**Ellie:**

😎

# 33

# Internal Screaming

In the main hall after school, I'm trying to cram some facts into my brain about ratio, proportion, and rates of change. Because any free minute should not be free. Any free minute needs to be spent attempting to force my brain to digest information I can regurgitate in an exam.

'Hey,' Benji says, as he appears in the hall next to me. 'What are you doing? Revising?'

'Um, yeah,' I say awkwardly. Because I haven't been alone with Benji since Hayley came out, and I know he liked her. Like, *liked* her, liked her. Hayley the heartbreaker.

'You seen Atwell today?' he asks casually.

'This morning,' I say. 'We had French together.'

I don't say, we also ate lunch together and we'll probably meet up this weekend, and she may even come to rehearsal later, just in case she's been avoiding him and he doesn't need to know that. Because heartbreak and avoidance, I get.

'She OK?' he asks, opening the door to the storage cupboard and pulling out pieces of his drum kit.

'I mean, yeah, fine,' I say uncomfortably. The truth is, most people have been really cool about Hay's news, but others haven't. The McQueen sisters have started a rumour that she just wants attention, that she's copying Jess to be cool. Others have insisted they always knew; mostly boys who've tried to kiss her when she told them she wasn't interested. As she said to one particularly obnoxious kid who tried to make this point: my lack of interest was specific to you, and your specific personality, not your entire gender. I didn't know I was gay then, I just knew I was anti-you.

'Cos I heard some rumours and stuff and I wanted to make sure she was all right.'

'You know Hay,' I say, raising an eyebrow. 'Not one to take anything on the chin.'

'More like punching someone else in the chin,' he grins.

'Hey, listen,' I say softly. 'I'm sorry things didn't work out between you. At least you know why now.'

'It's fine,' he says, shaking his head, and I wonder how I ever thought he was intimidating, with his penchant for slogan T-shirts and his shaved head. He doesn't trust people straight away, he doesn't let people in straight away, but when he does, when you're in, Benji's the best. Funny and kind and lovely. Not that he'd ever want you to know it. 'She told me when she was writing that speech thing.'

'Oh,' I say, surprised. And I know Hay gets annoyed with me for making everything about me (am I doing it again?), but why was I the last one to know? Why did she talk to James and Jess and Benji about all this, and not me?

'Anyway, as long as she's OK,' he smiles. 'So, I guess your parents were cool, given we're all going to New York next week.'

'My mum talked my dad into it. I have to stay with my aunty, though.'

'We're staying with Shawn's dad,' he says, looking up at me. 'I guess all the parents want someone to keep an eye on us.'

'I can't imagine you with parents. I assumed you were hatched out of a pod or something,' I joke.

He adjusts his drum pedal.

'Close,' he says quietly. 'I live with a foster family, so technically, they're not my parents.'

'Oh,' I say slowly.

Oh God. Why am I such an idiot? Why do I say things without thinking about the consequences? Not everyone has the same set of circumstances I do. Not everyone is the same. I should know that better than anyone.

'I'm sorry, that came out wrong.'

'It's cool, Ellie,' he smirks. 'I'm fine. You don't have to worry about me. Especially if it means following me around and harassing me, the way you do your other friends.'

I say nothing, so he goes on.

'The family I live with,' he says, continuing to set his kit up, 'the Petersens. I've been with them since I was twelve, and they've let me stay, even though I'm eighteen. I help out with the other kids, and I volunteer at school for some stuff, and it keeps them happy.' He smiles. 'They're great. I'm lucky.'

'Oh,' I say again stupidly.

'I wasn't always lucky,' he says darkly, 'but I am now, and that's what matters, right?'

'I like being your friend,' I admit. 'You're annoyingly wise for a pod baby.'

'Are you going to start following me around?' he says humourlessly.

178

'Maybe. I could do with someone new to stalk.'

'Why don't you just focus on yourself?' he says kindly. 'On not doing things you're not supposed to.'

I stare at him, the words strangled in my throat.

'You know what I'm talking about,' he says firmly.

'Heebeejeebeee,' I respond.

'At least Hayley told me the truth,' he replies to my incoherent mumblings.

'Heebeejeebeee.'

'I get the feeling he's just . . . filler for you. And he's better than filler. He doesn't deserve that, Ellie.'

Just as I'm about to start mumbling again, I see Shawn walk in. The *him* we're talking about. He's trimmed his hair a little, so it seems blonder somehow. He's wearing a green T-shirt with a cream overshirt and baggy jeans. I want to kiss him while simultaneously running away.

'Hey,' I say loudly, as Benji turns to look at him.

'Hi,' he says, walking over to me. He puts his arm around my waist and kisses me on the cheek, just as Hannah walks in with Ash next to her. And I can't tell who's more surprised. Me that Ash is with Hannah, or Hannah that Shawn's just kissed me, or Shawn that Hannah's watching him kiss me, or Ash that I'm staring at him while clearly silently screaming NO, NO, NO – PLEASE GOD, JUST NO, or Benji that he gets to witness this awkward love square first-hand.

Whatever way you look at it, there's a lot of internal screaming from everyone involved.

In fact, it's so loud, I can practically hear it.

# 34

# Siri, Play Dr Jada, Episode Five

**Ellie:**

ash saw shawn 💋 me!

**London Cousin – not annoying:**

where???!

**Ellie:**

on the cheek

**London Cousin – not annoying:**

not as exciting as hoped 😂

**London Cousin – not annoying:**

**London Cousin – not annoying:**

**London Cousin – not annoying:**
🥨

**Ellie:**
ty 4 ur help

**London Cousin – not annoying:**
why do u care?

**Ellie:**
i don't want 2 hurt him

**London Cousin – not annoying:**
he hurt u

**London Cousin – not annoying:**
hello?

**London Cousin – not annoying:**
hello??

**London Cousin – not annoying:**
u still there?

**Ellie:**
srry. 🐶 came in. dinner soon

**London Cousin – not annoying:**
don't worry abt it. u worry 2 much.

**London Cousin – not annoying:**
ur wifi is super slooooooww

**London Cousin – not annoying:**

taking ages to get ur replies

**Ellie:**

have 2 go. dinner w/ granny and the other 2 who live here.

**London Cousin – not annoying:**

almost 3!

**London Cousin – not annoying:**

k snack. i got u. jus chill. boys can wait.

**Ellie:**

♥

**London Cousin – not annoying:**

I put my phone down on the bed next to me and turn it over, covering it in revision cards. I figure the more revision cards I have, the better off I am. Also, if I can't see my phone, I won't have to think about the words Hope sent me.

*He hurt u.*

*Almost 3.*

Granny hasn't been in my bedroom, and dinner isn't ready either. I just can't stop thinking about everything. About Ash and Hannah and why they were together again. Why they both came to rehearsal. Why Shawn kissed me on the cheek like that in front of Benji, as if we were A Thing, when I said I didn't want to be A Thing. When I said I wasn't ready. Why I care about any of this when I'm supposed to be thinking about me. Why I *can't* think about me. Why this is not being a Better Person or Ellie 2.0.

'Siri, play Dr Jada, episode five,' I mutter.

I can hear my phone clicking and whirring from beneath the lined white cards covered in badly scribbled notes.

Dr Jada begins, her slow American voice talking about breaths both in and out.

Breathe, Ellie. Just breathe.

Just a few more days, and I'll be in New York.

New York, New York.

So confusing, you have to repeat it, just to be sure you know where you're going.

# ♡ Song 2 ♡

## Intro, Verse, Chorus, Middle Eight

I try to tease it out slowly. Carefully. As if paying attention to the three chords I have will coax the rest out.

*I'm not ready to let go*

And I wish I knew whether the chords I have are supposed to sound like this.

Anxious. Panicked. Fearful.

Or whether they should sound like something else. Feel like something else. The way chords do sometimes. Transmuting from dark to light, their ability to change meaning and purpose and feeling, with melody and context.

*I'm not ready to let go*

But I don't have melody and context – just this.

A feeling I can't let go of.

## 35

# If You Don't Know It by Now

**Hayley:**
GOOD LUCK 🚲🚲🚲!!!!

**Jess:**
GOOD LUCK 🍀!

**Jess:**
can't believe u r missing school rn!

**Ellie:**

**Jess:**
i'd b scared to miss school

**Ellie:**
...

**Jess:**
not that u shld b scared

**Jess:**

if u don't kno it by now, right?

Oh God. I don't know it by now.

**Hayley:**

if she wasn't scared before 🙀

**Jess:**

srry!!!

**Jess:**

u do kno it – don't panic!

But it's too late. Panicking is now my entire personality.

**Jess:**

i'll shut up now . . .

**Hayley:**

what if they offer u a contract??? & they want u 2 stay???

**Ellie:**

. . .

**Jess:**

she'll finish school 1st. obvs

**Hayley:**

school isn't 4 everyone. it's not the only education there is.

**Jess:**

school gives u options. options r good.

**Hayley:**

mayb not the options she wants.

I want to turn my phone off. Or go into a bathroom stall and scream. I've told myself to take everything one day at a time, just like Dr Jada says I should. This is the day I fly to New York. Tomorrow is the day we meet with someone called Gabrielle at Sound Records. Then we'll play a showcase and come home. But they keep talking about The Future. What happens next. What everything means when I don't want to know what everything means. When I can't think that far ahead without hyperventilating.

**Ellie:**

got 2 go. at airport & granny requires attn.

Gods bless Granny and the flexibility with which almost everyone views how she might behave in any given situation. Granny is a convenient lie for almost every occasion.

**Jess:**

safe travels 🖤

**Hayley:**

let us kno when u arrive 🛬

'Ellie, are you ready to go through yet?'

I nod.

'Mum, Dad, Granny – this is Shawn.'

Mum beams at him while Dad and Granny give him The Once-Over in the manner of a mob family considering whether or not to let him live.

'Nice to meet you,' he smiles. He has such a nice smile. Such a nice face. Everything about him is nice.

A woman turns and stares at me.

'This is my mum,' he says, pointing me towards her.

'Anita,' she says, putting her hand out. We all shake it, offering our own names in return.

'I've heard so much about you,' she says warmly.

'We never heard of you,' Granny offers grumpily.

I roll my eyes, trying to convey my apology through them.

'We'd better go,' I say, turning to Shawn. Which is code for: we should not be meeting each other's parents when we're just friends who sometimes kiss, or in my case, you should never be meeting my granny for any reason whatsoever.

Shawn takes my hand and I watch Dad look down at it.

'It was nice to meet you,' I say, turning to his mum; and she's looking down at our hands too.

As Shawn leads me away to security, I see the rest of the band with their families in line for the check-in desk.

'See you on the other side,' I say to Benji, touching his arm as I pass by. His foster parents wave at Shawn and say good luck to me, but I can't help but notice Benji look down at our hands too.

He gives me a look.

And I know I should probably just let go of Shawn.

But I don't.

# 36

# Random Spot Check

I get stopped in security the way I always get stopped in security. Randomly and for no reason whatsoever. I'm not wearing any metal. Not doing anything wrong. I'm just A Random Spot Check, even though I've abided by all their rules. Except it isn't random and the reason is entirely related to the amount of melanin in my skin.

It's hard to explain how tiring this is to someone who's never experienced it. Doesn't understand that you aren't being oversensitive, or seeing things that aren't there. That being brown in an airport is a reason to be held in suspicion.

In some ways, I'm embarrassed Shawn saw it happen; in others, I'm annoyed he didn't get it. That he didn't see it. Because how can he? How can anyone get it, who hasn't felt it? How can anyone know, who doesn't *know*?

I want to message Hope. I want to call Dad and hear him get angry on my behalf. I want to do anything other than laugh it off. Because the laughter feels like a knife. Like the pretence that it didn't happen, cuts more deeply than anything else.

Next to me, Shawn is fast asleep, as are the other boys in the rows behind us.

I'm excited to be going to New York, but at the same time, not excited. I'm worried about missing school (thanks, Jess), about how I'm going to feel when I get there. About the pressure and what's expected of me.

For the millionth time, I play the clip that went viral online, the number of views still creeping up every day. A shaky-handed Hope swaying to the song I wrote as she films us, so that watching it makes me feel seasick.

I remember all the feelings I felt in that moment. Writing that song. Singing it out loud. The sense that I'd put my emotions somewhere safe. That however I felt, putting them in a song was one step closer to making sense of them. And now I can't write anything. Can't make sense of anything.

Like why I can't breathe. Right now. When I'm sat next to someone I really like, on the way to do something incredible, something I never thought possible. Why everything feels so crowded and messy and uncontrollable.

I want to make it all stop.

The world and the way it's spinning.

But I'm on my way to New York.

And in the words of Frank Sinatra:

If I can make it there, I can make it anywhere.

# 37

# Lady Gaga's Lawyer

When we get off the flight, we all look like we feel. Tired and hungry.

'Ellie!' Aunty Kitty calls, as she sees me coming out of the gate.

'Hi,' I say, as she hugs me. Benji looks over at her appreciatively.

Gross. Is there any woman who Benji doesn't look at like that? Obviously, he saves all his disdain for me, his 'would you like to be my groupie' spiel for every other female.

'This is Elliott, Lucas, Benji and Shawn,' I say, introducing her to the rest of the group.

'Hi.' She waves at them all.

I see Shawn step forward.

'Dad,' he says, throwing himself into the arms of a tall blond man.

'Hey, you,' the man replies into his shoulder tearfully.

'Jakub?' Aunty Kitty says, surprised.

'Catherine?' he replies, letting go of Shawn. Because of course Aunty Kitty's name isn't actually Kitty – that's just the nickname Granny gave her to make her sound like a sweet, well-behaved cat, someone who might do as Granny tells her, when clearly she's a badass lawyer type in a flame-red suit. I love it when she rocks her Lady Gaga's Lawyer

Look. Not that she actually is Lady Gaga's lawyer, but because she looks like she could be. She looks *cool*.

For a lawyer.

'Do you two know each other?' I query, as Shawn and I look at each other.

'We've worked together,' Shawn's dad says.

'On opposite sides,' Aunty Kitty laughs.

'Are you as scary as your . . .'

'Aunt,' I finish for him.

'Are you?' he laughs.

'I prefer *competitive*,' Kitty says, laughing again.

Shawn puts his arm around my shoulders, and his dad looks at me again.

'Ellie?' he says, smiling. 'Right?'

I smile back. 'That's me.'

The rest of the boys are yawning, jostling their bags and looking bored.

'Why don't we all grab dinner later?' Aunty Kitty suggests. 'Charles is busy for a few hours, but maybe nine-ish if you boys can stay awake?'

Jakub nods, as I suspect Shawn, Elliott, Lucas and Benji are busy planning their naps.

'Sounds good,' he agrees.

They swap numbers and we all head in separate directions.

'Jakub Kowalski,' Kitty says, shaking her head. 'What a small world.'

'How do you know him?'

'He's a lawyer too. At another firm. He's English – well, Polish, but

English, if you know what I mean. Charles knows him better than I do, but he's good. Good reputation. So,' she says, smiling at me, 'you're dating his son?'

'No,' I say quickly. 'We're just friends.'

Who kiss sometimes.

'Does he know that?' she asks lightly.

I don't reply.

'So, tell me everything,' she insists, squeezing my shoulder. 'I've watched that clip a million times. I'm so proud of you, Ellie.'

'I wrote it,' I admit. 'The song.'

She widens her eyes.

'Good thing you have an aunt who knows a thing or two about contract negotiation,' she teases. 'I'm coming with you to this meeting, and I imagine Jakub will be too. Right, let's drop these bags off at the apartment and go shopping. I've got the rest of the day off and I'm getting married next week,' she squeals.

It's hard to believe this is the same Aunty Kitty I've always known. She went through something so horrible and hard when Granny refused to accept her and Charles being together, but she went through it and came out the other side being truly honest about everything.

I wish I could be her. I wish I could already be through the horrible, hard stuff. That I knew all the answers, and I knew who I was and what I wanted, and that I'd made my choices.

Choices. Ugh.

For just one second, I remind myself of the Ellie I was before. The one who used to hide, who wanted nothing more than to be invisible. Who'd never be here, in New York, with Lady Gaga's lawyer, getting ready to meet a record exec called Gabrielle, and I let myself be proud of where I've got to. Of how far I've come.

I may not know all the answers yet, but the answers are out there, and Ellie 2.0 is going to find them, and try not to be afraid of them.

For the first time in a long time, I believe myself. I believe in me.

Even though The Voice keeps telling me not to.

Over and over again.

# 38

# People Are Starting to Notice

We meet for dinner in Chinatown. I'm wearing a new dress Aunty Kitty bought for me this afternoon: a long halter-neck, red with tiny white polka dots and a slit up one side. I feel overdressed for dinner with the band, but as I always do in these situations, I ask myself what Hope would wear, what Hope would say. And the answer seems as clear as if she were stood here next to me.

YOU'RE IN NEW YORK, ELLIE. THERE IS NO SUCH AS BEING OVERDRESSED IN NEW YORK.

Aunty Kitty's wearing a mid-length white slip dress with a long white cardigan and gold jewellery. Her hair, which she usually wears in a low ponytail or bun, is loose and free-flowing. She looks young and pretty and excited about life, while Charles, who we've met straight from work, looks like he might burst with happiness every time he looks at her. And even though I remind myself I don't want or need this feeling, I can't help but want it. That person who looks at you like no one else exists.

'Well, don't you two look beautiful,' Charles says, kissing Kitty.

She smiles and takes hold of his hand. 'I booked Jing Fong,' he says, walking purposefully towards a restaurant nearby; and I think about the last time I was in New York, at Christmas. How Hope and I ate dim sum with Shawn after the open mic at the Bitter End.

Even then, when I was falling madly in love with Ash, when I almost regretted being in New York because it meant being away from him, I felt connected to Shawn. I still do.

When we enter the restaurant, it's intimidatingly huge. Red carpets and big banquet tables. Waiters looking self-important, muttering into walkie-talkies. We spot the boys straight away, waiting to be seated.

'Jakub!' Charles calls out.

Shawn's dad turns and smiles at him, reaching out to grab his hand.

'I booked a table,' Charles says. He turns to one of the waiting staff and begins talking to him in Mandarin. The waiter nods, picking up a large stack of menus.

'Do you know where the bathroom is?' I ask Aunty Kitty, feeling suddenly shy of eating dinner with the boys; with Shawn meeting my family, and me meeting his.

'I need to go too,' she whispers back. She taps Charles on the shoulder to let him know where we're going, and we walk towards the back corner of the restaurant.

Inside, the bathroom is overlit, the lighting unfriendly, the mirror huge. I can feel the weird people in my pores singing, *You're ner-vous, you're ner-vous*.

And I don't know what I'm nervous about. There are so many things. Tomorrow at the label meeting. Tonight with Shawn. The wedding. The baby. Exams.

197

'Ellie,' Aunty Kitty says, as we both emerge from a stall at the same time. 'Are you OK?' she asks carefully. 'You're breathing quite heavily.'

'I'm fine,' I insist.

'Are you nervous about tomorrow?' she asks sympathetically.

'It's just the smog,' I say dismissively. New York is seriously smoggy.

'OK,' she says, sounding concerned. 'But you've got a lot going on this year, Ellie. Nobody would blame you if you were struggling.'

'I'm not,' I say firmly.

'OK,' she says again slowly. 'But if you ever need to talk to anyone, I'm only ever a phone call away.'

'I know,' I reply gratefully. I turn and hug her properly. 'I don't want to ruin your white dress,' I say, moving my head to the side awkwardly. Brown make-up is both a blessing and a curse (it stains everything).

'I don't care about that,' she says sweetly. 'Just remember, you don't have to do anything you don't want to do. It's about working out what *you* want, Ellie. Come on,' she says after we've both washed our hands. 'Let's go eat.'

It's easy to spot our table when we walk into the dining hall. Loud and English, arguing over what appetisers to order, the boys dressed in their usual band attire, Charles and Jakub in suits.

As we approach the table, Charles and Jakub stand. The boys turn and stare at us, all of them rushing to their feet in an effort to emulate the older men. But all I can see is Shawn, his face watching my face.

'Hey,' I say under my breath.

'I saved you a seat,' he says, ushering me to sit next to him.

'Hey, Ellie,' Lucas says. 'You look nice.'

'I was going to say that,' Benji complains. 'Then I was going to ask her when the flamenco dancing starts.'

'You look beautiful,' Shawn says, taking my hand. 'Really beautiful.'

And I'm blushing so much I may have turned the same colour as my dress.

Benji feigns a sick noise, while Lucas and Elliott grin as if we're adorable.

'So,' I say, trying to change the subject, 'how are you all feeling about tomorrow?'

'Sick,' Elliott admits, his red hair sticking out at odd ends as he rakes his hands through it. 'I mean, excited, but sick.'

'Ditto,' Lucas says, watching one of the waitresses.

'It'll be fine,' Benji says dismissively.

Shawn smiles carefully. 'It'll be what it'll be,' he says wisely.

'Boys,' Aunty Kitty says to our side of the table. 'Charles is going to order. We can share everything – but is there anything in particular you want? Any food allergies?'

They all shake their heads, jet-lagged and hungry and happy to try anything.

When the food arrives – bamboo steamers piled high with dumplings and dim sum, bowls of delicious fried rice and golden noodles, plates of duck and pork covered in sweet, sticky sauce – we attack it all as if none of us has ever eaten before, barely a word passing between us.

I can see the grown-ups chatting at the other end of the table, politely waiting to take a piece of this or a piece of that, as the rest of us dive straight in. My leg's touching Shawn's under the table. Every so often he puts his hand out, drawing a circle on my knee with his finger.

'Shawn knows New York pretty well,' Jakub's saying to Kitty and Charles. 'I make sure the kids come out at least twice a year; and Anita and I try to share Christmas and the big holidays. It doesn't always work out, but we try,' he says, looking down at his plate. 'Anyway, he's been offered a place at Berklee in the fall, so I figure I'll see more of him then. Paster & Walker has offices in Boston, so there's even a chance I could transfer.'

I can feel Shawn tense next to me.

'Berklee?' I offer, surprised. 'That's, like, the best school for music in the world, right?'

'I mean, it's good,' he says modestly, 'but I don't know if I'm going to go yet.'

'Why wouldn't you go?' I ask him. 'Have they offered you a place?'

He nods.

'Shawn, that's amazing,' I say, kissing him on the cheek.

He stares at me.

'It is, isn't it?' Benji says pointedly.

'It's a massive expense,' he says, looking down. 'And I'm not sure I can leave my mum, and there's other stuff I don't want to leave too.'

I feel myself tensing.

'The band,' he continues, looking up at me. 'Who knows what's going to happen next.' But it feels like he isn't talking about the band.

'That's true. But Berklee, Shawn. I mean, wow.'

He says nothing.

At the end of the meal, we're all stood outside the restaurant, Chinatown thrumming around us.

'I love it here,' I sigh, feeling the noise and the colours and the movement in every molecule of my skin. Everything feels so alive here.

Shawn puts his arms around my waist suddenly. 'I wish I could kiss you.'

'Might be a bit weird with all these people around,' I say uncomfortably.

'I'm not sure I care any more.'

I look over at Aunty Kitty, watching us out of the corner of her eye.

'Shawn, I thought we agreed to be friends?'

'Did we?' he smiles. 'Friends who kiss sometimes,' he says, pecking me on the lips, 'and hold hands sometimes,' he says, squeezing my hand, 'and write songs together, and meet each other's parents,' he continues.

'I like you, you know that,' I interrupt, 'but you said we'd be friends. You said you'd wait.'

'I know. I am.'

'I don't want you giving things up for me,' I say awkwardly.

'I'm not,' he says, looking away. 'I'm still thinking about it, that's all.'

'OK,' I assent. 'I'd better go.'

'See you tomorrow,' he says, letting go of me.

'See you tomorrow,' I say uncomfortably.

And he's looking at me the way Charles looks at Aunty Kitty, and I wish I could look back at him the way he wants me to; but thinking about real things feels overwhelming. Because I'm starting to realise I'm Not OK, and that at some point, People Are Going to Start Noticing.

As we walk away, Aunty Kitty puts her arm around my shoulders. 'Are you OK?'

'Fine.' I nod.

She gives Charles a look over the top of my head.

'OK,' she says, squeezing me.

Note to self: people are starting to notice.

# 39

# A Girl Called Ellie

My name is Ellie. Ellie Pillai.

But sometimes I wish it wasn't. Sometimes I wish I had blonde hair and pale skin and no reason to be stopped in airports. Sometimes I wish I could walk into a room and not be the only non-white person in it.

I wish I could appreciate my family more. My heritage. That I could wear a sari and feel like I'm respecting tradition instead of wishing I was wearing something else. Something I've been told by everyone else is acceptable for the country I live in, for who I should be. I wish I could stop trying to assimilate and just *know* who the real me is.

My name is Ellie. Ellie Pillai.

I want to love myself and all I am. But I don't know who that is any more. Not without all that stuff. The pressure to pick a side, East or West, when really, I'll never be either.

My name is Ellie. Ellie Pillai.

I wish my head wasn't so full.

I wish I could stop thinking, for just a minute.

# 40

# Frontwoman Energy

We're sat in a room waiting for someone called Gabrielle. Benji keeps humming the opening bars to 'Thunderstruck' by AC/DC.

'THUNDER, waaaa waaaa wahhhh wahhh wah.' He taps on the table, mimicking the drumbeat with his fingers.

'Benji,' Elliott says, looking slightly sweaty, his red hair sticking to his forehead despite the overly air-conditioned office we're currently sat in. 'BENJI,' he repeats. 'Can you just . . .'

'Stop,' Lucas says, staring at him. 'Can you STOP. Thanks.'

'Why are you all being so weird?' he notes drily. I admire him so much in this moment because I can see how real he is. How he isn't trying to impress anyone. How he genuinely is just: yeah, let's see what happens, and whatever that is will be fine. I wish I could be Benji.

'Sorry I'm late.'

Someone I can only assume is Gabrielle walks in and sits on the other side of the desk we're at, facing a laptop. Tan, interesting face with big brown eyes and little round glasses, wearing a relaxed blue suit with a plain white T-shirt and expensive-looking trainers.

'Hey, man,' Benji says, standing up. 'We spoke on the phone.' He extends a hand and Gabrielle returns it.

Aunty Kitty, who it's been decided between her and Jakub is chaperoning this meeting, grins to herself. I can tell she likes Benji.

'Technically,' Gabrielle smiles, 'I'm nonbinary, so I'd prefer hey, you, hey, there, hey, Gabrielle, you get the point. I'm they/them.'

'Sure,' Benji replies without missing a beat. 'Cool.'

Gabrielle waves at him to sit down. 'I'm so excited you made it. Sorry about the coach flights, but my boss already hates that I've flown you here. But with the showcase tonight, I wanted him to see you in real life. It's downstairs, in our bar. They'll probably be on about eleven-ish' – Gabrielle motions at Aunty Kitty.

'P.m.?' Aunty Kitty asks in a slightly shrill voice.

'That's right,' Gabrielle smiles. 'So, tell me about yourselves. Who writes the songs?'

'Ellie and I do,' Shawn says, sitting forward.

'And who wrote "As It Seems"?'

'Ellie.'

'Do you speak?' they ask kindly, looking at me.

'Um, yeah,' I reply, swallowing.

'You have a good look,' they say, surveying my lime-green tie-dye vest top and baggy white jeans. 'Strong. I like the female frontwoman thing.'

'I'm not the frontwoman.'

'Are you they/them too?' they enquire curiously.

'No, I just mean, I'm not the front anything. Shawn's the lead singer and front . . . person.'

'He's good too,' Gabrielle says, eyeing him up. He looks super cute

205

today in tailored white suit trousers and Converse with a wide-striped orange-and-purple shirt; our trousers make us look worryingly matchy-matchy. 'But the two of you together are better.'

'Right, I mean . . . but I'm not.'

'Let's just watch the video again,' Gabrielle announces. They turn their computer towards us and press a link. For the millionth time, I hear the song I wrote. The words that stopped my heart from breaking.

'That's you,' they say, pointing at me. 'Frontwoman.'

I feel slightly sick.

'Anyway, you've gone viral, and I'm sure you're going to get lots of calls, but what we do here is develop talent. We work with you to create a sound, a look, something marketable. We see you for what you could be, not what you are. Now, I like you. But your numbers aren't that big, you don't have much, if any, experience, and this –' they say, pointing at the screen – 'could be a one-off. So, I need to hear more songs. Get a better sense of who you are.'

'What they are,' Aunty Kitty says primly, 'is very, very young. They're all in the middle of exams.'

'Like I said,' Gabrielle responds, 'this isn't about Right Now. It's about the future. Credibility. If you've got something we want to develop. Nobody needs to drop out of school,' they say, rolling their eyes.

'So, what now?' Lucas says, leaning forward.

'Play some good songs tonight, and we'll see,' Gabrielle smiles. 'Now, who wants to get some lunch?'

They take us to a pizza place, and we get to know them. About how hard they've worked to prove themselves in a male-dominated workplace. That they want to be respected for spotting and developing raw talent, but half the people they work with can barely be bothered to learn their pronouns.

'You see – we're all outsiders. And there's nothing wrong with that,' Gabrielle offers, taking a bite of pizza. 'In fact, it's the people who think like outsiders who are changing the world. Making everyone realise there is no inside or outside, right? And that's what *some* people,' they whisper, '*certain* people, are afraid of. Because they no longer wear the crown.'

We all nod. Sold, sold, sold on this incredibly impressive person.

'So, tonight. Be your best, OK? Do your best. Do not,' they say, looking over at me, 'be afraid to embrace your inner frontwoman energy.'

I nod again. If only I wasn't so jet-lagged. If only I wasn't starting to feel so terrified.

We part outside the pizza restaurant and go back to Shawn's dad's apartment to rehearse.

'Ellie, this is all about you,' Lucas says unhelpfully.

'You and Shawn,' Benji corrects. 'You two need to be like you were that night at Cinema, when people were, like, chanting for you.'

'No pressure,' I mutter.

'Pretend that it's just you and me,' Shawn says, taking my hand.

And I look at him. At the way he's looking at me. At the way I can't look back at him. And honestly, I think that advice might be so annoying and unhelpful, it could have come from me.

# 41

# Outsiders

The jet lag's seeping in, and it's bad. Bad. We're all on our knees. In a bar watching what seems like a million other bands who are all better than us. Shawn's trying to keep our energy up – but the best he can get out of any of us is to keep us awake.

Awake. I am not awake.

Or maybe I am. Maybe this is my living nightmare. Maybe I'm half asleep and half awake, which seems like the worst combination of any halves of things, ever.

Lucas, Elliott and Benji are all drinking coffee, and Shawn's on Coca-Cola. I'm not going to lie. If we weren't being chaperoned, I'm pretty sure we'd be using the fake ID Benji showed us on the flight over to buy tequila shots – which, to be honest, wouldn't be helpful either. A drunk Ellie is about as useful as a not-drunk Ellie.

Oh God. I can feel the nerves creeping in, the sweat running down my top lip and into my mouth. I want to run away. Or be sick. Or possibly both at the same time. I've always gotten nervous; it used to stop me from doing things. Literally stop me, like I'd been put on pause. But lately, I've tried to use those feelings. To push past them.

Onstage with the band, I'm in the background, but I'm there, right there, in the moment – and I can sing and play and be OK; something I'm learning to do better and better every time I do it. But there's never been anything at stake before. There's never been anyone to let down apart from me.

I look over at the boys. At how excited (but mostly exhausted) they are. They want this so much. Shawn's deciding whether or not to go to Berklee based on this; or at least, partly based on this. Everyone needs something from me, and I'm the person that lets people down. I'm the person that chokes.

I have to remind myself. Literally. Not to choke on the water I'm sipping.

Note to self: don't choke.

'Are you OK?' Shawn whispers.

I nod.

Arrrrrrrrrrggggggghhhhh.

Am I OK?

Internal screaming isn't helping.

THUNDER, waaaa waaaa wahhhh wahhh wah.

Internally singing 'Thunderstruck' by AC/DC isn't helping either.

'Why don't you have some coffee?' Benji asks, from over his fifth cup. And of course, they don't know that I hate coffee and I never drink it.

'I hate coffee, and I never drink it,' I inform him.

'What?' Elliott says, his head snapping round.

'I don't like it. I've never liked it.'

'You just haven't tried the right *kind*,' Benji says knowingly. 'Some of it literally tastes nothing like actual coffee.'

'Why drink it then?' I ask bluntly.

'Because it wakes you up, my little friend.'

And I don't like being called *little*, even if he does follow it up with the word *friend*.

'Do you like milkshakes?'

'I mean, yeah. Sometimes.'

'What kind of milkshakes?'

'I don't know, but you're starting to sound slightly Child Catcher-y,' I say, thinking about Dad and his obsession with the villain from *Chitty Chitty Bang Bang*.

'Just give me a minute,' he says, standing up from the table.

In ten minutes, he returns with an enormous plastic cup with a straw.

'Starbucks,' he says, as if in explanation.

'It's ten p.m. . . .' I murmur.

'It never shuts,' Lucas monotones from over his matching cup.

I take a sip of the drink from the cup Benji hands me. It's so sweet I can barely taste anything but sugar.

'Brown sugar, oat milk, iced latte,' he explains.

'It's . . . not horrible,' I admit.

I finish it in about five minutes – and he's right, I do feel slightly more awake. Slightly less nervous. Slightly more alive and ready for *something*.

'I'm going to get another one,' I whisper. 'Anybody want anything?'

They all shake their heads, while Aunty Kitty offers me some money. I shake my head. I brought my own money.

As I step outside the bar, they stamp my hand so I can get back in and put a green wristband on me that says ARTIST.

Artist, I think. I'm an *artist*.

Across the street, Starbucks is glowing, still filled with people. I queue and order two of the same coffee again, so I don't have to come back out. They ask if I want extra shots. I say yes. Because extra can only be good.

When I get back inside the venue, I'm halfway through my drink when I see Gabrielle at the bar.

'Hello,' I say, walking over to them.

'Frontwoman,' they respond. 'Did you bring your A game?'

'I brought coffee,' I respond stupidly. 'Starbucks never closes.'

'Okaaaaayyy,' they say, watching me. 'How many of those have you had?'

'Just one.'

'Oh, OK. Good. You don't want to get all hyper.'

'Hahahahahahahahahah,' I start laughing hysterically. They don't seem impressed.

'Are you OK?' Gabrielle asks, taking hold of my elbow. 'Because if this is all too much, you just need to say so. I don't need to be embarrassed tonight. Ed's already knocked one of my bands out.'

Note to self: do not let Gabrielle down.

Or Shawn.

Or Lucas, or Elliott, or Benji.

Or Mum and Dad.

Or Granny.

Or Aunty Kitty.

Or Ash.

But how could I let Ash down? We're just friends and he saw me kiss Shawn and he thinks Shawn and I are A Thing, and maybe Shawn and I *are* A Thing, because he's nice, and nice could be good for me. Nice could be just what I need.

Is this what being hyper is?

Note to self: Shawn is nice.

I suck hard on my straw, the sugar entering my veins like an electric bolt.

Sugar is great.

Sugar is the best.

SUGAR. YEAH.

'I know what it's like,' I say to Gabrielle, my eyes wide. 'To be an outsider.'

Suck.

They look down at me. For some reason, I hadn't noticed how tall they are. Maybe because they do such a good job of putting themselves at your level. Of making you feel comfortable.

'Oh, yeah,' they say.

'Everyone looks like that where I come from,' I say, sucking my drink again, and pointing at the band. 'Most people are white.'

'Most people are,' they say, arching an eyebrow.

'And I'm not, and I've always felt it. Like I don't quite belong. Not with them. Not even with my own family sometimes.'

They nod.

'That's why I write songs,' I explain. 'Because music is universal. Something that brings us all together. That makes me feel like I belong somewhere.'

'I get it,' they say softly. 'That's why I got into this too. Even if sometimes it feels like nobody wants me to be who I am,' they sigh.

'I want you to be who you are.'

Suck.

'Thanks,' they respond, 'but bring what you just told me. That vulnerability. That pain, and I know there's anger in there too,' they say, pressing me on the nose, 'to what you do tonight. You write to be heard. To be seen. So, go do that. For you, and for every other outsider.'

They turn back to the bar and I walk over to our table.

'Are you OK?' Aunty Kitty asks as I sit down. 'You've been gone a while, I was starting to get worried.'

'I'm fine,' I say, putting my spare coffee on the table.

Suck.

'How many of those have you had?' she asks.

'One.'

I've had one. This is two. The spare is three. So, it's not a lie. And the sugar and the caffeine are definitely starting to wake me up. Definitely starting to make me feel like I can do this.

'I told you,' Benji mouths to me across the table. But none of the band are speaking, because a guy's up there playing a guitar and singing, with the kind of voice that feels like a mix of Tim Buckley and Al Green. Which sounds like a weird combination but isn't. It's sort of silky soft and soulful with a folk heart. His song has a seventies feel. Like it should only ever be played on vinyl.

I finish my drink quietly and pull the third one over. As I push the empty cup away from me, Aunty Kitty gives me a look. I decide to ignore it. I may need to wee urgently, but at least I'm awake.

I can feel my leg pulsating under the table, my heart accelerating to a speed that feels almost like flying.

I just want to get up there. Get this over with. And at the same time, I also don't want this amazing man to stop singing. Except I do, because he's making me feel the way Jessica used to make me feel when we walked into school together in Year 7. Very Bad in Comparison.

'We're next,' Shawn says, turning to me.

Oh my God.

Oh my God.

Oh my God.

Breathe. Then suck this coffee in faster. I don't know why. I don't think it's helping. In fact, I suspect it might be making everything worse.

I can do this.

I am doing this.

We are doing this.

Everything is going to be fine.

FINE.

Gabrielle approaches us and tells us to get ready; that the drum kit's set up and the keyboard's in the corner. And usually, I wouldn't care what I was playing on, although I know Benji isn't happy about playing on a different kit and has brought his own sticks, but for some reason, it's all I can focus on, as I try desperately to breathe in, and out, in, and out.

I don't think I can remember how to play the keyboard. I don't think I know how. Did I ever know? I'm not sure. I'm trying to remember where middle C is and if I'll know on a different set of keys. I can't remember the words to my song, and we have to sing that first. .

Oh God.

Lead Energy. Frontwoman Energy. Come on, Ellie. You can do this! Gabrielle puts their hand on top of mine momentarily.

'Breathe,' they say. 'You were born to do this.'

And everything about the way they say it, so confident, so firm, so certain, makes me rethink everything. Re-*feel* everything. Because I've been writing songs for as long as I can remember – at least up until now, until the well ran dry and the words ran out. But I won't think about that now. I can't focus on that now.

Because I've been singing those songs, the ones I write, to myself at home, in the shower, in the music room at school, in my head, always. And all of it, everything, has been leading up to this.

Meeting Shawn at Christmas. Writing songs together. Singing onstage. Being in the band. Every step of it has been going somewhere. Somewhere I'm not sure of yet, but somewhere I was born to be.

I was born to do this.

And this pep talk would be very life-affirming and comforting, and definitely help me get onstage and at least look like I knew what I was doing, if I hadn't ingested more sugar and caffeine in the last twenty minutes than I have in my entire life. As we head toward the stage, my legs are shaking. So violently that as I take a step forwards and up in an effort to get onstage, I overshoot it, my hands desperately trying to stop me from falling, and in the process finding Benji's back, who's just behind Elliott, who's just behind Lucas, who's just behind Shawn. We fall like a pack of dominoes, one on top of the other, the sound of guitars and drums and high hats soundtracking our descent.

Oh. God.

# 42

# When I Fall on the Floor

We're all lying there as I look across at Gabrielle, their head in their hands.

I have to do something.

Anything.

There's murmured laughter and the sound of glasses clinking, people talking. It feels worse than everyone staring at us. They're pretending we don't exist.

Shawn pulls himself up to standing, and behind him Lucas and Elliott and Benji stand too, and from where I'm partially still lying halfway up a step, I start singing.

*Tonight, I'm going to be mine*
*You won't get in my head*
*With the things that you said*

At first, they're still talking over us, ignoring us, but Shawn puts his hand out and pulls me up, my leg still pulsating from all the caffeine. He swings his guitar in front of him and plays a chord. Just one for each line, my voice carrying us.

*If I would have known*
*That it would hurt like this*
*Then baby I would never, never, never*
*Never have let you in*

And suddenly they recognise us. The band from that viral video thing. That song. You know the one. From that clip. Those British kids.

They're getting quieter, Shawn starting to strum now, adding a rhythm, taking us where we should be.

We all move behind our instruments, quickly, lightly.

Everyone's watching me. My voice rising and falling, the notes expanding around glasses and cups and bottles, until I can feel it. The complete control I have to make them listen.

I put my fingers to the keyboard. I feel its weighted plastic keys. I remember where middle C is, and simultaneously that I don't need to play it, that most of it's at least an octave lower than that. I play heavily. With all the feelings I feel every time I play this song. Broken and angry and heartbroken – and something more. Something bigger.

And the rest of the band are starting to join in – finding a place to add the bass and lead guitar, building, building, building until Benji comes in on the drums.

*Ripped at the seams*
*Like nothing I knew before*
*I don't know what it means*
*Just know I'm in pieces*
*On the floor*
*I'm not what I seem*

*I'm not who you knew before*
*Don't you know that I'm mine?*
*Yeah, you'll know it in time*
*All is not as it seems*

In that moment, we're exactly what we always hoped we could be. A real band, playing intuitively together. Knowing that to keep them with us, we'll need to play the chorus again; we'll need to take it up an octave to a different register. Slow it down, speed it up.

*Tonight you will see*
*My heart doesn't bleed*
*Though I'm ripped at the seams*
*I find my way back to me*
*I won't hurt any more*
*When I fall on the floor*
*Tonight, I'm going to be mine*
*Don't you know that I'm mine?*
*All is not as it seems*

They're with us, on our side. When I sing about falling, I look straight out at them, at Gabrielle, at Aunty Kitty. I let myself be vulnerable. I let them in on how hard it is to belong to yourself.

'So, like I said,' I say, as the song finishes. 'When I fall on the floor, it doesn't hurt any more.'

# 43

# So Tired, But Also,
# So Not Tired

They're laughing at me. Or maybe not at me, with me. The band grinning at each other, lit up. And Shawn tells them what else we're going to sing, and we launch straight into another number, finishing with our duet, 'Tell Me the Truth'.

When we come offstage, I feel lighter than air. Or maybe that's just the caffeine buzz.

'I could have killed you,' Benji says to me, 'but then when you started singing, it just worked, you know, it just came together.'

He's drumming in mid-air, his sticks flying.

Shawn kisses me.

'That,' he says, taking his guitar off his shoulder, 'was amazing.'

The room's packed, other green-wrist-banded people coming over to say hi. To say they liked our set.

'Well done,' Aunty Kitty says, giving me a hug. And unbelievably, we seem to have pulled it off. A showcase in New York.

'Do you think we can leave now?' Elliott asks, yawning.

'No,' Gabrielle says, appearing at our shoulders. 'You need to stay until the end. How would you feel if people had left after they'd done their set and you didn't have an audience?'

'We might have had less people watch us fall over,' Lucas mutters.

'They think you did it on purpose,' Gabrielle whispers. 'To get noticed.'

'Oh God,' I intone.

'No, it's good,' they insist. 'Good recovery. Although maybe lay off the sugary drinks next time. Those iced lattes have an insane amount of caffeine in them. You probably won't sleep tonight.'

'Oh. Right,' I say, embarrassed. 'Is it that obvious?'

'Your leg,' they say, pointing down. 'Hasn't stopped moving.'

Benji smirks.

'So, what happens now?' Shawn asks.

'There'll be a meeting next week, and we'll talk about what we've seen.'

'OK . . .'

'But I'd say,' Gabrielle responds, 'that you have as good a chance as anybody of getting a development deal. You were pretty great tonight.'

'What exactly does a development deal entail?' Aunty Kitty asks.

'If it happens, we can talk options,' Gabrielle replies. 'You're based in New York, right?'

'I'm a senior partner at Roth & Meister,' she says, eyeing them in an adversarial manner. 'We handle most of Warner's contracts, so I'm sure I can find someone to advise my niece and her friends.'

They stare at her, impressed. The woman who should be Lady Gaga's lawyer.

'I'll be in touch,' Gabrielle says, shaking her hand, and then each of ours.

We walk out of the bar around 1 a.m., barely able to stay upright.

Shawn puts his arm around me.

'Sit next to me on the flight tomorrow?' he whispers.

'I want to sit next to Benji,' I joke.

'You were great tonight.'

'So were you. We all were.'

'No,' he says. 'Your writing, it's good. It's better than half the stuff we heard tonight. You need to know that.'

'It's not that good,' I say, embarrassed.

'It is,' he insists. 'We wouldn't be here it if wasn't for your song.'

The last song I wrote. The one that might actually be my last.

I bury my head in his shoulder and yawn.

'I'm so tired,' I complain, 'but also, so not tired.' I can feel a buzzing behind my eyes, like the sugar I consumed has turned into live bees.

'Come on,' Aunty Kitty says, hailing a cab. 'It'll be a miracle if you get any sleep tonight.'

'Goodnight,' I say to the band.

'Goodnight,' they yawn.

And as I get into the cab, all I can think is: I was born to do this.

But also: why does it still feel so hard?

# 44

# OK

The flight home is pretty uneventful, other than the fact I sit next to Shawn and don't tell him that this is getting confusing. That we're not together. That we should probably stop kissing, even if he is nice.

This is possibly because I barely slept last night due to the five thousand shots of espresso I ingested, and pretty much fall asleep as soon as I sit down on the plane. I wake up when we're not far from landing, my head tucked into Shawn's shoulder, his blanket over me, the meal they've clearly served while I've been drooling on him balanced on the tray table in front of him.

'I saved you something to eat,' he says gently, as I lift my head off his shoulder.

'Thanks,' I say, embarrassed.

'Do you think I could have my hand back?' he asks.

I look down at my hand, intertwined with his on his lap.

'Taking my headphones on and off has been pretty challenging,' he teases.

Why does he have to be so lovely? Why, even in my unconscious state, am I confusing everything by holding his hand, putting my head on his shoulder, behaving as if we're a couple? What is my unconscious state trying to tell me?

'Look, Ellie,' he says, turning to face me. 'I really like you. I think we should just give this, whatever this is, a try.'

I want to say, no. I want to say, I can barely cope with what's happening on a day-to-day basis. I want to say, I can't breathe, Shawn, don't you understand that?

But my unconscious state says it all. That I woke up holding his hand. That whenever I need him, he's been there. Someone you can rely on. Someone who says what they mean, who's easy and uncomplicated. So instead, I say: 'OK.'

'OK?' he smiles.

'OK,' I repeat shyly.

He leans forward, his hands around my face. I kiss him, and he kisses me back.

My boyfriend.

Only the second one I've ever had.

'Ugh,' Benji snarks from the other side of him. 'Get a room.'

# 45

# Must. Stay. Awake.

The wedding – or THE WEDDING, as Granny likes to call it – is happening in two parts. The Catholic service, which is happening this Sunday, followed by dinner and a party, and the Chinese celebration, which is happening in a month's time.

I've arrived at Hope's house straight from my flight, and I'm exhausted. I've got three nights of sleep before Granny drives me completely off the rails on Sunday, and I'd like to not look like I've carried my bags home under my eyes.

Aunty Kitty invited the whole band to come to the party on Sunday as the next day's a bank holiday. Lucas and Elliott already have plans, but as Shawn was coming to the wedding as my guest and now Benji has his own invite, the two of them are staying with a friend of Shawn's for the rest of the weekend. I'm nervous to let the two of them into my world, to see my family and my culture up close; as though the act of seeing who I am outside of the band and school will somehow show them a person they can't understand. That they won't want to understand.

If I'm totally honest, there's also the fear I have surrounding The Sari, and the way I felt the last time I put it on – which was Not

Good and Not Like Me, and now my boyfriend's coming (I have a boyfriend . . .) I think I'd prefer not to feel like that.

'So, Ash and I have decided to give things a go,' I say to Hope as I lie on her bed, my eyes closed. Must. Stay. Awake. Apparently, this is the only way to beat jet lag. To stay in the time zone you're in and stay awake.

'Ash?' she says, shocked, as she jumps on to the bed next to me. 'What do you mean? When? How? Why? What?'

'I mean,' I say, keeping my eyes shut, 'he was just so great while we were away, and I woke up holding his hand on the plane, and he'd saved me a meal because I was asleep when they served it, and I love those little aeroplane bread rolls with the plasticky cheese and ham.'

'What?' she queries again. 'Why was Ash on the flight? Why did they only give you a bread roll on an eight-hour flight? What class were you flying in?'

And then it hits me.

'I meant Shawn,' I say, opening my eyes, panicked. Of course I meant Shawn. Shawn is now my boyfriend.

'Whoa there, cuz,' she half laughs. 'That is *some* Freudian slip.'

'Since when do you say Freudian slip?' I ask irritably.

'Since you just called your new boyfriend by your ex-boyfriend's name,' she says plainly.

Oh God.

'Hope, can you not read anything into this, please? Can you just say, great. Well done. He's nice. And move on?'

'He is nice,' she says firmly.

'What does that mean?'

'You know what it means,' she says pointedly.

225

'I like him, Hope. You know I like him. He's kind and he's sweet and he's a brilliant writer, and I feel like I can really rely on him. I feel like he isn't going to hurt me.'

'Hmmmmmn,' she says, unconvinced. 'What happened to your No-Romance Policy?'

'What happened to you pushing me into going out with him?'

'That was before. I'm just not sure . . .' she says gently. 'I think you want a distraction from other stuff, and I don't think that's fair,' she continues.

Oh God. Why is she suddenly so wise and all-knowing?

'He's my boyfriend,' I respond. 'I'm excited about it. The end,' I insist. 'Now what's happening with the sari situation?'

'In hand,' she says, bouncing off the bed.

Why is she so bouncy?

'Um, OK. What does that mean exactly?' I ask nervously.

'You'll see it tomorrow,' she promises. 'I had to get a tailor to make it, because there wasn't enough time, but I cut the pattern and designed it. It's going to be epic.'

'Hmmmmn,' I respond unsurely.

'Why don't you just go to sleep, cranky?'

'I have to stay awake, or the jet lag will get me,' I yawn. 'I slept for the whole flight, so I don't know why I'm soooo tired.'

'It's all the overthinking you do,' she says archly.

'You just accused me of *not* thinking about Shawn's feelings and using him to distract myself,' I say, annoyed.

'You're concentrating on the wrong things, is what I said,' she responds frustratedly. 'You overthink the stuff that isn't that important and just ignore everything else.'

226

'Can this therapy session please end?' I say, closing my eyes again.

'FINE,' she says testily. 'But don't come crying to me when you have some kind of meltdown when it all catches up with you.'

'I won't,' I say, opening my eyes and glaring at her.

She walks out the door, slamming it shut behind her. And I don't know why we're arguing. I don't know why I'm being so . . . so . . .

It's the jet lag, I tell myself.

It's the leftover adrenaline from the showcase, the thought of what's going to happen next and what any of it means.

It's my new boyfriend. It's *having* a new boyfriend.

I'm just tired, that's all.

Everything will make sense soon.

Everything's going to be OK.

Isn't it?

# 46

# Ellie Has Left the Group

**Ellie:**
jet-lagged ✈

**Ellie:**
also …

**Ellie:**
shawn & I are official ♥♥

**Hayley:**
officially what?

**Ellie:**
together … he's my bf … ♥

**Hayley:**
why??

**Jess:**
what?

**Jess:**
why?

**Ellie:**
because i like him . . .

**Hayley:**
what hppnd 2 no ♥? & getting to kno urself?

**Ellie:**
tx 4 the support

**Jess:**
we r worried abt u.

**Jess:**
r u ok?

**Ellie:**
i'm fine

**Ellie:**
I jus made a decision. i chose shawn

**Hayley:**
i thought u chose u?

**Ellie:**
. . .

**Jess:**
r u still there?

**Ellie:**

...

**Jess:**

e??

**Ellie:**

jus because u have blown up ur love life don't blow up mine.

**Jess:**

...

**Ellie:**

u shouldn't hav broken up w Elina & u kno it

**Ellie:**

why do u get 2 decide what she wants & what is best for her?

**Jess:**

we r talking abt u. not me.

**Ellie:**

why can't u just support me?

**Hayley:**

we r trying 2 support what *u* said u wanted.

**Ellie:**

u just think we won't work out.

**Ellie:**

because i fail at everything

**Hayley:**

we never said that e. calm down.

**Ellie:**

i am calm.

**Hayley:**

what's happening???

**Ellie:**

i don't need this.

**Hayley:**

need what?

**Ellie:**

u constantly criticising my decisions.

**Hayley:**

u just told ur broken hearted bf that she did it 2 herself. pretty harsh. even by my standards.

**Ellie:**

according 2 u, i'm annoying & self-centred, so i guess that's me, right?

**Hayley:**

i didn't mean any of that stuff

**Ellie:**

it's what u said tho. isn't it?

**Hayley:**

this isn't like u. i'm worried. can i call u?

**Ellie:**

keep ur secrets. I don't care.

**Hayley:**

what secrets?? what r u tlking abt??

**Ellie:**

u don't trust me

And I'm thinking about the fact that she came out to everyone before she came out to me. That she talked to Jess, and James, and Benji, and she didn't trust me enough to talk to me about it. That she seems further away from me than ever before, even though I keep trying to be there for her, I keep trying to reach out to her.

What's the point of being friends with someone who doesn't want your friendship? Who constantly pushes you away.

**Hayley:**

that's not true

**Ellie:**

i have to go. wedding stuff.

Ellie has left the group.

# 47

# Return of the Smiley Face with Sunglasses

I don't know why I've gotten so angry all of a sudden. I can feel the tears working their way through my eyes, a strange stinging in my eyeballs.

First Hope, now Jess and Hay.

I wipe my face with the back of my hand and try to breathe. Why is it so hard to breathe these days?

All I want is to talk to Mum. To hear the soothing sound of her voice. To feel my dad's arms around me.

I pick my phone up from where it's lying on the bed next to me and go to my favourites screen and dial home.

'Hello?' Mum says breathlessly. 'Pillai residence.'

I smile. I love this line. Pillai residence. As if we're foreign diplomats or cousins to a queen.

'Hi, Mum.'

'Hi, darling,' she says excitedly. 'How did it all go? How are you feeling? Kitty said you were amazing.'

I can hear Dad grunting in the background.

'It's Ellie,' Mum says in reply to Dad's grunts. 'I'm just putting you on speakerphone.'

'So, how was it?' she asks again.

'It was good. Scary. Strange.'

'OK,' she continues, coaxing me. 'That's to be expected. I heard about the coffee . . .' she says, trying to suppress a giggle.

'I knew I hated coffee,' I grump.

'Are you OK, *sina pillai*? You don't sound like yourself?' Dad asks gently.

'Just jet-lagged,' I say quietly.

I can almost see them turning towards each other. Making that face they make. The one that says: something is wrong with our daughter and we're not sure what to do about it. Maybe we'll start with shouting at her. At least, that's how it used to be.

'We'll be there tomorrow,' Mum says mock cheerfully. 'We can talk about it all then.'

'I had an argument with Hope,' I reply uncomfortably.

And Jess. And Hayley. And basically, all the people I love the most in the world other than you.

'You two will work it out,' Mum says soothingly. 'You always find your way back to each other.'

'You know my boyfriend's coming on Sunday?' I ask in a hopeful voice.

'Boyfriend?' Dad barks.

I feel Mum giving him The Look.

'I mean, oh. Yes. You did say you were bringing your friend from the band. I didn't realise he was your, ahem . . . boyfriend,' Dad reconsiders.

234

'He wasn't. But he is now,' I say, trying to be light.

I don't need Dad scaring Shawn off the way he did with Ash.

'I'm looking forward to getting to know him better,' Dad says quickly.

Which is code for: I look forward to interrogating him and ultimately deciding he will never be good enough for you.

'When did this happen?' Mum asks more astutely. Damn Mum and her astuteness.

'On the way back from New York. We decided to give things a try.'

'Right,' she says slowly. 'And Ash is OK with that?'

'It's got nothing to do with Ash,' I say defensively. 'Ash and I are just friends.'

'Friendships are much better at your age. Much, much better than, you know, other things that are more than friendships,' Dad says, trying to sound wise. 'You need to focus on yourself, *sina pillai*.'

'Well, it'll be nice to meet him properly,' Mum says kindly. 'And I can't wait to see you tomorrow. We've missed you.'

'Hello? Hello? Who is this?'

And Granny has entered the chat.

'Hi, Granny,' I reply. She sounds grainy. Like she's standing too far away from the phone.

'Hello, Ellie,' she says, suddenly very loudly. Like she's screaming in my ear.

'*Amma*, you don't need to stand right next to the speaker like that,' Mum says.

'Ellie, can you hear me?' Granny screams in response.

'Yep,' I say, holding the phone away from my ear.

'Was good? All good in New York?' she asks a little more quietly.

'Yes, Granny. It was all fine.'

'Hmmmmn,' she responds, unconvinced.

'Anyway, I'd better go,' I say, feeling slightly better.

I feel tethered. Grounded. Like talking to them has given me a sense of stability. A time and a place and a version of myself not everybody hates.

'OK,' Mum says, sounding sad.

'We'll see you tomorrow,' Dad adds quickly.

'Yes,' Granny shouts. 'For final try-on.'

Ugh. The Sari Situation.

'See you tomorrow!' I try to sound cheery. Like one of those morning television presenters.

When I hang up the phone, I take a deep breath and try to relax. Just another few hours and I can legitimately go to sleep.

**Shawn:**
hi ♥

**Ellie:**
hi ♥

**Shawn:**
u managed 2 stay awake then?

**Ellie:**
just about . . .

**Shawn:**
i kind of miss u

236

**Ellie:**

i kind of miss u 2

**Shawn:**

did u speak to ur parents?

**Ellie:**

✓

**Shawn:**

do they know about us? me?

**Ellie:**

✓

**Shawn:**

ur dad is a bit intimidating

**Ellie:**

ur taller than him . . .

**Shawn:**

he has big energy

**Ellie:**

will tell him u said that 😁

**Shawn:**

falling asleep. wish u were here.

**Ellie:**

me 2

**Shawn:**

r we really doing this?

**Ellie:**

✓

**Shawn:**

think i'm falling 4 u

**Ellie:**

**Ellie:**

see you sunday

He's back. The smiley face with sunglasses. The emoji that is the answer to all things uncomfortable.

He can't be falling for me. We've been together less than a day and he doesn't even know me. Doesn't know that I'm the kind of person that is horrible to her best friends and the cousin that has spent weeks working on a design for her bridesmaid sari thing, when she has exams and a life and friends of her own. He doesn't know that sometimes I wake up and I can't breathe. That I feel overwhelmed in a way I have never felt overwhelmed before. He doesn't know me, because I don't know myself. Because I'm lost right now. I'm lost.

And it hits me then, like a wall of bricks is falling on me. That I've never felt quite this lost. Even before. Even when I was trying to be invisible. That just because I can stand onstage and sing now, just because people can suddenly see me – it doesn't mean I'm OK. That everything else has fallen into place.

238

I stare at my phone, knowing how I must have made Shawn feel with my response. Knowing how badly I'm getting everything wrong.

But I can't think about that now, or I'll just fall apart. And falling apart won't help anybody. Not Mum or Dad or Granny or the baby, or Shawn or Jess or Hayley.

So, I push it all down. Into that box. The one I reserve for all the things I can't think about. Which is a lot of things. I force the box shut, put my earphones in, then turn on an episode of Dr Jada.

Note to self: feeling is for losers. Only losers fall apart.

# 48

# The Sari Situation

By the time Mum, Dad and Granny arrive the next day, Hope and I still aren't quite speaking. By which I mean, I keep trying to talk to her, and she keeps ignoring me. Which is for the best because I have nothing to say. If only smiley face with sunglasses was a phrase. A group of words that could be the answer to anything awkward or uncomfortable that happens.

You're wearing your sari backwards.

*Smiley face with sunglasses!*

You've failed all your exams.

*Smiley face with sunglasses!*

You have no friends, and everybody hates you.

*Smiley face with sunglasses!*

Ugh.

'*En anbe!*' Mum says, clutching at me as soon as she gets into the house. 'Let me look at you,' she says, pulling me upright and tweaking my chin so I'm straight.

'I've been gone four days,' I mutter.

'You've been to the other side of the world, *en kathal–*' and I don't know why she's using so many terms of endearment. Next, she'll be calling me her bae and posting selfies of us on Instagram.

'Mum,' I huff. 'I'm sixteen. I'm not a baby.'

'You'll always be *my* baby,' she says, rubbing her stomach, filled with her real baby. The Baby. The one I can no longer pretend isn't coming until I'm ready. Because he's coming when *he's* ready. Which, by the size of Mum, is soon.

Dad pulls me into a little hug and sniffs my hair. Which is dad language for: I missed you, I'm glad you're here.

Something about my dad's hugs, maybe because we got so close to losing him, feel very soothing. Not stifling like Mum's can be sometimes but sort of half firm, half gentle, like you solidify in his arms. I hug him back as Mum looks at us.

'Is Kitty here yet?' she asks Aunty Christine, who's spent the morning acting as a conduit between Hope and me. (Can you tell Ellie breakfast's ready? Can you tell Hope I can hear her.)

'Thomas is picking her up now. We're going to meet at the bridal shop. Her flight was delayed.'

Mum nods her head.

'What time do we need to go?' Hope asks.

'In about twenty minutes,' Aunty Christine replies.

'Can you tell Ellie to bring the shoes she's planning to wear, so we can make sure everything's the right length?' Hope asks her.

Aunty Christine rolls her eyes irritably.

'Ellie . . .' she begins.

'I can hear her, Aunty. I'll go get them.'

Mum and Aunty Christine exchange a look. One that seems to suggest they will both be discussing this over wine later.

I wander up to Hope's bedroom to collect my wedding shoes, or WEDDING shoes as Granny would call them. They're silver. A high-heeled single-strap sandal that I will most likely fall over in, which Hope picked for me in the days before we had to communicate via her mother. From the window I can see Granny outside on her mobile phone. Watching Granny shout into her tiny phone always makes me laugh, as though the tinier the phone, the harder she thinks she needs to work to be heard. At least here, where Hope lives, the sight of a small, shouty brown woman evokes little to no response; Granny seems to be watched by our neighbours like she's either something to be feared or something to be laughed at. A something, not a someone.

But it's not Granny that draws my attention for long, rather the black SUV she's standing by. It's not Uncle Thomas or Aunty Christine's cars, and definitely not mum's Mini either.

Granny opens the back seat and pulls out her handbag, still on the phone. Is it ours? Do we have a new car?

I run down the stairs, my shoes in my hand.

'Mum! Dad! Whose car is that outside?'

They turn to me, a smile registering on their collective faces.

'It's ours,' they say.

'It's so fancy,' I say, rushing outside. 'What made you get a new car?'

They shake their collective heads.

'Just time for a change,' Dad says. 'I don't put all those hours in for nothing.'

'And we thought maybe you could start practising in my old car,' Mum grins. 'For when you turn seventeen.'

'What?' I ask incredulously.

'There has to be some benefits to living in the middle of nowhere,' Mum continues. 'We'll find somewhere off-road to practise, so you can learn in the same car you're going to drive.'

'What?' I ask again, launching myself at her.

'OK, OK,' she laughs, as she strokes my hair. 'I love that car, so you'd better take care of it.'

'I will.'

'Harrumph,' Dad says, sounding concerned. Admittedly, I don't have the best track record when it comes to cars. The accident Ash and I were in almost got me killed.

'I'll be careful,' I say to him.

'If anyone's likely to drive like a little old granny, it's Ellie, Uncle. I'm sure she'll be fine,' Hope says, almost normally. I turn to smile at her, and she looks out of the window moodily.

'OK, everyone,' Aunty Christine says, looking at her phone. 'We better head to the shop. It's time,' she says, smiling.

'Time for what?' says Granny, appearing next to us. 'And who says driving like little old granny? Grannies drive very well. Is nothing wrong with being a granny who drives.'

We exchange looks.

'Of course not, *Amma*,' Mum says sweetly. Granny eyes her suspiciously.

'Kitty is almost at shop,' she responds, ignoring Mum's tone. 'We must go. Is Time.' Which is exactly what Aunty Christine just said.

We pile into Aunty Christine's car, because Mum doesn't like driving in London, and head to the shop in Wembley. From the outside, it looks like a reasonably nice sari shop, but on the inside, it's one of those places where everything seems to cost approximately one million pounds. Like they've lured you in, and once you're in, you can't leave without selling a kidney.

'*Amma?*' we hear Aunty Kitty call from the fitting room at the back. 'Are you here?'

Granny disappears into the room, from which point we begin to hear grunts and heavy breathing, like they may be engaging in some kind of WWE-style wrestling match.

'Huuuuuurrrgh,' we hear Granny say.

Hope and I look at each other and stifle a giggle. Then remember we aren't talking.

'Stand still,' Granny commands. 'Look better when you stand still.'

'I have to be able to walk, *Amma*!'

We're all starting to get slightly nervous from the enormous amount of sighing that seems to be coming from Aunty Kitty. As if she's unhappy. As if she's just doing this to make Granny happy, and not because it's what she's choosing to wear on her and Charles's day. The day she's going to marry someone who loves her. Who looks at her like she's the only person in the world who exists.

I start feeling twitchy. As if this is portentous. As if this is only the beginning of people having to do things to make Granny happy – including me and the sari situation. Which I know is selfish, but as my boyfriend's going to see me in it, I'd really like to feel not awful in it.

We wait with bated breath as the curtain to the fitting room is pulled back, even though we've seen her in the sari before. Readying our faces for gasps of delight now we can see the complete look, with her wedding jewellery and the handmade lace blouse that was just finished yesterday. As the curtain pulls back, I can see the blouse clearly. It's beautifully simple. White and gold, embroidered with tiny crystal stars. Her hair's pulled back from her face into a low bun. Large gold earrings and necklaces and bangles piled artfully on her ears, across her chest, up her wrist and almost to her elbow. She looks beautiful. She looks perfect.

'Thank you, Hope,' Aunty Kitty says, beckoning her towards her. 'The blouse is perfect. Exactly what I wanted. Hope had this made for me,' she says, turning towards me and Mum.

'You look . . .' says Mum, speechless.

'Exactly,' agrees Aunty Christine, smiling.

I look over at Granny. Waiting for some remark about what could be different, better. How she should stand up straighter. How she should be wearing her hair differently. But it never comes.

Instead, Granny's eyes are full of tears.

'Are you OK?' I ask her.

'Yes,' she says, looking at Aunty Kitty. 'I just very, very proud of you.'

And with that, Aunty Kitty's crying, and Mum's crying, and Hope and her mum are having a hug and I'm crying too.

We're all so weepy it's starting to feel slightly hysterical.

'It's OK, *Amma*,' Mum says, putting her arm around her shoulder; and Mum needs no excuse to cry these days. Pregnancy has turned on an unstoppable tap.

'Why don't you girls try your outfits on now,' Aunty Kitty says, wiping her eyes and pulling the curtains back so she can start unwinding her sari.

I walk tentatively into the fitting room next door, where the shop assistant has laid out the outfit Hope designed for me. All I can see is the sari fabric. Dark pink and silver.

'It's pink,' I say, picking it up. 'What about the turquoise that Aunty Agnes picked out?'

The Aunty Agnes who told me there were certain colours I shouldn't wear because I was dark. That dark was bad.

'Hope and I thought pink would be better,' Aunty Kitty says.

I hear Granny grousing as Mum shushes her.

'We thought we should choose a colour that made us feel happy, because that's what makes us feel beautiful,' Kitty continues.

And it's unsaid that they've deliberately ignored the rules. Because we don't believe it matters what shade of brown you are, just that we should celebrate every, single, one.

I pick the fabric up, expecting it to fall to pieces in my hands, but it becomes clear it's a dress. There's a neckline at the top, so I pull it on over my head, watching as it drapes over my frame to the floor. A little long, but probably just right with my heels.

'Is it on?' Hope asks.

'Kind of,' I reply.

'Can I come in?' she asks, coming closer to the curtain.

I pull the curtain back just enough for her to come inside without anyone seeing me.

'OK,' she says, getting to work. 'There's a belt just here, see? And there's no separate top, it's all built into the fabric.' She pulls the belt tight and rearranges the top half, standing back to let me see myself in the mirror.

It looks like a sari, but also not like a sari. Like a beautiful cerise-pink dress, with a delicate deep V-neck and just the hint of my waist showing at the side, along with a split up one leg. It feels grown-up and elegant and kind of sexy, but also respectful. Like a mix of me and the version of my culture that I represent. Something different and new, but no less Asian. No less Tamil. Just me. Like she knew exactly.

I turn to her, tears in my eyes. 'I don't know what to say.'

'Try – thank you,' she says, and I can hear the lump in her throat.

'I look . . .' I say, trailing away.

'Beautiful,' she finishes. 'You always looked beautiful, but now you look comfortable too.'

'How did you know?' I ask, turning to look at myself from different angles.

'I just knew the whole turquoise thing was throwing you off. It's just a pre-draped sari really,' she says modestly. 'It means you won't be worried that you've done it wrong, or it's going to fall apart. It's easy to put on, and it's got some little modern touches,' she grins, pulling it at the thigh slit. 'I've done something similar with mine, but they're both slightly different. Mine's higher at the neck, more waist, fuller skirt,' she continues.

'I don't deserve you,' I whisper.

'I know,' she whispers back. 'Put the shoes on before you show them.'

'Must see,' Granny tsks from outside. 'What taking so long?'

'She's going to hate it,' I hiss, pulling my sandals on.

'No one could hate you in that dress. Trust me,' she says, looking satisfied with herself.

'OK,' I say, taking a breath. 'I'm coming out.'

Hope slips out before me, and I pull the curtain back, revealing the dress.

Mum starts sniffing, and then Aunty Kitty.

'Is not sari,' Granny says, horrified.

247

'It's better,' Aunty Kitty says, stepping forward.

'I mean, is not *bad*,' Granny says, inspecting it, her tiny face screwed up as she pulls at the fabric. 'Is clever,' she admits.

Mum begins wailing, her words indecipherable.

'I think those are happy tears,' Hope says, giggling.

'I'm so proud of you both,' Mum wails.

And it seems like it might be catching. I think we might all be unstoppable taps now.

# 49

# Rebecca

I get his message about an hour after we get home from the bridal shop.

**Ash:**
ru free 2day?

**Ellie:**
depends on ur definition of free

**Ash:**
available-2-meet free

**Ellie:**
...

**Ash:**
staying with bec. she wants 2 say hi.

**Ellie:**
...

Rebecca.

Ash's beautiful best friend who sometimes thinks she's in love with him, and who I sometimes wonder if he loves back. The girl who did everything she could to break us up, then, just as we were starting to become friends, left. The one it turned out was really insecure, who was running away from a boyfriend who had hurt her, straight to the one person who never had: Ash.

Which is ironic given how he treated me after she arrived.

**Ash:**
srry. is that weird?

Is it weird that I kind of want to see her too?

**Ellie:**
no

**Ellie:**
don't kno if i can tho. WEDDING stuff . . . 😣

Not exactly true. Granny is literally ignoring us now Aunty Kitty, the subject of all her advice, prayers and instructions, has arrived.

**Ash:**
how was nyc?

New York. Where my new boyfriend and I performed with our band. The new boyfriend that's coming to the wedding with me tomorrow. The one my ex-boyfriend is attending with his sister, my best friend's ex-girlfriend. God, this is complicated.

**Ellie:**

good. tx.

'Who are you talking to?' Hope asks, craning her head over my phone as I lie next to her on the bed.

'No one,' I say, trying to remove it from her view.

'Aha!' she says, pointing a finger at me accusingly. 'It's ASH,' she says in a suspicious voice. 'Why are you messaging Ash?'

'I'm not,' I respond defensively. 'He's messaging me!'

'To which you are responding,' she says in a matter-of-fact way. 'What's he saying?'

'He wants to know if I want to meet up.'

She sits up. 'Why?' she whispers, widening her eyes.

'Because we're friends.'

'Hmmmmn,' she says, sounding like Granny.

'You sound like Granny.'

'Hmmmmmn,' she repeats.

'Why does he want to meet?'

'Rebecca wants to see me.'

'Rebecca?' she queries, putting her head back against the headboard. 'As in his quasi-ex-girlfriend-your-evil-nemesis Rebecca?'

'We sort of got over all that,' I say dismissively. Because once I realised Rebecca was just trying to protect Ash, in her own weird, warped way, that actually she was going through stuff of her own, I started to realise she wasn't the villain I thought she was. That maybe we could even be friends – not that she stuck around long enough for us to find out.

'Do you think they're back together now? Do you think that's why they want to meet up? To tell you?' she asks, watching my face closely. 'Or *show* you,' she continues theatrically.

And I haven't thought about that – because why would I want to think about something that makes me feel physically sick?

I try communicating with words but fail.

'I mean, you probably need to tell him about Shawn. Unless you've already told him?' she asks, continuing to watch me.

Oh God. I'm going to have to tell him at some point. I'm going to have to say: I'm with someone else. And I am completely and utterly fine with you moving on too. Even if the person you've moved on with is the exact person I told you was trying to break us up and you always took her side.

Ugh.

'We've got some time,' Hope says innocently. 'We don't have anything major to do until tomorrow. We could meet them for a couple of hours?'

Say words, Ellie. Say any words.

I look at my phone again.

**Ash:**

And I can't tell whether he's trying to be funny or trying to communicate that he's feeling really awkward; I just know I am. Feeling really awkward.

'I don't know, Hope, I'm still really tired, and we should probably help with dinner.'

'We're having a takeaway . . .'

'I don't know if I want to know if they're together,' I blurt out.

'Which is why you should know.'

'Do we have to?' I cajole.

'Yes. I'm dying to meet them both. And I'm bored. Come on,' she says, putting her arm around my shoulders. 'It'll be fun.'

I don't believe her.

But still.

**Ellie:**

where do u want 2 meet?

# 50

# Hope & Ash & Rebecca

When we get to Covent Garden tube station, I stand in the lift, feeling slightly ill. Partly because of the collision of all the different parts of my life that is about to happen. Ash. Hope. Rebecca. Did I mention Hope, Ash and Rebecca? Together? But also, partly because this lift smells a bit like wee.

'Hi,' I say, trying not to vomit when I see Ash and Rebecca.

'Ellie!' Rebecca says, pouncing on me.

Rebecca. Annoyingly beautiful, strikingly cool Rebecca. In London. Her hometown. Looking cool as a cucumber (never understood that expression – cucumbers are only cool when they've been in the fridge, and everything's cool when it's been in the fridge – maybe London is the fridge, maybe London makes everyone cool).

'Hey,' I say awkwardly as she hugs me. 'How are you?'

'Good,' she says, staring at me. 'How are you?'

'Fine, yeah.'

'Ash told me about New York. Your record contract thing. Sounds amazing,' she says excitedly.

'This is my cousin, Hope,' I say, introducing them all.

Hope and Rebecca glare at each other, like a scene from *Into the Spider-Verse*, like they could be the same person from different versions of time.

'Nice to meet you,' Hope says, narrowing her eyes.

'You too,' Rebecca replies.

'Hey, Ellie,' I hear a voice from behind me.

I turn towards it and give her a hug. So happy to see her for so many reasons. The girl I was friends with, then not friends with, then kind of friends with, and now am . . . something with. Jess's ex-girlfriend – Elina.

'Hey, Elina,' I say happily.

'This is Dev, my boyfriend,' Rebecca announces, as Elina rolls her eyes skywards.

I turn towards a good-looking light-skinned brown man, then at Ash, who smiles awkwardly.

Rebecca definitely has a type.

'Nice to meet you,' I say, relieved – because they're not together, her and the one that's my type, or was my type, but isn't any more because I have a boyfriend.

'Hi,' Dev says back.

'Are you based in London?' Dev asks Hope, paying her way too much obvious attention given his girlfriend is next to him.

'Mill Hill,' Hope says obliviously. She isn't encouraging him; I think she's just used to people acting like this around her.

He doesn't ask where I live. Clearly, I'm of no interest.

'Hi,' Ash says, walking towards Elina and me as the other three chat – which involves Rebecca eyeing Hope, and Hope pretending not to notice.

He pulls me into a hug. 'How are you feeling about tomorrow?' he asks. 'How's Granny?'

255

'Her usual happy-go-lucky non-judgemental self.'

He grins as Elina takes my arm and hugs it.

'She's really excited. It's super cute.'

'It's going to be great,' he says as we start walking towards Covent Garden itself, the square of shops in the middle, a magician doing tricks on the cobbles.

'Yeah. I hope so.'

We walk silently for a minute, until Rebecca turns around and beckons Ash to join her.

'So, how are you?' Elina asks, squeezing my arm.

'I'm OK. How are you?' I ask meaningfully.

'Honestly,' she says, looking away, 'I haven't been great.'

'I'm sorry,' I reply uncomfortably.

'It's OK,' she says quietly. 'I'm sorry I haven't spoken to you. It just feels kind of weird. You being Jess's best friend and everything.'

Jess's best friend. We haven't spoken since I left our group chat.

I don't reply. I didn't exactly love seeing her after Ash and I broke up either.

'It's OK,' I say gently. 'I understand. It takes time.'

'Do you think we're destined to be alone forever?' she says jokingly.

Technically, I have a boyfriend. Although she has a point. I do feel alone. I don't know why.

'It's not that I'm not happy being on my own,' she continues. 'It's just, well, you know. It's nice having that connection.'

'I don't think you need to worry,' I reply uneasily.

She ignores my response, lost in her own thoughts.

'For what it's worth,' I say into the silence that follows, 'she is heartbroken. Jess, I mean.'

'Jess?' she says bitterly. 'Why is she heartbroken? This was all her choice. She decides we're not going to make it. She decides I should go to university on my own. She decides we're holding each other back. Not once did she ask me what I want. How I feel.'

'You know,' I say slowly, 'Jess has had so little control over anything in her life up until now. She's so used to looking after other people, putting them first. I think she really believes it's what's best for you; even if it's not what she wants, even if it hurts, she thinks she's putting you first.'

Elina says nothing for a second.

'That's the thing, Ellie,' she says unhappily. 'I know that. That's why I love her so much. But she won't listen to me, and I don't want to be with someone who doesn't listen to me. I finally understand why you can't forgive Ash. Some things you just can't get past.'

'What about me?' he says, turning up next to us suddenly.

Elina looks over at him guiltily. 'Nothing,' she lies smoothly.

'Your cousin seems nice,' he says to me.

'She's great.'

'*Unlike–*' Elina nods to Dev unsubtly, as Ash says nothing.

'I know. He's awful,' Rebecca says, joining us. I look ahead at Hope to check she's OK, but she seems fine. 'But we're never going to end up together, so I figure at least I know what he is.'

It seems depressing logic. That you'd rather be with someone terrible than no one at all.

'I'm not convinced you need to be with anyone,' Ash says to her quietly but firmly.

'That's what Ellie and I were just saying,' Elina agrees. 'About being on your own.'

Just tell them. Just tell them you're with Shawn.

'Poor Hope,' Rebecca whispers. 'Dev's doing his best to make her fall in love with him.'

'Hope's not that easy to win over,' I say quietly. Although I'm worried that she might be – ladies and gentlemen of the jury: Ethan.

'So, tell us about New York,' Ash says, watching me. 'How was it?'

I tell them about how cool Gabrielle is, about the showcase and falling over after too much coffee. How we're waiting to hear on a development deal, whatever that is. That I can't believe how much people have connected to my song.

'Yeah, I saw it,' Rebecca says, turning to me. 'By the way, Shawn is *still*–' She does a chef's kiss. 'Anyway, it's a beautiful song, Ellie. Heartbreaking.'

Ash looks at the ground.

'It's not supposed to be heartbreaking,' I say unsurely. 'It's supposed to be sort of, I don't know, anthemic. About things getting better.'

'After heartbreak,' she says matter-of-factly.

'I mean . . .'

'So, how is Shawn?' she asks.

'Who's Shawn?' Dev asks, turning around to look at her. 'And why is he–' He does an exaggerated chef's kiss.

'I didn't realise you cared.' She smiles sarcastically.

'I do,' he says, turning around to kiss her quickly, as Hope slips back towards me.

'He's a guy Ellie's in a band with,' Rebecca explains.

'You mean, her boyfriend?' Hope asks, looking at me.

'Your boyfriend?' Elina says slowly.

I look over at Rebecca. At the shock on her face. And I can feel the anger returning. The way she behaved with Ash when we were together. What happened on my birthday. The way she was hanging all over Shawn. It's like I'm over it and I'm not over it, which seems to be my thing. Thinking I've dealt with something, but really just boxing it away, waiting for it to reopen at some horribly inconvenient point later in time.

That's right, Rebecca, I think. *My* boyfriend. The one that chose *ME*. Not you. Who cares about me and lets me know how he feels and what he wants, who never makes me feel insecure. Not like before.

'Yes,' I say defiantly. 'We're going out now.'

I try to see what Ash is doing next to me, but I can't bear to look at him.

'It's really new,' I backtrack. 'We decided to give things a try when we were in New York.'

'Oh,' Rebecca says carefully. 'Cool.'

'In fact,' I continue, 'he's coming to the wedding with me tomorrow.'

'Great,' she says, smiling. 'I'll get to see him then. I'm going with Ash,' she says, looking over at him.

'Oh,' I say calmly. 'Great.'

Hope gives me the eye. The one that says: I don't like Dev and WTF is going on here.

'Should we get a coffee?' Dev asks, as we pass a coffee shop with chairs on the square.

'Sure,' I reply quickly.

After all, I already feel sick. What does it matter?

# ♡ Song 2 ♡

## Intro, Verse, Chorus, Middle Eight

The line is running round and round my head, like the prelude to something that never happens.

I want to know what I'm feeling. Why the words won't come.

Everything feels wrong except the three chords in my head.


*I'm not ready to let go*


I try to push past the feeling, but I can't.

I don't hear anything beyond that line.


*I'm not ready to let go*


Why can't I let go?

# 51

# Hair, Make-up, Sari, Jewellery

I get woken the next morning by a frantic Granny making as much noise as humanly possible.

'Need to get up,' she hisses at Hope and me as we both roll over and ignore her.

'It's six a.m. . . . .' Hope says from under the covers.

'Wedding is at eleven!' she shouts. 'Hair, make-up, sari, jewellery. All take time. Car arrives at ten thirty. There is only four and a half hours to get ready.'

'Four and a half hours,' I groan. 'I need twenty minutes.'

'Yes, Eleanor. That is why always look mess.'

'Bit harsh,' Hope says on my behalf. 'But she's probably right. We should get up.'

'Oh,' I say, annoyed. 'Because I'm such a mess that it'll take four and a half hours to make me look OK.'

'No,' she sighs. 'Because there are a million people in the house, and we only have two showers.'

'Ugh. Fine,' I grump. 'Since when did you get so reasonable?' I complain.

'Is good girl,' Granny says, patting Hope's head like a dog. 'Now up, up!' she says, pulling the duvet off us.

'I hate this day already,' I moan.

'Is it because Ash is bringing Rebecca?' Hope says astutely.

'No,' I say too quickly.

'Who Rebecca?' Granny asks suspiciously. Because she is in love with Ash and will probably fight Rebecca for him. Which I would like to see, film, and possibly sell online and make myself a millionaire.

'Just a friend of his.'

'Hmmmn. Friend,' she says suspiciously. 'You and Ashar are friends. Why are you not going together? Why are you bringing white boy?'

'Grannnnnny,' I say, trying to contain myself. 'You can't not like Shawn because he's white. Also, you don't need to mention what colour he is at all.'

'That is not reason I don't like him,' she says imperiously.

'How can you not like him when you don't even know him?' I ask frustratedly.

'He is not Ashar,' she says stubbornly.

'That's not a reason!'

'You aren't going to win this one . . .' Hope says, poking me with her big toe.

'Oh, whatever,' I concede.

Why is everyone so annoying today. And every day.

We take turns in the shower, and when I come out, I find Mum standing on the landing outside, queuing to get in.

'Ellie, move a bit quicker,' she says, trying to squeeze past me. 'I need to wee. This baby is literally sat on my bladder.'

262

'OK, OK,' I say, moving out of the way. She slams the door shut behind me.

'What is everyone's problem today?' I mutter.

Dad shuffles down the stairs from the loft room he and Mum are sleeping in.

'Morning,' he says, rubbing his eyes.

'Morning,' I reply.

'So, who's your date today?' he asks menacingly.

'DAD,' I say in the voice he knows is a precursor to me screaming: PLEASE STOP TERRIFYING AND VILIFYING ANY BOY THAT SHOWS THE REMOTEST INTEREST IN ME.

'What? I can't ask a simple question?' He pauses. 'But a new boyfriend, Ellie? Isn't it a bit soon?'

'A bit soon?' I repeat shrilly. Why does everyone have an opinion about this?

'A few weeks ago, all you did was mope around in your room listening to that terrible Jada woman and playing *Rumours* on repeat. I had to buy earplugs.'

'I thought you liked Fleetwood Mac?'

'Not from eight till eight,' he says, eyeing me. 'And personally, I prefer *Tango in the Night*, it's less obvious, but that's not the point, *sina pillai*.'

'We're just worried about you,' Mum shouts from inside the bathroom.

For the love of God.

'Mum, just wee!' I shout back. 'I don't need any advice. I like Shawn. I'm fine,' I say, turning back to go into Hope's room.

'Just think about it,' Dad says.

'About what?'

'About what you're doing with this boy.'

'But we're very excited about meeting him if you want us to meet him!' Mum shouts from inside the bathroom.

FFS.

My parents, who never talk about their feelings or my feelings, or feelings in general, who never want to talk about *anything*, seem suddenly incapable of Not Talking.

I walk into Hope's bedroom, where she's half dressed in some kind of weird body-shaper thing that looks like an instrument of torture.

'Why are you wearing that?'

'It takes two inches off my waist.'

'You don't need two inches off your waist,' I say worriedly. 'Your waist is perfect.'

'Whatever,' she says, trying to roll the material up her torso.

'How are you going to go to the toilet in that thing?'

'It's got snaps down here,' she says, pointing to the gusset.

'Seems like a lot of effort.' But when I see her put the sari over the top, I have to admit it looks good.

'Do you want one or not?'

'One what?'

'Body shaper. I bought one for each of us, but as you're so *comfortable* as you are, and it's too much *effort*,' she says sarcastically, 'you don't have to bother.'

I look at her again.

She looks amazing – and I have to stand next to her in photos. I have my ex-boyfriend and ex-nemesis coming, as well as Shawn and Benji and dare I say Ethan, whose opinion I don't really care about, but who'll make it known regardless. I need to look the best I can. Even if it means having to prise myself into what looks like sausage casing.

'FINE,' I say, glaring at her, 'but this is a bad idea.'

'What could go wrong?'

But we both know it's *us* we're talking about; and therefore, quite a lot of things.

# 52

# Glowy Skin, Fluffy Brows & a Pink Lip Gloss

I've managed to wrangle myself into the body shaper Hope bought me, but I'm not going to lie, I have no idea how I'm going to get it off. With both our sari dresses now on, we put our dressing gowns over the top and wait for the hair and make-up artist Aunty Kitty hired to get round to us.

I've never had my make-up done professionally, not unless you count the woman at Superdrug who told me I was wearing the wrong colour foundation then proceeded to advise me that my eyeliner was wonky.

'You seem nervous,' Hopes notes.

'No, I don't,' I reply quickly. 'Why would I be nervous?'

'Because you're going with Shawn ... and Ash is going to be there,' she says, watching me from the corner of her eye.

'I honestly don't care.'

'You couldn't even look at him yesterday.'

'What do you mean?' I ask, turning to her.

'After you said that you and Shawn were together. You couldn't look at him,' she states.

'Heebeejeebeee,' I respond.

'I'm just saying, it's pretty obvious you felt awkward about it.'

'Heebeejeebeee.'

'But if you like Shawn as much as you say you do, then you can't worry about how Ash feels.'

'How do you think he feels?' I ask out of nowhere.

She turns to me triumphantly. 'Aha!' she crows. 'Why do you care if he cares?'

'I don't care. I told you.' Then after a beat, 'But how do you think he feels about it, just, you know, out of curiosity.'

'I think he's fine with it,' she says honestly.

'Oh.'

'Which is good. Right?'

'Right,' I agree.

'Because you're just friends now,' she continues.

'Yes. Friends.'

'And Rebecca has a boyfriend, so she's not with him, so you don't have to worry about that, and you can just have a nice day. Right?'

'Right.'

And I feel like she's leading me in some kind of affirmations process, as if we're manifesting all of this being true. I should have brought my crystals.

'Good,' she says, taking my hand, 'but if it happens that you're having a meltdown, I'm here. OK?'

'I thought you said you wouldn't be?' I say, repeating her line from our fight. That she was sick of me focusing on the wrong things, which would inevitably lead to me having a meltdown, and she wasn't going to put up with it.

'I didn't mean that. I could never mean that,' she says, squeezing my hand.

When the hair and make-up woman arrives, we sit at Hope's dressing table, and she puts our hair into two matching buns with wispy tendrils around our faces. It feels grown-up and pretty and weirdly like the end of something. Like childhood is over, and we're becoming something else.

She keeps our make-up simple, minimal. Glowy skin, fluffy brows and a pink lip gloss that feels like things might stick to it in a slightly unappealing way.

When she's gone, we stand in front of the mirror and look at ourselves. And despite all my worries and insecurities, my fears that I'm not going to look like me, that compared to Hope I'll seem like the before photo in one of those makeover programmes – it's a version of me I like. A version of how I see and feel and experience my heritage. Not in exactly the same way as my parents or my granny, but my way. Like we're creating a new subculture. A new generation.

Hope turns to hug me. 'Well, I'm not sure this is going to make your situation any easier,' she says.

'What situation is that?'

'Ash might have seemed fine when he saw you yesterday, but wait till he sees you looking like *that*.'

'I want him to be fine,' I say quietly.

'I want *you* to be fine,' she says, taking my hand again.

'I am,' I lie.

Note to self: be fine.

# 53

# WEDDING, Part One

We're outside the church, waiting for Aunty Kitty to arrive with Granny. Inside, the aisles are packed with various Sri Lankan relatives and relative-adjacent people we call aunties and uncles when technically we're not related to any of them.

Also, Ash, Shawn and Rebecca.

Ugh.

'Stop fidgeting,' Hope hisses. 'You're making me feel sick.'

'Why do you feel sick?' I ask, surprised.

'I'm not sure I like all these people looking at me,' she explains.

'What?' I demand. 'You love people looking at you. You live for people looking at you.'

'I know, but the dresses,' she says, gesturing at herself. 'What if people don't like them? What if they think the design is bad? You know what the aunties are like. They're not exactly known for being subtle about these things.'

'Hope, they're gorgeous. You're talented. This is what you should be doing.'

She blushes. 'You really think so?'

I nod. 'I know so. Besides, Granny will take down anyone that criticises anything about this day.'

She grins. 'True. Honestly, I thought she was going to hate them,' she admits.

'I think Granny might be . . . kind of cool,' I say, biting my tongue. 'She's so much more open these days.'

'It's the Ellie effect,' she says fondly.

'Heebeejeebee.'

'You make everything better.'

'No, I don't.'

'Last year I felt like such a failure. I was dating that idiot Vikash. You just made me see who I could be, E, who I am.'

'You did that, not me,' I say, embarrassed.

'You're a good person.' And as soon as she says it, all I can think about is Jess and Hayley. Who've done nothing but try and look out for me. To make sure I'm OK. How I said what I said to Jess. To the best friend who's always been there for me. That isn't a nice person. That's the real Ellie effect.

I try to swallow the feeling down, but it keeps resurfacing. The way it has since it happened. Like forgetting you have a bruise, then pressing against it without meaning to.

Breathe, Ellie. Breathe.

I give myself a minute to try and suppress it. It's not as if I'm not an expert in this area; it's just I'm starting to feel like a pot on the verge of boiling over. Like every pot boils over whenever my mum tries to cook almost anything. Luckily, Aunty Kitty's car arrives, which makes it hard to think about anything other than what's happening right now. How beautiful she looks. How happy Granny stood next to her looks, in her aquamarine-blue sari.

We rush over to the car and help them both out.

'You girls look gorgeous,' Aunty Kitty says to us.

'I mean, wow,' I breathe, looking at her.

'And Granny,' Hope says, taking her arm. 'You look like Madhubala.'

Granny blushes and waves her away.

'You do!' Hope insists. And I wonder who Madhubala is. 'She was the Marilyn Monroe of Bollywood,' Hope explains, and I feel suddenly ashamed that I didn't know that. That I need a Western comparison to understand who a South Asian actress is.

'OK, OK, are we all ready?' Hope asks, taking charge. 'If so, I'll let them know to start. Ellie and I will walk first, and then Granny, you'll walk with Aunty Kitty. OK?'

We all stare at her and nod. As if she's the only one who knows how to do it – which may be true. We walk into the back of the church together, and as always, take the holy water in the entrance to dab across our foreheads in the sign of a cross. I've been doing this for as long as I can remember. The same way I can say the Lord's Prayer forwards and backwards, as if it's ingrained in my brain. And even though I'm not sure what any of it means, if I really believe any of it, in that moment it feels soothing and ritualistic. The smell of candles burning, the heavy wood beams, the cold flat stone of the church walls. Like I've come home to all the people I love most.

And I don't let myself think about the last time I went into a church. That even though it was a long time ago now, I haven't been able to go back into one since. The day we buried my brother. His tiny coffin sat to the side of the altar while the priest talked mournfully about sorrow and grief and loss, my mother wailing, my father stoney-faced, my grandmother holding his hand.

All I want is to forget it, but it's right there. The water inside me, the fire lit beneath it. Burning, burning, burning. Begging me to boil over.

Breathe, Ellie. Breathe.

'Come on,' Hope says, pulling me along, as Aunty Kitty and Granny stand hidden in the vestibule. 'Time to go.'

The organist begins playing and Hope starts walking up the aisle. Around her I can see the church packed with aunties and uncles, kids dressed in formal dresses and suits, fidgeting, bored already when the service hasn't even started yet. I can see Charles's family to the left, with a group of chic older Chinese women and the men who carry their handbags. Everyone's watching Hope, the way everyone watches Hope. She looks serene, almost ethereal. I love her so much in this moment it hurts. The dresses she's designed, the way she carries herself, how kind she is.

Now it's my turn to start walking, so I do.

I can hear a little gasp from Mum, Dad sat with tears in his eyes as he watches me walking towards them. I see Shawn sat with Ash and Elina and Rebecca – and Mrs Aachara and Mr Green. Mr Green!

Mr Green and Mrs Aachara are holding hands. My favourite teacher/my ex-boyfriend's mum is holding hands with one of my PE teachers. The super-hot one. Who looks hot. As expected. In a shirt with a Nehru collar and a dark blue suit.

They're all smiling at me, Shawn doing a little wave as I smile back. But it's Ash's eye I catch, even though I don't want to. There's a smile on his face, but his eyes look unhappy. It feels like looking into a mirror. Like he can see right inside me.

I take a sharp breath and avert my eyes, locking mine with Hope, stood at the front, waiting for me to arrive next to her. When I do, she takes my hand as we watch our beautiful aunt and our brilliant, if sometimes scary, unforgiving, rigid grandmother make their way up the aisle to the front of the church.

Opposite us, Charles is stepping from side to side nervously, Ethan stood next to him looking annoyingly handsome, which doesn't bode well for Hope, who seems to be catching his eye more than I think is entirely necessary.

When Kitty arrives at the front, Charles leans down to hug Granny. I see her fingers tighten across his back, her lips mouthing words into his ear that probably go something like: if you do anything to hurt my daughter, I will hunt you down and kill you, because I've killed before and I'll do it again, so don't mistake my tiny stature for cute decrepitude, because I Can Take You. Or something like that. And when Hope tells me later that she just said *you are my son now*, I don't believe her.

Throughout the service, I keep looking at Mum and Dad. They look so different to the last time I saw them in a church together. So happy, holding hands. Her head on his shoulder, the way they kiss when Aunty Kitty and Charles do. And I don't know why I don't feel happy too. What this nagging feeling inside me is. Like I'm looking at an airbrushed picture, and I've seen the original, and I prefer the original.

Hope nudges me. 'They did it,' she whispers happily.

And we watch Kitty and Charles walk down the church aisle together. Man and wife, everyone taking pictures.

'They did it,' I smile.

But just like Ash, it doesn't quite reach my eyes.

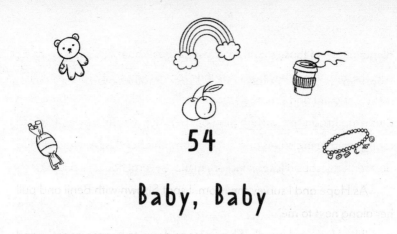

# 54

# Baby, Baby

We've made it through the wedding, which seems like a miracle given the last few months. My face hurts from all the smiling I've done for the photographs, but now we've arrived at the party everything feels slightly more relaxed. It's a huge room with floor-to-ceiling windows looking out over Camden Lock. The sun's shining, flooding the floor with light, music playing, people perched at tables as a DJ plays music in a corner.

The party seems to be the one area Aunty Kitty and Charles have had any control over. The church they married in is the one my family grew up going to when they moved to London. It was a full Catholic service – the same as the one Granny had when she married her husband, that Mum had when she married Dad – you get the picture. The flowers, the hymns, the organist, even Aunty Kitty's jewellery, was all picked out by Granny. She had some say in her wedding sari, but I know what she really wanted to wear was a dress, which is why Hope stepped in and designed the blouse for her. The Chinese wedding, which is happening in a month, was completely arranged by Charles's family, so this, the party that Granny actually wanted to be a formal sit-down dinner at one of those slightly soulless purpose-built banqueting suites, was the one thing they both put their foot down about. They wanted it to be relaxed and simple and welcoming. Drinks and bowl food and music, no organised seating plan or speeches, which, having been to many banqueting suites and sat at many children's tables and had to deal with my cousin Joseph kicking me for several hours, is a relief.

As Hope and I survey the room. I spot Shawn with Benji and pull her along next to me.

'Hey,' I say awkwardly. Shawn leans down to kiss me sweetly, and I swear, I spot the side-eye from every aunty in the room. But it's worth it.

'You look beautiful,' he says, taking my hands.

He doesn't look too bad himself, in a dark blue suit and tie, his blond hair pulled back into a bun.

'Shawn, you remember Hope,' I say mock formally.

'But of course, I'm impossible to forget.'

'True,' he grins and gives her a hug.

'So, what's happening with Berklee?' she asks curiously.

I give him a look. How does Hope know about Berklee, when he never told me?

'I got in,' he replies quickly, 'but I'm still thinking about it. We're waiting to hear from Gabrielle next week.'

'Right,' she says, looking over at me. 'The label people.'

'You remember Benji,' I say to her, trying to change the subject, because I don't know how to feel about any of this. Him going or not going. That I might have anything to do with him going or not going.

Benji's staring at Hope, speechless. Not doing his usual groupie speech or tweaking his nipples.

'Hey,' Hope says, waving at him. 'Nice to see you again.' Because they've met before. In the Easter holidays when she came to rehearsal and took the video that got us our shot with Gabrielle.

'Heebeejeebee,' he says, copying my turn of phrase. Shawn and I sneak a look at each other, trying desperately not to laugh.

'Okaaaayyy,' she says, knitting her eyebrows. 'I'm just going to say hi to Ethan.'

'OK,' I respond, concerned. I hope Ethan hasn't managed to convince the bar staff here that he's old enough to drink.

'What was *that*?' Shawn asks Benji, laughing. Benji puts his head in his hands, the colour rising in his face.

'I've *never* seen you do that before,' I tease. 'You were literally agape.'

'Good word,' Shawn says, congratulating me. 'He was totally agape.'

'She's just . . .' he tries. 'I mean, she's so . . .' he continues.

'I know,' I reply without the need for him to add an adjective. 'She is.'

I've never seen Benji tongue-tied. I almost feel sorry for him. Almost, but not quite.

'I'm going to get a drink,' he says forlornly, as if he's blown his chance, which honestly, he may well have, because: heebeejeebee. 'Do you two want anything?'

'No, I'm fine,' I reply. 'And would you mind . . .' I begin.

'I'm not planning to drink in front of your parents,' Shawn says. 'If that's what you're going to ask.'

This time I lean up to kiss him.

'Have I told you how much I like you?' I ask, putting my arms around his neck.

'No,' he says, kissing me again. 'How much do you like me?'

'Get a room,' Benji says irritably. 'It's bad enough I'm at a wedding with two teachers without you two sucking each other's faces off.'

'What are you guys up to?' Rebecca says, appearing next to us with Ash and Elina in tow behind her. We let go of one another quickly. Sharply. Or maybe that's just me. Putting space between us.

'Hey there,' Benji says, looking from her to Ash to Shawn to me, and suddenly seeming less irritated.

Shawn puts his arm around my shoulders.

'Weren't you going to get a drink?' I ask Benji.

'No,' he says, smiling. 'I'm fine now.'

'Really,' I say through gritted teeth. 'Because I think I can see Hope near the bar.'

He turns so quickly that Shawn and I can't help but laugh.

'Not much,' I reply to Rebecca's question. 'We were just discussing Benji's crush on my cousin.'

Benji shoots me a look. 'I don't have a *crush*,' he replies. 'I'm not a thirteen-year-old girl, Pillai.'

'Heebeejeebee,' I say mockingly. 'Also, thirteen-year-old girls are much smoother than you are, Benjamin. Never, underestimate a thirteen-year-old girl,' I say seriously. Shawn laughs.

'Fine. I'm going,' Benji says, steeling himself.

'Good luck,' I grin, as he disappears.

'So, how's Granny?' Ash asks out of nowhere. I can feel Shawn's arm tightening around my shoulder.

'Living for today.'

'Clearly,' he says mock seriously.

'You'd better go say hi, so she can introduce you to all her friends,' I joke. 'I'm sure she's told them all about you.'

'Stop being jealous,' he teases.

'What can I say, she mostly tries to pretend she doesn't know me, so it kind of hurts,' I kid.

'You know she worships you,' he says, actually serious this time.

'Hardly,' I laugh.

'Most of the time we spent together at the hospital, she kept telling me how strong you were. How amazing you were after—' He stops suddenly. Painfully.

I want to say 'After what?' But I know. Even though I've spent all day fighting it. What feels like years fighting it.

'I'm sorry,' he says, shaking his head quickly. 'I don't know why I . . . I just meant that—'

'It's OK,' I cut him off. 'Don't worry about it.'

But he looks almost as sick as I feel.

'Come on,' I say, pulling at Shawn. 'We'd better check if Benji survived.'

I shoot Elina a smile and wave to them all as we walk away.

'See you later,' Rebecca says, her voice fading as we leave them behind.

As we get closer to Hope, I notice Ethan just behind her. He seems to be hanging off the wall slightly, like he can't stand, Benji to one side of him.

Not again.

'Are you OK?' I ask, putting my hand on Hope's shoulder.

'Yes, fine,' she says tightly.

'Hey, Ethan,' I say, waving. He nods.

'I was just saying to Ethan that maybe he should sit down,' Benji says to Shawn and me.

'Shawn, this is Ethan,' I say, introducing them.

'Hi.' Shawn waves.

'This is my boyfriend, Shawn,' I say to Ethan.

'Your girlfriend's cool,' he says to Shawn.

'I know,' he says irritably, and I don't know why he's annoyed.

'Ethan, your mum's here. And pretty much your entire family,' I say quietly. 'Maybe you should sit down. I'll get you a glass of water.'

He laughs. 'They all think I'm a screw-up anyway. That's why my dad never shows up. Because I'm a screw-up.'

'Nobody thinks that.'

'Come on,' Hope says, taking his hand. 'Let's go sit somewhere.'

He shakes her off. 'What would you know about anything, with your perfect family?' he snarls. 'With your perfect dad and your perfect little wedding.'

'Come on,' Shawn says, moving a little closer to him. 'There's no need to be like that.'

'Who even are you?' he asks him heatedly.

'You know what?' Benji says menacingly. 'Look around you. This room is full of people who care about you, so how about you stop thinking about yourself for once?'

'You don't know anything about me,' Ethan replies furiously.

'I know I never met my dad,' Benji says, meeting his fury. 'In fact, I don't even know who he is. I know my mum left when I was six. And I remember it. I remember her leaving and not coming back. But I don't use it as an excuse to get drunk and hurt the people that care about me,' and he's looking at Shawn, and Shawn's looking right back, and I understand what that means, that friendship, that feeling that someone has you. That someone knows you. Because that was Jess and Hayley for me, and I've thrown it all away. I've ruined everything. 'I know what it's like to have no one,' Benji continues, 'so when people show up for me, I tend not to be the kind of brat that throws stones at them.'

Ethan stares at him, his shoulders sinking. 'I j-just,' he stutters, his eyes filling with tears before he wipes them away angrily with the back of his hand. 'I just don't know why I'm not good enough for him.'

'You are,' Benji says, touching him lightly on the arm. 'It's him that's not good enough for you.'

He puts his arm around Ethan so gently, so kindly, it's hard to imagine this is the Benji that uses his drum kit like a punch bag, who can find the joke in anything. Benji, who's been through so much. Who, the more I get to know him, the more I want to earn his respect. Because being respected by him means something.

Hope walks round to Ethan's other side, mouthing 'thank you' at Benji across his chest.

'Where should we take him?' Benji asks her; and now that he's no longer interested in impressing her, he's impressing her. Like, a lot.

'There's a corner over there. We can get him some water,' she says, blushing.

'Thanks,' I mouth at Benji. He half smiles, half grimaces back.

'I think I'd better find my mum and tell her about Ethan,' I say, turning to Shawn.

'I'll go help them,' he says, nodding in Benji's direction.

He leans down to kiss me, and this time it feels suffocating, because however much I like him, I'm not sure I like myself enough to be doing this, and it feels like my body shaper is trying to kill me. There's a knot inside my chest, getting tighter and tighter. Or maybe it's not the body shaper. Maybe it's everything else.

Don't think about it, Ellie. Don't think about anything. Just breathe. Remember how to breathe.

I spend ten minutes looking for Mum and Dad but can't find them anywhere.

'Have you seen my mum?' I ask Rebecca and Elina when I pass them.

'No, sorry,' Elina offers apologetically. 'Are you OK, Ellie?' she says, pausing. 'You seem a bit . . .'

*A bit what?*

'I'm fine,' I reply distractedly.

'I'm sorry about yesterday,' she responds quickly. 'What I said about Jess, not being able to forgive her. It wasn't fair to say that to you, I know how close you are.'

*A bit no longer close to Jess.*

'It's OK. I understand,' I say robotically.

'You mean, because you can't forgive Ash?' Rebecca asks bluntly.

*A bit unforgiving.*

'I get he wasn't the best boyfriend in the world,' she continues. 'I mean, you weren't winning any awards for best girlfriend either, but he loves you – and for some reason, I thought you loved him too.'

*A bit not the best girlfriend in the world.*

'Stop it, Bec,' Elina says irritably, watching my face.

'You know he loves you. You must know,' she continues mercilessly.

'We're f-friends,' I stammer, turning to Elina. 'We're better as friends.'

'Maybe,' Rebecca says, staring at me. 'But I still don't get why you're with Shawn. What happened to getting to know yourself and being on your own, or whatever it is you said to Ash?'

'I, I, I,' stutter.

*A bit stuttering.*

'You're not being fair,' she says brusquely.

'Bec,' Elina says, her eyes flashing. '*Look* at her, she's clearly not OK. Just stop it.'

*A bit clearly not OK.*

'Don't you think Shawn deserves better than being used to get over someone else?' Rebecca persists.

I'm shaking. Barely able to see straight.

*A bit shaking.*

'It's none of your business, Rebecca,' I state, glaring at her. 'None of this is.'

'Of course it isn't,' Elina agrees. 'Ellie, are you OK? You don't look very well. Ellie?' she repeats loudly.

*A bit not very well.*

'Ellie,' Rebecca says suddenly gentle, her face registering something as close to concern as she's capable of. She touches my arm. 'I just want you to know how much he cares about you.'

'Why?' I gasp, the air no longer reaching my lungs. 'So I can feel worse than I already do? Because trust me, Rebecca, I don't think that's possible.'

I walk away, trying to push it all down. To take control of this feeling that's suddenly gripping me. Then I finally spot Mum in a corner, her belly so far in front of her she's practically in another room.

'Mum,' I gulp. 'Can I talk to you?

'Of course,' she says, rubbing her bump. 'You look so beautiful, *en anbe*.' She puts her hand out to stroke my arm, the feeling both soothing and painful simultaneously. 'But I forgot to give you my bangles this morning and your grandmother isn't happy you aren't wearing any jewellery. Be a good girl. Get them out of the car? Put them on? We're parked by the back door, near the kitchen.' She passes me the keys.

'OK,' I say compliantly.

*A bit of a good girl.*

I follow one of the catering staff towards the kitchen and ask where a car might be parked. They point me in the direction of the black SUV, and it takes me a minute to remember it's ours. Our new car. The one I haven't even sat inside yet.

I press the unlock button on the key and open the front door, thinking she must have left the bangles on the passenger seat. When I can't find anything, I open the back door. To one side I spot a red velvet jewellery bag, but as I reach to grab it, on the other, I see something else. Something that makes my mouth go dry.

There's a song that plays in my head sometimes. When I think about anything sad, anything that takes my breath away; and it's playing now. Everything in slow motion. Band of Horses, 'The Funeral'.

And I can hear those overplucked electric notes, Ben Bridwell's voice, high and needy; the way the oohs sound almost holy, like a choir, before the guitars and drums kick in, forcing your emotions to expand.

A car seat. A baby seat.

The real reason my parents bought this new car.

I'm breathing in time with the music inside my head, but then I'm not. Gulping and spluttering, my chest closing.

They didn't want a change. They didn't want me to have the Mini to practise in. They were making space. For the baby that's coming to take my brother's place – when my brother can't be replaced. My brother could never be replaced.

283

It's happening. Everything I've been trying to fight back, everything I've been trying to hold in, suddenly rushing forward so I can't take in air. My descent soundtracked by electric guitars and pulsing drums.

I slam the car door shut and lean against it.

Come on, Ellie. It's OK. Everything's going to be OK.

But it isn't. Nothing's OK. Nothing's ever been OK.

I'm gasping for air, like my lungs have given up. Like I can no longer process oxygen.

I turn around, doubled over, tears stinging my eyes.

'Ellie,' Hope screams. 'What's wrong? Ellie? ELLIE!'

I can hear Hope shouting my name, Shawn trying to pull me up off the ground from where I've fallen.

'Get her mum!' Hope screams at someone. 'Ellie, Ellie, please talk to me. Please.' I can hear the tears in her voice, and I want so much to tell her I'm OK, but I can't, because I'm not. I don't think I have been in a really, long time.

It's all so confusing. Just a mess of noise and shapes and emotions, things I can't wade through any more because I don't know how. Did I ever know how?

'ELLIE.'

His voice cuts through everything. The only voice I can hear.

He crouches down next to me, holding my forearms, forcing me to look up at him.

'Just breathe,' he says. 'Breathe with me.'

'I, I, I,' I stutter.

'Look at me, Ellie. Come on.'

I focus on his face. The face I've spent so long trying not to focus on.

'In,' he commands, 'and out, OK? Just in, and out. You can do it.'

284

I practise the gesture as if I've never done it before, forcing my brain to remember.

I can feel it all slowing down and speeding up again. I remember the car seat, and the way it made me feel sick. The thought of this new person. His cot in Amis's room.

'It's OK,' he's saying. 'It's OK. I know it hurts. I know you're hurting.'

'I miss him,' I'm crying. 'And everyone just wants to forget him. And it's too much. It's all too much. I'm not strong enough. I'm not strong. I think I might be broken. I think I might be broken. I think I might be broken.'

I'm muttering it over and over. Over and over. Sobbing. Until suddenly I'm in his arms and he's stroking the back of my head, and I'm boiling over, in my beautiful pink sari dress, at my aunt's perfect wedding, and I'm not strong. I don't think I was ever strong.

'Ellie,' I hear Mum say. 'I'm here.'

I can feel Ash lift me up to standing, my legs weak beneath me.

'I've got you,' Mum says, lifting me out of his arms. 'I've got you. I'm here.' And she's crying too. Her body shaking against mine.

'The, car, seat,' I gulp.

'*En anbe, en anbe, en anbe,*' she croons. 'I'm sorry. I'm so sorry. I meant to put it in the boot.'

'Wh-why?' I gasp.

'Because every time we say or do anything related to the baby, you get so upset.' She's moaning quietly, her body wracking. 'You had your exams. I didn't want to worry you, but I didn't know what to do any more. We started hiding things from you. Doing things when you weren't around.'

'I d-d-don't. I c-c-can't. We're, we're forgetting him,' I breathe. 'I'm forgetting him.'

285

'I'll never forget him.' She's weeping now, no longer able to hold it in. 'He was my son. My beautiful, perfect, precious son. I could never forget him, Ellie. Never. And you'll never forget him either. I won't let you.' I feel her collapse against me, the two of us folded into one another, holding on for dear life. 'But we haven't talked about him enough, have we?' she asks. 'We haven't talked about him together, have we?'

I shake my head, thinking about his birthday every year. The chocolate cake with its hard chocolate topping, the sprinkles all over the kitchen counter. The way Mum cries as Dad sits grey, stony-faced, the three of us on separate islands.

I'm crying again. More quietly this time. More in control, or as in control as you can be when you're crying in your mother's arms outside a wedding.

'You're OK,' she says. 'You're OK. I promise you. Everything's going to be OK, *en anbe.*'

And I don't know whether I believe her, I just know she can hear me.

That maybe, finally, it's about time I heard myself.

## 55

# A Girl Called Ellie

My name is Ellie. Ellie Pillai.

And I'm broken.

But the thing about broken things is.

They can be fixed.

# 56

# Therapy Voice

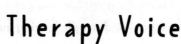

I'm in therapy. Which is something I haven't done in forever. Well, the last time I did I was eleven, which feels like a lifetime ago. Before I went to high school. Before I met Jess and Hayley. Before. Before. Before.

There's a before. And it's something I try not to think about now I'm living in the after. That there was a before, with a little boy called Amis. My chief tormentor, my best friend. And now, the therapist says, there's a new baby coming, which is bringing the before back. Reminding me of what I didn't deal with the first time round. That I lost someone. That we, Mum, Dad and I, lost someone, and we never talked about it. About what happened to Mum when she couldn't get out of bed, or how I buried everything I felt to try and protect my parents.

It's strange, because for a long time, I felt angry, so angry about it. About the way they'd left me out of their grief. But I thought I'd dealt with that. That I'd forgiven them. I thought Mum and I had moved on after we finally talked about it last year. But it seems all we did was open a Pandora's box. That all those emotions have been out there, flowing into the universe, that the closer Mum got to her due date, the more panicked I became – the more I suppressed that panic, the more the panic overwhelmed me.

I've never been good with change, and the therapist thinks that part of that is because the biggest change I ever experienced was losing my brother. That I haven't recovered from it. That I believe all change will end in something terrible and painful, which is why exams and change at school and people leaving me is something I struggle with.

I'm struggling.

She made me say the words out loud. I'm struggling.

It took a while, but there it is. The truth. I. Am. Struggling.

Which is OK. Because we all struggle. We all have those moments where everything feels immoveable. In a bad way. When it feels like the fear and trauma will never shift. That they'll always be in control of you. But they won't. Change is inevitable. Change means movement. Change, apparently, is a good thing.

My homework now is to reframe the way I think about change. To think about the language I use around it. To stop seeing it as something to be feared and start seeing it as something to get excited by.

Change is good.

If I say it enough times, maybe I'll believe it.

I've seen my therapist three times this week. Twice on my own, and once with my parents. After what happened at the wedding, Mum and Dad took me home and got me booked in with Dr Sharma, a local family therapist. I talk to her on my own, but she also runs workshops with families, and that's what we're doing. Talking to each other about what's happened between us since we lost my brother. Each one of us saying words out loud we've never dared say before.

Before. There was a before. And there is an after; and there is an After This. These are the things I know.

The worst thing is how bad I feel for scaring everyone, but Dr Sharma says I have to stop feeling bad. That now's a time for figuring things out. So here I am, trying to figure things out.

Here's what I know so far:

That night at the wedding, Hope, Shawn and Benji took Ethan outside to get some fresh air/avoid très chic Granny, who seemed to have her suspicions about an empty bottle of vodka she'd found down the side of their table, which is when they saw me having a panic attack, doubled over by the side of our new car.

Hope was trying to talk to me, reason with me, but I wouldn't listen. Honestly, I couldn't. I couldn't hear anyone. Shawn tried to lift me up off the ground, but I wouldn't budge. So, Hope sent Benji inside to find Mum, and he passed Ash and Elina, who came out to help. The two of them had been looking for me, because Elina was certain I was having or was about to have a panic attack. Turns out she was right. I'd been having a low-level attack all day, and then suddenly, it wasn't low level any more. It was something else. Something bigger.

According to Hope, Ash was the only person I'd respond to. He refused to leave me, even coming back to Hope's house with her parents and waiting until he knew I was asleep before he'd leave.

I haven't really spoken to anyone other than Hope since then. Mum took my phone away and said I needed space to think. She's right. I've distracted myself from so much by focusing on all the wrong things. Trying to fix other people's lives, when just like me, they need space to fix themselves.

The one thing I know outside of all this is a phone call Mum let me take from Gabrielle. The label are interested but want to hear another song. Something to prove we're not just one viral song, but something more. But I can't get any further than *I'm not ready to let go*, no matter how hard I try. Maybe I won't, until I actually do it. Until I finally let go of whatever it is that's holding me here.

Gabrielle says there's no rush, but I know there is. I know Shawn will be thinking about Berklee and trying to decide what to do next. Like, how to dump his girlfriend and leave the country as quickly as possible.

It's half-term, and Dr Sharma joked that I'm so accommodating of my family, I even waited until after the wedding and the start of the school holidays to have my big panic attack. I've been feeling anxious for months. Managing smaller panic attacks without really knowing what they were. And much to Mum's chagrin, it turns out Dr Jada's advice was helping. That breathing techniques and quieting intrusive thoughts with simple repetitive phrases are things Dr Sharma suggests too. And while she doesn't go as far as saying she agrees with everything Dr Jada recommends (Dr Sharma is definitely *not* a fan of crystals), she say there's merit in the fact I tried to help myself. That I knew there was a problem, and I tried to fix it. It's just, Dr Jada wasn't the entire answer. Apparently, fixing yourself doesn't mean you have to do it on your own. It means asking for help. It means saying to someone you trust: I'm Not OK.

Next week is my final week at school before going on study leave and exams, exams, exams. Which in my case means house arrest with Granny as an armed guard.

Mum and Dad have said I don't have to do exams this year if I don't feel up to it, that I could re-sit them next year – but exams were never the problem, or at least only part of my problem. It was me doing what

I always do. Distracting myself from the things that matter. So, here's me trying not to do that any more.

Note to self: focus on things that matter.

Must learn why Shakespeare made up so many words.

Also, why my new brother's cot makes me cry.

# 57

# The Promise

I feel nervous going into school on Monday. I know Mum's spoken to Mr Gorley and some of my other teachers like Mrs Aachara, and Shawn, Benji, Ash and Elina all saw me dissolve in front of them at the wedding. What I don't know is how any of them are going to react to seeing me again. Whether they've spoken to each other or formed some kind of support group for the friends of people who have anxiety and suffer from panic attacks. I don't want to be treated any differently. I don't want people whispering about me or acting like there's something wrong with me.

Also, I don't know what Jess and Hayley actually know. Mum hasn't called them, and when I got my phone back on Sunday, it was eerily quiet, virtually no WhatsApps or voice notes from anyone bar Hope.

I walk off the bus feeling heavy and strange. Like everything's slightly further away from me, or I'm underwater.

'Hey,' Shawn says, stepping forward, his blond hair trimmed a little, wearing one of his arsenal of Nirvana T-shirts, this one bright green. He puts his arms around me and envelops me in a hug.

'Hey,' I say tearfully.

'How are you feeling?' he asks, stepping back to look at me.

'I'm OK,' I smile. 'Thanks for coming to meet me.'

'I had no idea,' he begins.

'I know,' I say cutting him off. 'It's OK.'

'No,' he says forcefully, 'please let me say this.' He stands back, looking down at me. 'I had no idea what you were going through, Ellie, and I'm so sorry I didn't know. I'm sorry that I kissed you, and I kept kissing you, and I'm sorry if you felt like I pressured you into making a decision about something you clearly weren't ready to make a decision about.'

I stare at the ground. 'I really like you, Shawn,' I begin.

'But you need to focus on yourself,' he says softly.

I nod.

'I should have respected that from the start. I'm sorry.'

'Can you stop saying sorry?' I laugh. 'I didn't exactly *not* enjoy kissing you.'

He takes a breath. 'I really want to be friends,' he says, taking my hand. 'I promise not to kiss you.'

'And I promise not to kiss you,' I return, and looking at him right now, I wonder how hard it's going to be to keep that promise.

'So,' he says, 'are you ready for this?'

I look over at the school. All square lumpy concrete boxes. Somewhere I used to think I hated, but which in the last year feels like it's become part of my bones. Something that's helped build me, piece by piece.

'Not really,' I say quietly.

He takes my hand and walks me through the main gates, past reception to the door of my form room, without letting go.

'Will you be OK?' he asks, as he finally removes his hand from around mine.

'I think so.'

'I think so too,' he smiles.

And even though in that moment it feels particularly hard to keep my promise to him.

I do.

# 58

# I Don't Got It Just Yet

Hayley refuses to look at me in form room, and I don't attempt to force it. I'm the one that accused her of not trusting me. I'm the one that said she should have come out to me first; as if *I* should decide who she feels comfortable with, *I* should decide who she chooses to share herself with.

And I don't know whether it was the anxiety making me think like that, or just me being me, which is a much worse thought. But I should have been happy she had people she could talk to, not upset that it wasn't me.

I leave registration feeling defeated but remind myself that Dr Sharma says baby steps. That as hard as it is not to want to rush everything, to make it instantly better, you can't. In the same way I can't rush how I feel about the baby, I can't push aside what I feel about Amis. I have to wait. I have to do the work.

I walk down the hall, wondering whether I'll be walking down every hall alone today, when I see James and his girlfriend Sadie.

'Hey, Ellie.' He waves. 'How's it going?'

'Good,' I reply. 'Well, I mean, not bad,' I conclude.

'I heard a rumour that not bad is better than bad,' he grins. 'So, I was just wondering how Hayley was doing?'

'Er, yeah. Fine, I think.' I picture Hayley's impassive face sat next to mine and try not to cry.

'It's just, the auditions were kind of brutal last week. I was wondering if she'd heard anything yet? I've been messaging her, but she hasn't responded. I don't know if that's a good thing or bad thing with her,' he says worriedly.

Auditions. Of course. They were last week, during half-term.

'I'll check on her,' I say confidently, as if she's talking to me, as if I'm someone she turns to.

*HA.*

'Cool,' he replies, taking Sadie's hand. She turns to wave at me.

'See ya, Ellie.'

'See ya,' I reply.

I quite like Sadie. I don't really know her, but she seems nice. She seems calm and kind and not like the rest of the slightly shouty girls' football team who ignore you unless you know how to do a thigh and drive tackle, which, clearly, I do not.

I walk towards biology feeling slightly less bad, because Hayley's face means something other than just being upset with me.

Baby steps, Eleanor. Baby steps.

'Ellie!' I hear someone shout, as they run along the hall towards me.

'Hey,' I say, turning to face Elina.

'How are you doing?' she asks, taking my arm inside hers as we walk the length of the corridor.

'I'm OK.'

She looks at me, and then at the floor. 'I know you aren't, and I know you haven't been,' she says quietly. 'If you ever want to talk about it, you know where I am. Trust me.' She pauses. 'I really do get it.'

Sometimes I forget Ash and Elina lost their dad a few years ago. That it almost destroyed Ash. They seem so together now. Such a team. And I think that's what Mum, Dad and I are trying to do now. Deal with some of the things we should have dealt with together, as a team.

'Thank you for everything. For that night, for today,' I say softly.

'What are friends for?' She smiles. 'Where are you going now?'

'Biology,' I reply, making a yuck face.

'I like biology,' she responds, amused.

'It's Jess's favourite subject. You two really do belong together,' I joke. But the joke's out before I have a chance to think about it. Because she and Jess aren't together. She and Jess aren't perfect.

'I'll walk you there,' she replies, graciously ignoring my blunder.

'So, how's everything else going? Exams, life, stuff?' I ask.

'Well,' she says, clearing her throat, 'I got a conditional offer from Saint Martins.'

'That's amazing,' I interrupt.

'It is,' she says slowly, 'but I also got an unconditional offer from the University of the Arts here, and with Mum staying, it feels like a sign that maybe I should too.'

'Your mum's staying?' I ask happily. 'At the school, next year?'

'Maybe. We're still not sure whether Mr Grange is coming back yet, but she's met someone. She wants to see whether they can make something of it.'

'Whoa,' I say, looking at her. 'Do you mean –' I drop my voice to a whisper – 'Mr Green?'

She nods.

'How do you feel about that?'

She shrugs. 'He's nice. He makes her happy. It's super early, but it feels enough for her to not rush back to London. The school want her to stay. I think it's just about finding the right position for her.'

'Saint Martins is your dream though, right?' I ask bluntly.

'Dreams change,' she smiles. 'The Shelley want to make my internship official next year. A part-time paid position would really help with uni costs, and I'd be getting on-the-ground curatorial experience, working directly with artists and getting involved with how the whole gallery experience works. It feels like that might be more *me* than a Fine Art degree. Plus, I'd get to be with Mum. It's a lot to think about. It's the first time I'd be away from Ash, and I don't know how I'd do that. Anyway,' she sighs, 'that's my update on exams, life and *stuff*.'

'Well, that's a hard update to live up to,' I tease. 'I mean, what am I going to say to *you* the next time you ask *me* for an update? I'm still panicking about exams, life and stuff. I have no update on my update.'

'You have a potential development deal,' she says seriously. 'Stop selling yourself short, Ellie. You're amazing.'

I make a weird, indecipherable grunt noise in response.

'If I stay, we can hang out together next year,' she says gleefully. 'We will actually be *friends*,' she says dramatically.

'About time,' I say, as we arrive by the walkway to the science block, thinking about the fact we were friends, and then we weren't, and then we kind of were, but she was always with Jess and we never got the chance to talk just the two of us.

'Don't forget me when you're, I don't know, some famous art person,' I say, reaching for the door handle.

'Enjoy biology,' she returns. 'Remember, the nervous system enables humans to react to their surroundings and coordinate their behaviour. It comprises millions of neurons and uses electrical impulses to communicate. But you control *it*. It doesn't control you. It just takes practice, OK?'

I smile. 'Got it,' I respond.

And OK, maybe I don't got it just yet.

But I will.

I will.

# 59

# Beautiful, Strong, Funny, Brilliant You

At lunchtime, I walk into the canteen feeling uneasy. Like it's the first day of school and I'm looking for somewhere to sit. Someone to sit *with*.

My eyes automatically search for Jessica. My fail-safe. The one person I've always been able to rely on. Even when we've both been going through stuff, we've stuck together. We always have.

When I spot the back of her head sat with the McQueen sisters, my heart drops.

Since she and Elina broke up, I feel like she's done a lot of what my mum would call *backsliding*, which is when you return to previously undesirable patterns of behaviour after you've made a breakthrough.

I know this because apparently, I've been doing a lot of backsliding myself. Letting my intrusive thoughts take over, not talking to people about how I'm feeling, lying to myself. You get the picture.

I want to walk over to her and sit down confidently, not caring what the McQueens have to say about anything, but I don't think I'm strong enough yet. I don't think the voice inside my head could cope with hearing their barbarous little digs about my hair, or my skin, or my general overall me-ness.

Breathe, Ellie. Breathe.

'Hey,' Ash says out of nowhere, as I'm stood staring into the distance, considering whether I should take my lunch to the library. 'Are you sitting down?'

'It was one of my options,' I joke.

'Come on,' he says, steering me by my elbow to a table in the back corner of the room where Elina's sat with Jane. It makes my heart drop. Why is Jane here? Why isn't she Jess? Does Jess know Elina might be staying? Why can't this mess just fix itself? Should I do something?

Slow down, brain. Just slow down.

Elina and Jane look up at me and smile as I sit down next to Ash.

'So, how are you feeling?' he asks gently.

'Tired,' I state bluntly. And he feels like the first person I've been completely honest with today.

'You look better,' he says brightly. 'You look like you again.'

'Like a nerdy-but-not-actually-that-clever-sixteen-year-old brown girl?' I query, putting my sandwich to my lips.

'Name the first three tracks on disc two of the *White Album*,' he says, narrowing his eyes.

'CD or vinyl?'

'Vinyl. Side three.'

'"Birthday", "Yer Blues", "Mother Nature's Son",' I respond quickly.

He smiles, satisfied.

'Don't make me pick you up.' Which is a reference to when we were going out and I wasn't being very nice about myself. He'd pick me up and hang me upside down until I stopped.

I put my hands up in mock surrender. 'Fine. I look like me again, whatever that means.'

'It means you look beautiful and strong and funny and brilliant.'

'I'm not saying that.'

'Why not?'

'I'm not calling myself funny looking,' I joke. 'I'm trying to be nicer to myself.'

'You can leave the funny part out.'

'Ha ha,' I say drily.

'Seriously,' he says, looking down at his hands. 'I knew you were struggling; I just didn't know how to help.'

'You were my friend,' I say, grabbing his hand. 'You have no idea how much that helped.'

He smiles, gripping my hand.

I pick my sandwich up with my free side and take a bite, spilling it all over my face.

He uses his other hand, the one not holding on to me, to wipe me down like a child, then puts a finger in the cream on top of his apple pie and dabs it on the end of my nose.

'Ash Anderson, I will END you,' I laugh, as he grabs my other hand before I can retaliate.

'I think that's unlikely,' he teases.

'You'd better let go of me, or I'll tell Elina about . . .'

'What?' Elina says, turning towards us, suddenly interested. 'Tell Elina about what?'

303

'You better not,' he says, trying to put his hand over my mouth while holding my arms together.

'Mmmmnnnm mmmmm,' I attempt. 'Ash got paint on your blue scarf!' I say from between his fingers.

'What?' she says, crossing her arms. 'The one Nina made? I blamed Rebecca for that!'

Elina and I look at each other, a silent understanding passing between us.

She jumps up and pulls his arms behind his back while I advance with my own finger of cream.

'Stop it, you two. I don't like you being frieeeennnnds,' he shrieks.

'Hey, Ellie,' Shawn says, looking down at the two of us. 'Have you got a minute?'

I stop awkwardly, my finger covered in cream.

'Sure,' I reply.

'Hi,' Jess says, appearing next to Shawn. 'Can I join the queue?' she asks, smiling uneasily.

Elina stares at her, releasing Ash's arms.

'Sure,' I reply again.

'Ladies first,' Shawn offers. So, Jess and I head down to the music room. To the one place things usually make sense. I just hope this time, they make sense to more than just me.

# 60

# That's the Tea

As soon as we reach the music room, Jess launches herself at me.

'I'm sorry,' she says, pulling me into her.

'What are you sorry for?' I ask, surprised. 'I'm the one that was awful.'

I sit down at the piano, and she perches on the bench next to me.

'I knew you weren't feeling good, E. I just knew it. You're my best friend, and I knew. And I didn't do anything about it. Not enough, anyway.'

'It's not your job to look after me, Jess.'

'I could say the same for you,' she says, raising an eyebrow.

'Look, about you and Elina,' I continue awkwardly. 'It's none of my business. I should never have said anything. I want to support you, I just, sometimes I don't know how to do that without getting too involved.'

She looks down at her knees. 'It's OK. You were probably right.'

I sit back, surprised be her candour.

'Billie and Addy tell me what I want to hear. I guess that's why I've been spending so much time with them lately. You know me better than anyone,' she sighs. 'It's kind of hard to argue with your logic sometimes.'

'I am very sage,' I say seriously.

She pushes me light-heartedly. 'I said *sometimes*,' she jokes. 'But I'm sorry if I've felt a bit distant. I just needed to hear that I'd done the right thing. That I hadn't just ruined the one thing that's made me the happiest in my whole life.'

'Oh, Jess,' I say, turning to hug her.

'I knew you were freaking out. I just knew it,' she continues into my shoulder. 'It's like anything to do with the baby, or the end of the year, you just clammed up. But I had no idea you were having panic attacks again.'

Jess is the only person, other than my family, who knows about my panic attacks. I'd only just stopped having them when we started high school, and every so often I'd still occasionally forget how to breathe. Usually on Amis's birthday, when she'd sit me in a corner and hold my hand until it was over.

I sit back and look at her. 'I didn't really know myself,' I tell her. 'It was so slow at first, I didn't even know it was happening; and then I'd just be in the middle of one, and it was awful. Like nothing would ever feel better again.'

She squeezes my arm. 'Ash told me what happened at the wedding,' she says gently. 'He called me and Hayley. He wanted us to know what was going on.'

'Did he?' I ask, embarrassed.

'I think he's been calling your parents, like, every day to check on you.'

I ignore the comment. 'Hayley's still angry with me, though.'

'It's not personal. She's not talking to me either.'

'Oh,' I say, now worried.

'So, what's going on with you and Ash?' she whispers. 'I mean, obviously Shawn's in the queue behind me, so you need to spill the tea quickly. Or is Shawn the tea? Who have you spilled? What's going on?'

'Nothing's going on,' I say immediately. 'With either of them – and it never should have been. I need to focus on the exams, Jess. And therapy. And writing a song for Gabrielle. I used to find it so easy to write songs, but ever since "As It Seems" went viral, I can't seem to find the words any more.'

She hugs me again. 'You've got a lot going on,' she says sympathetically.

'So have you,' I reply, squeezing her hand. 'Have you spoken to Elina?' I ask delicately.

'She doesn't want to talk to me. And I never see her without Jane. Are they . . .' she asks, looking down at her hands. 'Are they together?'

'I don't know,' I offer honestly. 'But I could ask?'

She shakes her head. 'I messed up,' she says tearfully. 'I thought I was doing the right thing. I thought it would be easier this way. Less painful. Breaking up now, instead of when she's in London and she's met someone else.'

'You sound like me, Jess.'

Which is why, I realise, I didn't really fight her when she said she needed to break up with Elina in the first place. When everything was great between them. Because it's exactly what I would have done. Because when you know what it's like for people to leave you, when you know how much it hurts, you want to control that feeling, do anything you can to make it manageable; to at least know it's coming.

She smiles sadly. 'That's the tea,' she says quietly. 'I made a mistake.'

Should I tell her that Elina might be staying? Should I tell her that she may have lost her for nothing?

'Well, as you once said to me, Jessica Leigh King, you have to be honest about your feelings. Take a risk. Because whether it works out or not, if you care for someone, they're always worth putting yourself out for.'

'You really think so?'

'I really think so.'

'What should I do?' she asks.

'Go big or go home,' I say confidently, when we're interrupted by a sudden knock on the door.

'Hello?' I call out.

Shawn pokes his head in the door. 'Is this your new office?'

'Old office,' I smile back.

'She's ready to see you now,' Jess says, standing up.

I stand up and give her what seems like the millionth hug of the last ten minutes. I wish I could hug her forever.

'We'll talk later,' she says, holding my hand.

As she leaves the room, Shawn looks over at me.

'I thought we could try and write a new song,' he smiles.

'Together?' I ask.

'Together,' he clarifies.

'I don't know, Shawn,' I say unhappily. 'I feel like I've run out of songs.'

'That's OK,' he says gently. 'We all get writer's block sometimes, you just need to work through it.'

'I've tried,' I say, thinking about the hours I've sat, my fingers hovering over the keys.

'Remember what I said about harnessing the uncomfortable stuff. The fear and all that – and using it in your songs?'

'Yeah,' I say slowly.

'Maybe that's what's been blocking you,' he says carefully. 'The fact you haven't been harnessing it, you haven't been dealing with it. Maybe something's come unstuck now. Maybe now you're talking about it . . . Maybe if we try together,' he coaxes.

'I'm so tired, Shawn. I just don't know if I can.'

'What used to make you feel better? When you had stuff going on?'

'Writing . . .' I admit.

'I'll get my guitar,' he continues.

Baby steps, I think.

Baby steps.

# 61

# Something That
# Needs to Be Said

He was right.

Writing together feels like someone's given me an oxygen mask. Reminded me how to take breaths. Something's forming. Coming together. Something that needs to be said.

We spend the rest of the lunch hour in the music room, then agree to meet again tomorrow. To give ourselves until the end of the week to write something, then try it out at practice on Friday. We've got our gig at Blues Factory on Saturday, a kind of final blowout before we all go on study leave, and we want to try and play it then if we can.

I hug Shawn goodbye when the bell rings, feeling so lucky to have him.

'Thanks,' I say shyly. 'I really needed that.'

He's packing his guitar away, his eyes thoughtful. 'I'm going to miss writing with you.'

'Miss it?' I ask, looking up at him as I collect my bag from the floor.

He flushes. 'Ellie, I'm not sure yet, but I think I might be going to Berklee.'

I reach for his arm. 'As in Berklee School of Music, Boston, Massachusetts?' I probe.

'I wasn't sure about the address,' he teases, 'anyway,' he continues more seriously, 'I don't want you to think that's why I said what I said this morning. I didn't respect you when you asked for space, but I haven't stopped caring about you.' He puts his hand behind his head awkwardly. 'I really wanted things to work out. I still really, really like you, which is *not great*, to be honest, given, you know . . .' And he's almost talking to himself now. 'Look,' he says, coming back to me, 'I haven't told the band, because I haven't really fully decided yet.'

'Shawn,' I breathe. 'This is so exciting.'

'Really?' he says, his face breaking into a relieved smile.

'I would never have wanted to be any part of the reason you didn't go,' I say uncomfortably. 'And I kind of felt like maybe I was, at least, part of it.'

He looks at the floor.

'I need to figure some stuff out, Shawn, and it wasn't really fair of me, trying to be with you while I did that.'

He nods, still staring down.

'I still care about you too. And I really like you too, it's just, like, timing, or I don't know. There's so much going on.'

He nods again.

'I'd better run,' I say, looking at the time. The bell rang five minutes ago and even though Mr Gorley no longer seems to care what we're doing or where we are, given we aren't going to be his problem for much longer (his words, not mine), I still want to try and catch Hayley on our way to drama.

I lean up to give him another hug and kiss him softly on the cheek.

He pulls me into him, and we stand there a minute longer.

'Bye,' he says softly.

'Bye,' I say, squeezing his arm, and I run off to see the teacher who doesn't care about my existence and the friend who isn't speaking to me.

Because that's how today is going to roll. But I think I can handle it. At least, I know I can try.

# ♡ Song 2 ♡

## Not Done Yet – Intro, Verse, Chorus, Middle Eight

When you feel like you've been silenced, when the world can no longer hear you, sometimes you shut down.

You stop trying. You tell yourself you can't change. That the world can't change.

But it can.

Everything changes. All the time.

Scarily. Frequently. Against all odds, change happens. Life continues.

*I'm sorry I didn't do better*
*And I'm sorry I broke you in two*
*And I'm sorry I can't forgive myself*
*Until you forgive me too*

And this song is that feeling. Knowing you've made mistakes, but it's possible to fix them.

It's about being sorry. And scared.

Not being ready to let go.

Not being ready to give up.

Because someone once told me, when you love someone, you have to be honest about your feelings.

Which is a ballad and a pop song, and a bit of indie rock thrown in for good measure.

Because that's me.

And me?

I'm not done yet.

# 62

# Self-Protection

'Hi,' I say when I sit down next to Hayley, heavy breathing from my quasi-run up the corridor.

'Hey,' she says, refusing to look at me.

So, she is speaking to me. Even if it is monosyllabically.

'How are you?'

'OK,' she says, looking draw, in a way I should have noticed this morning.

'Are you feeling OK?' I ask, reaching out to her.

She nods, pulling away.

'Are you angry with me?' I whisper, as Mr Gorley walks in, his battered briefcase swinging beside him.

She shakes her head.

'Hayley,' I hiss, poking her. 'What's wrong?'

She shakes her head again, clearly fighting back tears.

Mr Gorley takes the register and we put our hands up, the two of us on different planets.

When we leave form and head towards drama, I grab her arm.

'We're going to be late,' she says angrily, as I pull her towards the girls' toilets on the first floor. They're particularly grim. A place you only go if you're desperate. Two out of three of the stall doors are broken and the toilets only flush if you push the handles at a specific angle with roughly the same amount of force it takes to cycle a bike up a hill, or what I'm guessing would be the amount of force required to cycle a bike up a hill – because I can't do that. Cycle a bike. Up a hill or otherwise.

'Hay,' I say, as she sullenly stands against a wall. 'Talk to me.'

'About what?' she says, staring out of the window. 'I hate these toilets,' she mutters.

'I don't love them either, but that's not the point.'

She turns towards me. 'I'm sorry. I've been horrible today. I'm sorry for everything you're going through,' she snivels.

'You don't need to be sorry. It's not your fault.'

'Well, I am. And I wanted to be a better friend today, I really did. I know you're struggling, and I think I've known it for a long time, it's just that . . .'

'What?' I ask gently. 'You're struggling too?'

She nods.

'I'm sorry if I've been following you around, Hay. I was worried about you. I wasn't trying to make it about me, or annoy you, I just didn't want to miss anything the way I did before.'

'I know that,' she says, crying. 'Honestly, I do. I don't know why I was being so mean to you.'

'You were fine,' I say, trying to put my arm around her. She shrugs me off.

'The reason I didn't talk to you about coming out wasn't because you were less important to me, Ellie.'

I cut her off quickly. 'I can't believe I said that. It's pathetic. I was being pathetic.'

'You weren't being pathetic. You were right. I was avoiding you. I wasn't telling you everything. Because you know me better than anyone, and I knew if you were watching me too closely, you'd know I wasn't doing very well.'

I stand still. Waiting for her to tell me in her own words, in her own time.

'I'm not doing very well, Ellie,' she says, starting to break down. 'I can't stop making myself sick. I can't stop thinking about my body, all the time. *All the time*,' she whimpers.

'Oh, Hay,' I say, pulling her into me. She collapses a little. As if she's been waiting to let herself. 'It isn't instant. Getting better never is,' and I'm crying myself now. 'But we're going to get better. Both of us. We're going to put the work in. We're going to try. And look, we're talking about it. That's a start, isn't it?'

'Yes, in this disgusting toilet,' she says, sniffing dramatically.

I laugh. 'But still,' I offer.

She nods, then looks me in the eyes.

'I got offered a place. At BackStage,' she says quietly. 'I got the offer letter this morning.'

'That's amazing,' I say, widening my eyes.

'Mum won't let me go,' she says, her eyes dead. 'She says I'm not ready to be on my own yet. I've ruined everything, Ellie. I've ruined everything because I can't get better. Because I'm not strong enough to get better.'

'Just stop it,' I say, facing her. I've got hold of her arms now and I'm shaking her. 'You are strong, and you will get over this. It's just

317

not the right time for you. Something else is supposed to happen at a different time, when you're ready for it – and it will happen, Hay, it will. But your mum's right. You can't go when you're not well. You have to focus on getting better. That's what you have to focus on. Nothing else matters, OK?'

'What if this is my only chance?' she asks in a tiny voice. 'What if I've ruined everything?'

'Then we're both ruined, because Shawn's going to America and the band's going to break up and the record contract isn't going to happen, and I can't believe this is my *only* chance. I have to believe that some stuff isn't supposed to happen yet. That it'll happen when it's supposed to happen.'

We're hugging and crying now, the two of us. Because sometimes things don't work out the way you thought they would; and you know one day you'll look back and know that's exactly how it was all supposed to be. That in that moment of disappointment, something else was hiding. Something you'll know later was the break in a timeline that made something better happen.

I hope.

We hope.

'I hate this place,' she mutters again. 'I used to come here a lot,' she says, her voice wobbly. 'To be sick and stuff.'

'Oh God, let's get out of here. I'm sorry.'

I pull her towards the door, her eyes streaming with tears, and down the corridor in the direction of the drama studio.

'I can't go in,' she says, her voice cracking.

'It's OK,' I say, grabbing her hand. 'I'll get Mrs Aachara.'

I walk into drama twenty minutes late, and everyone stares at me.

We're practising our final pieces, critiquing each other. Hayley's usually the first person in.

James looks at me nervously, as if he knows.

'Where have you been, Ellie?' Mrs Aachara asks, walking over to me.

'I'm really sorry,' I whisper. 'It's Hayley. She's . . . she's outside. She's not . . . very good.'

She nods her head at me efficiently, as if bracing herself for what she knows is about to happen. 'Should I call her mother?'

'Yes,' I say certainly, 'but I think she wants to talk to you first. I think she needs to know it's going to be OK from someone that isn't her mum.'

She nods again and heads out the door, just as James walks over.

'Ellie,' he says. 'Where's Hayley?'

I shake my head. 'James, she's . . .'

'She didn't get in,' he says in a soft voice.

'She did,' I state, 'but she can't go. She's not . . . she's not ready yet.'

He hangs his head.

'What about you?' I ask. 'Have you heard anything yet?'

'No, but I'm guessing if she's heard and I haven't, it can't be good.'

I put my hand on his arm sympathetically. 'You didn't hear it from me, OK? She'll tell you when she's ready.'

'Thanks,' he says, smiling. 'Do you think it ever gets easier?' he asks suddenly.

'What?' I ask, distracted by Jeffrey Dean's kimono. I wonder what he's doing for his final piece, and then I don't. Whatever it is, I'm pretty sure I'm going to be offended by it.

'Loving someone who doesn't love you back,' James says quietly.

I squeeze his arm. 'I think it does,' I say unsurely. 'I mean, it definitely does,' I confirm, watching his face fall.

And in that moment, I can't help but think about Sadie. About how much she clearly likes James, and how much he clearly wants to like her back. But you can't force feelings when they aren't there. Force yourself to be over someone when you're not. Even when things have changed, and you know you should be.

And for some reason thinking about Sadie makes me think about Shawn, and how really, they're not that different. That James and I, we're not that different.

How I hurt Shawn, trying not to get hurt myself.

But that's the thing about self-protection. Sometimes, when you try to protect yourself, you inevitably end up hurting someone else.

# 63

# Forever My Friend

I'm on my way to therapy after school when I run into Ash on the street.

'Are you going to the bus stop?' he queries. 'Is it OK if I walk with you?'

'No,' I say, suddenly embarrassed. 'I'm, um … I'm walking somewhere else. To meet someone else.'

'Oh,' he says, looking away. 'You know, you can just tell me if you're going to meet Shawn.'

'I'm not,' I say, staring at my feet. 'I mean, Shawn and I we're not, we aren't … we're not a *thing* any more.'

'A thing?' he questions.

'I need to get through the exams,' I explain. 'And he's leaving,' I say, blushing, 'there's no point,' I ramble, 'I'm not ready. The timing's just . . .' My attempts to finish a sentence fail horribly until he takes pity on me.

'I get it,' he smiles. 'But you'll see him in the holidays and stuff. It might work out,' he says reassuringly.

'That's not really what I meant—' I continue, but he cuts me off.

'So, where *are* you going, then?' he asks curiously.

Lie, Ellie. Just *lie*. You're good at that.

'If you really want to know, I'm going to see my therapist.'

Ugh. Why do you have to choose *now* to be truthful?

I stare at him, expecting him to run in the opposite direction.

'I'll walk you,' he offers.

So, now he thinks I'm falling apart. That he has to take some kind of *responsibility* for me, and offer to walk me places, just in case I fall to pieces on the way to wherever I'm going.

'Why?' I ask, irritated. 'I don't need a babysitter. I'm not going to have a panic attack just because Shawn and I broke up.'

'I didn't think you were.'

He's looking at me with that face, those eyes, the ones that say: stop doing this to yourself, there is nothing wrong with asking for help. Or maybe it's just me, telling myself that.

'But if you want to walk on your own, it's fine,' he continues carefully.

'I'm sorry,' I sigh. 'I guess I'm just a bit embarrassed.'

'About what?' he says without missing a beat.

'I don't know,' I say clumsily. 'It just feels like I'm, I don't know, *broken* or something.'

'I talk to someone,' he says, looking me in the eye.

'You never told me that before.'

The sun's shining, and I look up at him, the light cutting across his tan skin, his dark curls momentarily golden. I reach out to touch his arm, feeling weirdly maternal. Like I want to make sure he's OK. As if I'm not the one that's a mess, even though he's never made me feel like I am.

He's wearing a short-sleeved white T-shirt with the words, THE FUTURE IS FEMALE, on it. The colour accenting the line between where his sleeve ends and the darker skin on his forearms.

'I guess we weren't always as honest with each other as we should have been.' He looks directly at me. Into me.

'I've been seeing Dr Myers since my dad died. I'm still screwed-up,' he laughs, 'but I'd be a lot worse without him. Anyway,' he says softly, 'I'll let you go.'

'No,' I stutter. 'Walk with me. I want you to.'

He takes my bag off my shoulder. Something he used to do all the time when we were dating.

'I'll carry this,' he says, putting it over his own shoulder.

'You just want my Beatles bag,' I tease. 'That's all you've ever been interested in.'

'No,' he says bluntly. 'That isn't what I was interested in.'

I hear him stop himself from starting another sentence. I want to ask him what it is that he wanted. If it's past tense – or if he still wants it now. But I don't.

'So, how are you?' I ask, as we start walking. 'I heard your mum was staying.' I sneak a look at him, turning slightly as we go.

'Fine,' he replies dismissively. 'Everything's fine.'

'Why do I get the feeling that's the not-being-quite-honest-with-each-other thing we were just talking about? Your mum's staying. Elina might be staying. Your mum's dating. You must be feeling something,' I probe gently.

He sighs, his shoulders slumping. 'I always thought Elina and I would go to school together. We've always done everything together.'

'Then maybe it's time for something new,' I remark softly. 'You can't be together forever. At some point, your paths were bound to diverge.'

'Our paths,' he repeats slowly, 'were bound,' he continues in the same voice, 'to *diverge*. Someone's been doing their therapy homework,' he teases.

I hit him lightly in the chest. 'Shut up,' I say, blushing. 'You know what I mean.'

'You're right,' he says, holding his hands up. 'I know we can't do everything together, but it's what we planned. Going back to London. It feels weird doing it without them.'

'So, are you *definitely* going then? To Saint Martins?' And it's the first time I've realised I was hoping he'd stay. That he'd do what Elina was doing. Go to University of the Arts here, in the city. That I'd still get to see him.

He nods. 'I got in, and that's a big deal, Ellie. It's what I've always wanted. I can't even imagine going anywhere else. It's just strange to think of doing it without Elina.'

'You're not doing it without her. You're always going to be there for each other. You're *bound*,' I say, emphasising my therapy word. 'You'll visit. She'll visit. It's a couple of hours away on a train, it's not a different continent.'

'Not like you and Shawn,' he says, smiling.

'Not like me and Shawn,' I rabbit.

'I know you're right,' he smiles. 'But I'm going to miss it here.'

'Whhhhy?' I ask sarcastically. 'You're going to *London*. London, Ash. This place is exactly what this place is,' I sigh.

'It is, but everything I love is here,' he says meaningfully.

OK, heart, stop. I mean, don't stop, because stopping would make me dead, but, you know, *stop* because he's talking about Elina and Kyra, not me. And I don't want him to be talking about me. SO THERE.

SO THERE, HEART.

'So, Mr Green,' I continue, 'how's, er, that? The dating thing.' I imagine for a second that it's *my* mum dating a teacher at school and decide it can't be a good thing. Although Mrs Aachara seems happy, and they look ridiculously beautiful together, and Ash is leaving, and really, it's *her* life, and I want to mention all this to him, but he looks suddenly a bit angry.

'Mum seems happy,' he says, shrugging and looking away as his pace quickens. 'That's all that matters.'

And I want to tell him that's very mature of him, but I'm having very immature thoughts suddenly, so it feels wrong to say it.

'So, does he, like, sleep over a lot?'

Why am I being weird and childish and euphemistic when what I really want to say is: does he walk around without his shirt on? Have you worked out if he's a real human man, or an actual Greek god?

He gives me a look.

'What?' I blush.

'Eleanor Eve Pillai,' he lectures. 'I know you think he's hot. You're not exactly subtle about it.'

'I don't!' I interrupt, lying; and now I'm seriously concerned, because if I'm not very subtle about Mr Green, what else am I not very subtle about?

He gives me another look.

'I mean, he's not *un*-hot,' I admit slowly. 'He's not, like, cold or anything. He's a perfectly reasonable, decent form of a man.'

He grins.

'He's very fit. He takes care of himself. Which is good for your mum, and, like, you, because you don't have to worry if there are things that need doing while you're away that require, like, height, or weight, or *muscle*. I'm not being sexist. I'm sure Kyra can do all that stuff herself, but it's nice to have, like, the *help*. And I think he'll be very helpful.'

'Helpful?' he smiles.

'Yes,' I confirm. 'I think he's very helpful, that's all.'

'Riggggghhhhttt,' he says, rolling the word around in his mouth.

'Shut up, Ash,' I say, glaring at him.

'I didn't say anything.' He grins again.

'Whatever you're thinking, just stop thinking it. Immediately,' I reply, my skin flush like I've just been for a run.

Mr Green. Going for a run.

Stop it, Ellie. You are a sick individual.

'You don't know what I'm thinking,' he replies.

'I do. So, stop.'

He watches me, his eyes unreadable.

'Ellie?' he asks gently, as we continue up Weston Street. 'Maybe this isn't the right time to talk about this, but . . .' he trails away uneasily.

'Talk about what?' I ask, linking arms with him as we walk.

He stares at the ground and clears his throat nervously.

'Why do you think things didn't work out between us?'

I stop in my tracks and just stand there. Because I'm not expecting it. The directness of the question. The unsaid words that have hung between us over the last few months.

'Why do *you* think we didn't work out?' I ask, turning the question back on him as I move to face him.

'Because I was jealous of Shawn,' he says quickly, 'and weird about Rebecca, and I didn't visit you in the hospital after the accident. I wasn't good enough for you.'

'That's not true,' I say, tilting my head to the side to watch him. 'You were *never* not good enough for me. I just wanted you to talk to me. I wanted us to talk to each other. Like, after the accident.'

'At the hospital.' He cringes. 'When your dad said I hurt you. That my dad would be ashamed of me. I don't know.' He shrugs and turns away, refusing to look at me. 'I thought, maybe he was right. That I was hurting you by being with you. I know I haven't been the son my dad would have been proud of, but I'm trying, Ellie.'

I put my arms around his neck and pull him into me suddenly, his much taller frame momentarily lost inside mine

'I'm sorry,' I repeat, over and over. 'I'm so, so sorry he said that. And I know he's sorry too. He didn't mean it. Your dad would have been proud of you no matter what, Ash. You have to know that. You *have* to know that. And I don't blame you for not wanting to see my dad after that, or me, or for falling apart. I don't really blame you for anything. I guess I was just angry because I needed you. I just didn't realise you needed me too.'

And it feels so right to finally say the words out loud. That I was angry. Not just with him, but with myself too.

'I let you down,' I whisper into his shoulder. 'I'm sorry.'

He pulls away to look at me.

'You didn't let me down. You've never let me down, Ellie. And I'm sorry about Rebecca. She's like my sister,' he continues.

'Your Very Annoying Sister.'

He laughs.

'True. But she's family. I should have explained that, instead of using her as someone to hide behind because I was scared of how I felt about you. I just thought you'd think it was all too much drama.'

Now it's my turn to laugh.

'Life has been one long drama since you arrived, Anderson.'

'Coincidence?' he teases, screwing his face up.

'Mmmmm,' I joke.

He kisses the top of my head, like my dad does when he comes in to say goodnight, then looks suddenly awkward.

'Sorry. I didn't mean to . . .'

'Bend down,' I request, tugging at his T-shirt. He bends down compliantly, and I plant a kiss on top of his dark curly head.

'There. We're even. Think of it as more of a Granny kiss.'

'You'd need to squeeze my cheeks first.'

I stand on my tiptoes and squeeze them. Hard.

'Ow!'

'You *said* hard!' I protest.

'Are you still angry with me?' he kids, rubbing his face.

'No,' I say seriously. 'I'm not. And about Shawn.' He stops smiling and looks at me just as seriously as I'm looking at him. 'You were right to be jealous. I did . . . feel something for him, and I wasn't honest about it.'

'That's OK,' he half smiles. 'I like him. He's good for you.'

'We're not, we aren't,' I struggle. 'That's not how I . . .' I attempt.

'I like this honesty thing,' he says, starting to walk again as he links my arms back through his. 'I wish we'd started it sooner.'

'Anyway,' I counter. 'Are you coming to watch us at Blues Factory on Saturday?'

He nods. 'Yeah, I'm going with Hannah, actually.'

'Oh. Cool.'

Cool? *Cool?* Do I really think it's cool or is my nose growing at the speed of sound? Am I going to get to therapy and realise I'm a

328

female Pinocchio like my Aunty Deena who has a nose that looks like a hot-air balloon?

'Just as friends,' he says casually.

'Oh. I mean, yeah. Whatever. Friends,' I say, trying to emulate his coolness. 'Like us. We're friends. We're all friends now. Which is great really, isn't it? Anyhoo . . .' I go on.

*Anyhoo??*

'I'm just over there,' I say, pointing to a red-brick building on the corner of Abbey Street.

'I'll walk you over,' he says, gesturing towards the building.

'No, no, it's fine,' I say, shaking my head.

'I don't mind,' he replies, holding on to my bag.

'Don't worry. I can take it from here,' I say officiously, lifting the bag off his shoulder. I lean up to hug him lightly. 'Thanks for the walk – and the honest conversation. I'm sure Dr Sharma will be very proud of me.'

He salutes.

'Roger that,' I joke, saluting him in return.

'Anytime, Roger,' he smiles.

We're friends, I think as I walk away from him. Ash and I are friends now, and I don't want to ruin that. Ever. Because being friends with him means more to me than I want to admit.

I buzz the door for Dr Sharma, and Elaine, her secretary, lets me in.

She nods as she watches me walk in, marking my name off her list like it's the morning register at school. Ellie Pillai Has Arrived at Therapy. Ellie Pillai Is Committed to Getting Better. Being Better.

As I sit in the waiting area, leafing through an article about mental fitness, a message appears on my phone.

**Ash:**

'Forever My Friend', Ray LaMontagne

It's a link to a song. Our way of communicating; like ordinary people do through emojis and abbreviations.

**Ellie:**

I ♥ this song

I can feel my heart beating, thick and loud. In my chest. In my throat. The rhythm of my breath as it rises and falls.

**Ash:**

I press the link, my earphones already in.

And I listen to the sound of jubilant, soulful, folksy guitars riffs, Ray LaMontagne singing that maybe it's wrong, and maybe it's right.

Wondering.

If I'll ever know for sure.

# 64

# Oh

Shawn and I have been working on 'Not Done Yet' all week. The two of us. At lunchtimes. The one time of the day I don't feel guilty for not revising.

It's starting to take shape now. Starting to feel like something good.

'What do you think about this?' I ask, using one finger to create a riff on the piano.

'I like it. We could add this,' he says, mimicking the riff on his guitar. 'Maybe get the bass to echo the bottom note?'

'Yes,' I say excitedly. 'And I have some lyrics.'

I pass him the paper with the lyrics I handwrote on the bus this morning.

He peruses them, his eyebrows rising as he stares at the words.

'Wow,' he says slowly.

'Wow – good? Or wow – bad?' I ask nervously.

'Just wow,' he says, looking up to meet my eye. 'You know, sometimes I think you're better at communicating through songs than you are in real life.'

'Oh,' I say quietly, unsure of whether that's a compliment. It definitely doesn't feel like a compliment.

He stands up and walks over to me, sitting next to me on the piano bench. 'I just mean, I wish you'd been honest with me about how you were feeling before.'

'About what?' I ask stupidly.

'I mean, everything, but specifically, me.'

'Oh,' I say again, now sure this is Not Complimentary.

'I'm going to Berklee,' he says surely. 'I sent my acceptance off this morning.'

'That's great.'

'I think it is,' he smiles. 'I really think it is.'

'How's Benji taking it?'

'Not well,' he says, frowning. 'I mean, he's happy for me, but I think he was hoping that things worked out with Gabrielle, I'd stay.'

'And you wouldn't?' I clarify.

He shakes his head. 'I have to do this, Ellie. I've got so much more to learn before I commit to what I do with any of this.'

'You have to put yourself first, work out what you want, Shawn.'

He breathes out heavily. 'I know. The boys are just so disappointed.'

'If the band's meant to be something, it will be,' I say sagely.

He nods. 'And Benji will be fine,' he says, as if reassuring himself. 'I'll be home every holiday and we'll see each other all the time.'

'It's not the same though, is it?' I ask unhelpfully. 'You'll have all these things going on when he's not around. All these inside jokes and stories about things he won't know about.'

He gives me a look, cocking his head to one side.

'I guess so,' he says carefully. 'But Benji's always going to be my best friend. What we are right now isn't going to change. I mean, maybe it'll change in the future; maybe we won't be best friends forever.'

'Don't tell him that,' I joke.

'My point is, nothing can take away from what we are right now. He'll always be the person I was the most afraid to tell about Berklee,' he laughs. 'The person I knew would care the most.'

'You mean, unlike me,' I say quietly. 'That I wasn't upset.'

'No.' He shakes his head. 'I mean, I was glad you were so cool about it, but then I just thought, why doesn't she care? Why aren't you asking me not to go?'

'I'd never do that,' I say defensively. 'It's your life.'

He looks down at his feet. 'That's not the real reason though, is it?'

'Shawn, please,' I say, turning towards the piano, 'can we not?'

'It's OK. I'm not upset about it, Ellie.'

'About what?'

'About the fact I was never the person you were upset about.'

'Shawn, I told you. I really liked you. I still really like you, it's just—' I try to finish the sentence.

'You like me,' he says softly. 'But you love him,' he finishes.

'That's not true,' I say flatly. 'I mean, it's true that I like you,' I fumble. 'But Ash and I, we're just friends.'

'You've never been just friends,' he smiles. 'I saw it at the wedding. He was the only one you'd respond to. The only one who could get through to you; and afterwards, he wouldn't leave you. I was with him. He made your aunt take him back to Hope's house, just so he could be there when you fell asleep. So he'd know you were OK.'

'Because he felt guilty for what happened after the accident,' I say quickly. 'For not coming to see me, for Rebecca, and breaking up with

333

me on my birthday. He's trying to make it up to me. To prove something to himself, that's all.'

'I don't know,' Shawn says, looking at his knees. 'I just know whatever you feel for him, you never felt for me.'

I put my hand on his for a second and hold it. 'You're right,' I breathe. 'I'm sorry. It's just that when I'm with you, I know where I am. I know what you want – and I never knew where I was with Ash. It feels easy with you, and it should feel easy, shouldn't it? Liking someone?'

'Honestly?' he smiles. 'It's never felt easy with you, Ellie, and I've never known what you want.'

'Oh.'

'Look, I'm not saying any of this to get at you. I just think you need to be honest with yourself, and I think I deserve that too.'

'I'm sorry,' I repeat. 'I'm sorry if I hurt you. I didn't mean to.'

He leans down to hug me, and we hold on to each other for longer than feels strictly necessary; because I'm going to miss him, and it's the end of something, and the ends of things have always scared me, and it's like he knows that. Like he's holding on to me to stop me from falling apart.

'I'm going to miss you so much,' I murmur.

'Not as much as Benji,' he replies.

And at that, we both start laughing.

'I'll miss you too,' he says, letting go and leaning back to look at me. 'Promise me you'll keep an eye on Benji.'

'You couldn't stop me.'

'And that you'll tell Ash how you feel before he goes away.'

'I told you. We're just friends.'

He hands me back the paper I gave him, covered in the lyrics I scribbled on the bus.

'Maybe read this again,' he says, standing up.

He walks back over to the corner of the room and picks up his guitar.

'Let's give it another try,' he continues. 'Before we try it out with the band tonight. You're the leader now, you know that? You'll need to bring that frontwoman energy Gabrielle kept talking about.'

'Ha ha,' I say sarcastically.

'I'm serious,' he says solemnly. 'That was the last thing I was going to ask you. To look after the band.'

'Oh,' I say.

Oh.

# 65

# Wet Blankets

The Blues Factory is packed. It feels like every kid in years 11 to 13 is here tonight, and the band isn't feeling great. In fact, the sense of Not Greatness is palpable.

Mum and Dad were worried about letting me play tonight. About the pressure I'm putting on myself when I'm also still feeling Not Great. But Dr Sharma said if I felt up to it, I should try it. That I won't know what my boundaries are unless I test them. It also didn't hurt to point out that they were happy for me to take the exams. That when it's something they thought was important, they were more than happy for me to push myself. Hope said that was probably what pushed them over the edge, but I wasn't trying to push anyone over anything, it's just things have to change, and that's about me being honest. Saying how I feel about things, and not just swallowing them down.

Because I was never going to miss tonight. Not when it might be the last time we play together, all five of us. Not when Lucas and Elliott and Benji think this is the end. That without Shawn there's no development deal, no taking this any further. This is an ending, a scary

336

new place – or, as Dr Sharma keeps telling me, the start of a new story. Something I shouldn't be scared of, something I should embrace.

I want to be there for the band. For Shawn, who feels terrible for making a decision that's right for him, but like it's hurting the people he cares about; but also for me, to prove that I can. More than that, it's for Jessica. Because the song we wrote, the one Shawn keeps telling me I wrote about Ash, isn't about Ash. It's about Jessica and Elina. About all the things Jess told me she feels about breaking up with Elina. Because tonight is about helping my best friend too.

'Hey, guys,' I say cheerily. 'How are we all doing?'

A series of grunts accompanies my question, which appear to make up a response.

Shawn looks pained.

'This is going to be great,' I say overenthusiastically.

They ignore me.

'I thought we sounded great yesterday,' I continue. 'When we tried out the new song,' I say pointlessly.

'Yeah, it was good,' Shawn mutters unenthusiastically. There seems to be either a huge surplus of enthusiasm or a huge dearth of enthusiasm in this room; never an ordinary level of it, like there should be before a gig.

'Ellie,' Hope says, putting her face around the door of the dressing room we've been given as if we're actually important. 'It's really busy out there,' she says excitedly. 'Are you guys ready?'

Are we ready?

'Yep,' I say, trying to muster the lacking enthusiasm of my band mates.

'What's the point?' Lucas says irritably.

'Sounds a bit existential angst for me,' I joke. 'I don't know if there's a point in most things, but tonight, it's about having fun.'

'Fun?' Elliott says morosely. 'This morning I thought we were going to get a record contract; now our lead singer's moving to the other side of the world.'

'What about Ellie?' Hope pipes up.

They turn to stare at her. Benji more than the rest of them.

'Isn't she your lead singer too?'

'I mean, yeah,' Lucas says slowly. 'But they wanted all of us. Shawn and Ellie.'

'Who said they don't want you any more?' she asks snippily. 'Did this Gabrielle person say that?'

'No,' Lucas responds. 'But, I mean, it's pretty obvious.'

'What's pretty obvious is nothing's going to happen to anyone, if this is a terrible gig. So, buck up.'

*Buck up??*

'Buck up?' Benji queries.

'Yeah,' she says, faltering slightly. 'It's not over until it's over. It was Ellie's song that went viral – no offence,' she says, turning to Shawn.

'None taken,' he smiles.

'So, you still have every chance of getting this development thing you all want. So just Buck Up.'

'OK, OK,' Benji says, putting his hands up. 'Bucking.'

'She's right,' Lucas admits, as Elliott stares at me. 'Ellie's our best hope. You need to take the lead tonight.'

'Frontwoman energy,' Elliott declares.

'I'm not . . . I don't think I can,' I begin.

'If Ellie's not comfortable,' Shawn says gallantly; and he's always

338

been gallant. He's always been kind and sweet and thoughtful, and it would all be so much easier if I loved him, but I don't. I can't. Not when I'm in love with someone else.

Damn it.

But the least I can do is help out the band. Which means helping out Shawn. Making him feel less guilty about what's happening.

'No,' I say firmly. 'I'll try. If you help me,' I say, looking at him. 'I don't think I can sing lead on everything.'

He nods.

'Great,' Hope says sarcastically. 'Now that we've all decided not to be a big pile of wet blankets—'

'That would be a great name,' Benji interrupts. 'The Wet Blankets.'

She shoots him a look. 'You can get on with this gig and make it the best one you've ever done.'

They nod, slightly roused by her speech.

'I love you,' Benji mouths at her sarcastically.

'I know,' she says, and walks out of the room.

'Come on,' I say, now the pitch of the room feels closer to a normal level of enthusiasm. 'Let's go.'

We put our hands in the middle of us and maintain eye contact.

'WET BLANKETS,' Benji shrieks, as the rest of us roll our eyes.

'Let's just have fun out there,' Shawn says, turning to us.

'OK,' we agree.

So, we do.

# 66

# Not Done Yet

There's good energy in here tonight, almost like I brought my crystals (OK, I *may* have brought my crystals). I'm stepping up, singing lead on some of Shawn's songs, trying to talk in between numbers, shift the focus from him to me.

I'll be honest. It's not entirely successful. I can feel the anxiety rising up in me like a tide. I want to be sick. I want to sit in a corner and repeat that it's OK, over and over, until I actually am OK. I count the lights. But I keep going. Shawn steps in to help, and I realise I need it. That maybe I only have Frontwoman Energy like thirty per cent of the time.

I worry for the band. I worry for what it means for all of us. But I keep going.

Until.

It's the last song before we take a break. Our new song. Mine and Shawn's. But there's someone else we're here to sing it for.

'Sometimes,' I say, stepping out from behind the keyboard, 'we all make mistakes. We say or do something we don't feel we can come back from. And it's like,' I say, removing the microphone from the stand, 'you don't know how it happened, or why you did it. You just know it

340

ruined everything.'

The whole room's silent. Still. I'm holding them in the palm of my hands, in a way I never thought I could hold any room. Any crowd.

I look around at the faces I know. At Shawn, who I like but don't love, who I hurt when I didn't mean to. At James, still half in love with someone who can never love him back. At Hayley, in love with the idea of who she should be, what she should achieve, having to rewrite her story. At Jess and Elina, heartbroken, when all they were trying to do was avoid that exact feeling. We've all made mistakes. All of us. But we're not done yet.

As Shawn strums the first chord, I say:

'We wrote this song about the mistakes we make. About second chances. About change. And someone here tonight asked me to sing it for someone they hurt. Someone they love. Someone they need to say sorry to.'

I beckon Jess towards me and put my hand out, pulling her up onstage.

I can feel her shaking, her body quaking with nerves.

'Elina,' she says, looking out over the crowd. And I can see Elina stood with Ash and Hannah and Jane by the bar.

'I didn't listen to you, and I'm sorry. I'm so sorry I didn't hear you. I was just trying to do the right thing, and I got it so horribly wrong. Because I'm not perfect, and for everyone out there who thinks I've got it all together, I really, really don't – and not being with you just proves that. Because it's all my fault we're not together,' and suddenly she's crying, 'and I don't deserve a second chance, but if I don't ask for one, I'm going to regret it for the rest of my life.' She's holding the crowd in her hand too. Her hair golden like a halo around her shoulders. Her purple denim jumpsuit stark against her fair skin, the silver zip flashing in the light.

'Because you're my person,' she says, her voice cracking, 'and I don't care how far away you're going to be. I don't care how much it's going to hurt if you decide you don't want me. I have to try. I have to tell you how much I love you. That I'll always love you. That you changed my life.'

I'm watching Elina. The way I watched Charles at Aunty Kitty's wedding. Looking to see if she's got that strange shining light on her face. The one that says: you're all I can see. But it isn't there. Jane is. Looking awkward and unhappy, Ash turned towards the bar and away from me.

I take hold of Jess's hand as she moves to the side of the stage.

'Elina, this song is for you,' I say, looking out at her.

I walk back behind the keyboard, Shawn playing the opening refrain on his guitar.

*I ruined everything, it's all my fault*
*And I know that you*
*Don't have to forgive me*
*But forgive me*
*I'm sorry*

I want to see Elina walking towards Jess. I want to feel like the crowd are parting and they're going to find each other; but all I can see is the back of Ash's head. Like he can't bear to look at me, Hannah at his shoulder, her face frozen.

Elina's picking up her bag, putting on her coat, Jane just next to her. Oh God, Jane.

*I still carry all those notes you wrote*
*And that pen you left when you went home*

342

*You're my home*

*Please forgive me*

We haven't thought about her. About whether she and Elina are anything more than friends. Whether this song is going to hurt her. Whether Jess is trying to win a battle she's already lost; or one she can only win when there's a casualty.

Shawn's singing harmony now, his voice railing against mine. It's times like these I feel the most connected to him, like I can see inside him. I remember him telling me that I hurt him. That he deserved the truth. That I needed to be honest with myself.

I know I love Ash. I know it in a way I've never known it before. More than when we were dating, trying to make it all perfect. I know it because he drove my mum back and forth to the hospital when my dad was sick. I know it because he sat with my granny when she was scared. I know it because he takes my calls in the middle of the night. Because he watched me with Shawn and never judged me for not choosing him. I know it because I just know it.

But it isn't enough.

Things are changing, and I can't go backwards.

When the song ends, Jess is crying, and Shawn is telling the crowd we'll be back in twenty minutes. I watch Elina's back as she retreats through the exit.

I turn to Jess.

'Go big or go home,' I whisper.

She nods.

Then she starts running.

343

# 67

# You Broke My Heart

I'm running out the door behind Jess. I don't know why. To support her or to see what happens next, I'm not sure.

'Elina,' she screams, running after her. 'Stop, please.'

I can feel Ash just behind me, where he's left Hannah and Jane at the bar.

'Jess, don't!' Elina shouts, wheeling round to look at her.

'I'm sorry,' Jess says, dejected. 'I'm sorry.' She takes a step backwards, her spine bending in on itself.

I feel myself rushing forwards, my arm around her waist, trying to stop her from falling.

'You told her,' Elina spits at me. 'I thought we were friends, Ellie? I thought I could trust you.'

'What do you mean?' I ask, horrified. 'Told her what?'

'About me staying.'

'What?' Jess says, stunned. 'What are you talking about?' She looks from Elina to me, then back again, her face crumpling.

'I didn't tell her,' I protest. 'I didn't know what you were going to decide. I didn't want to get her hopes up.'

Elina turns to Jess savagely.

'You broke my heart, Jessica.' And she's crying now, the tears uncontrolled. 'I waited for you. I waited until you were ready, even when it meant hiding who I was. Do you know how hard that was for me? Do you know what I had to give up?'

'I know,' Jess whispers. 'I know.'

'No. You don't know, Jess – and then you just break up with me, out of nowhere, and you won't talk to me, you won't look at me. And I'm trying to study, Jess. I'm trying to get through the hardest year of my life, focus on my exams, my future – and my girlfriend, the person I'm in love with, tells me it's going be too hard to stay together if I leave. That she can't be bothered to put the effort in for me.'

Jess is full-on sobbing now, Elina in pieces in front of her.

'H-how,' Jess stutters, 'how can you say that? How can you think I didn't want to put the effort in for you? Look at you,' she says unwaveringly. 'How could *you* want to be with *me*? You were going to leave. You were going to meet somebody better. And I didn't want to stop you, Elina, I didn't want to hold you back. I didn't realise what I was doing. How much I was going to hurt you. And then it was too late, and it had gone too far, and you'd met someone else.'

'Jane's a friend,' Elina cuts in icily. 'She's going through a break-up too. She's been there for me, Jess. Which is more than I can say for you.'

'I wish I'd done it differently,' Jess whispers. 'But I didn't. I was scared. I was a coward. But this was never about you not being worth it. You,' she says, her voice shaking, 'you're everything.'

I watch Elina turn her head away, refusing to look at Jess, her eyes full of tears.

'You've always been everything,' Jess continues. 'But my mum left,' she says, dissolving. 'So it's hard for me to trust people. And I'm sorry. Because I've always been able to trust you. Always. And I don't know why I did what I did, other than I made a mistake. I thought it would end just like it did with her. That you'd go, and things would never be the same.'

'I'm sorry,' Elina says, softening. 'I'm sorry for the way your mum is, Jess. I just don't know if I can get past this.'

I can feel Jess's body slackening in my arms, Ash stood a little way behind us, his eyes boring a hole in the back of my head.

He moves forward and pushes Jess towards Elina gently.

'Just forgive her, Elina.'

Elina stutters in reply, her words lost.

He pushes Jess forward again.

'Just forgive her,' he repeats. 'You love her.'

Jess steps towards Elina.

'I don't care where you go, or what you do,' she breathes. 'I'm going to be there. However hard it is. I don't care. Please give me another chance. Please.'

Elina shakes her head tearfully.

'I'll wait,' Jess replies. 'I'll wait until you're ready to forgive me.'

Oh gods, please, no more waiting.

'You need to talk,' Ash says, watching them both. 'Just the two of you.'

Jess puts her hand out hopefully, and Elina takes it slowly, unsurely.

Ash pulls at my arm as we both step away, his hand slipping through mine as we walk back towards Blues Factory, leaving the two of them alone in the dark.

'You should get back to the band,' he says, as we reach the door.

'You should get back to Hannah,' I reply.

He lets go of my hand. We part ways.

As if nothing ever happened.

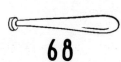

# 68

# The Light

**Hayley:**
👁 hav fallen out

**Ellie:**
revision is worse than school

**Jess:**
i like it

**Ellie:**
WEIRDO

**Hayley:**
WEIRDO

**Ellie:**
sent new song 2 Gabrielle

**Jess:**

**Hayley:**

**Ellie:**

jus need 2 get through next few weeks now

**Ellie:**

exams may end me

**Hayley:**

can't believe i missed sat

**Hayley:**

mum won't let me go *anywhere*

**Hayley:**

am prisoner in own life

**Ellie:**

i wld say u didn't miss much but ...

**Hayley:**

**Hayley:**

what's happening w shawn??

**Ellie:**

he leaves next month

**Jess:**

& ...?

**Ellie:**
will miss him as friend

**Jess:**
how's ur mum?

**Ellie:**
angry & pregnant

**Hayley:**
how ru?

**Ellie:**
ok. therapy helping. how ru?

**Hayley:**
still can't believe james got into backstage
and is ALLOWED 2 GO

**Ellie:**
i can believe it

**Hayley:**
I kno. he deserves it.

**Hayley:**
my life is despair personified

**Ellie:**
u will always be my drama queen @HayleyAttacksFilms

**Ellie:**
also – u promised 2 move to london with ME not james

**Hayley:**

true. u wld miss me 2 much if i wasn't here. u need 2 be watched.

**Jessica:**

she does. should we plan a rota?

**Ellie:**

HA HA

**Jessica:**

who is joking?

**Hayley:**

heard ash not leaving until end aug

**Ellie:**

from who??

**Hayley:**

Jessica ...

**Jessica:**

why don't u just talk 2 him?

**Ellie:**

need 2 focus on exams rn not ash

**Jessica:**

**Hayley:**

**Ellie:**

hav 2 go. granny harassing me.

**Hayley:**

revision tomorrow?

**Ellie:**

here?

**Hayley:**

✓

**Jess:**

c u then

I put my phone down on the bed, and Granny pops her head through the doorway. 'You OK, Eleanor?' she asks gently. She's been like this since the wedding. Careful with me, as though I'm a plate that might break.

'I'm fine, Granny.'

'You study?' she asks, walking towards the bed.

'Um, yeah,' I lie, trying to hide my phone underneath a pillow.

She sits down on the bed next to me. 'Your mother and father love you very much,' she says, reaching forward to sweep a tendril of hair behind my ear. 'The baby will not change that.'

'I know,' I say, feeling that familiar peppery feeling. Like there's something up my nose, stinging my eyes. 'But we never talk about him. We never talk about Amis, Granny.'

'Such a special boy,' she says, smiling. 'Such a naughty boy,' she laughs.

I laugh too. 'He was,' I smile.

'It is painful for your parents to talk about him, I think.'

'It's painful for me to talk about him too,' I protest. 'But he was here, Granny. He existed.' And I'm off. Crying. Trying so hard not to, but it's no longer just below the surface; but right here, where I can touch it and feel it and see it. My grief. Exposed to the world.

She pulls me closer, stroking my hair. 'Come,' she says, standing.

She takes my hand and pulls me towards the corridor and down the stairs, all the while wiping my eyes.

I walk into the kitchen, expecting to be greeted by the usual smell of spices that accompanies anything my grandmother cooks, but instead I see my parents at the table, surrounded by pictures of Amis, his favourite books and toys in piles around them. On the side, there's a bag of Chinese takeaway food and the chocolate cake Mum makes every year to mark his birthday.

'Do you remember when he hid the remote control in my briefcase?' Dad asks when he sees me. 'He'd wrapped it in one of your mother's sanitary towels,' he laughs, picking up a picture.

I nod. My eyes shining with tears.

'You were the only one,' Mum says, starting to cry, 'who could get him to eat at the end. Do you remember that? How you used to feed him with that spoon he loved. How you'd try to make him laugh so he'd open his mouth.'

My face hurts. Like my bones have disintegrated and I'm made of nothing but water.

So, I walk towards Mum and let myself disintegrate into her. Into Granny and Dad sat next to her.

I weep and I weep and I weep; and I hear Mum weep too. Feel her arms tightening around me as she holds me so tight it hurts. Like she needs me. Like for the first time ever, she needs me as much as I need her.

'He was funny and charming and so, so, naughty,' she cries. 'And I didn't know how to grieve him and love you at the same time, and I'm sorry,' she says, her face buried in my hair.

'Your brother,' Dad says, choking, 'was my sunshine, and I found it hard to find my light without him. I was angry. I'm still angry, Ellie, but I have you, and every day I have thanked God for having you. You're my light. My everything. You and your mother and Granny and this baby. This family. You're my light.'

Granny does her best Sri Lankan head shake, her head bobbing from side to side.

'My special girl,' she croons. 'We are always here with you.'

I don't think I can speak any more. There are no words.

But somehow there are.

So, we sit and talk about my brother, about how much we loved him and how missed he is. How blessed we were, by whatever gods we believe in, to have had him in our lives. We go through his toys and books and put aside the things we want to give the new baby, then carefully place the rest in boxes we can get to any time we want to feel closer to him.

We eat Chinese food out of the carton (Granny appalled – why we not use plates?), and laugh, and listen to the Beatles, 'I Am the Walrus', Amis's favourite song. And even though it doesn't make everything better, somehow the weight I've been carrying feels like something lighter. Something I can manage.

When it finally comes time to eat the cake, we light twelve candles, each of us feeling our own thoughts and fears and worries; then blow them out together, remembering those thoughts and fears and worries belong to all of us, always. That together, we can bring the darkness to light.

Because that's what family is.

What *my* family is.

The light.

# 69

# EXAMS

Exams have started.

EXAMS.

The things we've been preparing for, for the last five years. The beginning of the rest of our lives, as Jess likes to call it, just to make it more intimidating.

We see each other outside halls and classrooms, waiting expectantly for our lives to begin, then file in and sit quietly, leafing through page after page of questions, our eyes on the clock.

Part of me is finding it really hard. The part of me that wishes I'd taken the option to repeat the year. The part of me that woke up on the morning of my first exam and had that strange feeling in my chest.

But I've been practising the techniques Dr Sharma taught me. Ways to talk to myself. Ways to calm myself down. To quieten those voices. Granny made me tea. Mum and Dad made it clear that whatever I do, however the exam goes, everything's going to be OK.

Mum drove me to school, and I did my best, which I think was OK. Which is a word I've been using a lot lately.

OK.

Such a small, insignificant word, but being OK, feeling OK, means everything when you've felt nothing but the opposite for months, maybe even years.

Since that first exam, I've been mostly OK. Being in this weird bubble of time feels almost normal now. Existing from exam to exam, the days in between a blur. Staying at home, staring at record cards full of information, hoping I'll remember it all when I have to. I even enjoy the English exam, finding I can fill the pages with word after word after word, my thoughts and feelings channelled into Malorie Blackman's *Boys Don't Cry* and Jane Austen's *Pride and Prejudice*; as if I've finally connected to the texts in the way Mrs Bright says we're supposed to.

Days turn to weeks. I speak to Jess and Hayley most days, see them on weekends, sometimes with Elina or James or Benji in tow, sometimes just the three of us. I want to say I won't miss what we are in this moment. The way we feel about each other, the way we are together; but I know I will. Because nothing lasts forever, which is why I keep listening to Echo & the Bunnymen, 'Nothing Lasts Forever', over and over every night before I fall asleep.

James and Sadie broke up. He's going to be in London for drama school next year (a fact Hayley both loves and hates) and when I told him about Shawn, the way you do when you're trying to explain a story as if it's a parable, as if there's something the person listening to it needs to learn – I think he got it. That you can't use someone to get over someone else. That when you focus on the 'using' part of the sentence, you realise what you're doing. That however much you might like them, it isn't really enough.

He and Hayley are still close, and I love that for them. That their friendship is starting to take over from whatever came before. Benji's friends with Hay too, and indirectly now James as well, much to his annoyance. He wants to hate him, but I caught him sending him a list of albums to listen to the other day, and they're all the good ones. Rage Against the Machine, Nine Inch Nails, Smashing Pumpkins, Stone Temple Pilots, Jane's Addiction. The ones Benji likes. Not the list of Kid Rock singles he sent me when I first joined the band, and which I now know he hates and only makes people listen to as punishment.

All in all, things feel OK. Like I said. It's a pretty big word for me these days. I haven't seen much of Shawn apart from our band WhatsApp group, where we've all been waiting for news from Gabrielle. Which eventually comes something like this.

They FaceTime us as a group, and explain they love the new song, but feel we aren't ready yet. That we haven't quite worked out who we are. With Shawn leaving, they want us to work on creating something that feels unique to us. They want to hear from us in a year, and from Shawn too. This isn't a no, it's just a Not Yet.

To be honest, I feel relieved. As much as I want to explore who I am as a songwriter, there's a million and one other things I want to explore too. I'm not done yet. I'm not ready to say who I am, I'm still figuring it out.

Exams go on and on, whiling away into the summer, and on the final weekend just before the last week of exams, Jess suggests a picnic by the river. I'm not sure I want to go. I've got my chemistry exam next week and if I stay home and stare at my notes, I might manifest an actual passing grade.

**Jess:**
ur coming E. the end.

358

**Ellie:**

CHEMISTRY jess. CHEMISTRY.

**Jess:**

i tested u last week & u were fine.

**Jess:**

why don't u *really* want 2 go?

**Ellie:**

stop therapizing me. i have enough of that already.

**Jess:**

therapizing is not a word

**Ellie:**

spellcheck says it is.

**Jess:**

ELEANOR

**Ellie:**

JESSICA

**Jess:**

he isn't going 2 b there

**Ellie:**

who?

But I know exactly who she means, and she knows, I know, exactly who she means. But still.

**Jess:**

**Jess:**
who do u think i mean?

**Ellie:**
. . .

**Jess:**
i thought u were friends now?

**Ellie:**
we r.

**Jess:**
so come.

**Ellie:**
but he isn't coming anyway, right?

**Ellie:**
is he??

**Ellie:**
IS HE??

**Ellie:**
JESSICA

**Jess:**
chill drama queen.

**Ellie:**

u r spending 2 much time w Hayley. u used 2 b nicer.

**Jess:**

I really wish I wasn't thinking about chemistry right now. As in the chemical reaction that seems to happen inside my gut every time I think about Ash lately. Because now isn't the time. Now Is Not the Time to start feeling like this again. If I ever stopped feeling like this in the first place.

STOP.

It's a picnic he won't be attending.

It's an exam I can handle because I'm prepared and ready for it.

It's a life of possibilities and new challenges and things I can cope with if I frame them in the right way.

Change is good. Change is good. Change is good.

If I repeat it enough times, it has to be true.

# 70

# Hold Back the River

Jess lied. Which in hindsight seems pretty obvious.

When I arrive, I almost fall into the river – which is basically how we all first met – when I see Ash stood with Elina by Jess's makeshift picnic basket, a Sainsbury's bag for life overflowing with vegan sausage rolls and mini cans of Coke.

Jess avoids eye contact and when I finally get her alone and hiss 'YOU LIED' at her, looks innocently at me, something she is annoyingly good at, and says she thought I was talking about Shawn, which seems A Little Close to the Bone given the current circumstances.

**Ellie:**

am going to kill u ☠

She ignores the message I send her from where I seat myself beside Hayley and some unknown person I'm not sure I like, because they're unknown, and Hayley is *my* best friend, and *yes*, I'm a child, but right now I feel a bit weird and I don't know what to do with my emotions.

'She's spending too much time with you,' I whine, as Hayley sits with her feet dangling in the river. 'You've made her mean. I can't believe she didn't just tell me he was going to be here.'

Hayley rolls her eyes.

'E – this is Rayden,' she says, pointing at the unknown person I've been ignoring. A white boy with shoulder-length dark hair tucked behind his ears wearing large, striking red sunglasses.

'Hey,' I respond dispiritedly. He nods back.

I pull at my black-and-white denim shorts as I sit down next to her, tucking my lime-green vest into the waistband and peeling off my black ballet slippers.

'Stop whining,' Hayley demands unapologetically. 'The sooner you realise the world doesn't begin and end with Ash Anderson, the better.'

'I don't think the world begins and ends with Ash Anderson,' I remark sullenly.

She shakes her head vigorously.

'Which one's Ash Anderson?' Rayden asks. He's got the kind of voice my parents would call Well Spoken, which is really just code for posh. Like he has tennis lessons and multiple homes and holidays in places that don't have swimming pools with things floating in them.

'That one,' I say, trying to point to Ash without him noticing. Ash looks over and half smiles, his brow furrowed from the sun.

'My world could begin and end with him,' Rayden says, looking Ash up and down over his sunglasses.

Hayley gives him a look. One I'm glad to see she gives to people other than me.

'Why are you looking at me like that?' Rayden asks, giving her an equally disparaging look back. 'How are you going to tell that library girl you like her with a face like that? You look like you're about to kill someone.'

'Maybe I am,' she responds grumpily.

'This Gen Z rage thing isn't working for you,' Rayden sniffs, looking away.

I'm starting to like Rayden.

Hayley sighs.

'Sorry,' she says, turning to me suddenly. 'You know I'm just joking, right?'

'No,' I say, miffed.

'Well, I am. And you're right. I can be mean. And I'm sorry if I've ever directed that meanness at you. Because I love you.'

I notice Rayden touch her hand momentarily.

'Who are you and what have you done with my best friend?' I ask, eyeing her suspiciously.

'Seriously,' she says, turning to look at me. 'I couldn't have survived this year without you.'

'And I couldn't have survived high school without *you*,' I say just as seriously.

'Having a popular, beautiful best friend probably helped,' she says, indicating Jessica.

'Having a mean, beautiful one was good too, though,' I joke.

She hugs me unexpectedly. Our tall girl, small girl embrace.

'So, how do you guys know each other then?' I ask when she lets go of me.

'We met at my group thing,' she says hastily. And I remember her mentioning him now. The boy who seems free. Happy to be who he is. And I wonder if any of us are really free. If any of us are really who we are.

'She was wearing all black and speaking in monosyllables. I knew I'd break her eventually,' he says, winking at her over his glasses. She smiles back. She seems lighter around him. More comfortable than I've ever seen her.

'Rayden helped me come out,' she says, staring at him. 'He was the first person to ask me if I was queer, and I just said yes, like I'd always known.'

'I didn't do anything,' he says dismissively. But I think he did. Even if he didn't mean to.

'You did,' she says, looking at him. 'You saw me, and now I feel like I'm starting to see myself.'

I look down at the ground guiltily. Looking back, Hayley always said she never wanted to be with James. I saw them together because it made sense to me. I assumed their friendship had to be a mutual attraction, because she was a girl, and he was a boy. And I'm upset at how stupid I can be. How small-minded. I need to be better, to really see things, and not make assumptions.

'I'm sorry, Hay. If I pushed you into anything,' I say, shamefaced. 'With James. Or Benji. I just assumed . . .' I trail away.

'You don't need to be sorry. I was hiding from myself, E. It's not actually a surprise I was hiding from you too. Besides which, I'm glad I got to know James.'

'Now, *he's* hot,' Rayden says, interrupting, and we both laugh, because a year ago, there is no way either Hayley or I would have allowed ourselves to be involved in a conversation where anyone was lusting after James Godfrey; but now it seems inevitable. Because we like him, a lot. And yeah, he is kind of hot. But please, gods, let no one ever hear my thoughts on this subject, like, ever.

I put my bare foot in the water next to Hayley's as Rayden lies back on the grass. I take Hayley's hand in mine, and we kick the water, the silence between us thick and comforting.

For a moment, I forget I have a chemistry exam next week. I forget that Mum's due date is around the corner and there'll be a new baby in Amis's room soon. I forget that sometimes, when I think about those things, I can't breathe properly. I just know in that moment, that everything's going to be OK. Because for the first time in a really long time, I forget to be afraid.

Jess was right. Of course I should be here. These are the people who make up my world. And Ash is my friend. We've decided. There's no reason to avoid him. To let the feeling in my gut be anything other than a feeling I know I can control.

'I'm going to say hi to Ash,' I say, turning to Hayley.

'OK,' she says, squeezing my hand.

'No further words?' I ask.

'I trust you,' she says simply. 'And he's not the same person who let you down. I just, I worry about you.'

I smile at her. 'Thanks for worrying about me, but I think it's time we both stopped worrying so much.'

'I concur,' Rayden says without moving from his spot on the grass.

I let go of her hand and stand up, slinging my bag over my shoulder, picking up my shoes with one hand and walking towards the bank where Ash and Elina and Jess are sat; an echo of an image from a time before.

As I walk, I pass groups of kids lounging lazily. Drinking Coca-Colas and eating bags of sweets. It's turned into an unofficial leaving party before any of us has even finished the year. James is sat with some football friends, and waves as I walk past. Later, he'll sit with Hayley and get to know Rayden, and he'll remember that how he feels right now won't be the way he feels forever. That he'll get over her. That sometimes, friendship is the best place to end up.

But in my situation, the problem with that sentiment is the song that starts playing in my head the closer I get to Ash on the bank. James Bay, 'Hold Back the River' – James telling me he tried to keep me close, but life got in between. I can feel my breath catching in my throat, my heart accelerating. Not from panic, but something else.

'Hey,' I say, as I look down at Jess and Elina and him. Him.

'Hey,' Jess says guiltily. I can tell she's starting to worry that maybe she should have told me he was coming. That she should have known there's only ever been one him when it comes to me.

'Hey,' Elina says, putting her arm up towards me. 'Sit down.'

I place my stuff on the ground carefully and sit down next to her as she pulls me into her side, her other hand holding Jessica's.

'I was just saying this doesn't feel the same without you,' she smiles.

I blush, not knowing how to reciprocate.

'Elina, I'm going to talk to Hay,' Jess says, pulling at her.

'OK,' she says, ignoring her tone and turning back to me.

'I'm going *now*,' Jess says, trying again with less subtlety. 'You should come too,' she says, motioning at Ash.

She looks over at him, his legs crossed, silently throwing twigs into the river.

'Oh, right, yeah,' she says, looking at Jess and standing up hastily. 'Back in a minute.'

'Oh, OK,' I answer awkwardly.

When they leave, Ash and I sit in silence. And it doesn't feel like it did with Hayley. It feels heavy and strange.

'I thought you were ignoring me,' he says, his eyes fixed on the river. He's wearing a worn yellow T-shirt, one he told me once belonged to his dad, with ankle-length, wide cream trousers, white socks, white trainers.

'I'm sorry. I just wanted to meet Hayley's friend, that's all.'

He turns to look at me, his eyes dark.

'OK,' I admit, looking at the ground. 'Maybe I was. Just a bit.'

'Why?' he asks, screwing his face up. 'I thought we were friends. I thought after everything, at least we were friends now.'

'We are,' I say quickly.

'Then why are you being weird?' he asks, throwing a rock into the water. 'I thought we were being honest with each other now?'

'I thought you liked weird?' I joke.

He turns back to me. 'Seriously, Ellie, why does it have to be so hard? Why are things always like this with us?'

'I don't know.' I shrug.

Because I'm not ready to be that honest with him yet. To tell him I'll always love him a little bit. That I'll always want to hold back the river and look in his eyes. I'll always want for us to be more, even when I know we shouldn't be.

I scoot towards him across the grass.

'I'm sorry,' I continue, taking his hand. 'I don't want to be weird. It's just who I am.'

'I don't want to lose you,' he says slowly, his thumb caressing my knuckles.

I feel selfish and angry then. That I'm focusing on how I feel. What I need. When he's been there for me, and now he needs that in return.

'You won't,' I say, putting my head on his shoulder.

368

He pulls me into the side of him, the way Elina did moments ago, and I settle into the feeling. His T-shirt soft against my skin.

'So, how are you?' I ask delicately.

'I can't believe I'll be gone soon,' he replies.

'Me either.' And I let myself drink the moment in. The way it feels knowing he's here. Right now. A permanent fixture at this point in time.

'Are you nervous?'

'Yeah,' he says, taking a deep breath. 'I am.' He withdraws his arm from around me and goes back to picking up rocks and twigs, throwing them into the water, watching them drift away.

'It's, like, going back to London,' he explains. 'To the person I was before I got here – without Elina or Mum. I'm scared I'll mess it all up.'

'What do you mean?'

'I mean, I'm not strong, Ellie. When my dad got sick – Elina was strong, I was a mess. Drinking and not going to school and not handling things – what am I going to do without her? Who am I going to be?'

I turn towards him, even though just then, he's refusing to look at me.

'You were my Elina,' I say quietly. 'This summer. You held me together when I was falling apart. My whole family, actually.' I look down at my knees. Trying to find the words. 'You are strong,' I say, looking back up at him. 'Don't you see that? You're one of the strongest people I know. And I'm going to miss you. Which is probably why I was being weird earlier, because being this close to you when I know you're going away, it's not . . . it isn't easy for me, Ash. But I know it's the right thing for you. And I'll be right here, on the other end of the phone if you need me. And so will your mum, and Elina, and all the people that love you.'

'The people that love me?' he asks softly.

'Yes.' I blush. 'Your family.'

'My family,' he repeats.

'Ash Anderson,' I say, prising his palm open. I pull out the stone he's been gripping and throw it into the water, placing his arm back around me. 'You're not getting rid of me that easily.'

I put my head on his shoulder, and he puts his on top of mine.

'Thanks,' he says into my hair.

'Thank *you*,' I say back quietly.

# 71

# All About Chemistry

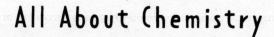

I'm not sure why, but the sweat has returned. Maybe it's because its summer and the school feels like a raging hell fire, maybe it's because my chemistry exam is an actual raging hell fire, or maybe it's because this is my final exam; no going back. No – I'll try harder in the next one, I'll do better in the next one – this is it. Exams are over.

This morning, Mum reminded me that if things don't go as planned, I can re-sit next year. I can reconsider my A level options if I need to. Because there are options, whatever happens.

I wanted to remind her that this is the exact opposite of everything she and Dad have ever taught me. That my GCSEs are truly the be all and end all of everything. The culmination of generations of our families' sacrifices, all resting on me. The only child. But we've all changed. She's changed. And I know it's different now.

So much has happened. The fact we're talking to each other. The fact I no longer feel that pressure. I know I did, because Dr Sharma told me to release it, and when I let it go, I felt physically lighter. Mum and Dad were in the room as part of one our family sessions. We all cried. We all felt it. The sense we'd all let something go.

But back to the sweating. It's working its way through my hairline and down the side of my face. I'm collecting brown foundation on my white sleeve, every time I try and fix it. James's hair looks gelled back, when I know he doesn't actually wear hair gel, so at least this exam is a raging hell fire for all of us, and not just me. Then I remember I'm in an *exam*, and I should probably be focusing on the questions and the test itself, as opposed to how sweaty my peers are.

And at this point, I can practically hear Jess in my head telling me that this is all chemistry in motion. The study of matter (my face) and the analysing of its structure, properties and behaviour to see what happens when it changes in chemical reactions (the addition of heat).

Think about Jess, I remind myself. All the things Jess has taught me about chemistry.

I put my head down over my paper and breathe.

Here goes nothing.


A couple of hours later, we emerge from the hell fire of the main hall, our eyes shut tight against the brightness of the sky.

'I feel like I've been in prison,' Hayley moans.

'I would tell you not to be dramatic, but it seems like that's your entire life's purpose,' Jess says grinning.

'I feel so seen,' Hayley replies, deadpan.

'So, about Jane,' Jess continues.

'What about Jane?' I ask, my spider senses on alert.

Hayley makes a face, as if to say: not in front of *her*.

'What's going on?' I continue. 'Why are you making *faces* about me? Is it because I'm sweaty? Because I can't help that. It's genetic. It's my *hair*. I have a lot of hair. Like, everywhere. And that exam was stressful. Also, why are you talking about *Jane*, and why don't you want me to *know* about Jane or whatever it is you are or aren't doing with Jane?'

'Can you stop saying *Jane*,' Hayley hisses. 'I told you she was going to do this,' she says to Jessica.

'What?' I demand. 'What am I doing?'

She shoots Jess a look as Jess grins back at her.

'Remember what Rayden said about your *looks*,' I say to Hayley. 'You need to give off less serial killer vibes if you want to catch Jane.'

'I'm not trying to *catch* anyone,' she says through gritted teeth.

'Just tell me, and I promise I'll shut up,' I reply.

'Ellie, I don't want you to play matchmaker,' she begs. 'I know you love doing it, but please don't. It's not me. I just want to talk to her in my own time. I think she's interesting, that's all.'

'She's intense,' Jessica chimes in.

'I like intense,' Hayley says, blushing.

'Hayley is the dictionary definition of intense,' I reply to Jess, who nods in agreement.

'Shut up, you two,' Hayley says awkwardly.

'Anyway,' Jess continues, 'Elina is bringing Jane to meet us now.'

My phone pings.

**Ash:**

'Chemistry', Semisonic

I put my earphones in and press the link, the sound of drums and upbeat guitars making me realise all the things I've learned about chemistry. The experiments I've conducted. Some successful (me and

373

Ash for a bit, me and Shawn for a bit), some not so successful (Hayley and James).

I feel a pair of arms around my middle, forcing me to pull my earphones out mid chorus to see who it is; wondering if Hayley's finally succumbed to her desire to kill me.

'Hello,' he says, turning me around.

'Hello,' I respond shyly.

'How are you? It's been weird not seeing you for a few weeks.'

Experiment number two. Aka Shawn. Looking particularly cute in his yellow Converse trainers, straight blue jeans and a black Neil Young T-shirt. I love Neil Young.

'I just finished my last exam,' I say, motioning towards the hall behind me.

'How are you feeling?'

'Free. Sort of.'

'Sort of free,' he grins. 'I know the feeling. I finished yesterday. I just came to pick some stuff up from my locker.'

'Oh. Right,' I say, my heart pounding. 'So, you're really going then.'

'I'm really going.' He grimaces.

'You don't look happy about it,' I remark worriedly.

'I'm nervous,' he admits. 'I just hope I'm good enough.'

'You are,' I say, punching his shoulder. 'Stop being all *me* about it. What happened to the boy that used his fear to be better? To not be afraid of being afraid,' I ask, recalling how he told me that he used his nerves to help him, the first time I saw him perform at an open mic night in New York.

'Are you really going to quote me?' he asks, embarrassed.

'I remember everything you say,' I tease.

374

'Which is ironic,' Hayley says, cutting in. 'Because she ignores everything I say.'

I roll my eyes. 'That's because it's mostly sarcasm and irritation.'

'True,' she notes.

'Anyway, I should get going.' Shawn motions to the building behind me.

'When do you leave, leave?'

'Next week. I'm spending the summer with my dad, so he can help me get settled in over there.'

'So soon,' I say quietly.

He makes a face, then clears his throat awkwardly.

'Hi.' I hear Elina from behind me, the sound of her and Jess kissing, then the feeling of awkwardness I assume is emanating from Hayley and Jane.

I turn to say hello to them all. To say goodbye too, because I assume I won't be wanted on their double date, but he's there too. Ash Anderson and his mop of dark, curly hair. White T-shirt, black jeans, chequerboard paint-spattered Vans.

Hayley and Jane are hugging self-consciously, Hayley's back as straight as an arrow, leaning down to Jane and patting her on the back like a small child who's swallowed something they shouldn't.

'Hey, Ellie,' Ash says, eyeing Shawn and me. 'Hey, Shawn.'

'Hi,' Shawn says, watching him.

And it strikes me that the last time they spoke to each other I was having a panic attack at my aunt's wedding.

'I was just going,' Shawn says into the silence that follows.

'Me too,' I say to the foursome. 'Have a good time.'

Elina watches me uncomfortably. Because the foursome is

currently plus one. The foursome has Ash, and maybe he's just a fifth wheel, or maybe he's here to see me; and I don't know why I think that, I just know I think it. That he's here to see me. My friend Ash, when I'm here with my friend Shawn.

We all look over our shoulders, as if desperately looking for a way to make the numbers make sense.

'OK, see you,' Shawn says, waving at everyone.

'I'll come with you,' I pipe up unexpectedly.

He smiles.

'Ash, are you busy? Do you want to come with us?' I add out of nowhere. 'Go get a coffee?'

Jessica stares at me as I watch Hayley physically hold back the words *but you hate coffee.*

'Er, sure,' Ash says.

'OK,' Shawn replies, looking slightly appalled.

Jess widens her eyes at me, as Hayley hides a laugh. Friends with my exes, and now making my exes friends. How very modern and mature of me. But probably not. Probably a stupid, awkward mistake I'll have to recount over WhatsApp later this evening and potentially for the rest of my life.

'See you then,' we say to the foursome, as we all slope off towards reception.

'I have to grab some stuff from the changing rooms,' Shawn says, as we walk down the hallway. 'Meet in the common room?'

'I can't go in the common room,' I note uncomfortably. 'I'm not in sixth form yet.'

'It'll be fine,' Ash says. 'It's your final week. You're practically a sixth former already. I doubt there'll be anyone in there anyway.'

We peel off in a different direction to Shawn, heading down the sixth-form corridor, somewhere I've always thought of as out of bounds.

'I feel like such a rebel,' I whisper.

'Why are you whispering?' Ash asks, laughing. 'It's not a church.'

'You don't whisper in a church,' I inform him. 'They want you to pray as loudly as possible.' He laughs again.

At the end of the corridor, I hear a guitar, a voice humming.

'Someone's in there,' I hiss.

He pulls me into the room, and I hate how much holding his hand feels right. Like I don't want to let go. Like I want to turn to him, like I did on bonfire night, and kiss him. The strains of Lorde, 'Green Light,' playing in my mind.

But I don't. Because we're meeting Shawn in a minute. Because we're friends now. Because the person in the room playing the guitar is Hannah, both of my ex-boyfriends' ex-girlfriend.

'Oh,' I say, surprised to see her. 'Hi.'

'Hi,' she says steadily. 'Sorry, I didn't think anyone was coming in here today.'

'We're, um, we're, er,' I respond, flustered.

She raises her eyebrows, her eyes searching our still-clasped hands.

'I have to say, I'm not surprised. I kind of figured you'd get back together when you and Shawn broke up.'

At just the moment she mentions his name, Shawn walks in.

'Hi,' he says, looking from her to us, then back again.

I let go of Ash's hand hastily.

'We're not,' I say, trying to finish my statement. 'This isn't . . .' I try.

'OK,' she says, going back to strumming her guitar.

377

'Actually,' I begin. 'We're going for a coffee. Do you want to come?' My friends look at me, and then at each other, and then back at Hannah.

'OK,' she says breezily. 'Let me grab my guitar case.'

'Great,' I say to no one.

She leaves the room, and we all stand there saying nothing, hoping she doesn't come back. Not because its anything to do with her, personally, but because it's everything to do with all of us, personally.

But she does come back. And even walking down the street together feels awkward, like none of us know who to walk next to, or what it means if we make a choice about who we walk next to. But when we do sit down, when we do order some mint tea and some pretentious coffees and a bunch of cake and start talking, we actually start laughing. At all of it. At the awkwardness. At how we all quite like each other (some of us more than others), at how this shouldn't be awkward, until suddenly it isn't. We're too busy dissecting *Rumours* by Fleetwood Mac versus the songs in *Daisy Jones & the Six*. Too busy talking about the things we have in common. Because there's more of those than we thought.

And that's how I come to realise: there is nothing that can't be fixed by a cup of tea and a biscuit – and even though my mum told me this, and I refused to believe it, sometimes Mum knows more about life than I want to admit.

# 72

# WEDDING, Part Deux

We're in a pretty room above a small Chinese restaurant in Chinatown in London. Ethan's standing to one side looking handsome and moody, but not drunk, which is a good start. Hope is busy texting Benji (Benji!) and Ash and I are sort of hanging around waiting for everything to start, trying not to annoy Granny, who is visibly riled by the fact she has no control over this part of the wedding at all.

It's a small affair; not like the last wedding, which seemed to be filled with every Sri Lankan I've ever met. Just Uncle Charles's family, our family, Ash, Elina, Mrs Aachara and Mr Green; because Granny has ostensibly adopted them, so apparently my hot PE teacher is now a Pillai.

Having Ash sat next to me feels both weird and disturbingly normal. He's wearing a bright green suit with wide-leg trousers and a Nehru-collared white shirt beneath it, like he's a half-Asian Harry Styles, which, I'm going to be honest, is a good look for him. Hope and I are dressed in gold qipaos, as is Diana and très chic Granny, who is looking particularly stylish today with her long, neat bob.

The men are dressed in dark blue suits, apart from Charles, who's wearing a traditional red changshan and black trousers, the women in pretty, brightly coloured purple and pink dresses; Mum looking especially beautiful in a cerulean-blue trouser suit, her bump dressed in a matching stretchy fabric top, her hair tied neatly in a bun on top of her head.

I want to pause for a moment and take a picture of it all. These two different sets of people. These two different cultures; three if you count us second generations. But it would be impossible to capture it all in a photo, to bottle it or pin it down. I think this is what belonging looks like. Acceptance. In the face of these two families, in the beauty of looking forward at the life Kitty and Charles are going to build together.

When Kitty arrives, she's brought in by the uncles, wearing a long red qipao, elegant and ethereal. I watch Charles the same way I did at their first wedding. His face as she walks towards him. As if all of it, the years of not telling anyone, of having to pretend your relationship doesn't exist, was worth it. For this moment. The one where you get to tell the world you belong to each other.

They start with a tea ceremony, Charles and Kitty serving tea to Granny and his parents as a mark of respect and gratitude, each of them in turn handing the couple a red envelope to signify blessings for their new marriage. Then tea is served to everyone as Charles's family give Kitty twelve beautifully wrapped gifts, each with another red envelope. At the end, Kitty goes to get changed again and the rest of us head downstairs for the banquet that marks the start of their new life together.

In the restaurant, the tables have been covered in red-and-gold stitched tablecloths and printed menus that number the eight courses we'll be eating. I'm regretting not wearing a larger size qipao, but

Charles's family didn't really give us much choice when it came to our wedding attire, and the only thing I've been able to do to make any of it feel remotely me is wear green winged eyeliner and the necklace Mum, Dad and Granny gave me for my birthday: a delicate gold chain with an E hanging from it.

'Should we sit together?' Ash asks, as we head towards the tables.

I nod, wishing I could breathe better in this dress. It's fine when I'm standing up, sitting down feels . . . less fine.

Hope throws herself down next to me with Elina to her right.

'God, this thing is tight,' she whines. 'And it's, like, an extra-large or something. Do you think I'm an extra-large?' she asks, concerned.

'I don't think it matters what size you are, because you're beautiful, but I think we may be bigger than your average-size Chinese person,' I say quietly.

'Why does it make me feel so bad to see those letters?' she complains. 'It's so stupid. I hate how fatphobic this world is. I swear, the clothes I make are going to be for everyone. They're going to celebrate every type of body there is. And I'm changing the sizing system. I hate it.'

'Good for you,' I say, wriggling in an effort to make myself comfortable.

'I completely agree,' Elina says from her other side. 'The language around size is so . . . frustrating.' They launch into a conversation about how the fashion world is designed to represent a particular tall, thin, white aesthetic.

'So, last week was fun,' Ash says from the other side of me.

'Was it?' I ask, wriggling again.

'Yes,' he says insistently. 'It was. I'm glad you invited Hannah.'

Ugh. Why? Why is he glad I invited Hannah? Why is he always

trying to make me friends with his ex-girlfriends, like he wants us to start a members' club or something.

'This dress is way too tight,' I murmur.

'Well, you look beautiful.'

And suddenly, I'm not sure whether it's how tight the dress is, or the fact he's sat next to me, that's making me feel slightly sick.

'Oh, er, thanks. You look . . . um, nice yourself,' I say, gesturing towards his suit.

From the side, I can see Hope and Elina, straining to hear what we're saying.

'Why do I feel like we have an audience?' I whisper.

'So, this whole honesty thing we're trying,' he begins. 'I need to talk to you about something.'

'If you're going to tell me you and Hannah are an item, I'm fine with it,' I cut in. 'I mean, whatever you want. I just want you to be happy, Ash.'

'Why would you think that?' he asks frustratedly.

'I don't know. Because you seem so keen for us to be friends,' I say awkwardly, not for the first time wondering why I'm so quick to jump to conclusions.

'Ellie,' he says, shaking his head. 'There's only one person I like that way, and you know exactly who that is. Who it's always been.'

And I know it isn't the dress this time. That it's not anxiety, or panic. That the way my heart's beating, the way my head's swimming, is nothing to do with anything but him.

'I don't think I'm what you really want,' I say hastily.

'You don't get to tell me what I want,' he says firmly. 'I know you're not ready. I know you've got stuff going on. I know I hurt you. But you know it, and I know it. I love you.'

'You love me?' I offer.

'Yes,' he says, looking down at his hands. 'But I couldn't stand it if we weren't friends. So, I know it can't mean anything. I know the timing's off. I just wanted you to know. Before I go.'

'You're not going until the end of August,' I state clumsily.

'I think it makes sense to go sooner. I can stay with Bec until term starts. Have a bit of time to get used to being away from Mum and Elina and—'

'Ellie,' Hope hisses, leaning over. 'Your mum!'

I turn around to the table Mum and Dad are sat at. She's gone white, a colour a brown woman should never turn, grasping at Dad's hand as she writhes around in her seat, making a low moaning noise.

'Mum,' I say, pushing my chair back and running towards her. 'Mum! What's going on? Is she OK?' I ask, turning to Dad desperately.

'She hasn't been feeling well all day,' Dad says, stroking her hand. 'I think she's been having contractions for the last hour.'

'No. I. Haven't,' Mum seethes, while clearly trying not to explode all over Aunty Kitty's wedding.

'Nimi,' Kitty says, appearing next to her, looking beautiful in a new, cream-coloured qipao. I'm loving how many wedding dresses she's had. 'What's going on?'

'Nothing,' Mum says, breathing heavily. 'Everything's fine. Let's eat.'

'Eat?' Dad says angrily. 'You're in labour, Nimi.'

'I'm not,' Mum lies. 'It's a stomach ache. I'm not ready to be in labour. Today isn't the day.'

I kneel down in front of her and take her hand.

'Today's the day, Mum,' I say firmly.

'But,' and she's starting to cry now. 'Are you OK, *sina pillai*? Are you ready?' But she can barely get to the end of the sentence, her eyes are closing, her hand gripping Dad's so hard his knuckles are turning white.

'We need to get her to the hospital,' Dad says to Kitty.

Kitty nods, Charles getting up as she motions to him. They stand on either side of Mum and pull her to her feet.

'Nimi,' Granny says, rushing forward when she notices the commotion. 'I am coming.'

Mum grabs her hand, the two of them lost in some unspoken conversation.

'What should I do?' I ask Dad. 'What do I do?'

'We'll take Mum to the hospital. Get her checked out. It might be a few hours yet. He's not due yet; it might be nothing.'

'Should I come with you?' I ask worriedly.

'It might be better,' Dad says hesitantly, 'if you come a bit later. I don't want you to worry.'

I want to cry. I want to scream or shout or do something, anything, to explain how all this is making me feel. Scared. Isolated. Out of control.

'I'll bring her, Mr Pillai,' Ash says out of nowhere. 'Which hospital are you going to?'

He's holding my hand. His thumb stroking my thumb.

'UCH,' Charles says, tapping on his Uber app. 'It's the closest.'

Dad nods.

Ash looks at me, inhaling deeply, inviting me to replicate. Telling me to breathe, without telling me to breathe.

'Should we come with you?' Kitty asks anxiously.

384

'No.' Dad shakes his head. 'Finish your wedding, *thangachi*. I'll take Nimi and *Amma* to the hospital. Ash can bring Ellie later.'

'The cab's a minute away,' Charles says to Dad from across his shoulder, Mum between the two of them.

'I have had a baby before,' Mum gasps. 'I'm fine. I'll be fine. Enjoy your day, Kitty. I'm so sorry this had to happen today.'

Aunty Kitty laughs. 'I don't think you could help when it happened, Nimi,' she says fondly. 'And what better way to end my wedding than with a new baby.'

Ash squeezes my hand. I can feel it, but I can't feel it. Everything feels far away.

'Ellie,' Mum says, staring at me. 'Are you OK? Do you want to come with us now?'

And the fact that she's worrying about me, when right now all she should be worrying about is herself, and the baby. The fact she notices me. That she cares how I'm feeling, just soothes me in ways I can't quite articulate.

'It's OK, Mum,' I say, tearing up. 'I'm fine. I just want you and him to be fine.'

'We will be,' she says, leaning forward to grasp my hand. 'But this next bit won't be much fun. Maybe better that you keep your mind off it,' she says, suddenly groaning.

'We'd better go,' Dad says to us both.

'Car's outside,' Charles says, helping Mum walk.

I walk them out to the car, the sun shining on what's turned into a perfect summer day.

As they leave, I stand there. Trying to remember all the tools Dr Sharma gave me to manage my anxiety.

'Come on,' Ash says, pulling at me as they drive away. 'I'll take you over there in an hour or two. Just eat something first.'

I try to take my mind off things. I eat beef and lobster and scallops, or at least I try. I laugh when Charles feeds Aunty Kitty double happiness fried rice and ask Ash how happy fried rice makes him feel. I smile when très chic Granny says Hope and I look lovely in our qipaos even though we're both starting to resemble gold trash bags, our silk dresses now a myriad of folds and creases, when hers looks immaculate.

I try to pay attention when Charles gives a speech about belonging, or when Aunty Kitty cries when he kisses her.

I want to be present, but I'm not. Half of me is here, and half is me somewhere else.

'Do you want to go?' Ash asks, squeezing my hand.

It's only then I realise he's never let it go. Not from the moment he told Dad he'd take me to the hospital.

I try to remember what he told me before that. The you-know-I-love-you-but-the-timing-is-never-right thing. And once again, the timing isn't right. I just know he's still holding my hand.

That he always lets me hold his hand, whenever I need it.

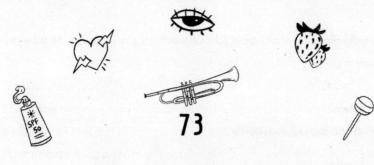

# 73

# All the Changes

He's home. My brother. It feels weird even saying it, but he's here. Beautiful and perfect and loud and already annoying, but here. The four of us running around after him like he's the king of a tiny little kingdom.

Mum was right, the way Mum's always right. By the time I arrived at the hospital a couple of hours after my parents and Granny, Mum was just about ready to push, and by the look on Dad's face, the last hours had been traumatic. For him. Possibly because Mum started listing off all the things Dad hadn't done to baby-proof the house yet, while screaming in agony and demanding he never, ever lie to her again or she was going to scream at him exactly like this, over and over until he stopped lying and told her the truth. Which seems harsh given how repentant he is about not telling us about his heart condition, but as Mum says, she was just about to give birth to his baby, and she was over walking on eggshells about it.

When we arrived, Ash waited with me until Kit was born. Then when he had to stay in hospital for almost a week with jaundice and feeding issues, he visited every day. But now we're home. In our house, in our village, Kit taking his first nap in his baby bouncer, right by my feet.

**Jess:**
when can i see him irl??

**Hayley:**
he's so cute 🐈‍⬛

**Jess:**
he is EDIBLE

**Hayley:**
eating babies is frowned upon.

**Jess:**
how r u doing E?

**Ellie:**
gd. just glad he's home now 🖤

So, I guess the one thing I didn't mention was that I'm back home, and so are Kit and Mum and Dad and Granny, but Ash isn't. He decided to stay in London for the summer, just like he told me he would. He'll be back to collect his stuff at some point, but I don't know when. And I'm OK with it, because All the Changes. They're here, and I'm handling them, and this is the way it's all supposed to be. Him there, and me here, and moving on, and growing up, and all the things they tell you come with changes.

Except.

When he walked me to the hospital, he never once let go of my hand. On the second day Kit had to stay in overnight he stayed with us, bringing us terrible tea from the canteen, letting me fall asleep on his shoulder listening to the sound of one side of his earphones. He was just there. Always. When Dad wanted a newspaper, or Mum wanted a bar of chocolate, or when he knew being in a hospital felt too much, had too many memories, he'd take me for a walk down Drummond Street, buying me sticky Indian sweets and talking to me about my favourite Cranberries songs ('Dreams,' every time).

But now he's not there, and I feel weirdly bereft. And it's not as if I need him, it's not as if I can't cope without him; I just miss him. We haven't spoken since he told me he wasn't coming back. Yesterday, when we were drinking mango lassi in the sun, laughing about the way Kit isn't crying yet, just mewing like a kitten. The most beautiful, glorious kitten you've ever seen.

I refuse to be sad about it. Because it's Ash's right to move on. Ash's right to have a life that doesn't include me in it. It's just, he's important to me. Because all the time we weren't going out, which is way longer than we were, he's become my friend. One of my best friends.

**Jess:**
u coming 2 last day of term next week?

**Hayley:**
✓

**Ellie:**
✓

**Ellie:**

come over after & meet the kitten?

**Jess:**

IN

**Hayley:**

r we doing all caps now?

**Jess:**

YES

**Ellie:**

u can bring Jane if u want . . .

**Hayley:**

we hav been on 1 date . . .

**Ellie:**

will buy new hat 4 wedding

**Hayley:**

only old people wear hats 2 weddings

**Ellie:**

does that mean u like her?

**Hayley:**

MAYBE

**Ellie:**

I ♥ that 4 u

**Hayley:**

ONE. DATE.

I want to message Ash and say Hayley's been on a date. Her first date since she came out, and it went well and I'm considering buying a new hat for her wedding, even though we aren't old enough to vote yet, let alone get married, but apparently, I behave like an old person, which won't come as a surprise to him.

I try not to think about how much I want to talk to him. Instead, I just send him a song.

**Ellie:**

'Changes', Emily Vu

Because he needs to know.

I'm not the same girl he knew before.

# ♡ Song 3 ♡

## Again - Intro, Verse, Chorus, Middle Eight

I don't even have to think about it, it just appears. As if it was always there, waiting to make sense of it all.

*Right back here with you, again*

That feeling.
The one that makes you feel like you're floating and flying and drowning simultaneously.

*Because I think it's true*

And I'm not afraid any more. I just know, suddenly.

*That I love you, again*

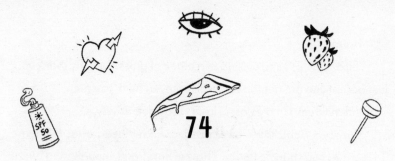

# 74

# The Last Day of School

School's swarming with kids – at least it feels like it's swarming. Every time I've been in for an exam it's felt quieter than usual, but today, everyone's back. To say goodbye, to sign shirts and homework diaries, to scream I hate you or I love you to the corresponding person and disappear into the summer a new being.

There's nothing to do but clear out our lockers and loll around on the green, thinking about next year.

'No more uniform,' Jess says triumphantly. 'I can't wait to wear my own clothes.'

'I don't know,' I reply. 'I think I'll miss it.'

But what I mean is, I'll miss not having to think about it every morning. Putting on the same thing as everyone else so it feels like there's less of a difference between us.

'If I had your wardrobe, I'd be very excited about non-uniform,' Elina says from her position on the grass, her head on Jess's lap. 'You've got great style, Ellie. It's one of the first things I noticed about you.'

'Me?' I guffaw. 'Style?'

'Yes,' she says seriously. 'You.'

I laugh.

'Ellie,' Hayley says, picking at a blade of grass. 'Just say thank you. Just accept you are not the colossal loser you think you are.'

'I don't think I'm a colossal loser,' I say defensively.

But she's right, that voice has been in my head a lot this term. Telling me I can't handle things. That I'm not strong enough. And I want to be better, but it's hard.

'In fact,' I say to them all, 'I think I'm pretty amazing.'

'YES,' Jess squeals, as Elina and Hayley applaud.

'And *thank you*, Elina.'

'You're welcome,' she grins.

'What a year,' Hayley says, lying down on the grass next to my crossed legs.

'I know,' I say, looking at my phone, at the songs I've been sending to Ash daily. Unanswered, grey ticked. Like they've been delivered but he hasn't read them.

Sunday.

**Ellie:**

'Light On', Maggie Rogers

Because I will leave the light on, whenever he needs to find me.

Monday.

**Ellie:**

'The Bones', Maren Morris

Because we broke, but it doesn't matter.

Tuesday.

**Ellie:**
'If You Leave', Nada Surf

Because I want every second with him to last.

Wednesday.

**Ellie:**
'Something Changed', Pulp

Because where would I be now, if we'd never met?

Thursday.

**Ellie:**
'Kiss Me', Sixpence None the Richer

Because, well, I think it's pretty obvious.

Friday.

**Ellie:**
'Friday I'm in Love', The Cure

Because I love him. Today. Right now. And it's the only way I know how to say it.

I'm not upset that he hasn't answered. That he hasn't read the code between the songs. He deserves to move on. To find the right timing with the right person. I want him to be happy, and I want to be happy too. Which is why I need to tell him, so that I can move on. Why I've been sending him my version of love letters. It doesn't matter if he gets them. It just matters that I tried.

'Hey, Ellie.' I look at the shadow over my phone and then up at its owner. 'I just came to say hello, goodbye.'

'You know that's one of my favourite songs,' I say, shielding my eyes as I stand up to give Shawn a hug.

'I'm going to miss you,' he says into my hair. 'Keep in touch, OK?'

'You couldn't stop me,' I sniffle. I've never been good at goodbyes, but I try to change the narrative in my head. I'm not bad at goodbyes, I just feel them, I allow myself to feel them, and that's a good thing.

He pulls back from me, holding my hands in his. 'I'm probably going to hate myself for saying this, but you should talk to him.'

'Who?' I ask, feeling myself getting warmer.

'Ash. He's on his way to the station.'

'What do you mean?' I ask, slightly hysterically.

'He was just here. Cleaning out his locker.'

'What?' I ask again, looking around frantically.

'He's gone. He had a train to catch.'

'A train to catch?' I parrot.

'He's in love with you, Ellie. And I'm pretty sure you're in love with him too.'

I look down at Elina and Jess, staring at the grass, avoiding eye contact.

'Did you know he was coming back today?' I demand.

'He didn't want me to tell you,' Elina admits guiltily.

'Why?' I ask, hurt.

'Because he doesn't think you feel the same way he does, and he wants to move on,' she says calmly.

'But I do,' I say wildly. 'I've been sending him love songs all week. Well, my idea of love songs. I thought he didn't want to know.'

'Well, what are you waiting for?' Elina says, sitting up. She looks at her phone. 'You have about fourteen minutes. Come on!'

'Come on, Ellie, move!' Hayley says frantically.

'I'll never make it,' I cry.

'Then MOVE,' Jess shrieks.

'You can take my bike,' Benji says, appearing behind Shawn.

'What? I can't ride a bike. And I can't do this. I can't—' I continue, panicked.

'You can,' Shawn says, squeezing my hand.

'What if it doesn't work?' I ask desperately.

'Nobody knows anything, E, but you have to try,' Jess says, standing up and pushing me forward.

'I'll give you a backie,' Benji says, grabbing my hand.

I turn around and stare at them all, doing my best impression of a goldfish.

'COME ON,' Benji says, pulling me, and this time I let him. I let him pull me towards his bike as he fumbles with the bike lock, and Jess and Hayley and Elina cheer us on.

Shawn helps me on to the seat.

'See you around, Ellie,' he says softly.

'See you around,' I say, giving his hand a squeeze.

And that's it. We're off.

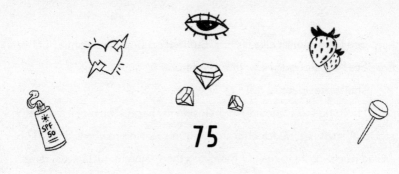

# 75

# The End

On the way to the station, I fear for my life. Benji's cycling is about as frenetic as his drumming.

'Do you think we should slow down?' I scream.

'You have twelve minutes!' he screams back – which means: no, you will arrive there in under twelve minutes either alive or dead.

When I see the front of the station, my heart starts pulsating at speed, like it's less of a beat, more of a hum.

What am I going to say to him? What am I going to do?

'You're here,' Benji says, jumping off the bike at the entrance. 'Go!' he shouts.

'But what do I do?'

'What would Hope say?' he asks, making a face.

And I think she'd say: go and do Not Nothing.

I start running, the station filled with families off to the seaside, people in business suits with newspapers and briefcases, teenagers looking bored sitting in lines with their phones in front of them.

I'm looking for him. Thinking if I see him, catch just a glimpse of him, that I'll know. I'll know it's him. But that's a stupid, romantic notion, because I've seen too many music videos.

Then it happens.

The song starts playing, right inside my head. The place it always starts. A rhythmic guitar chord and drums driving towards a riff. The crowd parts, as if Dolores O'Riordan's there, singing just for us, direct from heaven. The Cranberries, 'Dreams'.

And he's right there. Exactly where I can see him.

All my life.

'Ash!' I shout. 'Ash!'

He's got his earphones in. Music pumping out, its reedy echo audible even from here.

'Ash!' I shout again. 'ASH.'

He turns, as if suddenly he can hear me.

'Ellie,' he says slowly, pulling his earphones out as I run towards him.

'What are you listening to?' I gasp, trying to draw the breath back into my body.

I'm breathing, breathing, trying not to forget how.

'The Cranberries,' he says, smiling. '"Dreams".'

'Me too,' I manage.

He furrows his brow, taking in my lack of earphones.

'I could hear it, just now. When I was running. When I saw you,' I explain. 'In my head. Which sounds not normal, I know.'

He reaches forward, grabbing my hand. 'I have to go, Ellie. My train.'

'But I don't want you to.'

He looks pained.

'Why haven't you been reading my messages?' I demand. 'I thought we weren't trying to avoid each other. I thought we were

400

friends.'

'Ellie, I can't do this right now, I have to go,' he says, letting go of my hand and walking towards the train.

I run past him. In front of him. 'If you'd been reading my messages, you'd see I've been sending you songs.'

He stops.

'Maggie Rogers and Pulp and the Cure,' I say, gulping.

'Which ones?' he asks softly.

'"Friday I'm In Love",' I say. Because I'm trying to be clear, while being completely opaque.

'You're in love?' he smiles.

'Bad timing?' I ask, grinning.

'Always,' he grins in return. 'We have the best bad timing.'

'It's just, I don't know what's going to happen now,' I say seriously. 'I know you're going away, and I want you to go away, I want you to do whatever you want to do, I just need you to know you're my friend. I need you to know I'm in love with my best friend.'

He says nothing.

'So, you can spend the summer in London getting used to being without me, or you can spend it here, with me.'

'Is that what you want?' he asks softly.

I nod vigorously.

'Are you ready, Ellie? Are you sure this is what you want?'

'No,' I laugh. 'I don't know if I'm ready. But I know this is what I want.'

And I know if I don't do this, I'll regret it for the rest of my life.

So instead of regretting it, I lean forward and kiss him, my hands around his face, his bag dropping to the floor as he puts his arms around me. And that's where we stay, until a guard tells us his train is leaving, and we stand there and watch it go.

'You know, I rode a bike to get here,' I say, impressed with myself.

'I told you, you could cycle,' he says, kissing my nose.

'You did,' I say, kissing him again. 'Although technically, I did have a driver.'

'What are we going to do in September?' he asks.

'You're going to get on that train, and I'm going to stand here and let you go,' I reply.

'And then what?'

'I don't know.'

Here's the thing about endings. They're never really the end. Never really a perfect, seamless end of the story; but something else. Something more.

A wise friend once told me that endings are just beginnings in disguise.

So, I'll leave you there. At the beginning of the beginning, but also at the end. I don't know what's going to happen next – because who does? I just know that right now, I'm exactly where I'm supposed to be.

I. Am. Ellie. Pillai.

# 76

# New Beginnings

She steps out on to the stage and does that thing he used to do, leaning down into the mic, her voice dark and deep and tantalising. She says something serious, and I lean down into my mic and say something funny. She turns towards me, grinning. My new partner in crime. The new/old member of our band, both of us giving Frontwoman Energy.

And now I know her better, now I can see who she is beneath it all, I can even see why we ended up where we did. How our strange relationship square came to exist. The ex-girlfriend of my ex-boyfriends, or one current boyfriend/one best friend.

Hannah.

She of the voice and attitude and guitar skills that aren't quite Shawn's but come something close.

This is my new beginning. Our new beginning. Or maybe just the end of what came before.

I write a song and send it to Gabrielle.

They respond.

**Gabrielle:**

Interested. Send me more.

I get started on something else.
Or do I get finished?
Either way.

I'm not done yet.

# A Girl Called Ellie

My name is Ellie. Ellie Pillai.

And I'm gloriously chaotic. Confused. Frustrating. Angry. Sad. Happy. And all points in between.

I feel things without knowing them.

I love people deeply and sometimes too much.

I want to be better. I want to try harder.

But I'm doing my best at this moment in time – and that's enough.

My name is Ellie. Ellie Pillai.

And you – you're enough too.

I get the feeling you're not done yet either.

# Acknowledgements

All books create worlds, but for me, Ellie Pillai captured a world that existed yet was never really seen. As a kid that grew up without stories that reflected her experience, I often felt invisible, unable to breathe. As though I existed, but to the world at large I was less than. Not worthy of stories that spoke to who I was, what I was experiencing. I was an in-between. Not quite British enough, not quite Tamil enough either. As an adult, for a long time, all I really wanted was to feel seen. Really seen. To prove to the world I existed. Ellie Pillai became my literal 'I Was Here'. For that, I will always be grateful.

But these stories would not exist without the advice, kindness and encouragement of so many others, so a few thank yous to the village that helped me build Ellie's world. To Nathalie Morse who told me I could, and gave me the courage to believe I might actually be a writer, and to Makeda Gerressu who gave me such thoughtful insight – I can never impress on you how much these words would not exist without the two of you. Thank you to the brilliant Marina Rosova who let me 'borrow' and slightly botch her childhood vodka story, and for introducing me to the woman that would change my life – my amazing agent Thérèse Coen, who sent me the best email I've ever received, which involved many Beatles references and a shared love of George Harrison. To the team at Faber, publisher and editor extraordinaire Leah Thaxton (who only went and helped me win a prize!), the geniuses

Natasha Brown and Ama Badu, the amazing publicists Bethany Carter and Simi Toor and Emma Eldridge, art director of dreams – thank you. You made a fifteen-year-old brown girl feel seen. To Trisha Srivastava who brought Ellie to life in illustrative form – I still wonder how you managed to get inside my head and draw exactly what I was feeling. I'm convinced you have superpowers. Thank you, thank you, thank you.

To my dad who isn't here to read these words – you were the best. I'm eternally grateful you knew this book was coming and told every Sri Lankan across the world to look out for it. To my mum – thank you for everything. There are too many things to list here, but you know without words how much I love you. To Sarah Smith for believing in me enough to make me a notebook and express the belief that I was annoying enough to get published – thank you for being an early reader and a great friend. There are so many friends I could thank here for what I will euphemistically call *everything* – but you know who you are and how much I, let alone this book, would not be here without you.

Thank you too to the folk at BookTrust Represents (especially you, Emily Drabble) who took me to Cheltenham Literary Festival and not only introduced me to some other brilliant writers IRL (Clare Weze, Janelle McCurdy, E. L. Norry and Alex Sheppard – what a fun weekend!) but also taught me to take my place in the publishing world without using the word 'just'.

Finally, to my children Theo and Miles, who inspire me every day – sometimes to tear my hair out – but mostly to keep going, to insist on being heard. It's a privilege to be your mother. And of course to Ian. You know why in every way. Thank you my love.

To my readers – you are extraordinary. Please carry this with you whatever anyone else might tell you. These stories were written for you. Your magic inspired them.